# WAKING TO BLACK

V.H. LUIS

**Waking to Black**

Copyright © 2018 by V.H. Luis.

Front cover image by Victoria Cooper Art.

This is a work of fiction. Names, characters, businesses, places, events and incidents are either the products of the author's imagination or used in a fictitious manner. Any resemblance to actual persons, living or dead, or actual events is purely coincidental.

ISBN: 978-0-692-10143-8

https://vhluis.com/

*To my beautiful, baby boy.*
*I dare to dream, so one day you dare to dream too.*
*I love and adore you.*

# ACKNOWLEDGMENTS

I greatly appreciate all the talented women who helped me edit and polish this story. This novel is in part a reality, because of their valuable insight.

Ann Howard Creel, you gave me confidence when I wasn't sure I had any left—I will always treasure the advice and kind words you offered me. You made me believe I could write this story.

Heather Osborn, you are a grammar-goddess. The way you effortlessly simplify my sentences, while maintaining the integrity of what I'm trying to say, is magic. You give my words, new life. Thank you.

Tera Cuskaden, you made me work hard to smooth out the rough edges. You showed me what was missing and challenged me to make a story I thought was done, even better. You fought for my characters and I know the end product is so much better, because of you. Forever, thank you.

To my beta readers, thank you all for ignoring the typos and delving into the story. You caught what I couldn't.

To my family—my husband who had to listen to many conversations he wasn't necessarily interested in, my sister-in-law who helped me edit, my mother-in-law who took such good care of my son and gave me the opportunity to write, my stepfather who was always supportive in this endeavor and my cousin who was always so excited about the prospect of me publishing a book—thank you, I love you all!

Shivani, you are my sister from another mister, the most devote friend, and my number-one cheerleader. This story is as much my baby as it is yours. You read every page first. It's no secret, I continued to write because you demanded to read the next chapter, and the next. Every step I've taken towards the accomplishment of this dream, has been with you by my side. Words can't convey how invaluable you've been throughout this all so I'll simply say—thank you! I love you, chica!

My deepest gratitude and love to my mother, who read this story though it's not her genre of choice. I'll never forget your soft smile as you scrolled-down on my laptop, reading into the middle of the night, while I watched in secret from behind the door. I could write a book alone on all the wonderful things you've done for me, all the joy and opportunities you've given me. Suffice to say, you're an incredible woman and I'm blessed to have you in my life. I love you, with all my heart!

Finally, to my father… If I'm any good at writing, at being creative in any capacity, it's because I got the talent from you. Though you are no longer with me, you are forever in my thoughts. I hope you found peace.

# Chapter One

THE SHARP MOVEMENT of something in my periphery makes the hairs on my arms spike. With trembling fingers, I reach for the lamp and click it on. Startled marble eyes peer at me with feral interest.

I stare at my cat, Felix, my shallow breaths interrupting the silence of the lonely night.

I'm twenty-four years old and still scared of the dark. *Why shouldn't I be? Bad things happen when it's pitch black.*

The nuns at parochial school often said that idle hands were the Devil's playground. Given the countless sleep-deprived nights in my past, I realize they were right.

*What time is it?*

The neon-blue light emanating from my table clock glows 4:03 a.m. With a steady rhythm, I breathe in and out, willing myself to calm. *What the hell is wrong with me?*

Tossing and turning for ten wide-awake minutes, unable to sleep, I succumb to the inevitable and get up. After a quick stretch, I make my way to the spare room that for the last year has housed my art studio.

The rich scent of linseed oil floats in the air and though clutter surrounds me, I find comfort in the space. Picking up the palette full of still-moist paints, I sit in front of the easel.

I paint flowers because they tell all types of stories. A flower can make you smile, it can make you cry, and it can even be an unspoken promise. All the possibilities are enchanting, yet the painting before me lacks charm. It's an empty shell, and I don't possess the talent to make it whole. Frustrated, I scratch at the damp paint forming vivid lines against the canvas.

Light creeps into the dark room. *What time is it?* I rush to the bedroom clock. *Shit! Seven oh six a.m. I'm late.*

I hop in the shower, and five minutes later I'm clean and getting dressed. It's casual Friday, so jeans and a black shirt will do. I grab a hair tie and simultaneously cram my long curls into a messy bun and my feet into flats. Biting into a bagel, I start walking to the school down the street. Before any lingering thoughts about my failing artistic abilities can perturb me, I'm there.


"MS. SNOWE, look. It's pretty, right?"

The watercolor of a daisy is simple. Kate didn't spend much time mixing colors, but it does look beautiful—it looks happy. I smile at her. "It's perfect."

Time trickles by and the bell rings, signaling the end of sixth period. It's three thirty in the afternoon and as the students scurry off in an excited frenzy, I begin the dull task of cleaning up. Preoccupied with the mess, I don't hear Tina enter.

"Hey, girl, ready for happy hour?"

Christina Alba, an English teacher at the school I work in and my best friend since childhood, is not the type of woman to take *no* for an answer. Dark eyes narrow at me from under her mane of long black hair, and the *I'm ready for anything* smile plastered on her face makes it hard for me not to chuckle. I gesture around the room.

"Not exactly."

"No way. Leave it for Monday."

"I'll be another twenty minutes."

"Evie, you better not leave me hanging again." She leans against a desk, mischief sparkling in her eyes. "Besides, there's this cute bartender I want you to meet."

I groan while tossing an assortment of crayons in a bin. "Another charmer like last month's, whose opening line was—" I clear my throat and deepen my voice, "Tina didn't tell me you had such a nice rack."

She covers her mouth attempting to hold back a laugh, though it bursts from her lips anyway. "Yeah, okay. Not my best match, but you have to admit he was super-hot."

I roll my eyes at my bossy bestie. "Sure, so hot that when I asked him to name his favorite contemporary artist smoke practically fizzled out of his head like an over-fried circuit."

"Can it be we're setting our standards a tad too high?"

Ignoring her, I fish my bag out of the supply closet, and head for the door. "You go ahead and I'll meet you there. I need to stop at the bank and cash a check."

She points her index finger at me like a female Uncle Sam. "If you're not there in thirty minutes expect my pissed-off call."

"Yes, sir! I will be there, sir!" I give her a mock salute and her serious expression turns into one of exasperation.

AS I approach the bank, I spy a black Escalade parked by the curb, and a sentry-like man in a suit standing at attention. *Yeah, that's totally normal.*

I shrug, make my way inside, and grab a deposit ticket. Of course, the pen provided is out of ink.

A baritone voice breaks the monotony of my simple bank transaction.

"Everyone on the fucking floor! Now!"

*Oh shit!* My muscles lock in place and the pen I had begun searching in my purse for is clasped between my now-sweating fingers.

A blur to my left comes into my line of sight. The figure is wearing a ski mask, ripped jeans, and a stained sweater. The broad shoulders and physique make it obvious the robber is a man. However, the gender of my assailant is the last thing on my mind, because he has a firm grip on an enormous gun, which is pointed at me.

"Are you fucking deaf? Get on the floor, bitch!"

I close my eyes and bend my knees—or at least I think I am. I'm finding it hard to breathe, and the room is spinning. I must not be moving fast enough because the next thing I know, the man with the big gun grabs me and shoves the cold tip of the barrel against my neck.

*This is how it ends?* A pang of regret stabs deep within my belly. I wonder who will feed my cat when I'm gone, and the pathetic nature of that last thought is sobering. I haven't accomplished much in the last twenty-four years. My eyes begin to water, and my vision clouds.

"Hey, take it easy," a much calmer voice calls out from behind me.

I try to focus on the deep tenor of this stranger, who to my shock is defying a man with a gun, but my senses aren't cooperating.

Using me as a shield, my captor spins me and I get a blurry first look at my would-be hero. Through pooling tears, I see he's dressed in an expensive black suit, a crisp white shirt, and a solid black tie. He has hair the color of dark coffee, and because he defies the order to hug the floor, I notice he's tall. His sapphire eyes lock on mine, urging me to breathe, and for a split-second I forget I'm in the arms of a lunatic because it's this stranger's gaze holding me hostage.

Though his hands are in the air, like everyone else's, he seems to be humoring the robber rather than obeying him out of fear. And while not armed, his calm demeanor is more threatening than the creep jamming a gun against my throat. It's as if under the façade of composure something dark and dangerous lingers—the insight makes me tremble.

"Trust me, sir. You don't want to do this."

My mysterious hero speaks with disconcerting calmness.

"The next few minutes are going to define the rest of your life. Are you going to be the man who robbed a bank, or the murderer who shot an innocent woman?"

His tone is stone cold, and though I can't help but feel envious of his detached demeanor, I'm also pissed because that question is more loaded than the gun against my head. *You better have a plan, Mr. Black Suit...*

My potential murderer again digs the barrel of the gun against my neck and the pressure forces a guttural cough to escape from my lips. *Oh please God, let this be over soon!* Praying, even silently, is something I haven't done in years. It's pathetic to call on an abandoned faith in a moment of need, but as I stand there, petrified, I take comfort in words I have long since abandoned.

"Who the hell asked for your opinion?" the man gripping me snarls.

"You want money, don't you? Leave her alone and focus on the reason why you came here."

The thief's grip tightens around my chest. "Hey, how's it going back there with the money?"

*There are two of them?*

"We're running out of time. Hurry the fuck up!" The man pressing the gun against me is obviously unnerved by the slow progress of his partner in crime, along with the faint sound of sirens. Drops of his sweat are dampening the curve of my back, and his grip is bruising.

"Do you hear that? The police will be here soon. If you plan on getting out you better help your friend. You're wasting time."

Again, my hero speaks, and I swiftly come to the conclusion he's either a full-fledged idiot or ten times braver than anyone has the right to be under such circumstances.

*You're antagonizing a man pointing a gun at me, Mr. Black Suit. Roll the dice when it's your life on the line, not mine.*

"Maybe I should just shoot you *and* the bitch."

The thug pulls the gun from my throat, and a momentary spasm of relief pulses through me. I'm still in the arms of a lunatic, however, at least the gun is no longer burrowing its way through me.

"Where the fuck's that money?"

I know the sound of desperation, and this man is without a doubt desperate. Anxiety can cause people to do crazy things, and at this moment I'm being held by a ticking bomb.

For the first time, I dare to sneak a glance at my captor. He has his head turned so he can address his partner, and is holding the gun with an outstretched arm, his aim fixed on the cocky Mr. Black Suit.

Taking advantage of Ski Mask's inattention, Mr. Black Suit lunges for the gun, grabbing the barrel and shifting it to the side, while his opposite hand pushes against the criminal's wrist. A snapping noise following the hasty movement.

I'm thrown off balance by my abrupt release and stumble back, arms lurching forward as I join everyone on the floor. Thunderous gunshots echo throughout the hushed bank. Screams erupt as someone with a ski mask, who I assume is the other thief, drops near the teller line.

*Am I shot?* No, I'm still in one piece and my hero is in possession of the gun, now aimed at the thug beside me. The criminal is bellowing something about his wrist, which is twisted in an unnatural position.

My hero's voice reverberates against the marble interior of the room.

"Stay down!"

I'm not sure he's telling me or the groaning man beside me. Though it doesn't matter, because I don't possess the dexterity to move—there's no way I'm getting up.

Wide-eyed, I observe an armed man enter the bank. He's the guard who stood outside near the Escalade when I arrived. Peering to the left, I focus on the crumpled form of the shot man. Blood is pooling on the floor and I'm on the edge of a panic attack. *This isn't happening, I must be dreaming. Please, let me be dreaming.* I blink a few times, willing everything to disappear, but my attempts are futile.

Mr. Black Suit is conferring with the guard. My assailant's gun is in his grasp, still leveled at the thug who would've taken my life with little or no thought. The tears I've been harboring cascade down my face.

I've had panic attacks before. I try to count. I try to think of a comfortable place so the room can stop spinning, so I can stop shaking. *Take a deep breath from your diaphragm and hold it, focus, and you'll make it through.* My body trembles as I struggle to remain in control. *Get a grip!*

I hear the scatter of feet while the people racing toward the exit speed by like out-of-focus photographs. *Wait for me! I want to go, too!*

Mr. Black Suit materializes in front of me. He's crouched on the ground, speaking. His lips move, but I can't hear him. I'm still trying to slow my rapid breathing. His chest rises as he sucks in a deep breath of air, his lips parting in a charming little circle while exhaling. *Oh, so that's how it's done?* Slowly, we find a rhythm, and in no time I'm back on Earth, back in Miami, Florida.

I don't know how long we sit there doing the most basic of functions, but I'm grateful someone is next to me. And at the moment he doesn't seem like a full-fledged idiot.

"Everything's okay, you're safe."

His sapphire eyes are simultaneously soothing and threatening, like the flicker of fire. He offers me his hand, and when I place my palm against his, it's like I'm touching a fuse the second it blows. My muscles burn; it's hot around me, and I'm sweating.

*What the hell is wrong with me?*

I'm unable to move, and it's him who hoists me up. My knees buckle and I fear I'm going to fall, but his strong forearm curves around me, supporting my weight and holding me upright. Although the fabric of our clothing folds against our pressed forms, the defined ridges of his muscular chest push along the swell of my breasts and the image of ripping his button-down open and running my hands over his bare pecs flashes in my head.

Inhaling a deep breath because I'm obviously in desperate need of air, I'm hit by the decadent scent of his skin. The danger of going limp again becomes a real possibility. Before I sway, I dig my fingers into his toned shoulders, holding on for dear life.

"Steady."

He smiles down at me. It's a movie-star grin, teeth perfectly straight and white. The sight does nothing for my already shaky stance.

"Mr. Black, I'm sorry it took so long for me to respond. As soon as I realized what was going down—"

The sentry's apology is cut short by my hero, who is apparently his boss.

"You did fine. We'll talk about it later. This is neither the place nor the time."

*Mr. Black? Mr. Black Suit is actually named Black?* I can't help it, I laugh. Maybe it's the adrenaline still coursing through my body, the interesting coincidence, or that I'm in the arms of the most drop-dead gorgeous man I've ever seen, but I burst into a fit of giggles.

Again, he's staring at me, and though a second ago he was dismissive with his underling, there's gentleness in his gaze. It's an intriguing look that contrasts with the hard, chiseled features of his handsome face and before I can stop myself, my pointer grazes the line of his jaw.

A shadow crosses his eyes and his grip on the small of my back tenses. "Are you able to walk, or do you need me to carry you out?"

The deep grate of his words makes the already personal question boarder inappropriate, but damn, I'm tempted. So tempted I'm finding it hard to think about anything but being swept up in his arms.

Loud voices shouting orders and the scuffle of tramping feet jerk me back to reality. *Did I actually touch his face? This isn't me... I don't touch strangers, no matter how good-looking. Then again, I've never met anyone this good-looking... Focus, Evie!* I shake my head, trying to push through my embarrassment.

"No, of course not. I... I can walk."

I pull away from his arms, needing the distance to function. Steadying myself, I scan the room. The police have arrived and are everywhere, inspecting the area.

Mr. Black talks to his man though his eyes are pinned on me. "I'm going to have to speak with the authorities. It'll take some time. Take this young lady outside. The fresh air will do her good."

I don't move until Mr. Black's guard grips my arm, and as I am led out of the bank I can't help looking back at the man who is literally my hero. The thought once again brings me to irrational giggles.

# Chapter Two

HOURS LATER, I'M sitting with my back against a cold ambulance, retelling the events to a stocky, bottle-blonde policewoman who has yawned five times in the last ten minutes. Her disinterest in the entire ordeal is upsetting. *Well, excuse me, lady, but from my seat the experience was disturbing.* Officer Garcia, as her nametag declares, jots a few notes down as I speak, when we're interrupted by another cop.

"Do you know who that is, the guy who stood up to the perpetrator?"

His voice is casual, as if I wasn't standing there. *Hello. I was assaulted and nearly killed. Maybe we can spare the gossip until the donut break.*

"Someone important?" Officer Garcia's eyes perk up with interest.

The unknown officer, who has decided against wearing a nametag, scoffs.

"That's an understatement. Adam Black."

"Really?" responds Officer Garcia. "The guy from that *Forbes* article?"

My skin pricks at the mention of his name, because even I have read about him. At thirty-four, Adam Black is the owner of one of the most lucrative real-estate businesses on the East Coast. I vividly remember Tina obsessing about him at lunch a few weeks back. She was dead set on arranging a chance encounter with Mr. Eligible.

Officer Garcia coughs, jarring me back to reality. "Thank you for your statement. I believe we're done here. If we have any further questions we'll contact you."

The EMT has already given me a clean bill of health, so I get up to leave. My phone buzzes against my hip pocket. It's Tina.

"What the hell happened to you? It's been *hours*!"

"It's not my fault this time. The bank was robbed."

"*What*?" Tina squeals. "Like, no bullshit? Robbed? With guns?"

"Yes. Anyway, I'm still a little shaken. I promise I'll call you later and tell you everything."

"Do you want me to come get you?"

"No," I blurt out.

Tina has always done her best to protect me. She loves me like a sister, and while the sentiment is mutual, I feel like a burden.

"I'm leaving now. Trust me, I'm fine. I'll call you in like an hour."

"One hour, Snowe."

Tina only uses my last name when she's trying to make a point.

"I mean it. If you don't call me in one hour I'm driving to your house."

Hoping to sound casual, I force a chuckle. "If I don't call you in one hour I give you permission for a home invasion." I shake my head because I know I'm failing to reassure her.

"Evie," she whispers. "If you're not okay—"

"I'm f-fine," I say while swallowing the hiccup of my voice. "Stop worrying about me, okay."

I hang up, not bothering to hear her response. It may seem like a dismissal, but I'm far from indifferent to her feelings; I'm bound by them. I have been since that night years ago. A lurching sensation tugs at my stomach as I recollect the memory, so I suppress it, opting instead to focus my gaze toward the bank. I can't believe I survived that; I was held by a crazy man, on the verge of being killed, and I walked out. Maybe it's time I accept my mother's invitation to attend church. Too exhausted to keep contemplating, I shrug and turn toward the sidewalk.

"Where do you think you're going?"

His voice is stern, confident, and I imagine this is the tone he uses regularly, since it rolls off his tongue with precision.

Turning around with a frown framed between my brows, my gaze is again pinned by Mr. Black's startling sapphire eyes. I'm struck speechless. It's as if I'm staring into the depths and there's a rip current between us pulling me under.

"I…um…I'm going home." I want to sound assertive, but the slow heat sliding across my cheeks makes it impossible for me to think. I don't know if I'm coming or going.

He tilts his head to the side, sizing me up.

"I don't think you're in any condition to drive."

He's so arrogant, speaking as if there's no possible way anyone could disagree, and it's the shove I need to start talking.

"Well, luckily, I don't drive."

He glares at me, not amused, and my newfound poise disintegrates. I fiddle with my fingers, gathering my thoughts and then add, "I live nearby. It's not far."

"You live in Miami and you don't drive?"

*Yes! I surprised Mr. Black Suit. Finally, one point to Evelyn.*

He tightens his lips in a thin, hard line, and it's as if he bore a hole through me, leaving me exposed, with nothing more than a casual glance.

*Stop staring at me!* My thoughts are obviously more vocal than my actions, so I shift my shoulders in a meek shrug.

"I guess I've never found the need to drive…" I stop dead. This man rescued me from someone with a gun and I haven't shown him an ounce of gratitude. Yes, he's pushy, and from our brief conversation I gather he's demanding as well, but that doesn't excuse my behavior.

"Thank you for saving my life back there. You were brave and…" I catch myself before I can finish the statement. Without thinking, I was going to say he was brave and reckless. "You were brave and I appreciate it." I nod once, satisfied with my response.

The corners of his mouth pinch, as if he's holding back a smile.

"You're still nervous, and that's to be expected."

The husky rasp of his voice rubs against my skin, forcing me to fight a shiver.

"Not at all." I straighten, determined to put up a strong front. "I'm fine."

"Your cheeks are flushed and your entire body is tense. It's a perfectly normal reaction, you shouldn't be ashamed. You just went through a traumatic experience. I'll take you home."

"I'm not ashamed of anything." The sharp intonation of my words surprise me more than they surprise him. "And thank you for the offer, but I'm capable of getting home—"

He steps forward, his height daunting enough for me to lose all train of thought. "No one," he says softly, "should be alone after being in a bank holdup. Especially someone who reacted the way you did afterwards."

Craning my head, so I can clearly see into his eyes, I'm left awestruck by the intimacy of his expression—I fell apart in his arms and I can't hide from the reality, but still I try. "I…I'm fine."

Nodding, he takes a step back. "You've said as much already. And I, of course, believe you."

He flashes me a smile and though I'm upset by his placating words, I'm too stunned to string a sentence together. Fortunately, I don't have to because he breaks the silence.

"I, however, haven't recovered from the experience and since, by your own admission, I did save your life, you can't in good conscious abandon me in my hour of need..."

I blink a few times at his absurdity. *His hour of need?*

"The least you can do is keep me company for a while longer. So, I'm taking you home."

The deep timbre of his voice and his statement, which has been spoken as fact, makes resisting hard. *Careful, Evie. Men are by nature, trouble, it's the way of the world... But a clever man is downright dangerous.*

For a second, he appears as if he abruptly remembered something. "I'm Adam Black, and you are?"

His hand extends forward.

"Oh. Yes, of course. Sorry. How rude of me. I'm Evelyn Snowe."

*How rude of me?* Why am I apologizing to this man? He's the one who started the conversation. He's the one in charge of introductions. *What the hell is going on?*

He clasps my palm for the second time that day and a spark rushes through my body, prompting my toes to curl in the flats I'm wearing. The sensation making my nerves tingle is irrational and beyond intense. I have an instinctual, purely animalistic urge to lunge forward and rake my fingers in the lush strands of his hair so I can drag him down to my lips and savor him, bite him, completely make him forget about everything else in this world but me.

"Are you okay?"

*Shit...he's talking again.*

"Yes." I nod a bit too adamantly.

He squeezes my hand. It's the type of handshake I would expect from a businessman. Like Goldilocks's porridge, it's just right, firm yet not painful.

"It's unfortunate we've met under these circumstances."

Rather than linger on the frightening memory, he changes course by focusing on getting me to his Escalade, all the while holding my hand. With assured grace he opens the back door and ushers me inside.

Alone in the Escalade, I'm left wondering how I agreed to allow this stranger to take me home. *Oh, right, my agreement wasn't solicited.* The thought of darting out of the car and running comes to mind, but I've reached my quota of adrenaline for the week.

Out of the tinted windows I watch Mr. Black talk to his security guard. This man stood up to a gunman and he appears unruffled and utterly stunning, with his collar open and sleeves rolled to his elbows. No one should look this good after being in a bank holdup.

A scary thought hits—how do I look? Tilting my head toward the front of the SUV, I try to see myself in the rearview mirror. As my reflection comes into view the back door opens. I try for a casual pose as I fall back into the plush leather.

"Is everything okay?" Black's voice is calm yet probing.

"Yes," I whisper, attempting to regain my composure.

The omnipresent guard eases himself into the front of the Escalade. Mr. Black turns to me.

"Where do you live?"

His impassive tone makes me feel like a total idiot, because around him I'm anything but impassive. It's like I've been doused with pheromones. I finger the hem of my shirt while muttering my address.

"Parker, did you get that?"

The driver responds with a "Yes, sir."

In less than five minutes, we're at my house. Under normal circumstances I wouldn't be able to afford a home in this community. It's a sought-after location. By pure luck, I got the home in a short sale. It's a small two-bedroom house, but the lot is huge and I love the freedom owning my own place gives me.

Without uttering a word, Black opens the car door and steps out.

*Is he coming in?* I gulp louder than I anticipated and grasp the door handle. Before I can pull on it, the car door opens and he's standing in front of me.

He extends his hand and with a bemused expression I grab hold. Gingerly, he pulls me to my feet. The close proximity between me and this near-perfect specimen of masculinity is intimidating. My mouth is dry. I'm not sure why I simultaneously loathe his chivalry yet am drawn to it. *Have I become such a cynic?*

"Thank you," I breathe softly.

In a moment of clarity I push off from his warm embrace, the situation feeling too intimate, and move toward my front porch. The heat he's radiating makes it apparent he's standing behind me.

It takes me a few seconds to discover my keys in the depths of my purse. Reaching for the lock, I notice my hands are shaking. *Am I nervous because of today or is it because of him?*

I have little time to consider the random thought, because to my surprise, Black places his hand over mine, guiding me to the keyhole. In unison, we turn our hands and the door clicks open.

"Would you like to come in?"

I'm not even certain why I ask him to enter. Part of me finds him exasperating, yet I don't want him to leave.

He eyes his watch and nods. "Only for a few minutes. I want to make sure you're okay."

As I step into the house I cringe. Magazines I've read and discarded are strewn across the floor. Not only have I been a damsel in distress, but I apparently live in squalor. *Can this be any more embarrassing?* I survey the living room for a brief second and then start to grab the magazines. I pile them on the coffee table and give him a sheepish smile.

"Something to drink?"

He has a small frown perched between his brows as he stares at me. He runs one of his hands over his head until it falls at the nape of his neck, flexing, as if that small action is relieving pent up stress. After a beat he speaks.

"Water would be great."

I nod and drag my gaze away from him.

"I'll be just a moment. Please feel free to sit down."

I scurry toward the kitchen, happy I have a task, a distraction.

"You have a charming home," he calls out from the living room.

I smile to myself, because that's exactly what I think, although I wonder if his words have been prompted by his need to be polite.

"Thanks. Been here for about a year now. I'm fond of the area."

I finish pouring the water and head back to the living room. He's gone.

I blink a few times and shake my head in disbelief. As I scan the area I notice light emanating from my art studio. Placing the glass on the coffee table, I go to investigate.

Black is standing in the center of the room, his hands in his pockets as he studies one of my paintings.

*How rude! What an intrusive son of a—*

My thoughts are cut short by his deep voice.

"These are lovely."

He points to a set of rose paintings I've been working on, each of them identical, except for the color patterns. They look contemporary, or at least what would have been considered contemporary fifty years ago—very Andy Warhol. My cheeks burn and the muscles of my throat tighten. It's not that I have issues receiving compliments. It's that less than a second ago I was angry at him for intruding, and now he's pulled the rug out from under me.

"Um… Thank you." I mutter.

A small smile dances across his lips and I get the impression he knows I find the situation irritating.

"What happened here?" He points to the painting I was working on earlier in the day.

*What a personal question. It's obvious I took out my frustration on the canvas.* I shrug, trying to hide my discomfort.

"It didn't live up to my expectations."

He chuckles, and the action makes him appear less imposing.

"So when you're not being held at gunpoint you're an artist?"

"Not exactly…"

I lean against the doorframe, relaxed for the first time in his presence.

"I'm an art teacher, at the school behind South Bay Boulevard."

He opens his mouth to respond but is cut short by the buzzing of his cell phone. After muttering a quick *excuse me*, he answers the call.

"Black." He speaks his name with a severe tenor. "No. The property isn't worth that much…he's trying to put our backs against the wall. It's been on the market for over a year and the only offer he's received is ours. Send the contract with the price we discussed. He'll accept the deal."

Black is quiet for a moment as he listens to the person on the other end. His eyes dart toward me for a blink as he moves to pace around the room.

"I don't care, just make sure it gets done. I'll be in the office in less than an hour. Have comps and recent appraisals for both properties."

He ends the call, slips the phone into his pocket and turns to face me. "Sorry about that." Though his statement is contrite, his voice is not.

Once again he runs his hand over his hair to the nape of his neck.

"Is there a problem?"

He turns toward the painting I deformed in the morning hours.

"Not one that concerns you."

I'm appalled. Adam Black is standing in my house, in my art studio, my *happy* place, and he has the audacity to be short with me. I glare at him for a long minute, my mouth parted in astonishment.

"I only came in to make sure you were okay. I need to go." He looks at me and it is the first time since the bank I see softness in his eyes. "I don't mean to be short with you. Just having a bad day. I'm sure this isn't what you envisioned for a Friday evening."

I nod, because that's the best response I can come up with, and because he's right. It has been a long day and I suppose I could offer him some latitude. He did save my life.

"You live alone?"

The sudden shift in conversation makes me frown.

"Yes. Why do you ask?"

He shrugs and the action appears foreign on this man who is used to getting his way.

"Because I was curious."

He's amused again. The shifts of his emotions leave me confused. How can he be so coarse one moment and calm the next? Black moves past me toward the front door. I follow him, still reeling from the last few hours. He extends his hand toward me, and I extend my own.

The rush of energy pulses through my fingers again as we touch. No longer struck dumb by adrenaline I have the sense to pull away, but as I tug, his strong grip constricts, preventing my retreat. My gaze shoots up to his, and I can't gauge the expression he's wearing. *Does he feel this pull between us? Is he fighting against it, like me?*

"It's been my pleasure," he utters, his eyes locked on mine.

"Thank you for today, for everything. I...I don't know what would have happened if you weren't there."

It's the first time I've allowed myself to open up to this man, not because I find him inviting and warm, but because all the barriers I've built are crumbling under his penetrating gaze, his unsettling touch.

He squeezes my hand and I can't help it, I reciprocate the action.

"Are you sure that you'll be all right?"

His words may have been said with sincere concern, but what I hear is pity. I jerk my hand free.

"Yes. Of course."

His eyes twitch for a second before his features smooth out. "Well, in case you're not…" He reaches for his wallet and pulls out a card. "Call this number to reach me."

I palm the card, unsure of what to say, bemused by the oddity of what's happening, of what I'm feeling, because I haven't felt much of anything in years. When I manage to gather my thoughts, I notice he's already turned away.

In seconds, he's in the Escalade, and as I watch the SUV speed away, a sharp sensation claws at my chest.

*Goodbye Mr. Black, it was nice knowing you.*

# CHAPTER THREE

S TRETCHED OUT ON the couch with a pillow pressed to my chest, the strong scent of body wash circulates around me. It smells like him.

He's been gone for half an hour and yet I can't stop thinking about him. With my eyes shut, I picture Adam Black in my living room. His cobalt eyes gleaming at me with raw passion and his dark hair tangled between my fingers. My breathing slows and my muscles relax as I indulge in the harmless daydream.

Startled by a sharp banging on my front door, I toss the pillow on the floor. *Is he back? Did he forget something?* The possibility shouldn't make me this excited.

As I approach the door, the irate voice of my best friend calls out from the porch.

"Evelyn Snowe! You open this damn door."

*I forgot to call her.* I cringe at the realization.

I open the door, clasp her by the arm, and yank her inside. For a second, she's surprised and that big mouth of hers is shut.

Everyone should be lucky enough to have someone like Tina in their life. She would cross a glass-covered floor barefoot to help someone she loves. I adore Tina, but I can't deal with her reprimands tonight. So I do the only thing I can to disarm her—I tell her the truth.

"I was held at gunpoint today. My nerves are rattled. The last thing I need is a lecture from you."

In frustration, she throws her arms in the air and soon the gesture turns into a tight hug. "I know. It's all over the news. I've been calling you for the last hour. I was so worried. I even called your mom."

"You called my *mom?*"

Horror overtakes me. I rush to my purse and fish out my cellphone. I have six missed calls.

"Tina, I told you I was fine."

I curse under my breath and hit the call back button. Before I can utter one word, my mother yells into the phone. *That woman could burst an eardrum.*

"*Evelyn Marie Snowe!*"

"Mom, I'm fine."

"You're selfish. Tina and I have been so nervous. We had no idea if you were safe. A phone call, that's all I wanted. It is a simple enough task that I would assume you can manage."

"You're right, Mom. I should've called, it won't happen again."

I feign being contrite, though I know she's not buying it—she never does. The truth is, it's only in recent years that she's adopted this concerned persona. Ever since the "incident" three years ago she's kept a close watch on me.

"Are you listening?"

Her voice cracks like a whip, making me blink.

"Um…yes," I mutter, and we both know I have no idea what she said.

She sighs, and I don't have to be in front of her to know she's rubbing the sides of her head.

"I'm glad Tina is there; she'll take care of you."

*Wonderful… Because that's exactly what I want, to be coddled by my best friend.*

"I'll call you tomorrow." She pauses for a moment. "I love you."

*Oh, Mom, why is it always a fight?*

"I love you, too." I hang up and eye Tina.

"You left me no choice." Her voice is high-pitched, and though I know she's remorseful about the whole experience, she won't apologize.

It's infuriating to constantly be treated by the people in my life as if I'm some child who possesses little common sense. I understand why they do it—they love me, they worry, but every overbearing action serves one purpose—to push me away.

I suddenly want to tell Tina something to make her squirm with envy. "You'll never guess who was at the bank today."

Her eyes narrow at my sudden topic change and with apprehension she responds. "Who?"

"Adam Black."

She tilts her head to the side and it takes a moment for my words to register. "You mean the charming, rich guy from the article?"

I shrug, and though my stance is casual, the butterflies in my stomach make it apparent that even thinking about him thrills me.

"Yes. He saved my life." I frown as I recount the events in my head. "Though I don't think I would call the man charming. In fact, arrogant and egocentric are more fitting adjectives."

Tina has a huge smile plastered on her face. "Tell me everything. Don't you dare leave out any details."

She's relentless when her curiosity has been piqued. As quick as lightning painting the sky, the animosity between us fades.

THE bedroom is again pitch black when I wake. The blue neon light from the clock informs me it's four thirty-five in the morning.

Tina is still asleep. After our girl talk, she decided to spend the night. Tiptoeing out of the room, I make my way to my studio.

I stare at the painting I'd discarded, and I'm reminded of *him*. Adam Black stood here in this room and admired my work. Why the thought brings me comfort, I don't know. Maybe it's because having someone, anyone, believe in my talent is motivating. It makes me believe my dreams aren't lost at sea. They're washing up on the shore and I just need to grab hold of them, like a person picking up shells on the beach.

Tracing the outline of the vivid scratch marks on the canvas, I wonder if I can save this painting. I blow a strand of hair from my face and sit, determined to make this lump of coal a masterpiece.

The hours fade as I paint. I'm nearly done when a still somnolent Tina enters the room.

"Hey," she rasps.

I beam a smile at her. "Look, I just finished it."

She appears astonished at my enthusiasm. I can't blame her. I mean, it has been a long time since I've found pleasure in painting.

"It's beautiful. How long have you been awake?"

"I'm not sure," I say quickly, absorbed in the moment.

Tina rubs her head, trying to wipe away her drowsiness.

"Well, it's noon. We should probably eat something and then start getting ready." She grabs me by the hand and drags me to the living room. "Today's Art Basel and I don't want to get there too late."

Damn, she's overbearing. But she does have a point. I love Art Basel Miami—not because every year a slew of movie stars and musicians attend, but because it gives me the opportunity to do what I love—appreciate art.

"YOU have to wear this one!" Tina throws the little black dress on the bed before diving back into the closet to rummage for shoes.

"I'd rather wear jeans and a shirt."

Tina squeals and sways her hips in a happy-dance as she dangles a pair of too-high black pumps between her fingers. "These will go perfect with that dress."

"Are you even listening to me?"

"We can do something smoky with your eyes. Oh!" She snaps her fingers. "And some dark-red lipstick to match your auburn hair."

"Tina," I yell. "I'm not a doll you can play dress-up with."

Her eyes finally fall on me and her cheerful expression turns serious. "Evie... For months I've tried to get you out of this house. Every time I go out with friends I invite you and you always say no. I'm choosing to ignore you because yesterday my almost-sister nearly got shot. So tonight, we're partying it up and you're going to smile and go along with it because we both need this."

It's the watery sheen of her eyes that clues me in—Tina's worried about me.

"I'm fine," I say plainly.

"You're not." She drops the heels on the bed. "But I'm not going to argue with you because we're late and we still need to straighten your hair."

I grab the black dress and run the pads of my fingers against the soft, silky fabric. Maybe she's right and I *am* internalizing my feelings. Maybe I should be curled up crying about what happened yesterday. I could have died.

The problem is, I don't care enough to cry. I'm depressed, and I have been for years. Yesterday, I had a gun to my throat; I was at the edge of a dangerous precipice. I've been there before. I was scared, yet indifferent. *Stop thinking and enjoy the day.*

"Fine, we'll play it your way. Just don't cake the makeup on, okay?"

Again, she's squealing cheerfully.

THE cluster of bangles I always wear on both of my wrists jingle loudly as we saunter toward Tina's car. It's close to five on a cool December afternoon, and when we get there the sun will be setting.

We briefly talk about the exhibits and galleries we want to visit as we make our way to Miami Beach. Tina isn't interested in art, but she loves to people-watch. Art Basel Miami is definitely a great spot for people-watching.

As we make our way to the entrance a gust of wind rams against my body, causing my dress to twist up. I smooth my hands against the dress only to spy an attractive young man gawking at me. Our eyes meet and he bashfully turns away. I smile. Even though words haven't been spoken, I accept the compliment.

Once we're inside, Tina grabs my hand and drags me along to various exhibits. Sometimes I wonder why I tolerate her bossy behavior. *Oh, that's right—she puts up with me, too.*

After an hour of being yanked along, I finally put my foot down.

"I'm going off on my own. There are several exhibits I want to see that you obviously don't."

Tina rolls her eyes at me. "You mean several exhibits you want to stare at for *hours*."

Ignoring her sarcasm, I shoot her a huge grin. "As always, you are so insightful."

After giving me a somewhat playful scowl, she shrugs. "Fine, but leave your cell on; this place is a maze."

I give her a mock salute and scamper off. In less than five minutes, I'm staring at a set of photographs by Nick Vasquez, *Warhol's Flowers*. I'm mesmerized by them. The delicate way the artist has selected tiny ordinary objects and combined them into something extraordinary is beautiful. What's more, the artist arranged the items into one of the prettiest objects in the world, a flower.

*What is he trying to say? That there is a certain beauty in simplicity? That things, though they may appear simple, are in truth complicated?* I could stand here all night, transfixed, contemplating.

Art can mean everything and anything. I suppose that's why I've spent my life toiling over artistic pursuits. It's not about that egocentric rush a person gets when he or she creates something. Part of the allure is the pursuit of meaning. The infinite interpretations that can stem from one piece of art are captivating.

Unwilling to pull my gaze away from the photographs, I take a few clumsy steps back. My body collides with another. The impact, combined with the fact that I'm wearing high heels, makes me lose my balance. Before my graceless form can crash on the floor, strong fingers grip my waist and my hands grasp the stranger's forearms in an attempt to reclaim my footing.

The experience is beyond awkward, it's embarrassing. My back presses against a firm chest while I straighten my posture. When I turn, I'm greeted by the haughty countenance of Adam Black. He's in what I now consider his uniform, a black suit.

My apologetic expression turns into shock.

"Miss Snowe?"

His arrogant frown melts into a seductive grin.

"What a pleasure it is to see you again."

His words are fluid and his charm is unstoppable.

*How can I find him simultaneously alluring and infuriating? It's so damn confusing.*

I inhale a large breath to prepare for what I assume will be an uncomfortable conversation.

"Hello. Um…thank you." The response is ineloquent and my poise is waning with the passing seconds. "I'm sorry…for bumping into you, I mean."

He opens his mouth to speak, though he is stopped by the hands of a woman who decidedly invades his space. She's gorgeous, a life-size Barbie. Her hair is platinum blonde, her eyes crystal-blue, and her skin is a pale ivory. Standing in all her tall and slender glory, this mystery woman grabs hold of his arm and leans against him.

"Baby, let's go already. There's not much worth seeing here," she purrs.

I'm able to hold back the roll of my eyes but the stunned expression on my face is apparent. *There's not much worth seeing here? Are we at the same exhibit?*

Black grabs the mystery woman's arm, and by his scowl, I assume it is to pry her manicured nails away from his toned biceps. He places her hand by his side and in a collected voice speaks. "Victoria, if you want to go, find David and Melinda. We can't leave without them. We came together." He sounds as if he's reasoning with a child, condescension in his tone.

She gazes at him as she sulks. "Won't you come with me to find them?"

His sapphire eyes smolder as he stares at her. "You know the answer to that question."

Her mouth tightens and her beautiful features twist as she frowns. "I'll be back in a few minutes."

Sullenly, she leaves, never once bothering to address me. I apparently don't exist, not that I'm heartbroken over her dismissal.

"What brings you to Art Basel, Miss Snowe?"

Black's eyes, still dark with anger, focus on me. He grabs the lapel of his suit and straightens it, as if smoothing his appearance will wash away his annoyance. I want to laugh at the futility of the action, though I suspect such a reaction wouldn't be well received.

"Who wouldn't want to visit such an extensive collection of art, Mr. Black?"

My retort is emphatic because I'm horrible at hiding what I'm thinking. I'm aggravated at the attitude demonstrated by someone I assume is his date.

"As you can see, there are people who don't share your opinion. Victoria looked bored around this vast collection."

For an instant, a small, amused smile forms at the corners of his mouth, but as soon as I blink it's gone.

"Are you one of them?" My brazen question surprises me. When it comes to art, I've always been confident enough to care little about what others think of my tastes and yet the notion of Black finding me wanting, bothers me.

"No. I'm quite fond of art. My collection is extensive." He strides past me, his hands in his pockets as he moves toward the photographs by Nick Vasquez. "Are these what you were admiring?"

Why does he care?

"Yes. It's a beautiful exhibit."

His shoulders angle up in an off-the-cuff shrug.

"I see why you would find it charming. It's reminiscent of what you paint. You're enamored with flowers."

This man is insufferable. He happens to spend five minutes in my studio, idly regarding my art, while bickering about some real-estate deal, and he has the nerve to claim to know what I find charming. Yes, in this instance he's right. I do love the photographs, but the presumptuous nature of his proclamation is infuriating.

"I love the photographs because of the statement they make. The fact that the artist decided to form a flower with random objects is simply one of the many facets that draw me to this work. Frankly speaking, I find your generalizations insulting."

Oh, shit. Did I say that out loud?

"Name another facet. Explain to me why these photographs are so special."

His voice is soft. However, I can hear the undeniable challenge in his tone. My eyes narrow. He wants to goad me into a debate? Well, who am I to deny the man who has everything?

Stretching my arms toward the photographs as I speak, the passion imbued in every fiber of my being gets the best of me.

"The artist is obviously implying that while something may have a simplistic appearance, in actuality, it's intricate and multi-dimensional." I inhale sharply needing the air to continue. "We are surrounded by simple every day and yet we overlook it, preferring instead to revel in the intricacies of our narrowly-focused lives. And in surrendering to that narcissism we forget that even something common like a flower can hold mystery."

Self-conscious and annoyed by my outburst and flailing hand gestures, I cross my arms over my chest. I'm unraveling before him, finding it impossible to control my actions.

"Are you satisfied?" I murmur, trying desperately to avoid his gaze and not succeeding.

"Immensely."

The conviction of his one-word response makes me flinch.

He stares at me for a long minute, his dark glance enticing and enraging. It's a lethal look because it does perilous things to my self-control—a discipline that clearly under his presence is under constant assault. A throaty chuckle emanates from his lips, shattering the intensity of our standoff.

"I apologize for insulting you. That wasn't my intention."

He says the right words between a self-assured half-smile, but his manner suggests he's far from apologetic. It's as if he's purposely provoking me.

His gaze slips down my form, fixing on my breasts, which, due to my current pose, are suggestively pressed together. Unclasping my arms and letting them fall to my sides, I try for nonchalant casualness as I stand before him, even though I'm flustered.

"You look beautiful. That dress suits you."

My mouth drops open in surprise. Trying to recover my composure, I purse my lips. Before I can get it together, he's talking again.

"You seem to have a problem receiving a compliment."

The expression on his face, so cool and collected, brings out the worst in me.

"On the contrary, I receive them often enough to pay little attention to such arbitrary words." My mouth is dry, because the girl talking is one I haven't heard in years.

The sexy grin on his lips stirs a raging heat within me. I try to prevent the blush threatening to dominate my face. I fail.

"Maybe you only have a problem receiving compliments from me." He takes a few steps forward, invading my space and intimidating me with his height. "Does it bother you that I find you attractive?"

I straighten my posture, refusing to cower under his presence. "Not as much as it would likely bother your date."

A carefree laugh erupts from his lips and the transformation from imposing to effortlessly relaxed is so instantaneous, I don't have time to measure my response.

"I doubt she would be laughing if she knew how easily you stray when she's not around."

Again, he's shrugging. "It may come as a shock, but some people make no illusions about the relationship they have with others, or lack thereof. Their expectations are practical."

This man confuses the hell out of me, yet I'm reluctant to leave. "Are you implying, though you don't know me, that I'm not practical?"

"And if I was, would the implication upset you?" he asks, brow arched.

"No," I whisper, my confusion growing by the second.

Wanting to regain the upper hand in this conversation, I shift it so we focus on the only thing I've ever excelled at—art.

"What exactly catches your keen artistic eye, Mr. Black?"

"I don't subscribe to one particular genre. In fact, my tastes are diverse."

The statement, mingled with the sensual slant of his eyes, makes my pulse race. I'm beyond intrigued; I'm fascinated by the possibilities of his admission.

"Then I suppose you can easily supply me with the name of one artist you hold in high regard," I say with a touch of sarcasm, because I'm incapable of holding it back. My heart is thumping against my chest like an irritating drum.

He bites his bottom lip, a ghost of a smirk on his sinfully tempting lips. "I'm fond of Marina Abramovic's work. I find her study of the human body fascinating."

*He would!* Suddenly, I imagine Adam Black in a plush apartment, nude portraits adorning the walls. I blink a few times, shaking the image from my head.

"Have I left you speechless?"

His smugness rolls off him in waves and it's clear he's enjoying making me squirm by the sexy, provoking lean of his body. The man is without a doubt dangerous, because as frustrated as I am by his conceit, I'm dazed by the magnetism he's radiating. I suck a deep stream of air, committed to fighting his pull with every fiber of my being.

"No, not at all. In fact, your admission only serves to justify my initial assumption of your artistic taste."

"Now who is making sweeping generalizations?" His expression turns frigid.

We stand there frozen, staring at each other. He's right; I'm being judgmental. The truth is, yesterday, when we locked eyes at the bank, I found this man reassuring. However, the instant I knew who he was, I felt guarded. I don't trust myself around him. I'm being reckless in my speech, antagonizing in my actions, and I should walk away.

But I can't.

He grabs my hand and tugs me along as he treads ahead.

*Where are we going? Weren't we in the middle of an argument?*

In moments, we're standing in front of an oil portrait. The woman in the painting is slightly turned so you can only see her bare back, the faint outline of her petite breasts and her listless gaze. Her body is not the conventional image of female beauty, and yet the painting is alluring.

"How can you find such complexity in photographs of makeshift flowers, and yet not see the multi-dimensional aspects of this painting?"

*He's recycling my phrase!*

"She's standing there naked not because she lacks clothes, but because her emotions are raw for all to see." He focuses on the painting, an expression I'm not familiar with in his ocean-blue eyes. "I'm fond of Marina Abramovic's work because she shows us what we often hide. Yes, there's a perverse motivation behind my preference for this type of art, but it has nothing to do with pedestrian sexual desires. I like the honesty exhibited, the disregard for inhibitions."

I'm moved by his admission. For the first time, I get the impression I've misjudged him. A large lump forms at the back of my throat and I'm finding it hard to speak.

I turn away from the painting, unable to gaze at it any further. Standing inches away from him, I'm breathless, transfixed, only this time it's not a photograph that has me mesmerized. There's a spark between us I don't want to resist. A hot, unspoken desire is coursing through the air, saturating my senses and making it impossible for me to be rational. His chest lifts as he inhales, and the action betrays him. For a second I think he may act on the impulse hanging in the air. I think he might kiss me.

"There you are!" Tina shouts over the crowd.

The moment is lost. Black's eyes are reserved and guarded. He takes a step back and turns to regard Tina.

*Bad timing, Miss Alba.* I give her the darkest glare I can muster as I try to recover from the intense conversation.

"Mr. Black." I take a breath, trying to quell the burn in my chest. "This is Tina Alba, a good friend of mine." *A good friend who is currently on my shit list.*

Adam Black offers Tina one of his masterful handshakes. There's a smile on his lips, though I can tell it's a pretense. The smile never reaches his eyes and his body is rigid. I think he's mad at her, too, and the thought is comforting.

"It's a pleasure to meet you." Tina's response is a soft mutter.

"The pleasure is mine, Miss Alba." His voice has adopted a businesslike tone. "We were just discussing our opinions on the artists showcased."

"Yes." I laugh. "We have very different opinions about art."

A low chuckle erupts from him as his mood shifts. He places one of his hands in his pocket and his body resumes that casual stance I'm starting to like.

"I suppose that's a polite way of phrasing it."

Tina looks uncomfortable and out of place.

Black leans toward me and grabs my hand. My breath hitches and my pulse quickens at the movement. He brushes his lips against my knuckles in a tender kiss. It's such an odd gesture, formal and yet somehow intimate.

"Thank you for the stimulating conversation, but I should be on my way."

He shifts his gaze to Tina and inclines his head. "Miss Alba." He turns and disappears into the crowd. In seconds, he's gone.

"Goodbye," I whisper to myself.

*Why does he keep doing that?* This man has walked away from me twice in the span of twenty-four hours, and it's maddening. I'm flustered, and I don't know what I regret more—that I insulted him during our fleeting discussion, or that he's gone.

# CHAPTER FOUR

TO MY SURPRISE, Tina is quiet as we drive to my house. I was expecting her to interrogate me, but instead she drives down the interstate as silence envelopes us both. I thank God for the small favor, because even if I wanted to, I wouldn't be able to explain what happened.

Would I have responded if he had attempted to kiss me? Thoughts of his sexy smile provide me with the answer. I would be crazy to deny myself the satisfaction of kissing a man who undeniably possesses an edge of raw masculinity. However, something other than primal desire stirs within me. There was a moment during our conversation when I saw Adam Black for more than an exquisite example of his gender. There's a connection between us I can't explain. The first time we met he not only saved my life but also challenged me to finish a painting I abandoned. During our second meeting he called me out on my hypocrisy. This arrogant, infuriating man humbled me. The most maddening aspect of this entire ordeal is that as soon as the spark between us lit, the encounter was over.

Unable to withstand the hushed atmosphere and my frustrating thoughts, I turn on the stereo. One of my favorite songs blasts from the speakers and as I'm about to sing along, Tina turns off the music.

"Is something wrong?"

"What going on with you and Adam Black? Are you keeping something from me?" She glares at me.

*Is keeping something from you even possible?* I clear my throat.

"Nothing is *going on* between me and Adam Black. You honestly think I would keep something that huge from you?"

"No," she murmurs.

My body relaxes. I hate when there's tension between us. Although I'm glad her mood softened, her suspicion is insulting. I've never been known for my tact, so I opt for honesty.

"Why would you think that there's something between us?"

Tina puts on her indicator as she changes lanes. She shrugs as if she suffers from an irrepressible tick. "The way you both looked at each other. It seemed weird for a chance encounter. What were you talking about?"

"Why are you upset about this?" I shift the conversation to what's really bothering me, her interference in my life.

"I'm not. I'm *concerned*; there's a big difference."

"Would it be so terrible if something were going on between us?"

"No." She pauses for a moment and then states, "I'm not sure."

"Why do you always do this? You always meddle, just like my mother."

"I meddle because you don't know how to deal with certain situations. If something gets too stressful you fall apart. I don't want to find you in a thousand pieces." Tina turns at our exit and stops in front of a red light. "I don't want you to get disappointed."

I'm disarmed by her visible apprehension. Can I blame her for being concerned when I've always relied on her to put me back together? My hands instinctively trace the scars on my wrists.

"I'm never going to see him again," I say plainly, because it's the truth. *Why would I ever see him again?*

"That's the problem, isn't it? That you won't?" Small wrinkles form at the corners of her eyes.

"I barely know him." My voice raises. "Why should I care?"

The light changes from red to green and Tina focuses on the road. "You *do* care. Even if you don't want to admit it, you're bothered by the idea of never talking to him again."

"Well, since you know everything, why even bother asking me?" I cross my arms over my chest. She's so overbearing. At the moment, I can't stomach her intrusion.

"So you confront your feelings." Now it's Tina's voice that rises in volume. "So you don't internalize them and do something stupid."

"Well, thank you for having so much faith in me, for thinking a small measure of sadness will prompt me to do something stupid."

I hold back the tears pooling in the corners of my eyes. It hurts to be thought of as so weak and pathetic by my best friend. I've made mistakes, big ones, but not for senseless reasons. It made perfect sense to me at the time.

I gaze at my wrists, at the bangles that hide the marks of one of my *stupid* mistakes. Tina will never understand why, because she's never felt the need to escape. She's never been so overwhelmed with grief that the sheer thought of going on is suffocating.

We arrive at my house in record time. Tina grabs her purse and appears as though she's coming in. I don't want her to.

"I'll talk to you tomorrow." My voice is despondent and I know the tone will worry her.

"I think I should come in, just for a little while." Her voice is sugary sweet. It's her way of coaxing me free from the depression I've submitted to.

"Tina, I'm fine. I promise that if at any point I feel like I can't deal, I'll call you." I stare at her and hope she sees the sincerity in my eyes. "You can't always be here, watching my every step. I need to cope with things at my own pace, and right now, I want to be alone." I lean in to give her a reassuring hug and she squeezes me, prompting a smile to form on my lips.

She lifts her hand up, her delicate pinky raised. "You promise?"

I roll my eyes, and even though I'm still upset, I laugh. It's something we've done since we were little. I lift my own pinky, hook on to hers, and we shake. "I promise."

As I enter the empty, pitch-black house, I absently drop my purse on the floor and kick off my heels. I'm not tired and I don't want to sleep. All I want to do is paint and lose myself in a room that smells of linseed oil. My hands run over my body, grazing the beautiful black dress I'm wearing, and in a second it too falls on the floor. I think of Black as I discard the remnants of my attire, not because I feel particularly sensual, but because of what he said.

"I like the honesty exhibited, the disregard for inhibitions." I whisper his words because I agree with him. Being shackled by my emotions is not a life I want. So sitting in front of the easel, wearing nothing, I paint. I submit to the frustrations of being chastised by those I love, the sadness of the real possibility that I will never again speak with Adam Black, and the hours fly by.

THE phone startles me awake. I check the clock. Ten a.m. I'm surprised. It's been a long time since I've slept in. Lunging forward, I grab the phone.

"Hello?" I mumble.

"Evie, you're still sleeping?" My mother sounds astonished.

"Yes, Mom, I had a long night," I rub the side of my head and stretch. I'm still naked.

"I hope you had fun. I'm sorry I couldn't go with you girls to Art Basel."

"Yes, we had a blast." I try not to sound sarcastic. It was a fun evening, though I could have done without the emotionally draining encounters.

"Oh, that's nice." She pauses for a moment and I can sense the trepidation in her breaths. "I was wondering if you would like to go to Mass today."

The question doesn't surprise me. For the last two years, Mom has attempted to convince me that going back to church will make me feel better.

I'm silent for a long while, because for the first time in two years, the idea doesn't frighten me. I remember praying when I was held at gunpoint. It would be hypocritical not to at least attempt to worship when I'm not in imminent danger. *Maybe I'm not as faithless as I originally thought.*

"Okay, Mom. Eleven, right?"

"Yes." Her voice is astonished, only now I can hear a smile in her words. "I'll pick you up at ten forty-five." She hangs up—too quickly. She's scared I'll change my mind.

I hop out of bed and head to the bathroom. I turn the shower on and wait for the water to warm as I brush my teeth. Why am I so happy? The truth is that while my friends and family are constantly trying to determine what I'm thinking and feeling, I'm in the same boat. Half the time I have no clue as to the ebb and flow of my mood.

I enter the shower. Absently, I wash myself, my mind blank, then the face of Adam Black enters my head. I smile.

Thinking back on the events of the last two days, a random thought pops into my head. *How did he disarm that man? I mean, how could he do that so easily?*

I shuffle out of the shower and dry myself. It's ten thirty. *Shit. I'm running late.*

Opening the closet door and eyeing the large assortment of sundresses I've avoided for the last few years, I'm filed with nostalgia. I pick a white floral dress and in five minutes I'm ready. The loud horn of my mother's car blasts and, after a quick glance in the mirror, I run out the door.

In a few minutes, we're at St. Mary Magdalene's. Everyone is polite as they wave hello. Sunday Mass is something I'm familiar with. I've been attending since I was little. Or rather, I used to.

*That was a lifetime ago.*

We make our way to the pews and sit toward the front, near the altar.

I try to focus on the sermon. It's always been my favorite part of the service. When the priest stands and talks about how the story we've heard today can somehow relate to the events in our lives. But my heart's not receptive to the words being spoken and I want to leave. I look at my watch. *Only ten more minutes and it will be over.*

My phone vibrates against my hip. There are only two people who call me with consistency, Tina and my mom. Seeing as how one of my wardens is next to me, I figure it's Tina. Quietly, and under the narrowed eyes of my watching mother, I make my way out of the church.

Sitting on the steps outside, I stare at my phone. One missed call. It's a number I don't recognize. One of the parishioners I imagine is here for the noon Mass glares at me with visible reproach.

*Yes, I have decided to interrupt my worship to check my phone, I'm a heathen, I get it.* After I give him an equally cold glare, he turns away.

*I thought so.*

I press the redial button and the deep voice of Adam Black reverberates against my ear.

"Miss Snowe, I'm so glad you called back."

To say I'm surprised would be a vast understatement. *How did he get my number?*

"Are you there?"

"Yes!" I practically yell. "I'm sorry. I'm just a bit surprised by the phone call."

His warm laugh is smooth and seductive. It's like an unspoken promise.

"I was wondering if you're free this evening."

*He wants to see me?* My heart flutters, and it's as if I've time-traveled to junior high. I'm sure I have the goofiest smile plastered on my lips.

"Oh. What did you have in mind?" I try to sound reserved.

"I'd like to take you out for dinner."

"*Why?*" I realize after uttering the word that my tone is incredulous.

There's a long pause, and the silence makes me question if he's still at the other end of the line. His deep voice ends my speculation. "Are you always so distrusting?"

*Of handsome men who want to take me out to dinner? I wouldn't know, because it doesn't happen often.*

"Well, I don't exactly know you." *Good girl, Evelyn. That's a clever response.*

He laughs into the receiver, the low hum vibrating against the curve of my ear and even though its eighty degrees outside, I'm overrun with goose bumps.

"You're right. If only there was a socially acceptable practice in which a man and a woman could get to know each other, we could solve this problem."

Now it's my turn to laugh. "Well, since you put it that way, dinner sounds great. How should I dress?"

"The way you were dressed yesterday would be appropriate for tonight. You looked beautiful in that dress."

My cheeks burn at the compliment. "Okay, I'll see you at six." I say nothing else because my brain cells can't muster the creative energy.

He chuckles and I wonder if it's at my expense. "See you tonight."

I end the call. Did I just agree to a date with Adam Black? Should I be happy? Should I be nervous? A thousand questions cross my mind. Though I'm aware I'm not in the best place for this type of contemplation, I'm not willing to go back inside.

Mass appears to have ended. People shuffle out of the church, and my mother emerges with a deep frown between her eyes.

"Where did you go?" she murmurs, void of reproof. She must be under the impression that I stepped out due to racing, guilt-ridden emotions.

"I had a phone call," I say, hoping she lets the matter go. It's uncomfortable talking to my mother as it is.

"Who called you?" She asks the question I wanted to avoid.

"Tina." I smile at her as I lie. It's a believable fib and will spare us both an awkward conversation, so at least to me, it a considerate gesture.

*Okay, I'm probably lying to myself at this point, but I can live with that.*

She nods as we make our way toward the car.

I kiss my mother goodbye as she drops me off at my house, race up the steps leading to my porch, and go inside.

*Adam Black wants to see me.* In the blink of an eye, the world is filled with endless possibilities, with an enchantment that's been absent for years, and I welcome the change with a smile.

# Chapter Five

I'VE CHOSEN TO wear an above-the-knee navy-blue dress. It's low cut, with a plunging neckline that ends at the top of my sternum, right between my breasts. I bought the dress on a dare from Tina. She said it showcased some of my finer assets. Grabbing my two favorite wide-band bracelets, I hide the scars of my past.

At a quarter to six, I text Tina.

SPENT THE DAY PAINTING. I'M REALLY TIRED AND I'M GOING TO BED.

TALK TO YOU TOMORROW.

As I stand there lying to my best friend, I realize this is the second time today that I've been dishonest with someone I love. *Way to go. Soon you'll be able to do this in your sleep.* I frown as I shake off the remorse. This lie is necessary. Tina has spent the last few years scrutinizing my actions, and I'm not interested in her warnings. I want to take a risk on Adam Black, on whatever tonight may bring. The vibration of my phone captures my attention.

YOU'RE GOING TO SLEEP AT SIX IN THE EVENING?
GEEZ EVIE, WE NEED TO GET YOU A LIFE.
IS EVERYTHING OKAY WITH YOU?

Her silly comment about getting a life makes me laugh, because that's exactly what I'm trying to do. Maybe if I were honest with Tina, she'd support me, she wouldn't weight me down with warnings and concerns. A part of me wants to trust her and tell her about Adam, but the threat of being cautioned against him, is holding me back. And the truth is, I like the idea of keeping him my decadent little secret.

I shoot Tina another text, telling her I'm doing great and after her acquiescing response, I slip the phone in my purse. Sitting on the couch, I grab a magazine, attempting to distract myself with idle gossip. But a minute later, after reading the same paragraph three times, I quit the futile endeavor. I haven't been on a date in years, and I'm nervous. Before I can think more about it, a sharp knock startles me.

Inhaling a deep breath to steady my nerves, I open the door. The second I see him I'm struck dumb. Michelangelo's *David* is before me, only he's not naked. *Unfortunately.* I'm shocked by my hormone-induced thoughts.

Like yesterday, his eyes follow the contours of my form, pausing for a long moment at the gaping neckline of my dress. He's so blatant in his observation I can't keep quiet.

"Do you like the dress?"

His eyes meet my gaze and a slow smile forms on his lips. "I think you know the answer to that question."

I take a step forward, closing the door behind me.

"The polite thing to do, Mr. Black, would be to cater to my vanity."

He laughs, and like earlier in the day, the throaty texture of his voice ripples across my skin, giving me chills. He leans forward, pinning me.

"The color of your dress suits you. It contrasts nicely with your pale, smooth skin. It hugs all the right places."

He lifts his free hand and presses his fingertips on the arch of my neck. I gulp once as the muscles above my collarbone tighten.

"Your cheeks are flushed. It might be a result of the heat in the air, but my guess would be that our close proximity excites you. And I like that, too."

Sliding over the slope of my shoulder, he trails his fingertips until they rest at the bend of my arm. Teasingly, he rubs small circles against the tender skin, and my pulse quickens so that the roar of blood echoes in my ear.

"But if I had to pick the feature that most affects me, it would be your eyes, because they give everything away. They reflect exactly what you're feeling."

His lips hover above my ear and the warm caress of his breath makes my nipples peak against the thin fabric of my dress.

"Has your vanity been sated now?"

That's when I realize I'm playing for the junior varsity team and he's in the NFL—I'm so out of my league it's pathetic.

"Why did you ask me out?"

He flashes that movie-star grin that makes my knees go weak. "I've been told that things, though they at first seem simple, may in fact be multi-dimensional. I'm testing that theory."

"I'm not sure if I should be flattered or insulted."

He takes a step back and extends his hand. "Flattered, of course. Shall we?"

I hesitate. I don't know this man. He may be a complete psycho, the doppelganger of Norman Bates. Okay, that's probably not the case. He did save my life. However, in the span of five minutes he has me eating out of the palm of his hand—he's without-a-doubt dangerous. But who am I kidding? Cupid has long since shot me, so I place my hand in his.

He leads me to his car, a black Mercedes SLS, and before I can reach for the handle he opens my door.

"Thank you."

He winks at me, his way of saying *you're welcome*, and I know that if I stare long enough, I'm going to drown in those ocean-blue eyes. Though I don't let the fear cripple me, and in minutes we're speeding down Collins Avenue.

"I'm surprised you're traveling alone. I assumed you'd have some form of security." I press my thighs together, my palms resting on the soft leather seat. It's a rigid pose because I'm too tightly wound to relax in his presence.

"Why should I have security with me? Are you planning on assaulting me?" He glances at me with a playful grin as he shifts gears.

"That depends."

"On what, exactly? Let me guess, on my varied artistic opinions?"

The reference to yesterday's heated creative debate makes me smile. I shake my head.

"It depends on how long you plan to keep our destination a mystery, Mr. Black."

"Call me Adam."

The quick command makes frown. Does he want me to call him Adam, or are his good manners forcing him to allow the familiarity?

"Okay," I mutter, like a child who's been found with her hand in the cookie jar.

He stares at me as we pause at a red light. "As for where we're going, it's a surprise." He's adopted a matter-of-fact tone that implies the conversation is over and the ease I felt a second ago evaporates.

Peering out the window, I notice we're in South Beach. We turn on James Avenue, arriving at our destination. I'm familiar with the restaurant, though I never imagined I would eat there. Teachers don't exactly make big money.

Adam parks his car and a valet scurries toward him, while another opens my door. I step out, wide-eyed because the reality of my situation is hard for me to comprehend. I'm here, in a beautiful dress and in the company of Adam Black

"Evelyn." Adam's voice is soft, yet firm.

He grabs my hand. Maybe it's because he's addressed me by my first name or the charming setting, but around him I feel like a storybook princess and that's a perilous sensation.

As he pulls me along I scan the beautiful courtyard. There's a large tree in the corner decorated with lanterns. The inside of the restaurant is equally enchanting. It's reminiscent of a provincial Italian villa.

An impeccably dressed gentleman approaches us.

"Mr. Black, welcome back." He sounds genuinely pleased to see him.

We're led to a back room where a single table stands ready. Adam pulls out my chair and I smile at him in spite of my trepidation and nerves. He reviews the wine list with purpose and selects a bottle as I sit there, not sure of what to say. Finally, the servers leave us with our menus.

"You're quiet." He arches an enquiring brow.

I purse my lips for a beat, thinking.

"I don't know what would be appropriate to say. I'm not exactly sure why we're here or why I came in the first place."

I'm frowning at this point, and I can't put the brakes on my mouth.

"Part of me thinks you conjured up this evening to see me squirm, to make me uncomfortable. But the truth is, I don't know. Your actions have been a mystery to me since we first met."

He obviously finds me amusing because he tosses the menu on the table and throws his head back in a full-body laugh. I stiffen my jaw at the sight.

"I'm so glad you find me entertaining," I mutter.

Leaning forward, he eyes me with a predatory stare. "I find you more than entertaining, Evelyn, and that's a compliment."

The admission thaws my anger, though my body remains tense.

"I brought you here this evening because I thought the atmosphere would be one you'd appreciate."

His not so subtle reproach makes regret wash over me like summer rain. I cast my gaze down, a penitent expression on my face.

"As for the notion that I enjoy making you squirm…" He leans back in his chair, totally at ease. "I plead guilty. Although that's not the only reason we're here. I have a business proposition for you."

The sudden image of Julia Roberts in *Pretty Woman* flashes before my eyes.

"What type of proposition?"

His voice softens as he gazes at me. "I want you to paint something for me."

*What?* I wasn't expecting that. I wonder if this is how Leonardo Da Vinci felt when he was commissioned by the wealthy patrons of Europe. As I stare at Adam Black and his damn-near perfect features, a current of electricity flows through me. Nope, Leonardo probably didn't feel this way.

"You look surprised."

"Well…"

We're interrupted by our waiter, who goes over the lengthy specials. I didn't know there were so many adjectives to describe pasta. Adam, irritated by the interruption, cuts him off, informing him that we already know what we want. I haven't had time to review the menu, so when I'm asked what I would like to eat, I'm at a loss. I glance at Adam and he interjects.

"We'll have the Burrata with Organic Tomatoes and Petrossian Osetra Caviar as our antipasti." He focuses on me. "Do you eat meat?"

I nod, because the truth is, I'll pretty much eat anything. I'm a malleable piece of clay next to this man.

"Then we'll have the Gnocchi with Roasted Eggplant and two orders of Beef Tenderloin."

The menu makes a small snap as it closes and he promptly hands it to the waiter. He acts every bit the no-nonsense businessman, and the sight leaves me hot, because even the assertive way he orders dinner is a total turn-on.

The waiter scurries off as the sommelier brings out the bottle of wine Adam ordered. He takes a brief sip, inspecting its taste, and our glasses are poured. Once we're alone, I let the insecurities brewing within me spew out.

"Why would you want a painting from me?"

"From what I've seen, you clearly have talent."

I hate the compliment because it dulls the resentment I'm harboring.

"Why not tell me this business proposition over the phone or even at my house?"

"You don't like this setting?" he asks.

"That's not the point."

"What is the point?" He studies me with a sly smile.

A thought pops into my head. Maybe this was his intention all along, to make me burn. *The arrogant bastard wants me to fawn over him.* Well, I'm not going to give him the satisfaction. I reach for my wine, taking a welcome sip, willing myself to calm.

"What would you like me to paint for you?" My voice is much more put together than my thoughts. My eyes are fixed on his as I put the glass down.

Those deep blue eyes lock on mine challengingly.

"I would think the answer obvious. What you enjoy painting, something related to nature, a flower, perhaps. It's more a mural than a painting. I have a large space, an empty wall that could use some color. Of course, you will be compensated for your time and effort."

I nod wordlessly as the food arrives. It smells delicious, and yet my appetite is nonexistent. *He only wants me to paint something for him.*

"Do you have any family?"

The question is unexpected. One moment we're discussing a painting and the next, my family.

"Um..." I hate sounding so ineloquent. "Yes, my mother and a few cousins I rarely talk to."

"You have no siblings?"

I fidget in my seat as I scramble for an answer.

"No. My parents divorced when I was young. My mother did remarry, though she never had any other children."

"What about your father?"

Thinking of my father reminds me of sad times, late nights, and hours spent crying. "He died a few years ago." I don't whisper the statement, but there's a tremble to my voice I can't conceal.

The muscles in his forearms tense as he straightens against the seat. His detached features soften with what appears to be concern. "I'm sorry."

His expression makes me uncomfortable, so I shift the conversation. "What about you, do you have any family?"

He takes a deep breath. I get the impression he wants to persist with his line of questioning, but after a brief pause, he acquiesces.

"My parents live here in Florida, and my sister is currently studying at Columbia University, in New York." He takes a sip of wine while leaning forward abruptly. "You have beautiful eyes. They remind me of honey."

Caught off guard, I blurt out what I'm thinking. "Says the man with the most startling eyes I've ever seen." To avoid his gaze, I reach for my glass, downing the contents more out of necessity than want. *I can't believe I said that.*

A charming chuckle emerges from his lips as he watches me. "Are you always this honest?"

I blink in rapid succession as the flush of embarrassment burns against my cheeks. "No. Not really."

"That's interesting." He licks his bottom lip.

The husky purr of his voice mingled with the sight of his tongue makes my abdomen tighten. I push my thighs together in an attempt to subdue the burning ache between my legs, and the action makes the fabric of the tablecloth rustle.

I've lost this game of cat and mouse, because I'm a step away from writhing in front of him with unbridled desire and he knows it. *I need to get out of here before I really embarrass myself.*

"It's getting late," I say, while digging my nails into the tender flesh of my thighs. The sting of pain helps me focus.

"Would you like dessert?" It's an innocent statement that contradicts the sexy half-smile he's wearing.

*Are* you *on the menu?* Ignoring my naughty thought, I shake my head. "I should probably get home. I have to wake up early tomorrow."

He nods and the intense moment dissipates. In minutes the bill has been paid, the car retrieved, and we are on our way back. We talk idly about paintings we are fond of and books we like. It's the type of conversation you would have with someone on a first date. *Is this* a first date?

"Will you do it? The mural, I mean."

He's driving, his eyes locked on the road, which makes him easier to resist.

"I work every day. I'm not sure I have the time."

It's a poor excuse. The reality is, I'm terrified of being alone with him. What I feel toward this man is beyond attraction, it's an animalistic arousal that borders on inappropriate. And what scares me the most is that I'm not sure the sentiment is mutual.

"You could work on it in the evenings and during the weekend."

He's so practical, it's difficult to say no, and yet I have to. There's only one ending to this story, and it has nothing to do with fairytales.

We pull into my driveway and because I forgot to turn on the porch lights, it's dim. He shifts the car into park and I instantly reach for the door.

"I'm sorry. I just don't have the time to work on a project of that magnitude." Before he can respond I add quickly, "Thank you for a lovely evening."

Rounding the Mercedes as fast as my legs can bear to walk, my breath hitches at the sight of his tall frame in front of me.

"Taking you out to dinner has been my sincere pleasure."

Polite as ever, he leads me to my door, his hand brushing against mine in feather-light caresses as we move. *Is he doing that on purpose?*

The dull sound of my rapid heartbeat keeps me in pace, like a metronome. If I can make it in the house, everything will be fine. My life will stay the same. My days will continue being the gray I'm used to, and this crazy flurry of emotions will no longer plague me.

I climb the steps, and to my surprise, I have the dexterity to plunge the key into the lock.

"It must be difficult; constantly running away from anything remotely intimidating."

It's the dare in his voice that makes me turn my head, not the statement.

"Those are the words of someone who hasn't gotten what they want." Even as I'm speaking I know I'm the mouse in this cat and mouse game—I should walk away, but I can't.

"What do you know about what I want?" He climbs the last step of the porch, his broad shoulders flexed.

Refusing to take the bait, I give him my back. Reaching for the door with my right hand, I'm halted by the strong pull of my left.

Before I can focus, his lips press against mine while his body traps me between him and the door. One of his hands runs over the curve of my waist while the other tangles in the curls of my hair, pulling on the strands and angling me so that he can have free reign. I moan, loving the possessive way he grips my body, and he takes the opportunity to dip his tongue inside my mouth. His taste is divine; it's a heady mix of wine and passion. The remnants of my resistance melt as I meld against him, moving my hands over his stomach, and resting them on his belt buckle.

He pulls back with a quick nip to my bottom lip and my eyes pop open at the sudden jolt of pleasure-filled pain.

"Say you'll do the mural," he commands.

"Do you always get what you want?" I counter, gazing up at him from lowered lashes.

He rubs his cheek against mine so his lips hover over my ear.

"Persistence is a virtue."

"I thought that was patience."

He chuckles and I can't help it, I smile at the sound.

"I'll have a car pick you up tomorrow at the school. What time?"

"I haven't agreed to—"

"But you will." He pulls back, his gaze scorching and confident.

I'd like to attribute my desire to accept his proposition to pure obligation—he did save my life, after all. But no matter how much a person wants to, they can't lie to themselves. There are a thousand reasons I should decline, the main one being he's a rich, handsome, demanding man who can bed any woman he wants, and who likely does so indiscriminately. But I've tasted him and I'm lost. Playing it safe is no longer a possibility.

My mind comes back online. *I have therapy on Monday.*

"I have a thing tomorrow that I can't miss, but I can start on Tuesday after school lets out."

His body stiffens, giving me the impression he wants to know what I am doing tomorrow, but he lets the matter go. "Tuesday it is then." Holding onto the porch post as he walks backward down the steps, his voice lowers an octave. "Sleep tight, Evelyn."

Never has my name sounded more like a poem, than off the lips of the Greek god standing before me.

I will myself out of my daze to utter my own goodbye. "Good night, Adam."

He turns, making his way back to the Mercedes. Somehow I manage the energy to open the door and lock it behind me as I enter. Unlike every week of my life, I'm no longer wishing for Friday or Saturday, but Tuesday.

# CHAPTER SIX

*M*Y NAKED BACK *is arched as his hands run across my navel, caressing the skin of my abdomen. My muscles constrict. A chill cascades through my body, but I'm anything but cold.*

*I'm burning as if the sun is pounding down on me, only I'm not outside. He pulls me against him and our lips meet in a clash of tongues. It's a tender, yet practiced, kiss. The firm press of his mouth and teasing caress of his tongue makes me groan. I want this.*

*I'm straddling him, my knees bracketing his firm thighs. I steady myself by placing my hands on his muscular chest. The fine dark hairs on his torso are soft to the touch and I want to run my tongue across his tan skin, savoring every delicious inch.*

*Leaning down, I'm surprised when he grabs my elbows and spins me. I'm now lying on my back, staring up at those sapphire-blue eyes. He grins and I can't help it, I shove my body up to meet him, his erection thrusting into my writhing body.*

THE jarring noise blasting from the alarm clock startles me awake. My heart is racing and sweat is trailing down my spine. A deep heat throbs between my legs, makes me shift in bed. *What the hell was that?*

It's been years since I've had a wet dream. What is this man doing to me?

I want to sit and contemplate the events of the last few days, but it's Monday and the world doesn't stop spinning even if the chaos of your life has you dizzy. With reluctance, I stand.

Twenty minutes later I'm dressed and as ready as I'll ever be for the day ahead. I feed and pet my cat, Felix, who is starved for attention. "See you later, little guy."

Walking to work, Adam Black invades my thoughts, much in the same way he's invaded my dreams. The man is an interesting blend of contrasts. He's a detached real-estate mogul who radiates magnetism, while he still keeps you at a distance with practiced indifference. I don't know how to read him. Then there's the memory of that kiss—that remarkable, world-shattering kiss.

Why would he kiss me? Why was he so adamant that I paint him a mural?

The school day drags on. Tina tries to pry information out of me at lunch, but I'm tight-lipped. I don't want her interfering.

The bell signaling the end of sixth period reverberates through the room. The children scatter and I let out a long sigh of relief.

I begin the thirty-minute trek to Dr. Karena Davis's office, who I've been meeting with since the incident three years ago. I hate therapists. They ask invasive questions and stir up emotions you've long since bottled. They break down the barriers you forge and then leave you wondering why you can't deal with the fallout.

I greet the receptionist as I write my name on the clipboard, and in minutes I'm called in.

Dr. Davis looks lovely. She always does. Her black hair is pulled into a ponytail and her skin a hint of bronze, as if she tanned over the weekend.

"Evelyn, it's so nice to see you." Her voice is warm and welcoming. I'm always suspicious when people sound like that.

"Dr. Davis, it's nice to see you as well." I smile, because what else can I do?

"Call me Karena," she insists. She always insists.

*That's never going to happen.* Some people are able to forge friendships with their therapists. I'm not one of those people. Dismissing the thought, I sit and make myself comfortable.

"Anything in particular you would like to discuss today? How are you doing?"

Do I sincerely want to spill my guts to this woman who so often makes me feel like a pebble lost in the chasm of an evolving galaxy? Peering toward the floor, I sigh. Yes, I do, because though I hate talking to anyone about my feelings, I recognize bottling them up compounds the pressure—and I've never been any good under pressure.

"I was in a bank holdup this past Friday. This man grabbed me and pushed a gun against my throat." I frown. My hand rubs against my neck as memories of the encounter rush through my head. "I thought I was going to die."

My tone is plain and void of emotion. This apathetic attitude is what scares my mother and Tina. It scares me too.

Dr. Davis seems surprised. She probably wants to ask why I didn't call her emergency line for help. Of course, someone like me would need the emergency line. She settles on her favorite alternative—asking probing questions.

"How did that make you feel, to be in a situation where you don't have control?"

*What a ridiculous question. Like shit, of course.*

"I'm not scared of dying. There was a time when I welcomed the idea, and I rarely *have* control. In the chaos of the moment I was scared because the situation was new. Different things, *new* things, they scare the hell out of me."

I pause as a thought comes to my head.

"You know, when it was happening I was worried about my cat. I thought that if I died no one would be around to feed him. That's pathetic, isn't it? I don't have a fucking life." A bitter laugh escapes my lips.

"We have the experiences we want, Evelyn. You haven't been ready to go out and involve yourself in new things. For the last few years you've played it safe. Which is fine, but maybe now you're craving something more adventurous."

"Like going on a date with a stranger?"

She stares at me in confusion. "What do you mean?"

"I met a man at the bank. He's…" I pause, trying to organize my thoughts. "I don't think there's a word that can describe him. He knows about art. He's charming, intimidating, demanding, and handsome."

Dr. Davis laughs. "He sounds interesting. You've spent time with him, after the incident in the bank?"

I recount in detail the events of the last few days. As Dr. Davis listens, her gaze is annoyingly impassive.

"Do you want to pursue a relationship with this man?"

I answer the question without even thinking, surprising myself. "Yes."

"Why?" She shoots out quickly. "After years of avoiding experiences like this, why are you suddenly willing to try? What's changed?"

I open my mouth to respond, but I honestly have nothing to say. Fortunately, Dr. Davis interjects.

"It's natural to forge a relationship with someone who has shared a similar experience, especially when that person has rescued you from a difficult situation, though you shouldn't rush into anything."

I want to protest, because I can't stand her practicality. "What if I don't want to take it slow? What if I want to be reckless?"

Her eyes narrow and she nods. "Again, Evelyn… Why?"

"Because he makes me feel!" I half yell in exasperation. "He makes me excited, hopeful, and scared all at once." I pump my open palms back and forth from my chest in a beating motion as my muscles constrict. "He makes me believe that everything I've always found out of my reach is attainable."

The melodic bells of Dr. Davis's cell phone alarm signal the end of the session. "Disregard that. Let's keep going," she says impatiently.

Ignoring her, I get up and grab my purse. "I need to go."

"Reckless can be dangerous," she asserts. "You spent years doing reckless things like cutting yourself, which culminated in—"

"I haven't done anything like that in a long time," I say sternly. "Most of my scars are so faint they're unrecognizable, except for the ones at my wrists. And I didn't try to…" my voice shrinks into a whisper, "…kill myself because of my need to cut. The two things are separate."

Dr. Davis's chest rises as she inhales, and her eyes hold a softness that's perplexing. I don't know if she's upset, confused, happy, or concerned.

My father used to joke that heaven was a huge assembly line where angels would offer everyone who was yet to be born the skills they would need. He would smile at me and recount how when my soul finally reached the *emotional intelligence* aisle, the blushing angel attending the counter regretfully informed me they were all out. Therefore, I was sent down to Earth…incomplete. The *joke* used to make me sad because it made me think that my dad, someone who had many flaws of his own, found me lacking. And yet, maybe he was right. Maybe that's why I always have a hard time determining people's feelings… Maybe that's why often, I can't determine my own.

Suddenly, I feel like a small child. My insecurities are looming over me like shadows I can't escape. I'm scared of what the next few days will bring, and I don't want to go home to an empty house. I submit to impulse and hug Dr. Davis.

She returns the embrace, squeezing me tight. "If getting to know him is what you want, then I support your decision. All I ask is that you're careful. And if you find yourself unable to cope, don't forget I'm here. You have my number, use it."

I smile and nod even though we both know no matter what, I won't call.

As I exit the office, my phone vibrates against my hip. Adam has sent me a text message.

TOMORROW PARKER WILL PICK YOU UP AFTER WORK. WHAT TIME SHOULD HE BE THERE?

His text message is void of any emotion. It's professional and to the point. I try my best to sound equally as impassive.

FOUR IN THE AFTERNOON WILL WORK.

Seconds later my phone is again vibrating.

WHAT IS YOUR PREFERENCE IN REGARDS TO PAINT BRANDS?

The fact he's considerate enough to ask makes me smile. I respond and then it's radio-silence. The moment I think he's not going to say anything, the phone vibrates.

PERFECT. WHATEVER YOU DECIDE TO PAINT, IT WILL BE BEAUTIFUL.

The compliment makes me smile. For a few minutes I'm at a loss on how to reply. I want to say something witty but I'm drawing a blank. I settle on something simple.

YOUR FAITH IN ME IS REASSURING.

I'LL TRY NOT TO LET YOU DOWN.

Almost instantly I get a response.

YOU LET ME DOWN? NOT LIKELY.

HAVE A PLEASANT NIGHT.

I practically skip all the way home. After a quick shower I flop on the bed, exhausted. When my eyes close the welcome sight of Adam Black floods my head. For once, being in my pitch-black room isn't frightening. My breathing slows and the sweet taste of his kisses dominate my dreams.

IT'S a sunny Tuesday afternoon. The day thus far has been wonderful. The kids have been sweet and imaginative with their creations. Tina catches me as I'm leaving work.

"So, where exactly are you going?" She eyes me accusingly.

"Why do you ask?"

"I read your text messages during lunch," she blurts out. "You're going to his house!"

The anger in her voice startles me. She's my best friend and I love her like a sister, but her unsolicited interference in my life needs to stop.

"Are you serious? You went through my *phone*? You had no right." I head for the door though before I can clear it, she blocks my path.

"I shouldn't have gone through your phone," she says, attempting to appease me. "But I knew something was going on with you. And I'm worried—"

"That's why I lied about going out with Adam. Why I kept it from you that I was going to his house today. For the last few years you've been more of a nagging second mother than a friend and I can't stand it anymore. You're so busy making sure I don't make another mistake you make it impossible for me to talk to you."

She finches, her face appearing pained.

*Shit. I believe every word I've said, but I hate hurting her.*

"Tina…" I want to push her away, because it's easier to put distance between us and yet I know doing so after all the years she's stood by my side, would be unfair. "This isn't the friendship I want to have with you."

"What do you mean?" The sheen of her eyes, makes me hesitate, so she persists. "We've been friends for as long as I can remember."

"Yes," I say firmly. "But friends don't discourage, they encourage."

"I've never wanted to *discourage* you." She has a hard time getting the word out.

"I didn't tell you because I thought you would be against me talking to him, seeing him, and…" My voice trails off.

"And you like him," she whispers.

I'm surprised by her innocent statement, because it's reminiscent of something a teenage girl would say. Did my actions years ago freeze our relationship? Can anything thaw the ice? Will we ever get to the point where Tina doesn't feel the need to vet my actions?

"Yeah," I say honestly, "I like him."

"I just…" She stares at me, her eyes raw with emotion. "I don't want you to get hurt."

I laugh, to Tina's shock.

"I probably will, but is that so bad? Feeling pain has to be better than living my life in a bubble, too scared of taking chances."

Dr. Davis is right. I've spent the last three years afraid to live. I don't want to wake up one morning and realize my life slipped away. I want to do it all. I want to own every day, every second.

I narrow my eyes, trying to hold back the tears I had no idea were building.

"I'm sorry." Tina's says tightly. Apologizing has never come easy to her. "I had no right to look through your phone."

"No, you didn't." I rub my arms, hugging myself as I try to ease the tension in my muscles. "But I'm sure me lying didn't make the situation easy for you."

We're quiet for a long minute. I check the clock. It's five minutes past four, and I'm late, as usual.

"I have to go."

Before I can walk out of the classroom Tina calls out, "It's weird, between us."

I hate that she's right, so I spend five minutes I don't have telling her about my date with Adam. The intimacy is forced, and I'm worried our friendship won't recover from the obvious shift in power my recent actions have provoked, but if I don't trust her to rise to the occasion, if she doesn't trust me to manage my moods, we can't move forward.

THERE'S a black Escalade parked by the curb. A stoic man in a black suit is standing next to it. Wearing a sheepish smile, I wave.

"Miss Snowe," he says politely, though his face is stern. He opens the back door and ushers me inside.

"Thank you," I murmur softly because, like Adam, he's intimidating. "Your name is Parker, correct?"

"Yes." His one syllable is crisp and clear.

He's not much of a conversationalist. Drumming my fingertips against the soft leather seat, I try provoking him into some light small talk.

"Have you been working for Mr. Black long?"

"Long enough to know I shouldn't answer that question." His tone and posture is rigid, though his lips quirk in a smile.

"He's that much of a tyrant?" I say it jokingly, but as my mother has always asserted, there's truth in jests.

Parker shifts in the seat as he drives. "No."

*Oh, joy, we're back to one syllable remarks.* I nod, and we travel the rest of the way in silence. Fortunately, the drive is short. We pull up to a familiar building. Everyone knows it by the impressive water fountain— Eden Beach.

Describing this building could be a full-fledged architectural exam. The lobby has ultra-high ceilings, beautiful pale marble floors, and soft wooden accents. To say it's a gorgeous building is a vast understatement, and yet it lacks everything I believe necessary for a home. It's cold, barren of any true welcome. It reminds me of *him*. My heart sinks at the realization.

"Miss Snowe?" Parker extends his arm, motioning toward the open elevator doors.

I blink a few times and enter the elegant elevator.

*I don't belong here. I should leave.* It's as if I'm entering another dimension, one that will stifle the little creativity I have left. Yet, I must see what's on the other side of that elevator door. I'm bound by a dangerous curiosity. My fate was sealed when I entered that bank, the day I met *him*.

As the doors open, I see an impressive foyer. White walls outline the area and two large black doors with cast iron accents stand in front of me. Imposing, exactly like Adam Black.

Parker opens the door and I get my first glimpse of Adam's home. The furniture is modern and the color scheme matches the foyer, black and white being predominant.

I'm led to a big room that showcases a gleaming grand piano under a breathtaking skylight. It's lovely, but so out of place. It's the only object I see in this void-of-character apartment that's old and weathered. It's an antique.

The moment I see it, I want to play. My dad was a musician and wanted to teach his little girl to love music, too. He was successful. Though I'm a horrible piano player, I do love music of all kinds.

The room has a big black couch on the far end and a black-and-white patterned carpet. A few other random tables adorn the bare space. It's beautiful yet somber.

"You're here."

The voice of a woman surprises me. I turn to face her, unable to hide my astonishment. She has the appearance of a woman in her forties, with long black hair styled in a ponytail with curled ends.

"I see Mr. Black didn't mention I would be here." She smiles at me. "I'm Cadence Wright, I work for Mr. Black. I make sure this house stays clean, I cook any meals he desires, and generally take care of him." She speaks genially, yet there is a certain sense of finality in her statement.

"Oh." I finally recover my voice. "You're right, he didn't mention anyone would be here. Honestly, he didn't tell me much, other than that he wanted me to paint him something."

She nods and moves a few steps forward. "Yes, a mural of your own discretion right here." She points to the wall in front of the piano.

My eyes fall on the wall and unable to hold it back, I gasp. The wall is massive and, like the apartment, intimidating, though that's not what puzzles me. Adam is an enigma and yet deep down in my gut, I feel this room is the epicenter of who he is. *Why does a man who has everything want me of all people to paint him a mural?*

"Is everything all right?" Ms. Wright murmurs.

"Yes, sorry." I continue staring at the wall, contemplating all the possibilities it presents. "Is there some significance to this room? Do you have any idea why he would want me to paint something here?"

She laughs. "I rarely know why he does anything, not that I'm complaining. I prefer blissful ignorance."

I look at her, a small grin on my lips. She's frank, and I like that.

"He puzzles me, too." I shake my head and extend my hand. "Where are my manners? I'm Evelyn."

"It is a pleasure to meet you." She gives my hand a brisk shake.

"Is Mr. Black here?" I ask the question with my stare pinned to the wall, wanting to appear casual. My fingers fiddle with the bracelets on my wrists as I wait for her response.

"I'm afraid not. He was called away on business. I suspect he'll be gone for the next few days."

"Oh." I nod.

"He requested you be given anything you need while you work on the mural. Paint has been purchased, and if you need anything else Parker can be sent to acquire the items."

She moves to stand by my side. "I'm also more than happy to prepare meals and snacks for you as you work. I imagine a project of this nature will take several days, if not weeks, to complete."

I shake my head.

"I'll be fine. I'm sure whatever has been purchased will work for what I have in mind. As for the rest, that's nice of you, but I'd hate to be a bother."

Her dark eyes narrow. "Mr. Black requested you be well taken care of, and that's what I plan on doing."

There's no point in arguing. "Sure. Whatever works best for you."

"Good." She smoothes her skirt and looks around the room. "Well, I'll leave you to it. Parker will bring in the supplies." She strides off, her ponytail swinging as she retreats.

IT'S late on a Friday night and I've spent the last four evenings working on the mural. I'm exhausted, but I can't stop. I need to keep painting.

Parker and Ms. Wright have been accommodating. Most of the time I'm fixated on painting, and in the rare moments when I'm not, Ms. Wright insists on feeding me.

I've received no word from Adam. Not a text message, nothing.

*Maybe all he wanted from me* was *this painting.* The thought bothers me, though I try not to focus on the disappointment.

Taking a few steps back, I appraise the mural. I've painted a crimson flower. It's shrouded by an evergreen darkness that blends into ebony. The bright streaks of yellow scattered across the petals create a dramatic contrast. It doesn't resemble a flower found in nature, but is rather an amalgamation of many. It holds a mystery I find charming. And it's without a doubt the best thing I have ever painted.

"Beautiful." Black's voice is laced with wonder.

I turn to face him. I'm wearing simple jean shorts and a black tank, my hair is loose, and I've long-since discarded my sandals. I didn't expect him.

"Thank you. I'm glad you like it. I…I didn't expect you."

He's wearing gray pinstriped pants, a white button-down and an amused grin. "That's a reasonable assumption. Why would you expect to see me in my own apartment?" Adam purrs as he moves toward me. Every muscle in my body tenses as I stare into his hypnotizing eyes, and he notices.

"Do all men make you this nervous?"

*What a haughty bastard.*

"I think it's presumptuous of you to assume I'm nervous, Mr. Black." I speak his name with a heavy inflection.

"I believe I asked you to call me Adam," he says calmly, though a hint of anger burns in his eyes.

I tilt my head back and shrug. "Did you?"

He shakes his head. "Lying to me in my own home? I never imagined you to be so impolite."

"Says the man who asks the most inappropriate questions."

His laugh reverberates through the room. "They're only inappropriate if you subscribe to archaic models of propriety. I don't have the time or the desire to ask pointless questions. When I want to know something, I ask. When I want something, I take it. It's a simple philosophy."

How can I fault him for being so brutal in his honesty? I admire his lack of inhibitions, and yet that attitude is only possible for a select few. Of course, Adam Black always gets what he wants. He's rich, handsome, intelligent, and above all else, not hindered by the shadows that are in my past. Confused by my emotions, I try to organize my thoughts into coherent sentences.

"It's not easy to live like that. When you're reckless, people are bound to get hurt."

"You're too young and beautiful to be so jaded."

The confidence he exudes is threatening. It makes me question my opinions and beliefs. My legs tremble as I take a step back.

"Giving me a compliment directly followed by an insult won't make me agree with you."

He closes the gap between us. The smell of his aftershave and skin surrounds me and without thinking I take a deep breath.

"Why are you under the impression I want you to agree with me?"

My eyes widen under his scrutiny. The air around us is charged and it's hard to breathe.

"In fact, I would much rather you disagree."

"Why?" I can't help the genuine confusion resonating in my voice.

"I find you intriguing when you disagree with me. Not to mention, you're incredibly attractive when you're flustered. Your heart starts to beat faster and your breathing quickens."

He raises his hand and presses his index finger along the curve of my neck. His words come true as my lungs struggle to keep up with the demands of my body. Adam's lips curve into a soft smile as he trails his finger down my neck, resting it against my carotid.

My heart begins to race as a chill ripples down my body.

This man knows how his touch affects me, and he revels in the conquest. Part of me wants to deny him the satisfaction, a very small part of me.

"Do I make you nervous?" He places emphasis on the word *I*, his fingertips still pressed against my neck, against my pulse.

"Yes," I whisper plainly, because I can't manage anything else.

Adams hand grasps me behind the neck startling me into a gasp, as he hauls me against him. It's everything I've been dreaming about for the past week. There's an insatiable hunger between us. We both want this.

His tongue rubs against mine and I taste the faint remnants of whiskey on his lips—it's sweet, like candy. Wrapping my arms around him and entangling them in his hair, a heat begins to surge between my legs. One of his hands trails down my back, lingering along the hem of my cutoff shorts and my upper thigh. If he wants me here on the floor, I'll be unable to resist his charms, unable to resist this all-consuming passion burning throughout my body.

The firm clearing of someone's throat interrupts us, and Adam pulls away from me.

My fingertips reflexively rub at my mouth. The evidence of our passionate kiss is smeared on my lips.

Parker is standing by the door, his face apologetic.

If looks could kill, I suspect Parker would be in grave danger. Adam's eyes are dark as they focus on the guard.

Parker stares at Adam as if I'm not even in the room. He's an immovable statue, not even remotely fazed.

I have to give him credit for being composed. If the situation were reversed, if Adam was pinning me with that vicious glare, I'd probably cave under the pressure.

"Sorry for the interruption, Mr. Black, but Victoria Chase is here to see you."

I'm shocked to hear Victoria's name. Victoria was the vapid blonde at Art Basel.

Adam frowns. For a split-second he looks uncertain and then that decisive businessman returns.

"Please direct her here," he says steadily, no longer upset.

*Shit! No way he's bringing that blonde Barbie here. It would be way too cruel.* I'm not exactly dressed to impress. I glower at him.

"Is something wrong?" he asks with a quirked brow.

"Wouldn't you two prefer to have your conversation alone? Maybe in one of the many other rooms you possess in this massive apartment." Reaching for an open tube of paint, I close it before tossing it into a bag. I rub the smudges of paint on my fingers on the back of my shorts. I feel out of place.

"No, in fact *this* is becoming one of my favorite rooms." He looks toward the painting and smiles. "Besides, you being here might help the situation."

I scrunch my nose in what is probably an unflattering scowl. *Help* what *situation?* Before I can respond, Victoria Chase's voice cuts me short.

"What the fuck is going on here?"

# CHAPTER SEVEN

"**V**ICTORIA, YOU ARE as eloquent as ever."

By her stance, someone might assume she was posing for a picture. "That's because going through polite avenues has gotten me nowhere. I've been calling you for days. I spoke with your secretary and left several messages. I expected your call three days ago."

"So because your expectations weren't met, you decided to pay me a visit?" Adam shakes his head, annoyance on his face. "We stopped seeing each other several months ago. I don't owe you an explanation."

"We went to Art Basel just last week." She looks at him imploringly.

Adams eyes don't soften at her pleading expression. "We went as part of a group to an event. As I remember it, Melinda insisted you accompany us and I had no idea you were coming until after I picked up Melinda and David." He seems exasperated.

The piercing blue eyes of Victoria fixate on me. "What is *she* doing here?"

I stiffen at the intensity of her gaze, though I offer nothing else as a response. *What* am *I doing here? I should have bolted at the mention of Victoria's name.*

"That's none of your concern. This conversation is over. I've indulged your behavior too long."

"Are you sleeping with her? Are you so bored with your life you've resorted to bedding random women?"

"I think he would be better off with a random woman, rather than desperate ones who obviously refuse to take a hint." I give her a sarcasm-laced smile.

She has the nerve to appear appalled.

Adam glances at me, and for a second I see a touch of pride in his gaze. The adrenaline of the fight makes me want to lunge at him, to kiss him. I'm dragged away from my thoughts by Victoria's now-shrieking voice.

"He will use you and then *leave* you!"

She's probably right, though I would never give her the satisfaction of agreeing with her statement. The truth is, I've suspected as much, and come to the conclusion that being used may not be so horrible. After years of being a recluse I'm interested in the idea of putting myself out there.

*You say that now, but wait until Victoria's prophecy comes true.* I take a deep breath and shake away the fear invading my head.

"Maybe it's me who'll do the using."

Adams throaty chuckle makes me flinch.

*Is he laughing at me?* Both Victoria and I turn to face him.

"Mr. Black," Parker says cautiously.

"Parker…" Adam turns to the guard. "Victoria was just leaving. Please show her out."

Victoria opens her mouth to protest, but Adam's expression halts her. She turns and glares at me before stalking out of the room.

I focus my attention on Adam. I'm still angry at Victoria's harsh assessment, though I'm not willing to let my nagging insecurities win.

His voice is smooth as silk. "I do hope you plan on keeping your word. I like the idea of being used."

"Why?"

He saunters toward me. It's an elegant walk, one he has undoubtedly practiced.

"You wouldn't be here if you didn't want to. From the second I laid eyes on you in the bank I felt an attraction, and I know you feel, too."

"Victoria has been walked to her car."

It's reassuring to hear Parker. Being alone with Adam is an emotional rollercoaster.

Adam turns to face him. "Thank you." He eyes his watch. "It's eight already, why don't you take the rest of the night off? I'll take Miss Snowe home."

*He'll do what?* I stare at Parker, who for the first time since I've met him, has a grin on his lips.

"Yes, sir."

"Has Ms. Wright left for the evening?" Adam unbuttons the cuffs of his white shirt and rolls up the sleeves.

"Yes, an hour ago."

Adam nods. "Have a pleasant evening."

Parker turns and walks out of the room. The soft click of his heels against the marble floor quickly fades. He's gone.

*Damn it. Why am I so nervous around this man?* The question is stupid. He's a handsome, successful man who's always put together. I'm usually falling apart at the seams. *Of course* I find him intimidating. Most people would.

When I drag my gaze from my feet I'm an emotional wreck.

Adam stares at me with a gentle expression and I get the impression he knows I'm operating on pure adrenaline. He looks past me at the mural, appraising it with genuine interest.

"This is truly..." He pauses for a moment before completing his statement. "Stunning. The duality is what impresses me. The sharp contrast between the flower and its dark background is enchanting. While working, what exactly were you thinking about?"

The question takes me by surprise. Most of the time when I'm painting, my mind is racing, a hundred thoughts consuming my focus. However, while I worked on this mural I was oddly at peace.

"To be honest, I don't believe I thought of anything in particular. I'm sorry to disappoint you, but there is no definitive underlying message in this painting."

"Evelyn." He speaks my name softly. "There's always an underlying message in the things we do. People are just too scared of confessing their true motives, even to themselves."

This man consistently makes me question my actions and beliefs. He leaves me bewildered and grasping at straws. I try to form cohesive thoughts, and I settle on angry ones.

"Is that your subtle way of implying I'm hiding something from myself?"

The tenderness in his eyes has been replaced with arrogance. "I didn't think I was being subtle. Yes, I think you're hiding something from yourself."

He takes a deep breath and shifts his gaze away from me, back to the painting. "This flower is being consumed by the shadows." He speaks as if that simple statement proves his point.

"It's just a painting." I fidget with the hem of my tank, unsure of what else to say.

"Maybe." He steps close, his eyes narrowed and his penetrating stare so pervading a shudder runs down my spine. "But my guess is that it's something much more. And that intrigues the hell out of me."

The assertion, his proximity, the confrontation with Victoria—it's all messing with my head. How did this conversation get so intimate? I can deal with playful banter over the general merits of art, but the careful examination of my own work is uncomfortable. Needing to regain some measure of control over the situation, I shift the focus on him.

"They say people see in others what they can't confront within themselves. Maybe it's *you* who is hiding from something."

His jaw stiffens, though before I can press the issue he recovers, his features smoothing out into what seems like practiced impassivity. "That's a clever way of avoiding the subject."

A conversation with him is like a spar between boxing opponents, exhausting and relentless. Finally caving to the mounting pressure, I step back, lifting my arms in exasperation. "You know what the weirdest part of this experience is? The fact that you, *Mr. East Coast*, commissioned me, a *nobody*, to paint a mural."

"Mr. East Coast?" He laughs throatily. "That's cute."

"I'm serious!" Seeing him amused when I'm flustered pisses me off so without realizing, I'm yelling. "Why would you do that?"

His expression turns hard in a blink and sensing I've crossed a line, my muscles tense. Again he steps into my space, and though I'm nervous, I'm turned-on because there's something arousing in his imposing stance. The mystery he exudes makes me want to push boundaries—it makes me want to be reckless.

"I asked you to do the mural," he whispers low, "because I wanted you to paint something personal for me. I wanted a piece of who you are to call my own, because what I've seen so far is beautiful. And listen carefully, Evelyn, because more than anyone I've ever met I think you need to hear this—you didn't disappoint. So I'd rethink the whole *nobody* title, since it obviously doesn't fucking fit you."

The blunt confession leaves me frozen, unable to speak. The look in his eyes is so steamy it's sweltering around me. As my skin begins to burn, I'm overrun by emotions, though one in particular is stronger than the rest—desire.

"I… I'm happy you like the mural," I murmur, not trusting myself to say anything else.

The corner of his lip twitches into a half-smile. "It's a unique piece of art, though it is reminiscent of a Georgia O'Keeffe painting. The wide-open petals and the bright color make it an inviting flower. If you stare at it long enough, you could lose yourself."

His eyes glint seductively. "I think you were preoccupied with *interesting* thoughts when painting this flower."

Unable to resist, I laugh. Georgia O'Keeffe is often cited for her exploration of sexuality. Is this Adam Black's refined way of easing the tension and talking about sex?

I meet his challenging gaze. "Yes, I do believe you're right. Upon further self-reflection one particular thought *did* stand out while I painted."

Adam's mouth quirks up, wry amusement etched on his handsome features. "You've piqued my interest. What were you thinking?"

"That would be very telling, to confess something so personal." I take a cue from him and lean forward. "I don't think I'll tell you."

His tongue runs across his bottom lip. "You're forgetting that I always get what I want."

I inherently know his statement to be true. I can't imagine anyone denying him. Yet, I want to provoke some measure of insecurity in this overly assured man, because he throws me a curveball at every opportunity.

"I suppose you'll have to learn to live with disappointment."

I should have expected the kiss. It appears to be his solution for my defiance.

My thoughts urge me to struggle. *Push back, Evelyn; get the upper hand.* I should play hard-to-get, but who am I kidding—I'm totally gotten.

He pushes his body against me and I stumble back because I'm not prepared for the impact. We land against the black leather couch.

I rub my hands along the curve of his muscular back while his lips plant enticing kisses across my neck. It tickles, but I'm too overtaken by desire to laugh. I lean into his mouth, against the sweet, moist sensation of his lips, dizzy with the rush of being in his arms.

"Do you want this?" he rasps as his hands continue their exploration of my writhing body.

Provoked by the scent of his skin, I nip at his ear because I have a need to make every inch of him mine. He groans in response. *Oh, he likes that. I'll keep doing it then.*

"Evelyn," he persists. "Do you want this?"

In a moment of clarity, the word sputters out. "Yes."

He gives me a masculine grin of triumph. And then his hands are moving my thin black tank, raising it so it lies beneath my breasts. He kisses my stomach inch by inch, conquering me at an agonizingly slow pace. The sensation is too much to bear. I squirm against him, but his strong hands push me down, keeping me in place.

"Calm down, baby. We're going to take this slow."

His eyes lock on mine, and my muscles relax. Like that fateful day at the bank, the raw energy exuded by him ripples across my body, anchoring me.

He trails his tongue around my navel for several exquisitely long seconds. Then he takes a detour down my abdomen, until he's stopped by the button of my cut-off shorts.

My fingers are twisting in the silky strands of his dark brown locks. I want to bring his lips to mine but the slow roll of his tongue on my skin makes organized thoughts impossible.

With ease, he unbuttons my shorts. The zipper soon follows. He moves above me, his arms flexed in a push-up position.

This man is gorgeous. He's witty, intelligent, and he without a doubt wants me.

His touch is gentle as he guides the shorts off my legs, exposing my black satin underwear.

"Do you know how beautiful you are?"

I wiggle beneath him because the sincerity in his voice terrifies me.

He grabs hold of my chin, forcing me to stare into his dark blue eyes. "Maybe I should give you a reason to fidget, since you seem to love doing it so much."

I lick my lips at the threat and that's the only invitation he needs—he invades my mouth once again. I love the taste of this man.

Adam's hands move up, cupping my breasts underneath my tank top, kneading them, his deft fingers pinching my nipples with perfect, precise pressure. My back bows at the stimulation. Then his fingers are trailing the ridges of my ribs, sliding over the hills of my body and caressing the muscles of my back. He unsnaps the clasp of my bra, and in one fluid movement he yanks my clothing over my head. I'm practically naked in front of him, wearing only my panties, though to my surprise, I'm not nervous.

His sultry eyes fall on my bare breasts and then his lips are on me. The feeling of his wet mouth on my chest makes my nipples harden. My body convulses. Chills run across my skin as a pulsing warmth builds between my legs.

He's still fully clothed and the sight bothers me. I move my fingers toward his chest, pulling on the buttons of his shirt. I'm struggling, so he helps, and as the shirt falls to floor I finally view Adam's chiseled pecs. Fine dark hairs form perfect patterns on the defined muscle. Feeling possessive, I run my hands up his sternum, but before I can relish the experience he grabs my wrists, my bangles jingling at the touch and hauls me against him.

"Wrap your legs around me." His voice is gruff and so damn sensual.

I hug him close to my body, planting kissing on his neck as I tangle around him like a wild vine.

He stands, his hands gripping my thighs tight.

We're moving, though I have no idea where we're going. My back pushes against a door, a second after Adam's attentive hand protects my head from the impact. The sound of sliding leather echoes in the hushed darkness and then his belt thumps on the floor. The bulge of his growing erection rubs against my underwear, and I push against him.

Any man would take the action as an invitation to possess me, but not Adam Black. It's obvious he wants to savor the conquest.

His tongue lingers at the edge of my mouth, caressing my lips with leisure strokes. The tender action startles me, because I don't want him to be gentle. This is just sex. I won't let myself believe that he cares for me.

I pivot my chin, forcing his mouth to part from mine. In the darkness of the room only the faint outline of his face is apparent.

"What do you want?" he says softly, a hint of confusion in his voice.

I don't know why, but I'm honest. "I don't want to think too much."

I rub my cheek alongside his and the scuff of his stubble helps me focus.

"You were right when you said there was an attraction between us from the second we met. I want to run with this feeling." I dig my nails into his back and he gives me the sexiest grin I've ever seen. "I want you to lose yourself in me because that's what I plan to do with you."

"So you're using me?" Amusement warms his tone.

"We're using each other."

He opens his mouth to likely dispute my statement, but I don't let him speak. Leaning forward, I kiss him with a passion born from his caresses;

it's obvious that everything faded from his mind except the visceral urge to take what I've willingly given.

Sweat is misting over our pressed bodies. It's hot, sticky, and sinful—everything sex should be because it's based on primal instincts.

He pulls our tangled bodies away from the door and carries me over to a large bed at the center of the room.

I gaze at him as he retrieves something from the nightstand, though in the darkness I'm not sure what it is. He undoes his fly and discards his pants. Standing before me is a nude Adam Black.

My mouth dries at the sight. It's the type of image that provokes wet dreams, and for a second I wonder if I *am* dreaming. Adam's deep voice gives me my answer.

"Don't forget to breathe, Evelyn."

He leans down, towering above me and intimidating me with his large stature. All of a sudden his expression is serious. I gulp as I peer at this man who has so easily conquered me.

"I didn't think this would happen…that we would be in this situation." The words escape me before I can even think.

His response is absolute and confident, so him. "I did."

Then his lips are against mine, silencing me. I welcome the interruption. *You can shut me up like this any day of the week.*

Trailing his hand up my thigh, he finds the edge of my underwear and his fingers slip inside, brushing up against my opening. I arch my back and moan. Just that subtle touch has me throbbing with the need to come.

Adam pushes a finger inside me as he rubs my clit with his thumb, and I clench greedily around him.

"Fuck. You're tight." He groans as his lips press kisses between my breasts. "And so wonderfully wet."

I don't bother to answer because he's right.

His rhythm follows the swaying movements of my hips, which rise shamelessly to meet his hand. In and out, tantalizingly slow at first, and then his shallow thrusts increase. As he suckles the peaks of my hardened nipples in turn, he eases another finger into me, and a low whimper escapes my lips because I'm hovering on the edge of an intense orgasm.

"Let go, baby." His tone is urgent, yet tender.

At the endearment, my vision blurs and an effervescent sensation erupts throughout my body as I go over the edge. I've never orgasmed like that, it's so consuming it's hard to breathe. I'm glistening with sweat and my heart is racing.

He leans down and kisses me, triumph cast across his features. "You look so sexy when you come."

I stare at him wide-eyed. I'm exposed. My legs spread and his hand gripping me, his fingers still inside of me—I'm vulnerable. I want to regain some measure of control, but he has me mesmerized.

Adam's throaty chuckle reverberates against my chest.

Words haven't been spoken, but he knows I'm letting my insecurities torment me. *How can this man read me like a book?*

He grabs hold of my chin and rubs one of his fingers against my lips, smearing them with the evidence of my orgasm. "You have the prettiest lips, so full and smooth." He leans down and kisses me.

Tasting the saltiness of my release as our mouths press together, the trepidation I feel melts away under my arousal. It's not a question of want, but need. If he doesn't make me his now, I'm going to lose my mind.

Adam pulls back, tugging at my panties, and the caress of the fabric as it trails across my skin makes chills cascade down my form.

His eyes take in the sight of my naked body and the heave of his chest makes it apparent that he likes what he sees. Reaching for the item he previously retrieved from the nightstand, I now see it's a condom.

My swollen flesh tingles with renewed excitement. God, this man is perfect. Every inch of his body is rippling with muscles. My gaze lingers between his legs; he's hard like stone, a thick, long pillar of eager flesh tilting up in rigid readiness. The sight does more than turn me on—it scares the hell out of me because he's big, and I've never actually done this. *Is it going to hurt? Should I say something?*

Before I have a chance to think, Adam is moving between my parted thighs. The tip of his cock edges between the folds of my sex and in one fluid movement he thrusts deep. My muscles stretch, and I cry out in pain at the burning sensation.

Adam stills. He stares down at me and even in the darkness I can see his shock. "Are you a virgin?"

*He wants to talk about this now?*

The timing of his question, the taut inflexibility of his suddenly tense body blanketing mine, the sheer panic of knowing that my past is once again encroaching on my opportunity for even a sliver of happiness, makes me shake my head in denial. *This can't happen… I won't let it happen.*

I move my pelvis against him and bite back a wince. It does hurt, because I am a virgin and this is the first time I've attempted to be with a man in years, but I can't give him the real story. Doing that would be too intimate for what we're sharing. This is a random fuck, and nothing more. So I say the first thing that comes to mind, "Don't be ridiculous."

He doesn't seem convinced and he has yet to move. Tears begin to well in my eyes, and I know if we stop he'll see how fucked-up I am. *This can't end. Not now, not like this.* I show him through my ravenous kiss that I want this. I want *him*. I need *him*.

With his arms propped at my sides Adam pulls out so that the tip of his cock edges my opening and the next thrust is slow and gentle. My body acclimates to the intrusion and we quickly form a rhythm.

He grabs the back of my thighs and shifts them up so my legs wrap around his hips. It's different from this angle, sharper. I run my nails down his back because I want to elicit a response from him, and I'm successful. The tempo between us quickens as he pounds against me. My muscles convulse and I can sense by his ragged breathing that his own climax is building.

The sting of his drives is better than every cut I've ever given myself. It hurts, but in the most marvelous way, because in that moment I'm alive. All the shit haunting me shifts into the background and I let go.

"Oh…God…Adam!" I utter between gasps.

My cries make him increase his speed, his cock pushing against the clamping fist of my throbbing sex as he reaches his own orgasm.

"Fuck!" he groans. Then his broad shoulders shudder, his forearms flex, and those beautiful eyes of his dilate with sexual euphoria.

Spent, he lies on top of me, his cheek nuzzling against the swell of my breasts and his arms framing the curves of my body. He's heavy, but I love the heat he's radiating.

The only noise in the room is our labored breaths and as the afterglow fades, I wonder what will happen next. I don't know how to face him. I don't know what to say.

Adam rolls over on his back, withdrawing from me. The sensation is odd, and a brief pang of regret intrudes as our intimate moment ends. He pulls the condom off, tying the end and tossing it in the wastebasket by the nightstand. Again he's lying next to me on the bed.

"Fuck… That was amazing." His voice sounds young.

I blink a few times and then burst into laughter because his comment is so unexpected. My anxiety dissipates. "I never expected you to be so crass."

He grins at me wickedly. "You'll find that I am only on special occasions."

"Am I to assume that we will continue our tawdry affair for some time?" I sound calm, but I'm anything but.

He sits up and tilts his head to the side as he watches me. His expression is so serious it makes squirm.

"Don't do that," he clips out.

Startled by the reprimand, I whisper, "Do what?"

"Let your insecurities make you doubt what just happened between us."

I'm stunned by his statement. *Am I so transparent?* My eyes dart to the sheets because I can't bear to face him.

Adam grabs my chin, lifting my gaze to his unyielding eyes. "You're far too pretty to be constantly cast down."

I smile because the conviction in his voice almost makes me believe him.

He frowns. "The way you reacted when I pushed in, it seemed as if you were hurting. For a minute I genuinely thought you were a virgin."

I lunge forward, taking him by surprise with a passionate kiss because I don't know another way of avoiding the conversation. This moment is perfect. I'm wrapped in the arms of this smart, successful, and surprisingly caring man. I don't want the shadows of my past to ruin the moment, and to my delight they don't.

Adam allows the distraction and once again we lose ourselves between the sheets. The world stills, and for the next few hours only he matters.

# CHAPTER EIGHT

*M*ICHAEL'S MOUTH IS *open in awe. His shameless gawking makes me cover my exposed breasts.*

*"Stop staring at me like that. You're making me self-conscious."*

*"Babe, I can't help it. You have really nice boobs."*

*I laugh. Michael's never been much of a wordsmith but the fact that we're about to have sex has made his already questionable eloquence nonexistent.* Am I sure I want to do this? Do I want to go against everything I know—everything I've been taught—and sleep with him?

*Michael doesn't give me time to hesitate. He cups my breast while giving me a deep kiss—his tongue is plunging into my mouth repeatedly with pent-up need, and the quick way his chest pushes against mine as he pants makes it obvious he's ready to seal the deal.*

*My stomach swirls with apprehension. Should I feel this nervous? A small nagging fear lingers in the back of my head, as my Catholic upbringing shames me. I always assumed I'd wait until I was married to sleep with someone, but the truth is, I'm* tired *of waiting.*

*My cell phone vibrates against Michael's desk. I pull away from him. That's the third call in the last twenty minutes.*

Damn it, Tina! I told you I would call you after we did it.

*"Maybe I should get that."*

*I reach for the phone but he stops me before I get far with a soft push.*

*"Tina and your Dad can get by without you," he says impatiently. "They're always interrupting us. Don't let them ruin our big night."*

*Michael hooks a finger into the waistband of my underwear and again he's kissing me. Though he's trying to be gentle, his fast pace is intensifying my already spiking nerves.*

*Do I love Michael? I don't know. Maybe? I enjoy spending time with him. He makes me laugh.*

*Laying his body over mine, he pins me against the bed as his hands run over my body. A strong banging on the door makes me jump.*

*"Evie, Tina's here." Michael's roommate yells. "She says she has to talk to you. It's an emergency."*

*"Fuck! I knew they'd find a way to ruin tonight." Michael turns onto his back, his arm pressed against his forehead.*

*Frowning, I start to put on my clothes. "It's probably nothing."*

*"It's always nothing," he says. "I'm so tired of being interrupted."*

*"Come with me." I offer him a smile.*

*"I'm too pissed to go anywhere. I'll just..." He shrugs. "I'll call you later."*

*I sigh and nod.* Great. He's angry at me. *Maybe this is the universe's way of telling me that having sex with Michael is a mistake. Again my phone vibrates. Before rushing out I grab my cell and slip it into my pocket.*

*I step outside, ready to bitch at Tina, however her pale face instantly eliminates my anger.*

*"What's wrong?"*

*"Evie, we need to go to your mom's," she whispers, yet I can tell by her tone that something awful has happened.*

*"What is it? You're scaring me." My hands shake.*

*"I'll tell you when we get to your mom's. Let's go." She turns and heads for the car.*

*I don't move. It's getting hard to breathe.*

*A frightening thought comes to mind. I reach for the cellphone in my pocket and look at my missed calls. Several of them are from Tina and one is from my dad.*

*He called a few hours ago, probably while Michael and I were making out. Acid churns in my stomach, because I know what's happened.*

*"Oh God...no... Tina, is my dad okay?" I stare at her and the answer doesn't have to be spoken. By the expression in her eyes, I know he's made good on his threats. He's done it.*

*"Evie... I'm sorry..."*

*The world fades. Shadows consume me, and though I know I'm firmly on the ground, I'm weightless.*

*My daddy's dead.*

"EVELYN."

A voice calls out in the dark as I toss and turn against the sheets.

*"Evelyn!"*

I lurch my body forward into a sitting position, waking from the nightmare. I'm sweating and my breathing is irregular. Adam is beside me, his face furrowed with concern. My head shifts from side to side, taking in the shadows of the moonlit room.

Adam's strong hands reach for me, cupping my face. Then his warm mouth rubs against mine in a sweet, slow embrace. Tenderly, he trails his lips down my cheek and across my neck. The fog lifts and everything comes into focus.

"Evelyn, you're safe." He breathes against my skin.

I dip my head forward in a childlike nod. My eyes are brimming with tears.

How can I be safe when my world doesn't make sense? When my father took his life? When I tried to follow in his footsteps? Feelings of safety elude me because I'm haunted by so many mistakes.

Adam presses the pad of his thumb on my cheek and wipes away one of my tears.

*Why is he being so sweet? He barely knows me. I don't need his pity.*

The idea of being here is unbearable. I push off the bed.

"Where are you going?" He clicks on the lamp and I squint as light floods the room.

"Home. It's late and I need to get home." I sound crazy but I don't care.

"Calm down, Evelyn. If you want to go home I'll take you." He stands, his eyes scanning the floor for his boxer briefs.

"No. It's okay, I don't want to disturb you. I don't live far from here, I'll walk." I mimic his actions, trying desperately to find my underwear. *Where the hell are my panties?*

"I'm not taking no for an answer." He's adopted a businesslike tone. Only Adam Black could appear so authoritative and professional while wearing nothing.

I shouldn't argue. I should nod my head and accept his offer, but I can't.

"I'm perfectly capable of walking."

I turn to leave the room and to my surprise he's by my side, gripping my wrists and forcing me to sit on the bed. His jaw tightens as he presses his lips together.

"If you think for one minute that I'm going to let you walk out of here in the middle of the night, you are seriously delusional."

Frozen still by his cold voice, I stare at him, baffled.

"What was your dream about?"

He speaks with command, and I want to lie to him the same way I lied to Tina and my mother, but I'm unable to conjure the words.

"What was the dream about?" he demands, in an octave lower.

"The past, things I can never change. Mistakes…" Tears stream down my face and the urge to run is growing exponentially.

Adam kneels in front of me, his brow knitted. "That is the most ambiguous statement I've ever heard."

Of course it's ambiguous. He wants an elaborate explanation of my irrational actions, but you can't define crazy. My father spent a lifetime trying to understand the impulses that dominated his actions. In the end he quit trying. And what scares me is that I'm like him.

"I hate the look you're giving me right now."

"What look? My pissed-off expression?"

"Pity. Your eyes are drenched with it. Don't feel obligated to care because we slept together. Believe me, I won't hold it against you."

Adam's grip tightens around my wrists. "I've already said it, but you obviously don't understand so I'll repeat myself. I'm not the type of man who does anything out of obligation. My actions are motivated by my sincere desire to do whatever the hell I *want*!"

He realizes he's yelling and inhales deeply, muttering a curse under his breath. "I swear, you have the uncanny ability to drive me insane."

His admission halts my melancholy and a small smile crosses my lips. I can do that to him?

"You're not leaving now. In the morning, and I do mean *much later* in the morning, if you still want to leave I'll take you home. There's no way in hell I'm letting you leave while you're tired and upset."

I open my mouth to protest but his cobalt eyes are unyielding. I nod, too stunned to argue further.

"Lie down," he orders as he pulls back the comforter.

That's when I see it—on the center of the bed is a bloodstain. It's not big, but the contrast of the crimson mark and white sheets makes the image drastic. I freeze, a mixture of mortification and dread crawling through my body. My eyes dart to my thighs and at the sight of dried blood, my throat tightens and it becomes hard for me to swallow.

"You want to revisit the response you gave me when I asked if you were a virgin?" Adam says way too calmly.

"Just let me go home," I whisper, unable to face him.

"No fucking way—especially now!"

There goes his calm.

"You can't keep me here if I don't want to—"

"You staying, shouldn't even be a point of contention."

He shakes his head and drops his hands, which have been gesturing as he speaks. He's a poem, the effects of his irritation and exasperation adding flaws to his features that at least to me, aren't really flaws.

Lost in the thought I'm surprised when he cups my face, "Evelyn, explain it to me," he says slowly. "Why are you so desperate to leave?"

The direct question makes me shiver. Adam notices, and before I can answer, I'm in the cradle of his arms, my cheek warmed by the heat radiating from his chest.

"Don't ask me to let you go like this, because I can't," he whispers huskily. "Let me take care of you."

"I'm scared," I confess without thinking.

His arms tighten around my body. "Of what?"

My eyes are clamped shut, as the smell of his scent surrounds me. How can I explain what even I don't understand? I can't, so I don't even bother. Minutes pass and his reassuring hold manages to keep my panic at bay.

"Stay Evelyn. Stay so I can show you that when you're with me, you have nothing to fear."

Though I want to resist, the promise in his voice makes it impossible. I nod against him and he doesn't afford me the opportunity to change my mind.

"Lie down on the bed," he commands gently.

Using my hands to cover my bare breasts—a futile action, since he's already seen everything—I get back on the mattress. With care, he covers me with the comforter. It's cold in the room, but the stare he gives me is smoldering. I don't know what he's thinking. Is he pissed off because I didn't tell him I was a virgin? Is he angry about his sheets?

Adam turns off the light and then I hear the soft tap of his bare feet against the marble floor as he retreats to the bathroom. A slow burn sizzles in my stomach making me think for a dreadful second that I might throw up.

I'm so focused on keeping my anxiety in check, I don't notice Adam return until he's close, so close the heat of his skin radiates against mine.

"Spread your legs."

I stay motionless, not certain I've heard correctly.

"Baby," he says in a slow, sexy whisper while drawing the covers down, "Spread your legs for me."

I don't move because it's hard for me to process what's happening, so he helps, his knuckles gliding over the sensitive skin of my inner thighs. Then a warm washcloth is between my legs, rubbing against me, and my hearts racing, I'm panting softly and my hand has found its way to Adam's chest. I dig my nails against him, desperate to anchor myself from the reality of what's happening—my embarrassment over the situation, the familiarity of his actions, the incontrollable response his touch has over my body.

Needing to put a stop to this I mutter the first thing that comes to mind. "I'm sorry about your sheets."

His hand stops moving between my legs. "Evelyn," he says gently while tossing the cloth on the marble floor, "I don't give a fuck about the sheets."

He slides under the covers and shifts me so my back is pressed against his firm chest. The way he holds me shows his dominating nature, though his touch is tender. He took my virginity hours ago and yet this is the most intimate moment we've shared.

"Are you okay?" he murmurs.

I'm obviously not, though I offer him my stock response. "Yes, of course. I'm fine."

The hairs of his forearm tickle the skin under the swell of my breasts as he tucks me close. "Why do you do that?"

"Do what?" I say, trying to ignore the feelings I'm having over being held by him.

"Put up this front and pretend everything's okay when it's not. You just woke up in the middle of the night terrified because of a nightmare, a nightmare you're unwilling to discuss, and…" His chest pushes against my back as he breathes deep. "And you lost your virginity—"

"Adam, don't worry about me. I'm fine."

"You are annoyingly stubborn," he chides.

"I'm not the only one who falls into that category."

He squeezes me, and I squirm under the constraints of the tight embrace. His steady breath on the nape of my neck makes my muscles loosen. Wrapped around him, a scary realization hits—he makes me feel safe.

"Careful, I'm better at this game than you." While his tone is serious, I can hear the playful edge he's attempting to conceal.

"What do you care? If I want to leave in the middle of the night, why stop me?"

He laces his fingers with mine as he clasps my hand. His grip is steady and reassuring. "Because I wanted you to stay."

How can his arrogance be both something that drives me crazy with anger and passion? How is it that in such a short span of time he can control me? The entire notion makes me squirm.

"Stop fidgeting and go to sleep." He sounds distant, even though his hold is intimate.

I'm confused. I lie against him, trying to figure out the puzzle that is Adam Black. Unlike every man in my life, who has bailed on me at the mere hint of a complication, he's not willing to let me go and he barely knows me.

His actions don't make sense. Being in his arms is like taking a strong dose of Valium, and I feel like I'm floating. For a brief moment a nagging fear clings to my semi-awake consciousness.

*Don't fall from the cloud.*

# CHAPTER NINE

I WAKE UP curled against white sheets—alone.

*Where am I?*

*Oh, I decided to go with my impulses and sleep with Adam Black.*

I groan. My Catholic-influenced conscience still remains unforgiving.

As I put my feet on the cold marble floor, the large windows that wrap around the room capture my attention. The ocean view is breathtaking.

Standing, because I want to take in the sight, I wince. Muscles I've never used are tingling. I take a deep breath and step toward the en suite bathroom.

Since I can't find Adam and there's no way I'm leaving the room looking like this—a sex-tousled mess—I decide to shower.

The bathroom, a modern blend of black and white, is the epitome of Adam—intimidating.

Discarding my silver bangles on the stone countertop, I wait for the water to warm. A few seconds later I'm under the welcoming spray, bathing with his body wash. The smell floods me with memories of last night. My world is upside-down, but I love it.

The idea of lingering makes me self-conscious, so I hurry. After rummaging through his cabinets, finding a toothbrush, and borrowing one of his T-shirts, I set out in search of the sex god who has left me achingly aware that he's explored my body with vigor.

Approaching the kitchen, I hear the soft sizzle of something frying. *Oh shit, Ms. Wright is cooking.* I start speed walking in the opposite direction, when Adam's deep voice captures my attention.

"Read that line again… Send it back, the contract is shit."

Peeking around the corner, I see him standing over the stove, wearing simple black pajama pants and a white T-shirt. He has a cellphone pressed against his ear and is moving something in a skillet with a spatula.

The sight of a domesticated Adam is funny. Mr. Incredible can cook. I can't help it. I laugh.

He turns his head, his beautiful eyes focusing on me while the most adorable little scowl perches between his brows.

"I'll be in the office around two. Send them the contract with our adjustments. Change it so they're paying the closing fees. I don't plan on staying long, so make sure it's done by two." He ends the call and places the phone on the counter.

I laugh again. He can be so curt and commanding one minute and extraordinarily gentle the next. *Does he even realize he does this?*

"Is something funny?"

"You're a puzzle. I'm just trying to figure you out." With a smile, I move to the counter and lean against it, placing my elbows on the cold granite.

"Coming from you, that's ironic." He removes the pan from the stove and then leans against the counter, mirroring me.

"Hungry?" he says softly.

"Depends on what you're serving." My eyes take him in, from the lustrous waves on his head to the taut muscles his fitted T-shirt can't hide. One night in his arms and I'm lost.

He stands with a cocky smirk. "At the moment, I'm serving bacon and eggs."

I sigh at the disappointing response. "I'm surprised to see you cooking. I didn't think a man of your stature would willingly take on such a commonplace task."

"I should hope by now you realize I have *many* talents."

The comment makes my cheeks burn, which elicits a low chuckle from him. Returning his attention to the skillet, he takes two plates from a cabinet, serves us both, and sits on the stool next to me. It's surreal to be eating breakfast cooked by a man who spends his days dealing with multi-million-dollar business deals, so for what seems like forever, I'm quiet.

"Your silence is starting to worry me." He reaches for his glass of orange juice. "You don't like it?"

The fact he cares enough to ask is sweet. I scoop some eggs on my fork, take a big bite, and savor the flavor. "It tastes great, though I will reserve my final opinion until later, depending on whether I survive the day."

He puts the orange juice down on the counter, while his tongue glides across his bottom lip. "Are you implying my cooking will get you sick?" He looks appalled.

Leaning forward, he speaks with a husky tenor that makes the fine hairs on the back of my neck stand at attention. "Believe me, it's not my *cooking* you have to worry about."

I arch my brows at the cryptic statement. "What should I be concerned about then?"

"The fact that you're sitting next to me, wearing only my T-shirt."

His searing stare is nothing but carnal. My mouth dries as my pulse quickens.

"I still have no clue why I should be worried. I believe my virtue has long since been discarded with you."

"Why would you say that?"

The question sounds like a reprimand, which leaves me wondering how our conversation has derailed. Ignoring him, I stand and begin clearing the dishes. I place the plates in the sink, taking my time as I wash them.

"Evelyn—"

I interrupt him. "I have some questions I want to ask you."

Adam inhales a breath that turns into a soft snort. He's annoyed, though a hint of amusement gleams in his eyes.

"I'll answer your questions if you answer mine."

The dangerous purr of his challenge makes me hesitate, and he takes note.

"It's only fair," he adds.

Fighting against my inclination to buckle, I stare him straight in the eyes. "I have three questions. Shall we take turns?"

He nods.

I raise my index finger. "First, how did you disarm the bank robber? It's been bugging me for a week. I mean, everyone in the bank was terrified; you were calm."

Adam laughs. "Well, that's a random question."

He leans back on the stool and shrugs. "I was trained. After college I joined the Marines and spent four years active duty. I've been in situations where staying calm was the only way to survive. I was nervous that day at the bank, but I knew that showing I was would only make the situation worse. I kept it together because that's the best way to deal with a stressful situation."

His sincerity makes my mouth twitch in a smile. *Maybe this is why he's able to control his emotions so well.*

"It makes sense that you're an ex-Marine."

"I'm not," he says flatly. "You're never an ex-Marine. Once a Marine, *always* a Marine."

I nod, unsure of what else to do.

He takes a drink of his juice and then fixes his gaze on me. "My turn…" He raises his index finger. "How is it that a beautiful woman like you has never before slept with a man?"

"What?" I gape at him.

"You heard me."

"That's an intrusive question!"

"We never stipulated what we could and could not ask. I answered your question, now answer mine."

I'm irritated that he would ask something so personal. More than anything I'm angry I wasted a question inquiring about the bank robbery.

"Well?" He looks at me with impatience.

"Does everyone do what you want?" I glare at him.

"Yes," he says firmly, and I can tell he's getting cross.

"Don't assume it's because I never had the chance!"

"I would never assume that. In fact, that's the conundrum. You're a beautiful woman…intelligent, passionate, the list goes on. Why is it that you've never been with someone?"

I sigh with resignation because I have to answer this question. If I were to go back on our arrangement he would think less of me. *I* would think less of me.

"The one time I almost did, everything went wrong." My eyes sting as the memory flashes in my head. "I had this boyfriend in college and I liked him enough to think that maybe he was it. Fate didn't agree. Things fell apart after that and we broke up."

I grab his glass and drink the final sip of his orange juice while he watches, his gaze intense.

"Don't worry. It's not a big deal. I won't stalk you now that you've 'deflowered' me. I'm not that type of girl."

"You're lying to yourself if you honestly believe what happened last night wasn't significant. A person doesn't wait until they're twenty-four years old to fuck, just because."

The frank way he speaks makes me blush and he notices.

"That's exactly what we did," he persists. "I was the first man you've ever been with and it's a *huge* deal."

"I... I don't know what you want me to say," I offer lamely.

"I want you to look me in the eyes and tell me that you'll never lie to me again."

The statement makes me frown, and since I hesitate in responding, he continues.

"Last night I asked you if you were a virgin, and you lied. I don't deal with liars."

I focus on his eyes and see they're as hard as stone. My mouth dries, and when I do talk my words sputter out scratchily. "I didn't lie. I told you to stop being ridiculous. And I feel that's an honest enough statement since you asked that question in the middle of the act which is at least to me, ridiculous." His eyes narrow and he opens his mouth, though I don't give him the chance to talk. "I'm sorry, if you feel that was dishonest or unfair, I just..." I inhale sharply, "I didn't want you to stop." My cheeks feel like they're on fire because it's awkward confessing the extent of desire I felt for him last night—the extent of desire I've felt for him since we met.

He stares at me, as if he's trying to siphon my secrets with his glance alone, and then he sighs. The shift in his expression is like a sunset, slow and enthralling. His features soften as his tension dissipates. "You should have told me. I would have done things differently."

*You would have stopped.* Not having the courage to voice what I'm thinking, I nod slowly in an effort to appease him. It's apparent that Adam is not use to anyone contradicting him.

"I believe it's your turn," he says, his gaze annoyingly unreadable.

I rub the side of my head for a long minute, trying to recollect my original thoughts. "Um... Why did you break up with Victoria?"

I'm not sure why I ask the question, probably because I need to understand how a man who has everything can choose to spend a night with me instead of, quite literally, one of the most striking women I've ever seen.

"Victoria is a beautiful woman. She's incredibly sexy, and depending on the subject matter, quite intelligent."

I roll my eyes as he speaks.

"I'm not finished." He looks at me sternly.

"Sorry," I murmur. *Damn, I'm apologizing a lot in this relationship. Wait... is this a relationship?* Adam continues talking which makes it hard for me to think.

"Something was missing between us. We had different interests, and she was right when she said that I was bored."

My snippy thoughts cloud my head. *See, I told you so. He's going to use you, abuse you, and then lose you.*

"Are you always this insecure?"

*What an intrusive bastard. How does he know what I'm thinking?*

"That's your question?" I sound annoyed.

He shrugs. "Yes."

"I don't consider myself insecure. I just find you intimidating."

"I make you that nervous?"

"I believe it's no longer your turn to ask questions," I say with a smug smile.

He rolls his gorgeous eyes at me.

"Hey, that's not very polite."

Adam grins at me, and I'm surprised at how quickly he can make me forget he's an arrogant, domineering man who peels away at my secrets as if I were an onion.

I know what the next question will be, but the answer he may give scares me. After a deep breath I go with my impulse. "Where is this going?"

His grin fades as he stands up from the stool. His serious expression is void of emotion. He walks to the sink and stands next to me. "Where do you want it to go?"

"I believe answering a question with a question is cheating."

"We never specified the rules of this little exercise." He looks down at me self-assuredly.

I'm embarrassed so I lower my gaze, only to be halted by his hand on my chin. He tilts my head so I'm forced to face him.

"Answer the question, Evelyn."

"I liked what happen last night."

His lips curl into a satisfied smile. "I liked it, too."

He leans forward, kissing me, and it's the first time that the action doesn't catch me by surprise. As I wrap my arms around him, I'm vaguely aware that the T-shirt I'm wearing has risen, revealing my bare bottom to the attractive and seductive Mr. Black. He groans as his hands trail down to my exposed flesh, and in seconds I'm pulled against his growing erection.

He shifts back and whispers, "I think we're done with our question-and-answer game."

I nod up at him.

He has a smirk lingering on his lips that is piquing my inquisitive nature. He grabs my wrists, and for the first time in the last half hour I realize I don't hear the familiar chime of my bangles. *Shit! I left them in the bathroom. My scars!* I'm sweating, and it has nothing to do with arousal.

Adam pushes me against the refrigerator, his mouth still pressed again mine, and the cold stainless steel on my back makes me squeal. My thoughts scatter and the missing bangles are no longer a priority.

"I like that sound," he says huskily. "Maybe we can make some other interesting noises."

He grabs one of my hands and pulls me to the dining room. With a charming quickness, he discards his white T-shirt, leaving his bare chest in my view.

"I want you on this table," he utters as he towers above me.

I peer up at him between my eyelashes. "Am I to assume that I'm your dessert?"

"You are so perceptive."

He's forceful as he grabs my shoulders, spinning me so I'm facing away from him. I don't have time to be shocked because his hands invade my T-shirt, cupping my breasts and kneading them so my nipples harden. His actions are coarse and possessive.

Pushing me down on the table so my stomach is touching the cool, black wood, I'm aware that his intention is to take me from behind. The thought is exciting. Truthfully, I want him to make me his, because since last night, I *am* his.

I hear him rip the foil wrapper of a condom. *Where the hell did he get that?*

"Did you plan on this happening?" I say with a smile.

"I'm just perpetually prepared."

I don't have to see him to know that he's grinning.

Adam lifts the T-shirt I'm wearing so that it rests under my arms, leaving my back exposed. One of his hands moves along my spine while the other grabs my hips, pinning me in place. Then his lips are pressed against my skin, trailing kisses along the curve of my bare flesh.

The feel of his warm, wet mouth makes me whimper and writhe. I try to shift so I can face him, but he's persistent with his hold. He controls the situation.

His teeth graze my skin, nipping me between the shoulders and then he whispers, "What do you want, Evelyn?"

*What a stupid question. Obviously, I want you.* I continue to squirm against him without offering a response.

Adam makes a soft *tsk*-ing noise. "Tell me what you want, Evelyn."

Breathlessly, I answer, "You… I want you inside me."

He chuckles, as the hard bulge of his erection weighs heavy against my ass. "I want you to be exact. What part of me do you want inside of you?"

A low growl rolls out of my throat because I simultaneously loathe and love the way he pushes me out of my comfort-zone. "Your cock…. I want your cock inside of *me!*"

He thrusts into me hard. I'm wet, but the intensity of the movement and my soreness from the previous night, makes the friction painful. I cry out, and he stops.

"No," I say breathily. "Keep going."

He hesitates and I roll my hips, tilting them up, offering him a better vantage point. Then he's moving again, and my frantic moans only serve to excite him more.

This is precisely what I desire—the rough sensation of him conquering me, that perfect blend of pleasure and pain. My hands are moving against the table in a futile attempt to anchor myself, but there's nothing to grab.

Ecstasy ripples throughout my body as he slows his pace. His thrusts become shallow and I can feel every inch of his cock swell with pleasure as he sinks into me. I press my legs together and squeeze my muscles as he lunges forward.

"Fuck! Keep doing that."

Adam grips my ass as he thrusts deep, my body giving way to the forceful intrusion as his balls slap against my clit. A primitive groan escapes my throat and I'm about to come. His pace quickens and I can tell he's close.

We're at a precipice, about to fall together, when the sudden sound of a door opening halts our movements.

"What the hell?" Adam growls.

He pulls out of me roughly, making me wince. Before I know what's happening, he's yanking me upright, the T-shirt bunched under my arms falling so it sits high on my thighs and drawing his pants up, the condom still wrapped around him, though now it's concealed.

I stand behind him, unsure what's going on, my body still burning with need.

We both look toward the foyer entrance. A beautiful young woman in designer clothes appears, the sharp clicking of her undoubtedly expensive heels reverberating in the now-silent room.

She appears strangely familiar. Then I see her eyes, those beautiful deep-blue eyes.

Her voice is crisp, and she sounds amused. "Hello, brother. Am I interrupting something?"

# CHAPTER TEN

"SARAH. WHAT THE hell are you doing here?"

To her credit, his sister isn't fazed by his anger.

"How did you get a key?"

She rolls her eyes.

*How does she manage to do that with such elegance? I better start taking notes.*

"You gave me a key over a year ago, when you went to New York to purchase that apartment complex in Manhattan. I was here for the summer, so you asked me to housesit." She has that same matter-of-fact tone that Adam so often exhibits.

"As I remember it, you gave the key back."

"Well, yes. However, I did make a spare." She finally appears somewhat apologetic.

Adam's body is rigid, and I can tell he's holding back his fury. I'm huddled behind him, my face pressed against the warmth of his back. I'm mortified. His sister busted in on us when he was enthusiastically making me his. My thoughts echo in my head. *You mean while he was* fucking *you on the dining room table.* I stifle a groan.

"Go to the guest bedroom, now."

Since I have no clue where the guest bedroom is located, I assume he's speaking to his sister, though the thought of retreating is appealing.

"Don't be mad. I just wanted to surprise you."

"Sarah, go now!" he yells.

A twinge of sympathy stirs within me for his sister. Being on the receiving end of Adam Black's ire is not on the top of my to-do list.

The loud click of her heels dissipates as she walks away. Adam turns to me and I'm sure at this point I'm beet-red.

"Hey," he says softly.

"Hey." I mimic his response, because I don't trust myself to say anything else.

I gaze into those sapphire eyes and my own water with suppressed tears.

"It's okay. She didn't see anything." Gingerly, he wraps his arms around me.

He has a small smile on his lips and I wonder if he finds my reaction funny. A vile thought comes to my mind. *How many times has Adam been caught with someone else? How many times has he laid a woman down on that dining room table?*

My thoughts are halted by his kiss. At first I still, unwilling to return the affection because I'm tormented by the thought that I'm one of many in his endless list of affairs. However, those sweet lips are impossible to resist. As he bites my bottom lip I open my mouth and our kiss is no longer chaste.

Adam pulls back. "It's time you change into something more conservative. As appealing as you look in my T-shirt, we're no longer alone."

He is stiff with frustration. Maybe the thought of explaining himself to his sister bothers him? Probably not. I doubt Adam explains his actions to anyone.

"Feel free to use any of my things. I doubt I have anything that will fit you, but you're welcome to it." He sounds impassive.

I hate it when Adam sounds so detached. I nod.

He turns to retrieve his cellphone from the kitchen counter. "Shit, less than an hour till I have to leave."

I don't want to be in this room; I don't want to be near him. Confusion washes over me. Where the hell did the kind, compassionate man who spent the last few hours with me go?

I move past him with the intention of going to the bedroom, but then I remember my shorts and tank are in the piano room. Once I'm there I see my clothing scattered across the floor. I grab the shorts and put them on minus my panties, because I can't find them. My purse is on top of a corner table and a sudden thought hits me.

*Tina!* I groan. She's probably *furious*.

I reach the phone, and as I suspected, I have several missed calls and a few texts.

ARE YOU OKAY?

CALL ME.

IF YOU DON'T PICK UP SOON I'M GOING OVER.

I'M AT YOUR HOUSE. WHERE THE HELL ARE YOU!?

NOT COOL, SNOWE! I'M PISSED!

I press the call back button. The phone rings once before she picks up.

"Evie!" She sounds surprised.

"Hey, I'm safe."

"You didn't call last night or respond to my texts. What's going on with you?" The sliver of relief I heard has now switched to reproach.

"It's a long story. Are you still at my house?"

"Yes. I raided your fridge. Feeding me is the least you can do after ignoring me for hours."

"Did you call my mother?"

"No," Tina murmurs. "And I'm pissed you'd ask. Contrary to what you think, I don't call your mom to give her a play-by-play of your every action."

"Sorry," I say more to shut her up than anything. "I'll be home soon. I'll tell you everything when I get there."

"You spent the night with him, didn't you? No way! You slept with him?"

Her squeals as she asks the questions makes me lean away from the phone.

"Let's talk about this later. I'm not exactly in the best place to have this type of conversation."

"Are you okay?" Tina's voice has shifted back to concern.

"Yes. I'll tell you everything when I get home. I need to go." I hang up the phone, recognizing I probably left her with a thousand unanswered questions. I couldn't care less; I'm reeling from the emotional rollercoaster of the last few minutes and still trying to catch up.

I sit in the piano room, eyeing the painting I've created. The dichotomy is interesting. Part of it is beautiful and bright, hopeful even. Then the portion cast in shadow is scary. *Adam is right.* This painting is a reflection of my own emotions, of the feelings I struggle with daily. I close my eyes, unwilling to look at it further. I hate that Adam is right, and part of me is unable to fathom how a man who's known me for only a week can so easily see me. *Why can't I do that?*

"It's a beautiful painting," Sarah says from the entrance.

"Oh." I stand, startled. "Thank you."

"I'm sorry. We have yet to be properly introduced." She approaches and I notice she is no longer wearing heels. Her clothing has completely changed; she appears relaxed in jeans, a T-shirt, and sandals. With a smile, she extends her hand.

"I'm Sarah."

I nod at her and we shake. "Evelyn."

"Oh, that's a pretty name. I bet all your friends call you Evie."

I laugh, because it seems like the best reply.

"Are you dating my brother?" Her gaze scans me, overtly studying my actions and mannerisms. I get the impression she wants a certain answer.

"I believe you need to ask your brother that question."

"Oh. So he's the one who determines the answer?" She has the same infuriating arrogance that Adam exhibits.

"No." I pause, thinking about my response, because the next few minutes will determine the type of relationship, if any, that I will have with Sarah Black. "I'm not comfortable discussing something so personal with someone I barely know. However, he's your brother. I'm sure if you ask, he will happily supply you with an answer." I smile at her, though it is stilted.

A small grin forms on her lips. "I think you already know that Adam will likely not divulge much information." She walks over to the painting and inspects it.

It's as if everything about me is being measured. I stare at Sarah with resolve. "Yet another reason why I should stay silent on the matter."

"What is it you do?" She turns to face me.

I place my hands in my pockets, taking a cue from Adam's handbook. *That's right, Evie, look relaxed.* "I'm an art teacher." Before she can utter her next question I interject with my own, remembering what Adam told me about his sister when we were talking at dinner. "What is it you study at Columbia?"

Her eyes widen with surprise. After a pause she responds. "To the chagrin of my parents, I'm studying Art History."

This time my smile is genuine. "I can certainly relate; my mother was disappointed when I chose to get my degree in Art. Are you solely an art enthusiast, or do you paint as well?"

She blinks a few times and then shakes her head. "I've never taken an art class, though perhaps one day." She bites her bottom lip, lost in thought. "You know, Adam usually dates women who are much different than you."

"How exactly are they different?" I glance at her, hoping my curiosity isn't too apparent.

She does a casual, off-the-cuff shrug that instantly reminds me of Adam. "I'm sure you can imagine. They are usually very tall, very put together."

I take a deep breath. I refuse to let this girl push me into a corner. "I assume you are implying that I'm not tall and put together?"

She laughs outright. "I can see what he likes in you."

I tilt my head in confusion, still wanting her to answer my question, though I doubt she will.

"Do all the women he dates get an interrogation from you?" I arch a brow at her.

"So you *are* dating." She grins.

*Damn it. That's not what I meant.* I open my mouth to say something, but Adam's voice pulls my attention to the entrance.

"What are you girls talking about?" His hair is wet and slicked back. He's showered and is wearing dark navy-blue pants and a white button-down shirt. The top two buttons of his shirt are open, revealing his tanned skin.

"Nothing important. We were just getting to know each other." Sarah moves toward Adam and leans up to kiss his cheek.

Though I can tell he's still irritated at her, he bends down as she kisses his cheek. I smile, because it's wonderful to see this man who is so often restrained be affectionate with his sister.

Adam looks at me. "Are you ready to go?"

My right hand moves against my left wrist, an action I've adopted as habit, and I'm reminded about the bangles I've left in his bathroom. "Oh. I left something in your room that I need to get." It's awkward saying that in front of his sister, but it's unavoidable. I need those bangles. Any moment now, Adam will grab my hand, he'll look down and see my past, and his opinion of me will change. The thought alone makes my stomach turn sour.

"Okay, we'll be in the living room."

I nod as I walk past them both, toward the bedroom. Everything feels so uncomfortable now that his sister is here. *Maybe he's bored of you already.* Victoria's words haunt me. What could a man who has everything want in me?

I grab the bangles from the en suite bathroom and put them on. As I enter the bedroom I can't help the smile that emerges. *At least if it ends now, I'll have the memory of last night.*

Exiting the room, the muffled sound of conversation makes me stop dead in my tracks, not because I'm nosy, but because the voices sound angry.

"I don't like him for you."

"Well, you honestly have no say. Who I date is my business."

"You're right, though if you want to date a man who's only interested in sleeping with you, I have to question why exactly I'm paying for an Ivy League education when you obviously lack the intelligence to benefit from it."

I cringe at the statement.

"Are you saying that if I don't stop dating him, you'll stop paying for my tuition?"

"Don't be dramatic," Adam growls. "I'm simply making a point. You deserve better than being with a man who doesn't care about you."

"And do you care about the many women you sleep with?"

"What a smart defense, pointing at me and my actions, so we can disregard yours," he says with sarcasm. "Not that you deserve an explanation, but I'll offer it nevertheless. I have never once lied to a woman I have been with, which is more than what Markus can say."

"I thought he was your friend."

"Someone I knew in high school, an acquaintance, but certainly not a friend." His voice becomes tender. "Sarah, trust me. He's not the man for you."

I'm appalled that I eavesdropped on their private conversation. At the same time, a jealous thought tugs at my heart. *How many women has Adam Black slept with? Am I just another number?* This isn't the time or the place to be thinking about his past conquests.

Adam and his sister are probably wondering why I'm taking so long. I force a smile as I move through the hallway and into the living room.

"I'm ready."

Adam looks at me, his face flushed with anger. He turns to his sister and then stands. "Will you be staying here?"

Sarah shakes her head. "I'm going to Mom and Dad's. I just wanted to pop by for a visit."

"How did you get here?"

"I took a taxi from the airport."

Adam rubs the back of his neck with a hand, flexing his forearm. "As always, you act without thinking." He takes out his phone and presses a button. "Parker, I need you to take my sister to my parents' house." A few seconds later, he snaps the phone shut. "Parker will be here in twenty minutes."

Adam walks past me to the foyer. He doesn't utter a word, though I get the impression I should follow.

I smile at Sarah, because it's obvious she could use some compassion.

"Evie, it was a pleasure meeting you. I hope we'll have the opportunity to see each other soon." She sounds heartfelt.

I'm surprised that she uses my nickname, though I don't mind the gesture. "I would love that." I turn and follow Adam.

When the elevator arrives we travel down in silence. Why did this have to happen? Yesterday was perfect. The way he stared at me and the words he spoke gave me hope that whatever was happening between us was more than a fling. I'm broken at the thought that this is how our time together will end. The elevator doors open and I'm about to resign myself to my pathetic fate when his hand wraps around mine. I love the way he holds my hand, the grip firm and steady.

He leads me to his black Mercedes and opens the door without uttering a word. It's a sweet action, but the silence between us is like an insurmountable wall.

Shifting the car into gear, he pulls out of the parking garage.

I can no longer take the deafening quiet. "Please say something."

Adam frowns, though the action is more in confusion than anger. "What exactly would you have me say?" His tone is bland and uninterested.

I tap my chin in thought; an action that makes him smile ever so slightly. "Tell me something about you I don't know."

He arches his brow quizzically. "I don't like broad questions; they're a waste of time. I would rather answer a defined question."

I laugh, because in the short time I have spent with Adam Black, that's the one facet of his personality I understand. He's practical to a fault, and expects everyone to do what he wants. The mere idea of going against him makes me shiver.

My thoughts are cut short by his voice. "I'm beginning to get the impression, Miss Snowe, that you enjoy laughing at me. You do it often."

I shake my head at him and feign an earnest expression. "I would never laugh at you, Mr. Black."

He grins, his eyes still on the road. "Oh. Before I forget, I have something to give you." He reaches into his pocket and pulls out a small envelope. It's addressed to me.

"What is it?" I'm apprehensive and I suspect it has everything to do with being far past my comfort zone, thrown into a world both alien and addicting. *He's* addicting.

"Open it and you'll find out." His expression is expectant and the smile he wears makes a shiver cascade down my body. *Does this man have any idea what he can do to me just with a look?*

I run my finger underneath the seal and peer inside. It's a check, addressed to me, for twenty-five thousand dollars. My jaw drops. I'm speechless, unable to formulate a coherent thought, and then like an open flood gate the blood rushes my head.

"Why would you give me this?" I sound angry and in that instance I realize I am.

"I told you that you would be well compensated for the mural."

He sounds incredibly logical and it drives me crazy, because this is anything but logical. "I don't want it."

"That's unfortunate, especially considering you have no say in the matter." He speaks without even looking at me, his dark eyes glowering at the road.

"No say? You don't decide what I can and cannot accept." I drop the envelope on his lap as he drives.

We pull up to my house and he parks. "I said you would be well compensated for the painting and in doing so I gave you my word. This is not up for debate."

"I didn't go to your house because I had the desire to paint you something. Thinking back, the only reason I did go was because I wanted the opportunity to know you better, because you intrigued me."

He grabs the envelope and holds it up. "Evelyn—"

I interject. "Could you not accept the painting as a gift?" *Good girl, being tactical might work.*

Adam's body tenses. "It was never supposed to be a gift."

"I believe several things happened that weren't supposed to," I say in an agitated whisper.

"What exactly is this about?"

He sounds annoyed, and his direct way of phrasing questions makes me squirm in my seat. "It's about you flaunting your money and making me uncomfortable."

"*Flaunting?*" he snarls. "I hardly think paying someone for a service can classify as *flaunting* my wealth."

"That's just it. I don't want to be paid for a *service*," I say with fervent passion, because I'm not fixating on the hours I spent painting, but the hours I spent entangled in his arms, between his ultra-high thread count sheets.

Adam blinks a few times in surprise. "I'm paying you for the painting, not the night."

I blush and slump farther into my seat. He's said exactly what I was thinking. I don't want to be paid for the painting because it makes me feel cheap and opportunistic. "I don't want it." I say with conviction, though the original vehemence I harbored has been extinguished.

He leans forward and I still. "I believe I already told you to get over this, Evelyn. Stop doubting what happened." Adam appears exasperated, though he is keeping his feelings under control, for my benefit.

This man can be so sweet and considerate. I don't think he realizes those traits in himself. He's obviously not a patient man and yet with me he makes an effort. I know it's dangerous to think myself special, but around him I do feel special, and it's not something I can or even want to control.

Flooded by feelings too intense to articulate, I kiss him. Though I've taken him by surprise he smoothly adjusts, his mouth parting so that he can suck on my upper lip before thrusting his tongue and brushing it with mine.

Then his arms are circling my waist, pulling me against him and the narrow confines of his car become an obstacle we easily overcome. Now perched on his lap, I bite at his lips, wanting everything he can give, the gentle tugs, the powerful pulls, and the pure perfection I've only ever experienced in his arms. Adam groans against me, his grip tightening on my skin.

"If you keep this up I'm going to fuck you in this car." His sexy rasp is laced with desire.

"I wouldn't mind."

He grins, pulling back with regret. "As tempting as the offer is, I'm late for an important meeting."

I run my fingers behind his ear, brushing his hair back and he leans into the touch. "I don't want the money. Please."

His face hardens. "If you won't accept the payment, then you'll have to accept a gift."

He's so damn stubborn. But I know this is his way of compromising, something I imagine he rarely does.

"What type of gift?"

He shakes his head. "One of my choosing, that you will be unable to deny."

"I don't like the terms of this compromise," I say dryly.

Adam grabs my chin and his eyes command my full attention.

"I honestly couldn't care less if you like the terms. Agree to them or you're taking the check."

I'm not going to win this argument.

As I lean my body back against the driver's side window I resign myself to the fact that Black currently has all the power in this relationship. *But is this actually a relationship?* I brush off the thought.

"You win. Fine. I'll accept a gift of your choosing, no questions asked."

"That's more like it," he says with a half-smile.

"I better let you go," I murmur.

I open the driver's side door and in an unladylike scramble, step out. I'm missing my purse, so I use the opportunity to rub against him. I lean my body across his, reaching for the purse in the passenger seat. He smirks, his eyes silently saying *I know what you're doing.*

"Sorry, had to get my purse."

I bat my eyes at him, and then my vision blurs because his strong grip pulls me toward him. He spins me so my legs are still out of the car but my upper body is resting on him, his arms cradling me. His kiss knocks the wind out of me. It leaves me panting and craving more. When he pulls away, my knees buckle as I stand.

*Don't you dare fall, Evelyn. That would be beyond embarrassing.* I lick my lips and blink a few times, trying to remember how to walk.

"I'll call you later." His eyes narrow with amusement, no doubt at the dumbstruck expression on my face.

"Bye, Adam." Walking to the porch, I hear the revving of his car and feel panic, because he's leaving, and even though I want to believe him, I'm not certain he will call.

He drives off and I shelve my insecurities long enough to open the front door. Tina's in the living room wearing a guarded expression. She must be pissed because I didn't respond to her texts and calls. I open my mouth to cut her off before she starts bitching at me, and that's when I see her.

My mother is standing by the kitchen her face flushed and her petite nostrils flared—she's livid.

"Where the hell have you been?" She shoots me a reproachful glare.

I have the smarts to realize telling her I've been spreading my legs for a handsome, charismatic man won't go over well. I gulp as I stare at my mother. *What am I going to tell her?*

# CHAPTER ELEVEN

"**M**OM, WHAT A pleasant surprise, I wasn't expecting you."

"Quit with the games. I want answers and I want them now. Where have you been?"

The nerve of this woman is astounding. I understand she's my mother and she cares about me, but I am twenty-four years old. I'm not some teenager who's missed her curfew.

"I spent the night with a man I'm seeing." The thrill of adrenaline racing through my veins makes me want to laugh out loud though I have the foresight to resist the urge.

My mother is stunned into silence for a long minute and Tina herself looks shocked. I inwardly celebrate surprising them.

"I didn't even know you were dating someone."

"We only recently started seeing each other." I want to act casual, as if the notion of me seeing a man is common, but it's not, and everyone in the room knows it.

"And you're already sleeping with him?" she snaps.

I cross the room quick, tossing my purse on the dining room table ignoring her question, because my patience is nonexistent. Last night, drama and all, was the best night I've had in ages. The last thing I want is my mother to ruin the high I'm coasting on.

Tina interjects. "I believe she's been working on a mural for him. You know how she gets. She probably spent the night painting."

*Oh, great. More lies.*

"Stop it!" I yell, exasperated.

Tina is trying to protect me, like always. But the truth is, I am sick and tired of being protected. For the first time in years I feel brave, and I know it's because of him. Adam makes me believe that second chances are not only found in fairytales.

"Look, I'm not in the mood for a lecture. I'm spending time with a man I really like, and this is not something that merits an apology." I rub my eyes and my hands slap my legs as they fall. I'm so exhausted they're too heavy to hold up. *Of course I'm tired; I spent the night doing other things...not sleeping.*

My mother is speechless. Yes, in the last few years I've allowed her to make serious decisions for me. I've been a lump of clay and she has molded me as best she could. However, today I'm more myself than I have been in the last few years. I won't let her put the brakes on my life anymore.

"You're acting strange. I think we need to call your therapist."

"I spoke with her recently. She's of the opinion that I should explore this relationship."

"I doubt she meant you should sleep with him."

"Mom..." I take a deep breath to measure my tone because I want her to understand me. "I don't think it matters what she meant. The only thing that matters is *my* happiness, because this is *my* life." I shake my head. "He makes me smile. Do you know I never smile?"

"You smile all the time."

"No, you see half-hearted attempts."

For the first time in ages, my mother really looks at me and it's as if she can see the pain I'm harboring, the pain I try to bury. Her eyes widen and she appears as if she just got the answer to a difficult math equation. "You're happy about this relationship?"

"Yes." I give her the reassurance she needs, even though I'm not certain what I'm feeling, because I need her to trust me. I need my mother to believe that if Adam and I fall apart, I'll be okay.

She steps forward, wrapping her arms around me in a tight hug. "Well, tell me about him."

I squeeze her softly and stare at Tina, whose bewildered expression mirrors mine. My mother is rarely this affectionate with me.

After a long pause, she pulls away from me, moves toward the couch and dusts off a spot with her hand before sitting. "What is this mystery man's name?"

I begin organizing the room as I speak. It's both a result of my growing anxiety and a defense mechanism. If I'm busy working on something, my mother won't be able to gauge my reactions.

"His name is Adam Black. He works in real estate."

"Adam Black, the founder of the Eden Corporation?" She arches a brow in disbelief.

*Gee, thanks, Mom. It's not like my confidence isn't already in choppy waters.* I nod as I move some glasses to the kitchen sink, needing the added distance.

"Yes, Mom, that Adam Black."

"If you drive down Biscayne you'll see his name all over billboards. I mean, Evelyn, he owns properties all over South Florida, all over the East Coast. If there's a piece of land in Miami, he's developing it… How in the world did you two meet?"

"At the bank, the day of the hold-up. He was there making a transaction."

"And *now* is when I'm hearing about this?" My mother glares at me, an annoyed expression on her face.

"It slipped my mind. I'm sorry," I say reflexively, but I don't mean it.

"Men like that expect women to act a certain way, dress a certain way."

She straightens in her seat, her eyes narrowed in disapproval as she assesses my cut-off shorts.

"You were with him wearing *that*?"

She doesn't give me time to respond.

"We need to go shopping. I'm sure we can find a few outfits that will look lovely on you. If you plan on dating a man like Adam Black, you need to dress a certain way."

I was wondering how long it would take her to suggest shopping. If my mom could, she'd live in the mall. I shake my head. "I can't make it to the mall today. As you can see, my house is a mess; I need to clean up. Besides, he doesn't seem too concerned with what I wear."

My mother's expression hardens and she opens her mouth to respond when she's cut short by the ringing of her cellphone. "Hello?" She pauses for a few seconds. "Already?" She stands. "Okay, give me a few minutes and I'll go outside."

"Nicholas is here, I need to go," she says while cramming the phone into her purse.

*Yes, saved by my darling stepfather.* "You have to go so soon?" I try my best to sound sad about it.

"I don't know how to feel about any of this," she says, obviously not ready to end the conversation. "I don't know if you seeing this man is a good idea, and I think I should meet—"

"No." My stern interjection makes her eyes twitch with start. "I won't have you talking to him and cautioning him. I won't have you dictating what I will and won't do with *my* life."

"You're getting agitated, and I think—"

Again I interrupt her. "I haven't hurt myself, and I won't." I step into the living room, lift my shorts, and point to my thighs. Then I arch my neck and brush my hair to the side, revealing my nape.

Tina and my mother just stare at me in silence as I continue to show them the many places on my body I used to conceal cuts on—cuts I gave myself for years—cuts they never knew about until the pressure was too great to contain.

"Just because you haven't yet doesn't mean that you won't," my mother yells.

"And just because you micromanage my life doesn't mean that I won't!" I counter.

The silence that surrounds the room is suffocating. Again, my mother's phone rings. Sighing heavily, she walks over to Tina and gives her a hug.

"Bye, Mrs. Aaron," Tina murmurs.

My mother whispers something to Tina. She eyes me as she does and I try in vain not to feel insulted; she's no doubt telling her to watch over me. Tina nods. My mother walks over and embraces me. I say nothing—I don't move. She leaves and as the door closes behind her I shift my gaze to Tina.

"I didn't call her," she quickly says.

"Why did she come?"

"She's worried about you. We both are."

"Well, stop!" I shout because this conversation is tiresome.

"Okay, don't get so upset. Maybe if you would've told me ahead of time what you planned on doing, I could have covered for you."

"I don't need you to cover for me. I'm twenty-four years old. I can sleep with whoever the hell I want."

"Stop taking out your anger on me!" Tina raises her voice to counter mine.

I place one of my hands against my head. "Let's drop it…I don't want to fight."

Tina has her arms crossed over her chest. She still looks angry, though my words have curbed her fury. "Well, are you going to tell me what happened?"

"What exactly is there to say? We slept together."

"I want every last detail," she says shamelessly.

We stare at each other for a long minute and in perfect unison we burst out laughing. I flop on the couch and for the next hour I recount the events of my steamy night with Adam.

"Did he say when he would call?" Tina asks.

I shake my head. "He just said sometime later."

"And you're okay with that?"

My laugh is touched with bitterness. "Of course I'm not okay with that. I want him to call me now. But I'm not going to pout about not getting my way." I lean against one of the pillows. "I understand that in sleeping with him, I may have lost the only card I had to play." I shrug at the thought. "But I wanted to do it and I don't regret it."

Tina has a grin on her lips. "I've never seen you so… Carefree."

"Is that your nice way of saying I'm being a promiscuous little tart?" I'm amused by her expression.

"Because you slept with a guy for the first time when you were twenty-four? If you're promiscuous, I can only imagine what I must be." She pauses. "Did he you know, make you…"

I feign innocence, even though it's obvious what she's referring to. "Did he make me what?"

Tina rolls her eyes and her unflinching nature takes hold. "Did he make you come?"

Smirking at her, I give a slow nod. "*Multiple* times. I've been missing out."

"I'm so jealous. I spent my Friday night with Daniel and Michael."

"I gather they didn't make you come?" I say jokingly.

Daniel and Michael, whose names are uttered as a pair because they are never without the other, are our two very gay friends from college.

"You're so funny. I was a third wheel."

"What happened with Dean? I thought it was pretty hot and heavy between you two for a while."

"He's an irritating ass who can't keep it in his pants." Tina rubs her forehead with the back of her hand, and although she is trying hard to stop the tears from falling, they do.

I lean in and hug her. It's unnerving to be in this situation, because it's new to me. Tina is always the one comforting me.

"What happened?' I whisper.

"The bastard slept with someone else. He didn't even have the smarts to toss the condom out. He just left it lying on the floor. What a fucking idiot." Her watery eyes focus on mine. "I honestly didn't even like him much. But why would he cheat? I mean, grow a pair and own up to not wanting to be with someone."

"When did you find out?" My mouth is dry. Did this happen while I was with Adam? *I guess I'm not winning any friend-of-the-year awards.*

"It happened last night, but I'm fine." Tina rubs her eyes and gives me a brave smile. "Daniel and Michael helped me burn all of his shit. He's lucky I didn't set *him* on fire."

I kiss Tina's cheek and she pulls back in surprise. "Don't ever get that angry at me, please."

"I don't know, Evie. You certainly try my patience pretty often," she says with mock seriousness.

We both laugh. Sitting there with my best friend, discussing the ups and downs of our lives makes me feel so normal, so content. And yet, even in the wake of my happiness a somber thought infiltrates my mind—if Tina, who has tried to find love numerous times, has been denied her happily-ever-after, why should destiny be kinder to me?

TINA has left and I've been busy cleaning the disaster zone that is my house. For the first time in years I'm embarrassed to be living in clutter. The music is cranked up and my iPod shuffles to Usher's "Scream". I grin because Adam pops into my head. *How the hell does the man get me hot and bothered when he's not even here?*

I hop on the couch and eye my phone. *Why hasn't he called?* The nagging fear I've been suppressing all day is making its way to the surface. *Stop thinking about this.* I stand, determined to heed my own advice.

Thirty minutes later, my kitchen is spotless and the iPod Shuffle is now playing Mika's "Relax". I roll my eyes because I can't. I'm wiping the counter for the third time in a row, when I see my cell flashing on the coffee table. *It's him!*

I dart toward the living room, rushing to get the call before it goes to voicemail and stub my toe against the kitchen peninsula. "Shit!" I grab the phone and utter a flustered, "Hello?"

"Evelyn?"

His calm, deep voice makes my already racing heart throb wildly.

"Hey," I say breathily.

"Are you okay?"

"I stubbed my toe reaching for the phone." *Why would you confess that, you graceless idiot?* I stifle a groan.

His chuckle vibrates against my ear. "I'm sorry I'm not there. I would kiss it better."

*Adam Black kissing my toe? The idea has promise.*

"How was your day?"

"Good, and yours?"

"I've spent the afternoon trying to convince an infuriating man that selling me his property was in his best interest."

I grin at the thought. "I'm sure you were successful. I can attest to the fact that you're very convincing."

He laughs. "What are you doing tomorrow?"

I blink at the shift in topic. "I'm not doing anything in particular."

"You are now." That decisive tone reverberates against the receiver. "Be ready by noon."

"Ready for what?" I'm annoyed, because I hate how he states what I will and will not do. As if I have no options and must comply with his decrees. He doesn't own me.

*Are you sure about that?*

Adam's interrupts my internal argument, his tone clipped. "It's a surprise."

"You don't like it when I question you."

"No one appreciates being questioned," he says pointedly. "Since you obviously need to be convinced, I will inform you that it has to do with your gift. The one you agreed to accept, no questions asked."

I frown because he's right, as usual. "Okay, I'll be ready at noon."

"Sleep well."

I want to tell him not to hang up, to please keep talking, because I miss him. However, every phrase that comes to mind sounds desperate and clingy. I don't want to be perceived as some insecure girl who is growing dependent on his touch, on his presence. *Am I becoming that girl?*

My mind shifts back into gear. "Sleep well, Adam; I'll see you tomorrow."

Our conversation is over too soon. I'm hopelessly falling for this guy and he probably thinks of me as a pleasant distraction. I toss the phone on the couch and walk to my room. I'm alone and the thought is draining. In minutes I fall asleep, unwilling to dwell on concerns that I'm obviously not ready to face.


IT'S five minutes to noon and I'm sitting on my couch waiting for Adam, wearing a burgundy dress with simple black heels. The sharp knock at the door startles me.

I open the door and to my shock, Adam is not the person standing on the other side.

"Parker?" I can't hide my disappointment.

"Hello, Miss Snowe. Shall we?"

His tone is matter-of-fact.

I walk behind him, and as we come to the black Escalade he dutifully ushers me inside. His actions are always respectful. Why do I find him aggravating? *Oh, that's right…it's his total lack of personality.*

He enters the SUV, and after a few moments of silence I can no longer contain my curiosity. "Parker, where is Adam?"

"Mr. Black is busy with business."

The lackluster response makes me frown. Why would Parker pick me up if Adam is busy?

"Will he be meeting us somewhere?"

"I'm not sure, Miss Snowe. I was only directed to take you to the location."

I roll my eyes. "Am I allowed to know our destination?"

"Bal Harbour Shops."

"What? Why are we going to a mall?" I hate malls. I worked in one for a few years. They're busy and loud.

Parker takes out an envelope and hands it to me, his eyes never wavering from the road. "This should explain everything." His tone indicates the conversation is now over.

"Thanks," I mutter while eyeing the letter. It's addressed to me and written in fine script.

*Dear Evelyn,*

*I'm sure by now you're fidgeting in your seat wondering where exactly you're going, and most importantly, why. Since you refuse to accept the payment for your mural, which is rightfully yours, I have decided on a gift I believe you might enjoy.*

*Currently, you are en route to Bal Harbour Mall. I have left explicit instructions for the sales attendants. You are to buy several outfits, at my expense. I look forward to watching you try on the outfits purchased, but more than anything, I can't wait to take them off you.*

*Remember, you agreed to accept this gift without question. Don't overthink everything; that's a bad habit you possess. Try to have fun and I will see you later.*

*Adam*

Are you kidding me? He's gifting me a shopping spree. What a wonderful way not to flaunt his money at me.

I read the letter again and one sentence stands out. *He wants to see me try on the clothing...and he wants to take them off me.* The idea of Adam watching as I try on clothing makes me shiver.

"Are you cold? I could raise the temperature."

Parker says, startling me. I gulp once and manage to find my voice. "I...um...am a bit chilly, yes. Thank you." *Damn it, Evelyn. Stop thinking about Adam and get ahold of yourself.*

We drive the rest of the way in silence while I contemplate my current situation.

Adam consumes me. My thoughts are constantly of him, of the way he effortlessly dictates my actions. My body responds to his touch in a primal way and I'm not sure if I'm finding or losing myself.

I'm conflicted. I don't want the clothing, because spending his money makes me feel cheap. And yet the idea of his control makes me feel alive. I want it—I want him.

Then the questions hit like a sudden hailstorm. *What does he want from me? Why does he offer me such overwhelming gifts? Do I mean something to him?*

Adam's the type of man who gets his way. I refused the money so he gave me a shopping spree. He must have known I would hate being in this situation. When I see him today I'm going to make sure he understands I won't tolerate his domineering ways. Even as I think the words, I know I only possess such bravery within the confines of my own mind. *How can I deny him? Should I even try?*

The black Escalade pulls up to the mall and we stop in front of the entrance to Neiman Marcus.

"They're waiting for you, Miss Snowe."

I offer Parker a halfhearted smile while stepping out of the SUV. Upon entering the store, I'm greeted by three well-dressed women. The person I assume is the ringleader of this trio greets me.

"Hello, Miss Snowe?"

I nod as I consider walking out. Before I can make my escape, she speaks. "I'm Marian Carter. I'll be assisting you today. Mr. Black has left instructions about the type of clothing we should consider."

*I bet he has. I bet Mr. Controlling has left a bulleted list of what we can and can't do.* I nod politely at her. "Oh. What type of clothing should we consider?"

Her eyes widen at the question. "Why, only the best, of course. Please, follow me."

Instantly, designer dresses are shoved in my face—Escada, Emilio Pucci, Aidan Mattox, the list goes on. On rare opportunities when I brave looking at the prices I have to rein in my shock. *Are you shitting me, $1495 for a Fluted Ribbed Dress? What exactly does "Fluted" mean?* I'm ashamed to admit I asked Marian that question.

"Oh, a fluted dress means that the fabric fits snugly around the hips and then opens near the hem." She smiles.

*Well, duh! Of course that's what it means.* I nod, my senses overstimulated. More dresses are thrown at me and time crawls by.

I'VE spent the last four hours trying on hundreds of dresses, pants, shirts—everything you could imagine. At one point Marian drags me to the intimate apparel section of the store, and to my chagrin helps me select several sets of bras and panties. The experience has been an irritating blend of awkward moments.

I'm in the fitting room staring at the mirror in only heels and black lace underwear, going through the monotonous task of trying on yet another dress, when I hear the door creak. *What!* I turn to give Marian a piece of my mind, and to my shock Adam is the intruder.

He closes the door and presses down on the lock, without a flinch of remorse. Then he's against me, his lips pressed over mine and his tongue plunging into my mouth, devouring me.

I kiss him back, because even though I'm upset he's made me go through this uncomfortable experience, I'm ecstatic to see him. I can't deny that my body longs to be alongside his.

He leans back and whispers against my cheek, "I like the heels."

"Marian thought you might." My hand trails down his back to his dark blue jeans. His casual attire makes him appear younger and so damn sexy

"Where have you been?" I don't bother to hide the pout in my voice.

"I've been busy working." He kisses my neck and slowly makes his way down to my chest. As his tongue caresses the curves of my cleavage, he pulls my breasts out of the bra.

I don't have time to be shocked, because instantly his mouth is against my skin. The way his teeth graze my nipples makes me whimper.

He pulls back an inch, a devilish smirk on his lips. "Careful, someone might hear you."

I know the warning is in jest; I doubt he cares if anyone hears us. The beat of my rapid heart thunders against my ear. We're in a dressing room in Neiman Marcus. *He wants to do this here?*

Adam moves his hand down between my thighs, his fingers trailing over the thin material of my underwear, and I tremble.

*Yep, he definitely wants to do this here.*

With his sapphire eyes fixed on mine, he slides his hand inside my panties and rubs the pad of his index finger against my clit. My body comes to life. A scorching heat erupts between my legs and I can't control myself, I push my hips into his skilled touch.

"I think you're happy to see me."

I nod wordlessly, because I'm practically dripping with happiness.

In a steady, circular motion he massages my clit and my breath stutters. He has a smile on his smug face, and he's no doubt reveling in the fact that I'm completely his. If he wants to fuck me in this dressing room, I won't resist.

He pushes a finger inside of me, in and out, tantalizingly slow, while his thumb continues rubbing. Before I can resist the urge, a soft moan escapes me.

A sharp knock comes from the dressing room door.

"I've found the most beautiful dresses for you to try. They're a little short, but you have great legs; you can pull it off," Marian says excitedly.

Adam wears a wicked grin as he slips another finger inside of me. My lips part and I'm about to cry out when his tongue invades my mouth. The kiss is all-consuming.

"The door is locked." Marian twists the handle.

It's hard to think. I pull back from his lips and attempt to speak calmly. "Leave the dresses on the hanger outside."

Adam's rhythm quickens and I dig my nails into his shoulders, because the pressure is building, and I'm reaching my limits.

Marian's voice again intrudes. "Okay, I'll be back in a few minutes. I'm going to go get you a pair of white heels for the pastel dresses."

*Who the hell cares where you go? Just leave already.* "Okay," I groan, and to my delight, the response is silence—she's finally gone.

I'm writhing against him, at the edge of my orgasm. As I'm about to let go and find release, my eyes flutter open, meeting his, and the intensity of Adam's gaze makes me self-conscious. I pull back, but there's nowhere to go. I'm between him and the wall, and he's relentless. His fingers slick through the folds of my swollen flesh and my muscles constrict greedily around him. They spasm. They tighten. They begin to tingle with unassailable need.

"Come for me, Evelyn."

His husky command is my undoing. I cry out against his shoulder, reaching my climax, no longer caring that I'm in a dressing room and others may be hearing this intimate encounter. My knees buckle and I think I'm going to fall, but Adam's strong arms hold me up, the same way he did at the bank the fateful day we met.

We stand there for a few minutes as my frantic breaths find a natural rhythm. The world fades and only he and I matter. Our eyes lock and I realize *inhibition* is a dirty word around him. In his presence I don't have any.

"Do you think you can stand?"

The tenderness of his tone makes me smile. "Yes."

He pulls back to test the theory though one of his arms is still wrapped around my waist in a proprietary fashion.

As I get it together, standing on my own, he does something to threaten my stability. His eyes fixed on mine; he slips the tip of his thumb in his mouth, licking up the proof of my pleasure.

"That's such a good taste," he whispers, and as if to reinforce his point he runs his tongue across his lips, savoring the flavor.

"I'll meet you outside." He turns to the door, opening it and winking at me before it closes.

I stare at the dresses hanging on the numerous racks lining the fitting room. *Like hell, I'm trying anything else on.* I reach for my own simple burgundy dress. As I turn to leave, I spot my reflection in the mirror. My hair is tousled and my face has a rosy flush. I run my fingers through my hair and after a few seconds I quit trying to appear composed.

Stepping out of the fitting room I glance at the other customers and my cheeks burn. *Do they know what I've been doing?* Who cares if they do.

Adam is leaning against a counter, talking to Marian. She's fluttering her eyelashes at him and laughing at something said. A sudden pang of jealousy hits me. *Back off, lady, he's mine. Maybe.*

As I get closer to them, Adam sees me, and his eyes darken with what I think is lingering desire.

"There you are. I was looking for you." He sounds sincere, and I wonder how he can do that. He knew exactly where I was, and yet he can so effectively lie. It makes me wonder if anything he's told me since we've met is true. He's made me assure him that I'll never lie, because he doesn't associate with liars, but does that rule apply to him?

"Mr. Black, thank you again. Evelyn will look wonderful in the selections we've chosen," Marian says elatedly, and while I suspect the large commission she'll be receiving from this sale has something to do with it, I get the impression her intentions toward *Mr. Black* are anything but chaste.

I flash her a fake smile, and Adam notices. Grinning, he grabs my hand.

"Thank you, Marian." He speaks to her but his gaze is fixed on me. "Parker will be here within the hour to retrieve the items. Please make sure they are ready." Then he's tugging me and we're walking.

"What did you buy?" I ask sullenly, still affected by jealousy.

"Everything Marian said looked good."

"*Everything?*"

He glowers at me. I blink a few times, feeling remorseful for yelling, but not for the sentiment. All my doubts come to the forefront and I begin to recollect everything I wanted to tell him throughout the day.

"You just spent a small fortune on me, Mr. Black." I say his surname with a heavy inflection because I'm annoyed, and I want to distance myself from him. "Why would you do that?"

"Mr. Black? I would think, especially considering what just happened in the fitting room, we'd still be on a first name basis, Evelyn."

The ways he speaks my name, in a hushed tone, makes me flinch. It's as if he can caress me with only words, and part of me hates him for it. He breaks down the barriers I've built. And I need those barriers, because without them I'm not strong enough to keep going. *Can't he see that?*

"As for your question, I bought the items because I owe you some type of compensation for the mural you painted. And because, frankly, I wanted to."

His ambiguous response brings out the worst in me. "I'm just some girl to you, some distraction." I know I should put the brakes on my runaway freight train of a mouth, but I can't. "So this is all because you had to settle a debt?"

He leans forward, his height as always intimidating. "No, I would never be that obtuse. If it makes you feel better, my motives are purely selfish. The idea of undressing you, peeling off the clothing I've purchased for you, then having my way with you, excites me. It gets me hard just thinking about it."

How can he say things like that? He's so bold and wicked. Peering up at him, I whisper, "Do you buy clothing for every woman you fuck?"

His body stiffens. And although anger clouds his eyes, his voice, unlike mine, is of someone in control of their emotions.

"No, not every woman. In fact, only you."

"Why me?" I say, breathlessly.

Adam flashes me a masculine smile, the type that implies something dark and decadent, something only talked about in whispers.

"Maybe because I know you don't want the clothing."

"So you do it to upset me?"

"I do it to stack the cards in my favor. To rile you up and make you uncomfortable." His face is impassive and unyielding.

"You don't own me," I say with steadfast resolve.

His hand runs across my cheek and I hate that I shiver.

Haughtily, he states, "Not yet."

Adam wants to possess me? To own me? My thoughts echo in my head. *I think we've established he already does. May I remind you of the fitting room incident?*

My pulse quickens at the realization.

*Oh, shit.*

## Chapter Twelve

"**W**HAT THE HELL does *that* mean, Adam?" From the corner of my eye I notice a couple on the far left gawking at us.

Adam grabs my hand and yanks me away from our sudden audience. Turning into a narrow and apparently abandoned corridor of the open mall, he pins me against the wall.

"It means everyone can be bought. Everyone has a price," he says angrily.

"I don't," I murmur. The callous way he's speaking is breaking my heart.

A derisive laugh erupts from his lips as he leans forward, caging me with outstretched arms.

"I never stated that the price had to be monetary. Maybe you're the type of girl who needs flowers, sweet words."

"And you're not the type of man willing to give that?"

"I'm the type of man who doesn't *have* to give that."

I frown. The type of bitterness he's exuding resonates of someone who has been hurt before. I know the sentiment well.

"Some woman must have screwed you over big-time to make you such a…" *Arrogant prick. Stubborn ass. Egocentric bastard.* The words echo in my head, but I can't voice them.

"Say what you're thinking."

The warm caress of his breath against my cheek as he speaks is both exciting and dangerous. It's all the fuel I need.

"I don't care how much money you have, I'm not for sale. If you want some girl to fawn over you, to shut up instead of speak up, then you don't have that in me."

My fingertips tingle and I'm sweating, though I'm not sure if it's anger that has prompted the reaction or desire. I don't have time to consider the issue.

Adam tangles his hand in my hair and jerks me against him. The coarse action hurts, and I have the sense to pull back, to deny him the satisfaction.

An expression of shock crosses his gorgeous face. He's stunned I would refuse a kiss from him. *That's right, mister, you don't own me.*

Again he moves toward me and before his lips can claim mine I slap him. A short, shallow gasp escapes me as the vivid red mark of my handprint against his cheek becomes visible.

The passion radiating between us saturates the air. While I suspect my rejection is fueling his ire, a part of me thinks my brash statement holds some truth, and a woman did screw him over. Then I see it. For the first time in our brief affair I see vulnerability in his gaze, a hint of insecurity. *This imposing man in front of me is thrown off balance by me?*

My chest tightens and the bitterness of regret makes it hard to swallow. I don't know what to do, because I've crossed a line.

We're both panting. There's an energy building between us, like two stars about to collide. For the third time in less than a minute he moves forward, only this time I can't refuse him.

His kiss is drenched with a need I've never before experienced. Pulling my hair back so my chin tilts and my neck is exposed, he has complete control.

The truth is, my impetuous nature is urging me to leave, to run far away from this man who has stated he wants to possess me, because intrinsically I know such a notion is ludicrous. But the expression in his eyes makes me feel close to him and I haven't felt close to a man in a long time. In his arms I'm lost to reason.

His hands move to my hips, to the hem of my dress, and with a feral passion he grabs hold of my ass. I think he's going to lift the fabric, move my panties to the side, and take me right here in Bal Harbour. *Do I honestly mind?*

"Adam?" Sarah's voice bursts the bubble we currently inhabit.

*Are you kidding me?*

Twice in a row, this girl has interrupted us. I've come to the conclusion that Sarah Black is the most effective form of contraception. And by the stiff way Adam leans back, I get the impression he agrees.

His gaze still fixed on me, he speaks. "I believe I was supposed to meet up with you later."

Sarah is wearing a mischievous grin that I now realize is one of her defining traits.

"Sorry, I assumed if I found you, we could get to dinner quicker."

Adam shifts, focusing on his sister, and I let out the breath I didn't know I was holding. The way he moves is precise, as if all his actions are calculated ahead of time. That type of forethought is foreign to me. In a lifetime of careless actions and capricious decisions I've never met anyone so in control.

"Hello, there."

I jump at the sight of the man offering the greeting. He's standing next to Sarah, and until now I hadn't noticed him. He has blond hair and is dressed in designer slacks and a polo shirt. He's not to my tastes, but he's what most people would consider attractive.

I'm about to respond when Adam steps between us, like a lion defending his territory. His jaw is set, and I can tell he's containing his anger—and to my surprise, for once, it's not directed at me.

"Markus, how nice it is to see you again." Adam's voice has adopted a cold, businesslike tone.

*This is the infamous Markus?*

"As always, I find you in the arms of a pretty girl." Markus's voice is etched with an emotion I'm unable to gauge.

Adam grabs my hand and tugs me to his side. And it doesn't matter that seconds ago we were arguing. In the presence of his sister and her boyfriend, being surrounded by his dominating presence is a welcome protection.

Adam gives Markus a debonair smile, one that by its elegance I suspect he can offer at will. "Markus Krass, this is Evelyn Snowe."

I smile at Markus, though I'm unwilling to offer him my hand to shake.

"Are you hungry?" Adam directs the question to me.

I'm not, but among strangers I'm happy to let him take the lead.

"I am if you are."

He turns to Sarah and Markus. "How about we try some Italian food?"

They both nod at the idea. In minutes we've traveled through the mall and have arrived at a restaurant named *Carpaccio*. Briefly, I hear Adam speak with the waiter about the wines offered, and he settles on one called *Amarone*. Knowing his refined taste, I imagine it's a good wine.

Once we're seated, the overall mood of our table can be described as awkward. As always, Adam, with his cool and collected persona, takes charge.

"So what is it you currently do, Markus?" He tries for casual but the stiffness in his voice is apparent.

"I work in property development." Markus matches Adam's tone. "Currently, I'm working on the expansion of two buildings in the Surfside area."

"Oh. I was under the impression that with the recent decline in property value many developing companies were simply dropping projects, unable to acquire the necessary funding."

Sarah and I stare at each other; our apprehension mirrored in our rigid posture.

"On the contrary. Now is the most opportune time to develop property. The cost of construction is markedly lower and surely you, being in the real-estate business, know that property values are on the rise." Markus smiles at Adam, though it appears more like a smirk.

Our wine arrives. *Thank god, I have something to do.* I take a large sip as I listen to the conversation.

Adam's eyes take on a calculating glint. "So have you attained the funding for this project?"

Markus takes a long pause to drink from his glass. "Not yet, but we have some promising prospects."

"What are the names of the investors? Maybe I could put in a good word for you. As you said, I *am* in the business."

Markus shifts in his seat. His fidgeting quickly makes it obvious he doesn't actually have any viable funding prospects.

"Evie, you must promise to attend my birthday this coming Friday. It's being held at my parents' house; they live in the Gables."

With her interruption, I get the impression Sarah's trying to defuse the tense dinner conversation.

"I'm not sure."

"Adam, convince her to come," she pleads, her bottom lip protruding in a cute pout.

Adam looks at me as he places his wine glass down on the table. "Come with me."

His domineering tone makes it obvious that the statement is a command, not a question. I don't feel rebellious, so I nod. "If it will make you happy, I would love to go."

Sarah squeals with delight. Our food arrives and we eat while speaking idly about unimportant topics—disaster averted.

When the check is brought, Markus takes his time offering to pay. Only after Adam reaches for the bill does he halfheartedly interject.

Adam's features are cold and rigid as he says politely, "No. It's on me."

We all stand to say our goodbyes. Sarah leans over and gives me a big hug. I'm surprised by the action, but happy to return the embrace.

"It was nice seeing you again."

I'm starting to like Sarah. "It was nice seeing you as well."

Adam kisses his sister goodbye and shakes Markus's hand. As he turns to go, his fingers lace with mine. We practically sprint out of the mall.

"Will you slow down?" I mutter between hurried steps.

Adam doesn't respond, but reduces his speed. We reach the car and, polite as ever, he opens my door.

We drive in silence while I repeat a mantra in my head. *Keep quiet. This is not your business.* I decide not to follow my own advice.

"I understand why you don't like him."

Adam frowns. "How do you know I don't like him?"

*Damn it! I've pretty much confessed to being a nosy eavesdropper.* I bite my bottom lip. "It's pretty obvious."

Adam shakes his head. "Do you remember our conversation about lying? I don't like it when you're indirect with me."

"You and your sister were talking kind of loud back at your apartment," I say meekly. It is, after all, a weak defense.

Adam stops at a red light and gives me an intimidating glance.

"Don't look at me like that," I say nervously.

His expression calms. Adam sighs as he focuses on the road, the light having changed to green. "That guy is a fucking prick. He has no future prospects, he's known to gamble away any earnings he has, and he consistently cheats on the women he dates."

"Have you told your sister this?"

"Yes, but what little sister ever listened to her overprotective brother?"

"So you admit you're overprotective?" I say, unable to hide my grin.

"Not the right time to joke, Evelyn," he says with agitation.

"Sorry."

We turn, entering the Eden Beach complex.

"Adam, I need to go to work in the morning."

"So?"

"I don't have anything to wear here. I can't spend the night."

"We just bought you several things to wear." He pulls into his parking space and shifts the car into park.

"So you just decided I'm spending the night?" I say sarcastically.

He looks at me, his eyes weary. "If you want me to take you home I will, but I do want you to spend the night."

His expression is sincere, full of emotion. I'm unable to deny this man when he looks at me like this.

"Okay. I'll spend the night."

A small smile forms on his lips. We open our doors and move toward the elevator. It's odd riding in the elevator with Adam, going to his apartment to do…I don't know what.

*Really? You* do *know what, Evelyn.* I shake the thought away.

We walk through the foyer in silence, making our way to the kitchen, and I sense that Adam himself is confused. He's usually so assured. Now he moves as if he's unaware of his purpose. *Is the situation with his sister affecting him so much? Am I affecting him?*

Once we reach the kitchen he opens the refrigerator and pours himself a glass of water.

"Would you like something to drink?"

I shake my head and smile. Then a thought hits me. *Tina. I need to call her.* I place my purse on the counter and start to rummage for my phone. Randomly, I take things out as I search. I pull out a pen, my wallet, my cosmetics bag, my birth control pills, and finally, my phone.

"You're on birth control?" Adam's eyes widen.

"Oh?" I focus on the pill box. "Yes, I've been on it for years." I turn on my phone, scanning through my contacts.

"Why didn't you say something?" He sounds annoyed.

"Mentioning I'm on birth control is not exactly a conversation starter."

"That's the type of information you willingly supply when you're sleeping with someone."

I place the phone down, shifting my attention to him. "In that case, I'm on birth control, just thought you should know."

"Why would you be on birth control? We've already established that before me your experience was extremely limited."

"Well, Mr. Intrusive, I'm prone to ovarian cysts, so I've been prescribed birth control pills as a preventative measure." I sigh. "Why does this matter?"

"It matters because I'm the one who has to wear the condoms. They significantly reduce the overall feeling."

"Really?" I now regard him with a small smirk. "So are you saying you want to have sex without a condom?"

"I'm saying that the next time we have sex it *will* be without a condom." He takes a sip of his water.

*What a smug son of a bitch.* "How do I know you don't have any illnesses? Rich men are known to sleep around." I stare at him, a clear challenge on my face.

"Rich men are known to take care of themselves," he says emphatically. "I have a concierge doctor on retainer. You're more likely to have an illness than I am."

I narrow my eyes at him. "You are, without a doubt, *the* most conceited man I have ever known."

"Your opinion can't be trusted. You haven't known many men."

He appears so young when he is amused.

I laugh, because even though I find him arrogant to a fault, I find him charming. *You love punishing yourself...* Ignoring my nagging thoughts, I shoot him a coquettish glance.

"Is this how you treat all the women who are in relationships with you?"

"I wouldn't know. I don't do relationships." He steps around the counter, places the glass down in front of me and stands only a few inches away.

I frown, because he's confusing. "You don't call what we're doing a relationship?"

He tilts his head to the side. "We're dating."

"What's the difference?"

He inhales a deep breath. "You date someone, and as time passes, as you get to know them, you slowly forge a relationship. You begin to trust that person and they begin to trust you."

"And you never get to that part? You always just date?"

He nods as his eyes survey me, scrutinizing my face.

Adam has never been in a relationship? *No way.*

"I don't believe you."

"I was pretty certain you wouldn't." He has a challenging expression burning through his eyes.

I'm suddenly so tired. But I'm aware that I may never have the opportunity to broach this subject again. This is my chance to learn about the woman who screwed him over, because there is no doubt in my mind that there was at one point a woman in his life. A relationship.

"You're the one being indirect now. I thought you were a man who disliked lies."

"Maybe you're not asking the right questions."

I face him, my eyes narrowed. "Were you ever in a *relationship* with a woman? Did you ever move past the *dating* stage?"

"Yes, once."

"What happened?"

He shakes his head and a curtain has been pulled over his expression.

"I'm not going to get an answer, am I?" I say with resignation. "How long do your normal liaisons last?" I try to sound unperturbed as I change the subject, although the serious nature of our topic has left me sad.

"Liaisons? That's cute." He shrugs. "Usually they last for about a month."

"So this thing between us is a ticking time bomb? In three weeks it will all be over?" I whisper.

His eyes dart toward the floor for a second before shooting up to meet my gaze. "Probably."

"Why tell me?" I'm angry he would so boldly admit that I'm just a distraction, that he's bored with his life like Victoria proclaimed, and that he's using me. I can't face him so I look down.

"I tell you so you have a choice." He places a finger underneath my chin, making me face him. "I'm not interested in happily ever after. I'm more concerned with the here and now, but I *do* want to share that with you."

I pull away from his grasp. "I don't feel as if I ever had a choice."

He looks somber. "It takes two people to have sex, Evelyn, and as I recall, I did ask you if you wanted to do this."

I open my mouth to object but then quickly close it. He's right. I wanted this and I willingly jumped at the opportunity, knowing the risks. My mother warned me, Tina warned me, my nagging thoughts had told me I was making a mistake and I disregarded all of it.

"I don't want to fight," I say softly. "I did want this and I think part of me knew that eventually it would come to an end."

His hand rubs against my cheek; it's such a tender action that it gnaws at my heart. *Why the hell is he so damn sweet? He's telling me he's not interested in a serious relationship, yet he's being impossibly sweet.*

"I don't want to upset you. If you want, I'll take you home," he whispers.

The thought of leaving him, of never again seeing him, of being denied his honeyed kisses is too much for me to take. I'm not willing to accept it.

"You said you want to spend the *here and now* with me… Why?"

His eyes narrow. "Is that a rhetorical question?"

"No. I need concrete boundaries. I need to know if what's going on between us is an itch you need to scratch or if it's something more. If it's just sex then I can jump on that train, I'll ride it…" I cough and then clear my throat at the arched brow he gives me. "Um…that came out wrong but you get what I mean."

He shakes his head a low throaty laugh pulsing from his lips. "I haven't thought about it."

"Think about it. I'll give you a minute." I cross my arms over my chest.

"You're giving me an order?"

I straighten in the chair, giving him the most deadpan expression I can muster. "You shoot orders out all the time, so yeah, you would know how they sound."

"I'm not sure why, but I just got hard," he rasps.

There goes my poker face. Unable to resist, my gaze darts to his impressive package and for a long minute I stare at the bulge, arguing with myself over the desire I have to give in and let him fuck me senseless and my urge to define whatever it is we're doing together.

Again Adam lifts my chin. "I should take you home."

With five words, he's defined our liaison—sex. And he's right, I should leave, but leaving means it's over and I'm not ready for it to be over.

Framing his face with my hands, I kiss him. I run my tongue along his lips, tracing their shape. It only takes him a moment to run with it, his arms wrapping around me. Being in his embrace feels right, how can he ignore this burning intensity? As I'm giving in to my growing desire, he pulls away from me.

"Evelyn?" he says with a frown. "What are you doing?"

"Exactly what I want to. I'm a big girl; don't worry about me." I move my hands to the buttons of his shirt.

"You seriously want to do this? Knowing full well the consequences?"

"If we only have a few weeks, I don't want to waste time," I say in an effort to convince not only him, but myself as well.

He grasps my hands, pulling me away from his shirt and turns toward the bedroom. We don't, however, stop there. Adam leads me to the bathroom where he wraps his arms around me and undoes the zipper to my dress. It slides down my shoulders, leaving me in nothing but heels, bra, and panties.

I know this is wrong. What we're doing will lead to heartache, but I'm not willing to let it go.

Again, my trembling fingers move toward the buttons on his shirt. It falls to the floor. I see the chiseled lines of his abdomen and all I want to do is kiss every delicious inch, to trail my tongue over the ridges of his muscles.

Adam takes a step back as my hands move to his belt. He shakes his head, a lustful grin on his lips. *What is he thinking?*

"Take off the bra." His murmur is low as he watches me.

I lick my lips at the command, because knowing he wants to watch turns me on. My hands slide up my body as I reach for the clasp. I slide it off until I'm holding it out to him.

Adam gazes intently at my naked breasts, making a deep heat swell within me.

"Now take off the panties."

He speaks in that bossy tone that normally drives me crazy, though at the moment I like it.

I move my hands to my underwear, rubbing myself as I do, and my nipples harden at the feeling. Slowly, I slide the fabric down my legs until the black satin pools at my heels. With a grace I didn't know I possessed, I kick the scrap of fabric so it lands in front of him.

Standing before Adam wearing nothing but heels is liberating. I feel as if I have control over the situation, and though I probably don't, I revel in the thought.

"Now that you have me like this, what are you going to do with me?" I taunt.

Adam kicks off his shoes and pulls at his belt while moving toward me. "I'm sure I can think of something."

I think he's going to grab me, to hold and kiss me, but in actuality, he walks past me.

The bubble bursts—I never had the power. I hear the rush of the shower and in a blink he's in front of me. The button of his jeans is already open and his hands are on the zipper. The jeans and boxer briefs come off and Adam is standing naked and ready before me. Even with the heels I still have to look up.

"Get into the shower."

I step out of the heels and turn toward the shower because I want to be in there with him. My body has long since ignored the desperate pleas of my brain. *He will never love you, Evie. Run away while you still can. Don't be naïve.*

The water is warm as it cascades down my body. When I focus on Adam, he has a knowing smile on his lips, because it's obvious that desire has taken hold of me. He enters the shower and kisses me, his lips the only contact I am rewarded with. I want to wrap my arms around him and feel the press of his skin against mine, but I know this is all a game. Adam wants me to initiate the action; he wants me to lose control, to give in to my base desires.

I pull back from the kiss. With unbridled passion, I kiss his neck. I trail my tongue down his body, down his defined abdomen, and I don't stop there. I move to my knees and peer up at him as I roll my tongue over the tip of his cock. His breath hitches as his eyes darken. *Mission accomplished, I totally have the power now.*

I love the taste of this man, the weight of him against my mouth. He groans as I swirl my tongue around him. One of his hands is against my head, tangled in my curls, though he's letting me direct the situation. I run my lips down his length until the tip of his cock hits the back of my throat.

"I'm going to come in your mouth," he says between panting breaths.

I know it's a warning, but I don't care. *Please do, go right ahead.*

His muscles tighten and he grows bigger, so much the corners of my lips burn. I bob my head taking every inch I can; desperate to make him feel what I feel—what I don't have any control over.

A ragged groan erupts from his lips, echoing in the bathroom as he reaches his climax and a surge of warmth trickles down my throat as he spills. I swirl my lips over him a few times, savoring his taste, and when I shift back his eyes are fixed on me. *That's right, Mr. Black, maybe it's me who will do the owning.*

He leans down and grabs me by the hands, and with a sharp pull I'm on my feet and pressed against the marble tiles of the shower. *Maybe not.*

"What the fuck are you doing to me?"

He whispers the question, obviously not caring for an answer, because his tongue invades my mouth. He kisses me, his lips rubbing against mine as his hands run down my body, claiming me with every caress.

Adam grabs the back of my thighs, lifting me up and making me aware of the hard press of his cock against my stomach.

"Wrap your legs around me."

I happily obey, and he fills me. My cry echoes as he mercilessly continues his conquest, each thrust harder than the last. The sight of him pushing into me, invading my body, makes me thrash with uninhibited pleasure.

"Adam!" I cry, because at that moment, I'm his, and he owns me.

My breathing is erratic as I reach the precipice of my orgasm.

"Let go." There's raw need in his voice.

I come at his command and he follows. The room spins and my body convulses as a powerful surge of pleasure overtakes me.

I'm not sure how he manages the strength, but he lifts me out of the shower and gently lies me on the bathroom rug. Adam is still in me as I lay on top of him. My head is pressed against his chest and the rapid beat of his heart is like music to my ears.

"At some point we need to go in there and actually finish that shower," he says with a lazy chuckle.

"I think I need a few minutes to recover."

"That was unexpected."

"You're always shocking the hell out of me. It's only fair every now and then I get the same opportunity."

His chest rises as his laugh reverberates around the room. "I'm not complaining. In fact, whenever you feel the urge to do that again, you have my unequivocal permission."

His hands move up my bare back. It's an affectionate touch. A thought hits me.

*He's always rough when you have sex; it's always a conquest. He doesn't feel what you're feeling. He will never make love to you.*

I have to fight the tears welling in my eyes. I don't want Adam to see me like this. I don't want him to know I've been so careless, and that I'm hopelessly falling in love with him.

# Chapter Thirteen

I WAKE UP alone again. Tilting my head to the right, I focus on the clock. It's five past seven. I need to get ready for work. I stand and realize I'm naked. *Oh, Adam, since I met you, waking up naked is becoming a habit.*

I return to the scene of the crime—the bathroom—and I'm astonished at how easily I become aroused. Visions of the previous night play out in my head, distracting me. One of my trembling hands reaches for the faucet and in less than a minute I'm in the shower. My body is sore and the warm water washing over me makes me wince. Victoria's words echo in my head. *He will use you and then leave you.* I wrap my arms around my body.

Once I finish the shower I brush my teeth and rummage through Adam's drawers for something to wear. I settle on a pair of boxer-briefs and a T-shirt.

Peering out into the quiet hallway, I wonder if anyone is home. *Surely, he didn't leave me here alone.* I move toward the kitchen and soft humming startles me. I turn on my heels, prepared to go back to the bedroom, when Ms. Wright's voice halts my progress.

"Evelyn, you're up. What would you like for breakfast?"

"Ms. Wright, how are you?" I try to sound cheery but I know a blush paints my cheeks.

She measures me from head to toe, though her eyes don't appear to hold any judgment. "I'm doing marvelously. Come sit, have something to eat. Maybe some eggs?"

I shake my head because I've lost my appetite.

Sternly, and with motherly affection, Ms. Wright speaks. "Sit."

I nod and do what I'm told. With my eyes wide I submit to yet another bossy figure in my life.

"Let's get over the awkwardness. I'm busy, and I suspect you have to get ready for work. Now, what do you want to eat?" she says decisively.

"Um…fruit, I suppose, maybe an apple."

"That's all?" Her eyes are filled with disapproval.

I nod. "I'm already late."

Ms. Wright frowns. She walks over to a basket located on the kitchen counter and reaches for an apple. She cleans it under the sink faucet, dries it, and hands it to me.

I take the shiny apple a bit self-consciously. *I could have done that.* I do not like the idea of being served by someone.

After a long pause I ask her what I actually want to know. "Where is Adam?"

"Oh, he's probably in his office," Ms. Wright says while stirring something on the stove.

*There's an office?*

As if she knew what I was thinking she answers my unspoken question. "It's down the hall, third door on the left."

"Thank you." Still holding the apple, I stand and make my way down the hallway. As I walk in the direction of the office I notice the various paintings adorning the walls. I grin as I remember Adam boasting about his *vast collection* of art the night we happened upon each other during Art Basel.

The sound of Adam's voice at the far end of the hall cuts my thoughts short. I lean against the doorframe and peek inside his office. Adam is on the phone, standing near a window, a document in his hands. He's wearing simple gray pajama pants and a white T-shirt, the waistband of his boxer-briefs visible since the pants are resting low. I stare at him shamelessly. *Damn, this man is sexy.*

"This actually looks pretty good." He sounds surprised. "Get me the documents on the Korbin property. I want to close by the end of the week." He pauses for a moment and turns from the window, a grin forming on his lips when he sees me. "Okay, that will work. I'll be in the office by half past eight." He hangs up the phone and pins me with his gorgeous stare.

"I spend thousands of dollars on clothes and you're still wearing mine?"

The amused expression he wears is infectious.

"I have no idea where that clothing is!" I say playfully.

"It's in the guest bedroom closet."

I saunter toward a large chair in the corner of the room and flop down. This man is so puzzling. I suspect the brief response as to the whereabouts of the clothes is Adam Black's way of ushering me out of his office, but I'm not taking the bait. I eye him closely, because today is the day I reason out what type of influence Adam is on me, on my life. *Should I walk away?*

Adam's handsome face is marred by a frown as he looks at me. I feel as if those eyes can see straight into my soul, as if he can determine what I'm feeling before I admit it to myself.

"You seem pensive today," he says as he turns to his desk and picks up a document.

"I was thinking about some things." I try for a casual pose, but my muscles tighten with tension. *Am I angry at him?*

"Like what?" he says without looking at me.

"The origin of your name, for instance."

His lips quirk and I now have his undivided attention. "Let me guess, it's interesting because I'm named after the first man? Well, if you subscribe to Judeo-Christian beliefs."

I cross my arms over my chest and take a big bite of the apple in my hand, my gaze never wavering from his.

Adam walks over to me and places his hands on either side of the black leather chair. He leans forward. "The origin of your name is also interesting."

I tilt my chin toward him so we're only inches apart and nod slowly. The air is thick around us, and as I'm reveling in our close proximity an upsetting thought infiltrates my head. I wonder if this is how he felt with all the members of the One Month Dating Club.

He licks his lips and my jealous thoughts dissipate. I want to grab his cheeks between my hands and kiss him, but I feel a sudden pang of trepidation.

"Is there a reason why you're eating an apple as we have this conversation?" His eyes are mirthful.

*As always, Adam is finding me a pleasant distraction.* I take a deep breath and regard him seriously. "I'm looking for answers."

"And you're determined to find them in the Bible?"

"Many people find answers there."

He scoffs at the comment. "Who is the snake in this situation?"

Adam walks over to this desk and sits on the chair. He leans back, his powerful frame relaxed.

"I'm not sure." I sit up straight because I feel the conversation merits good posture.

"May I offer my own hypothesis?"

I nod. *Adam has an opinion on this?*

"You are the snake," he says without flinching.

"Me? *I'm* the snake? That's your opinion?" My cheeks burn, only the flush has nothing to do with desire and everything to do with anger. I stand, walking to the edge of his desk a hand on my hip.

"Yes. From the first moment I set eyes on you, I've been tempted to do things I know I shouldn't."

"From the moment I first met you, I have been tossed into chaos, and you, sir, are the cause," I say indignantly. "In your presence I have no clue if I'm coming or going."

Adam laughs outright. "I should hope that in my presence you're *coming*."

His strong hands encircle my waist and he pulls me to him. My breathing is agitated as he positions me on his lap. The mirth in his gaze is replaced with a serious expression.

"The roles we play don't matter. Not as long as we both eat from the forbidden fruit."

He whispers against me, and I know we're no longer talking about a Biblical story, but about our lives.

Adam leans down and takes a bite of the apple I'm still holding, the juices of the ripe fruit trickling down my hand. He licks at my fingers as he tastes, and I'm surprised by the warm sensation stirring between my legs. *He can make any conversation sensual. It's his superpower.*

My voice is soft and uncertain as I challenge him. "Doing something illicit can create precarious situations."

"That's true, though in my experience, nothing has ever been won without risk," he asserts.

"So you're the type of man who takes risks often?"

He gives me that movie-star grin. "What do you think?"

"Around you it's hard to think."

My fingers move over his smooth lips and I can no longer deny the yearning in my chest. I move my lips against his, only for the first time it's a tender caress. He moves to intensify the kiss but I move back. I deny him the control he's accustomed to, and I can tell by his reaction it's something he doesn't like.

Adam shifts, moving me off his lap, so I stand. His beautiful blue eyes are void of any emotion; I can't tell what he's thinking.

"You should get ready for work."

That is without a doubt a clear dismissal. I believe I've upset him, though I'm not sure why.

"Is something wrong?"

He shakes his head, and though his face is expressionless, I know something is bothering him.

"I have work I need to get to." His eyes go cold as he focuses on his laptop.

My head moves forward in a slow nod. "Bye, Adam," I say with a twinge of regret as I exit the room.

I'm more confused leaving than when I came in. *Does he want me to challenge him? Does he want me to take a chance on this relationship? Wait…it's not a relationship, it's just sex.* The uncertainty of my standing with Adam is overwhelming my senses, and unfortunately, I can't just sit here and think. I'm late for work.

In less than fifteen minutes I'm ready. With haste, I say my goodbyes to Adam, who's on the phone. He kisses me absentmindedly, on a reflex, more interested in his conversation than me.

Parker drives me to school. I climb the stairs to the fourth floor and I'm not ready to deal with the issues of the day. The world doesn't stop because you're not ready to face it, so as the kids enter I put on a brave expression.

TINA can read me like a book. She knows when I'm on the verge of falling apart and I don't want to make her worry. So throughout the day I keep myself busy and avoid her probing questions.

The bell signaling the end of sixth period rings, and in less than fifteen minutes I'm making my way out of the school, walking to my therapist's office. As I head out, I notice the familiar black Escalade parked at the curb. *What is he doing here?* I head over as Parker steps out.

"Why are you here?" I don't bother to hide my annoyance.

Parker's isn't fazed by my attitude. "Mr. Black was adamant you be picked up from school, Miss Snowe."

"Oh. Where exactly did Mr. Black stipulate I be dropped off?" I know I shouldn't take my anger out on poor Parker, but I am fuming. *Why does Adam care where I go? I'm just some girl he's fucking for the month.*

"He wanted you dropped off at his apartment," Parker says hesitantly.

"Well, tell him I'm busy. At the moment I can't be his beck-and-call girl." I turn and walk away, leaving Parker with a befuddled expression on his face.

DR. DAVIS looks at me as she listens, her expression clinical, void of any emotion.

"I slept with him. I knew he wasn't interested in a relationship, that I'm just a diversion, and I slept with him."

"What do you think prompted you to do that?" She crosses her legs, calmly staring at me.

*I hate when you ask these questions, that even in my own mind, I can't answer.*

"Why does anyone do anything, Dr. Davis? I wanted him. I knew I would feel like shit afterward, and I still did it because I couldn't deny myself the satisfaction of being with him."

"Why feel bad about it then?"

I narrow my eyes in confusion. "He'll use me, and once he's done he'll throw me away as if I don't matter."

"That is only an issue if you allow it to be."

"I don't know what you mean." My breath is racing and I feel a panic attack coming. My lungs are shutting down on me as my chest and abs tighten. Thinking about how careless I've been, how inconsequential I am to him, is paralyzing.

"Evelyn. Stop. Calm down and talk it out with me." The edge in Dr. Davis's voice matches her stern expression.

My eyes water over with tears. "I don't want it to end. He's going to leave me and the thought scares the hell out of me."

I have long since taken my shoes off and am rubbing my feet against the grain of the carpet. The rough feel of the material against the soles of my feet helps me concentrate on the conversation.

"Sometimes we don't have control over what happens. You know that. We have to live with not only the choices *we* make but the choices other people in our lives make," she says definitively.

"You're talking about my father now. I don't want to talk about my father," I say stubbornly, because I know where this conversation is headed.

"It all comes back to him." She is relentless.

I place my finger in my mouth and bite at the nail, not breaking it, but rubbing my teeth against it. I stopped biting my nails years ago, but when I'm anxious the urge resurfaces. "I know what you're thinking. You think because my father decided to shoot himself, because he decided to leave, it's somehow connected to the situation I'm in with Adam."

Dr. Davis bobs her head forward in a measured nod. "Tell me how the two instances *aren't* related. Make me understand."

My sobs overtake my shaking body. *She is so annoyingly logical. So annoyingly* right. "They keep fucking *leaving* me," I say bitterly. "Every man in my life picks up and leaves."

"Adam hasn't left yet." Dr. Davis's voice is soft.

Unsettled by the sudden shift in her tone, I blink a few times and shake my head. "But he will. He said it's only a matter of time." I wipe away the tears on my face and take a deep breath.

"From what you've told me, it seems he's as confused as you are. I doubt he knows *what* he'll do." She pauses for a second. "Not everything in life is set in stone."

"So I should just continue the relationship and see where it takes me?" I throw my hands up in the air. "Look at me. I'm falling apart! I'm on the verge of a nervous breakdown and I've only been in this situation for a week."

Dr. Davis shakes her head. "No, Evelyn. You're currently in the middle of a minor panic attack, that's all. Honestly, it's to be expected."

*Are you kidding me? You expected this?* I narrow my eyes at her. "How is this normal?"

"Life hurts. There will be moments that feel intolerable. You can't keep shielding yourself from relationships because you're too scared to see them fall apart." Dr. Davis sighs. "I encouraged this relationship because I want you to test the waters, I want you to start living again. Only you can gauge what you can take. If it's too much, end the relationship. But I believe you'll come to the conclusion that regret hurts far more than trying and failing."

We sit in silence for a few minutes as my breathing calms. Everything comes back into focus, and my heart begins to beat at a steady pace. *Is she right? Have I closed myself off to the possibility of being happy? Have I let my fear decide what I can and cannot do?*

"I think I'm falling in love with him." I say the words aloud for the first time.

"Then can you honestly leave at this point?"

"No...I can't." I'm tethered to this ship, and if it sinks, I'm going down with it.

Dr. Davis's alarm rings, indicating the end of the session. With what I think is annoyance, she grabs her phone and turns the alarm off. "We can extend our session. You don't have to leave."

I shake my head. "I'm fine. Actually, I need to go. I'm sure Tina and my mom are worried about me. I've avoided talking to them, so I imagine they're letting their imaginations go wild with all sorts of concerns," I say with a roll of my eyes.

Dr. Davis smiles at me. "They care about you; it's natural they should worry."

"I'm not going to hurt myself."

She nods slowly. "If I thought for a moment you might, I would do something about it."

I smile, because having the trust of at least one of the people in my life is reassuring. We say our goodbyes and I leave the room. As I stroll through the halls of the building I check my cellphone. Three missed calls, and they're all from Adam. I groan. *Great, like I don't already have enough problems.*

I step out of the building and call him. *This conversation should be fun.* To my surprise, I hear the loud ringing of a phone from the left. When I turn in the direction of the sound, a pissed-off Adam Black is glaring at me.

I blink a few times, registering the sight. He presses a button on his ringing phone, sending my call to voicemail.

"I thought I should come see what my *beck-and-call girl* was doing." He moves with purpose toward me. "Though for someone who claims that title, you rarely do what I want."

I gape at him. *How the hell did he find me?*

# Chapter Fourteen

"**H**OW DID YOU…?" Words fail me.

I ball my hands into fists, trying to coax my breaths to circulate so my stiff muscles can get the oxygen they need. It doesn't work. I finally manage to stammer out the question.

"How did you find me?"

He steps close so we're inches away from each other. His stiff mannerisms make it obvious he's straining to retain control of his feelings. Though I'm not sure what emotion he's favoring—anger, disappointment, concern… His question ends my speculation.

"That's the first thing you want to say to me?"

*As always, he's overwhelming me, unsettling the fragile control I work hard to maintain.*

I move past him and start heading toward my house, because I have no idea how to deal with this situation. What do I tell him? *The circumstances of our liaison have me going bat-shit crazy and I needed to talk to my therapist? Nope, that's not going to work.*

I imagine people don't normally give Adam Black their backs. It's not that I want to be an exception to a rule, but I just don't have the courage to face his knowing eyes.

"Where the hell are you going?"

Before I can respond his hand has already claimed my wrist. The bangles I always wear chime as he twists me to face him. His arrogant stance erodes my initial panic and moves me to anger.

"Why are you here? How did you find me?"

"Parker followed you at my request," he says without any regret or shame.

"And you think that's normal? That you had your lackey *follow* me?"

Adam raises his finger.

"First, he's not a lackey but a highly trained security guard who has been working for me for years. He's also a friend."

He lifts a second finger.

"Second, if you'd told me where you were going, communicated with me, I wouldn't have felt the need to have you followed."

"Why do you care where I go? I'm just some random woman you're fucking." My anger prevents me from curbing my words.

Adam takes a step back, releasing his grip on my wrist.

"Evelyn, you're not a stupid girl, but sometimes you say the stupidest things. Would a man who was merely fucking you drop what he was doing to wait outside a building for you?"

*Maybe, if he was in the mood to fuck you again.*

"What do you want from me?" The sting of my watering eyes blurs his image.

"I want you to get in the car."

"Adam…" I say contritely, because I feel some remorse. He has the ability to make think everything I believe is wrong.

"Evelyn, get in the fucking car. Now."

I gulp and make my way toward the Mercedes double-parked in front of the building. I grab hold of the door and pull, but it's locked. Almost instantly, Adam is beside me, unlocking it. Then he opens it for me.

Wordlessly, I get in, jerking in surprise when he slams the door shut. He enters the car and in minutes we're at my house. The drive was filled with deafening silence. *Is this my punishment? Why won't he say something?*

I try again to reason with him, to perhaps apologize for my comment, but he raises his index finger to my lips, silencing me. Adam exits the car and walks to the passenger door, opening it for me. I take a deep breath and make my way to the front door. Mutely, I open it and turn on the lights in the living room. Adam follows me in and closes the door behind us.

"Sit," he says as he points to the couch.

I want to argue with him, to yell and protest that this is my house and at least here he can't tell me what to do. However, the expression in his eyes cautions me against the idea. I take a deep breath and sit as commanded. Adam sits in a chair opposite me. He looks at me as if he's pondering a perplexing question.

"I want to know what you were doing in that building."

I'm coming to the conclusion that Adam deplores not knowing every facet, every detail, about the people in his life. I take a deep breath and respond the only way I know how—with hesitation.

"And if I refuse to give you an answer?"

"You do have that choice. However, if you refuse to give me an answer I'm walking out that door and whatever we have going on between us ends."

His face is impassive, as if the notion of terminating our association means nothing to him. I feel like I'm a deer cornered by a hunter. When I tell him I'm in therapy, when he realizes how messed up I am—he's going to leave me. *We already established he's going to leave you anyway. At this point it's only a question of when.* I blink once to focus.

"I matter that little to you?" I whisper.

He straightens in his seat, and I get the impression my question makes him uncomfortable.

"The *truth* matters that much to me. I don't do business with people who lie to me or keep secrets from me, and the same rule applies to women I date. It applies to everything I do, a guiding principle I follow stringently. Do you understand?"

"I'm not lying to you."

"You're also not telling me the truth."

"Adam, no matter how hard you try, the world will shock you and so will the people in your life. You can't control everything," I say with sincerity, because my experiences have proven them to be an undeniable truth.

"What were you doing tonight?" he says, disregarding my statement.

I shift in my seat as the anxiety of the situation makes my stomach churn.

"The way you talk to me is so cold and reserved." I rub my fingers against my temple because I'm trying to hold back tears. "Do you even care about me?"

"You're trying to change the subject." He leans forward, his forearms resting against his thighs. His gaze captures mine and sincerity shines in his eyes. "Of course I care. Your insecurities are clouding your judgment if you can't see that I care about you. But I won't be with someone I can't trust."

That last statement cost him. He's been hurt, I know that much. But I want the full story. If he demands my dark secrets it's only fair I own his. Feeling brave, I ask him the question that has been at the forefront of my thoughts for the past day.

"Adam, what did she do to you? The woman you once were in a relationship with, how did she break your heart? What did she do to make you have this need for control?"

He leans back in the chair, his muscles tensing. "Stop trying to make this about me."

"But it is. It's about *both* of us."

We stare at each other, our stubborn natures making us unwilling to turn away. A ringing phone shakes us from our standoff. Adam curses but still reaches for it and snarls a perfunctory greeting as he stands.

As Adam diverts his attention to the phone call, I allow myself the opportunity to breathe. When he ends that call he's going to return to this subject. How do I make him let it go? Maybe I can distract him with seduction? At first I chuckle at the thought but the idea slowly becomes less absurd.

I eye him in that perfectly fit button-down shirt. Even when he's upset, he's incredibly handsome. The idea of kissing those angry lips is beyond tempting, it's irresistible.

I kick off my shoes and saunter over to him. He's mentally in the office, but a curious mix of confusion and intrigue moves across his face. *I'm so going to win this argument.*

"If we lose that property because of a hundred-thousand-dollar difference, I'm going to be furious. The location is perfect. Agree to the damn conditions and close the deal."

He rotates his shoulders as he holds the phone to his ear and plops back down on the couch. *It's now or never.* I slide my hands under my skirt and take off my panties. Without taking my eyes off him, I toss them on the floor by his feet. I have his attention now. He blinks a few times, trying to retain his composure, and then speaks into the receiver.

"He asked for *what*?"

Lifting my skirt so it rides high on my thighs, I straddle him. The fear that he might reject me crosses my mind, but the press of his hand at the small of my back tells me this is not the case. I lean against him and begin to lick the contour of his ear, nipping the lobe. He swallows hard, but manages to continue speaking.

"I agree to the price increase, but not the extension on the closing. I need possession of the property by the end of the week."

While my lips continue the relentless conquest of his ear, I undo his belt. Adam breathes deep, my actions affecting his concentration.

"Read that line again."

I undo his pants and pull down the zipper, freeing his growing erection straining under the confines of his boxer-briefs. I can't resist the urge to plunge my hand inside. My fingers grip his width as my eyes fix on his.

His tongue slips out of his mouth, moistening his lips, and the muscles between my legs constrict at the sight.

"I'm going to have to call you back." He taps the end call button and tosses the phone on the coffee table.

Adam grips me by the wrist and pulls my hand out of his pants. Hauling me forward so my breasts are flattened against his firm chest, he kisses me, his teeth biting at my lips as his tongue dips into my mouth. Unable to control the urge, I groan. His free hand tangles in my hair, pulling on my curls and tilting my chin up. I gaze at him between my eyelashes, panting with desire.

"I know what you're doing," he whispers in a low, menacing tone.

"I have no idea what you are talking about," I say innocently.

Adam's hands move over my chest, over the buttons of my blouse, and with a rough tug he yanks it open, the buttons scattering over the floor like confetti. Then the ruined blouse is on the floor and he's unclasping my bra with quick, deft fingers, leaving me with only my skirt that looks more like a belt.

"Do you trust me?"

"I thought trust comes only after you date someone for a while. Isn't that in the Adam Black dating manual?" I don't bother hiding the teasing curve of my lips.

Adam pushes me so my back arches like a bow. My head hangs inverted, one of his hands supporting me at the small of my back while the other runs up and down my chest, the tips of his fingers grazing my neck and then caressing the sides of my breasts.

"Stop being cute and answer the question," he says throatily.

My mouth opens as I struggle to breathe, though he doesn't give me time to recover. He jerks me up against him and his warmth envelops me like a blanket. My barriers down, I let my instincts govern my response.

"Yes, I trust you."

Content, he flashes me a sexy smile while his hands palm my breasts. My nipples harden and he takes the opportunity to pinch them, spurring a moan from my lips.

Pulling away he grips the buckle of his undone belt and yanks the leather free from his pants.

"Put your hands behind your back."

Intrigued, I do what I'm told, and at the sight of Adam slipping the tip of the belt strap into its loop my chest begins to heave. He positions my hands inside the clasp of the belt and pulls, forcing my posture to straighten as the leather encircles my wrists. Wrapping the remaining length around my waist he holds on to the end, his wrist twisting once around the length, so he can maintain the hold.

My pulse quickens, because the idea of not being able to touch him both excites and petrifies me.

Adam pulls himself out of his pants, his other hand controlling the belt strap. He strokes himself a few times, and the sight makes my throbbing muscles react. I'm wet—soaking wet. Releasing his erection, he moves my body up and positions me so I slide down on his hard cock. My mouth opens in a drawn-out sigh as I feel him slip inside, inch by delicious inch, though before the last of his length is embedded deep his forearm flexes underneath my ass, halting my descent.

"Eyes on me, Evelyn," he commands, and the thought of resisting doesn't even filter through my fogged mind.

In this position I should have control but obviously I don't, and for a blissful second, I don't care because submitting to him feels right. Before I can process what I'm thinking, his hips buckle, his forearms moves and he thrusts the last of his length sharply into me, mercilessly, stirring a cry from my lips.

"I still want to know what you were doing today." Adam's gorgeous eyes search mine as he shifts my body.

His thick cock is lodged to the hilt, his balls resting at the base of my ass. The look in his eyes, determined with a hint of lust, makes it impossible to think. "Adam…" I say in a breathy plea.

Cutting me off, he pulls on the belt, straightening my back and forcing my shoulders to arch. Once again his hips buckle and his heat momentarily slips out of my sex before again he rams deep into my depths. I whimper as my muscles stretch around him. *Fuck! This is not how I envisioned this experience.*

"I won't stop until you tell me."

As if to reaffirm his point he continues to move, lunging into my body while his grip tightens against the belt and the rush of so many sensations— the bite of pain, the burn of arousal and the sizzle of anger—leaves me defenseless. *This is coercion. This is how he wants to interrogate me? This isn't fair—*

Adam's strong fingers dig into the tender flesh of my hip as he slams me down his cock while simultaneously pivoting up. With relentless persistence he torments me, orchestrating my movements while he rubs against the spot inside of me only he's ever discovered, and my orgasm builds and builds. I reach the pinnacle. This exquisite tension overruns me and as I'm about to burst, Adam shifts, changing his tempo and denying me release.

A low growl rumbles in the back of my throat and he flashes me a smile that though beautiful, isn't friendly.

"What. Were. You. Doing. In. That. Building?" he says between slow, powerful drives.

My anger wins the battle of emotions raging within me, because it's not right that he demand so much of me when he's not willing to reciprocate. I clench my muscles, squeezing his cock tightly and he hisses.

"Fuck you, Adam. I plead the fifth." I flash him my own version of his taunting smile noting the beads of sweat on his forehead. He's struggling, and I'm loving the sight. I roll my hips against him, biting my lip to prevent the groan that's itching to break loose from my throat.

Adam's grip on both the belt and my hip tightens and the twinge of pain that radiates from the contact is heaven, because I've never been one to run from pain, in fact, I've chased it. He leans forward and when I try to do the same because I want to taste his lips, he tugs on the belt, reminding me I'm not in control.

"I've said it before," he rasps. "I'm better at this game. More experienced. I will win. It's only a matter of time, unless of course, you're willing to forfeit."

The subtlety of his challenge isn't lost on me. I can end this with one word—*stop*. But in saying it I lose him, and I can't bear to lose him. This leaves me with one option, telling him the truth and then watching him leave me. Unable to make a decision, he continues tormenting me, fucking me, bringing me to the edge only to pull me away at the last second.

*Death by mind-blowing sexual torture? There are worse ways to go.* Submitting to his control, I let my moans escape—he's earned them. Even still, I'm too stubborn to answer his question, though he continues to ask.

Time blurs, leaving me uncertain as to how long this dangerous game between us lasts—hours, maybe? My body becomes sore and my groans are becoming soft, helpless whimpers under the strain of his skilled touch.

Adam pushes his still-clothed body against me, making me hyperaware of the vulnerability of my current position since I'm practically naked. The musky scent of our heated bodies mingled with his aftershave has me lightheaded. Wanting to savor his skin, I part my lips, planting kisses along his jaw, reveling at the opportunity to finally touch him. He leans into my kisses and whispers in my ear, "Why are you resisting?"

Drained by his assault, I respond honestly. "Because I'm scared."

His tongue runs along the curve of my cheek, licking at a stray tear and culminating in a fleeting kiss before again he asks, "Where were you today?"

Maybe it's the rush of his caress, of the hope inspired by the fact that Adam has been the only man I've ever met who chases challenges instead of running away from them, or resignation over what I think is inevitable, but I'm unable to hold out anymore. It's over.

"At therapy, Adam. At therapy." I sob helplessly, my body fatigued from the surges of pleasure. The entire experience is oddly cathartic.

Frowning, he tilts back, his gaze assessing mine. "You were speaking with a therapist?"

I nod as I sway, my body sticky with sweat.

He releases the hold on the belt and it falls on the tile floor. My arms, finally free, wrap around him, clutching him desperately because I'm terrified it's the last time I'll ever hold him and to my surprise he reciprocates my affection, one of his arms wrapping around my waist while the other curves around the nape of my neck.

"Why didn't you just tell me that?" He sounds confused.

"I didn't want you to think less of me," I whisper.

He shakes his head. With tenderness he's never before shown, he kisses me. His lips, though soft, are demanding. They take everything I have left, claiming and owning what I know in the depths of my heart is only his. It's as if after stripping me bare, he's breathing life back into my tattered bones.

Abruptly, he pushes me down on the living room carpet. Then he's moving, thrusting into me again and again. I wrap my legs around his hips, crossing them at the ankles, feeling as if the floor is falling away from me. Having been on the edge for so long, my orgasm comes swiftly and with ferocity. Seconds later he's crashing with me, his body shuddering above mine as he spends himself, a warm sensation spreading between my legs.

The corners of the room come back into focus and when I look up Adam is staring at me with an expression I can't gauge.

"Don't keep things from me," he commands, while softly rubbing his fingers against my cheek.

I unclasp my legs from his hips suddenly self-conscious. "I'm sure there are things you don't want to know."

"Like the fact that you go to therapy?" he says grabbing hold of my thighs and halting my retreat. "*Everyone* goes to therapy, and if they don't, they probably should."

I laugh because his words and actions allow relief to wash over me. My tension evaporates.

He smiles at me. "I want to know everything about you."

I stare at him wide-eyed. "Why?"

Adam shakes his head. "I don't understand how a beautiful, intelligent woman like you can be so self-doubting."

Releasing one of my thighs, he grabs my chin so I can't turn away. "I want to know everything about you because even though you piss me off with your statements, your stubborn actions, your insecurities…you inspire me."

I close my eyes because the emotion I see in his scares me.

"Adam, you say things like that and I have no clue how to respond."

He rolls onto his side, taking me with him. "Why do you have to overthink everything? Why can't you just smile and take the words for what they are—a compliment?"

I press my head against his chest, his smell again intoxicating my senses. In his arms I'm safe. "Because you say you want to know everything about me, and knowing someone like that takes longer than a month."

Adam's fingers trail down my stomach, grazing my navel. "I take it our conversation yesterday upset you." He avoids my gaze as he speaks.

I fidget at the question. "What woman wants to hear that the man she's seeing has a four-week expiration date on relationships?"

Adam presses his lips against mine abruptly. It's a quick kiss, the type that burns fast and leaves you hot and panting. He pulls back and stares into my eyes. "When I'm around you I'm confused, and that's new to me. You throw me off balance and make me lose my focus. I haven't felt like that in years. What I said yesterday was a warning. I don't want to hurt you, and it's been a long time since I cared enough not to hurt someone."

I squeeze his biceps, rubbing my thumb against the definition of his muscle. "Why do you think you'll hurt me?"

He cups my cheek and I lean into his touch, relishing in his warmth.

"Because of the way you react when I touch you. You're naïve. You don't know how the world works when it comes to men and women."

"Maybe the problem is that you think you know it all," I say defiantly.

"Happily ever after doesn't exist." He releases his hold on my cheek, his body tensing. "The concept is nothing more than a bargaining tool people use to manipulate, and I'm not interested in playing that game."

He must see something in my face because he curses under his breath. "I meant it when I said you're the first woman in a long time I cared enough about to warn. I don't want to hurt you."

"If you care so much, then why not stay away from me? Why come get me tonight?"

"Because I couldn't stay away!" Moving my body away from his, he sits up. "I'm a selfish man who goes after what he wants and what I wanted tonight was *you*. I readily admit I'm an asshole. I've always been upfront with women—told them exactly what to expect. Even still, I've made countless women cry and never once thought twice about it... But shit... The thought of making you cry..."

He goes silent, and because I can't tolerate the cynicism and sadness that has washed over him, I sit up and wrap my arms around him. "Adam..." I know I should say something. Finally, a thought registers in my head.

"Do *you* go to therapy?"

He laughs. "Is that your subtle way of implying I should?"

Before I'm able to respond he counters with a question of his own. "Why do you go?"

I'm not ready for this type of honesty, for the intimacy of telling someone your deepest, darkest secrets. So I shake my head, smile at him and instead decide to ask him a random question. "Are you hungry? I'm famished."

Adam frowns. "Evelyn..." His phone rings, interrupting us.

Silently, I thank whoever's on the other end the phone. I lean toward Adam and kiss his cheek. "I'll make us something. Would you like a sandwich?" I whisper as he reaches for the phone. Already too distracted to care, he nods at my question.

I stand up from the floor and stretch. I slide the wrinkled skirt off and head to the kitchen. Adam continues to talk as I prepare the ingredients I've taken out of the refrigerator.

"What are the taxes on the property?" He rubs the back of his neck, the phone firmly pressed against his ear. "That's going to increase once we get the new appraisal." His forehead creases in a small frown. "Did you talk to Jacobson? What did he say about the Korbin Property?" After a long pause

Adam emphatically curses. "I'll do it myself." He looks at his watch. "I want to be in the air in two hours; make sure the flight is cleared."

*Two hours? He's leaving already?* I stand there naked in the kitchen, unable to move. *He's always going to leave. Come to terms with it.* Unwilling to dwell on the thought, I step into the living room and he's gone. A sudden feeling of deja vu hits me. I put the plate with the sandwiches on the coffee table and walk toward the light emanating from my art studio.

Adam is standing in the middle of the room looking at the painting I had deformed in frustration. It's now a dark, blooming iris, on the verge of opening its petals to the world.

"You finished it." A hint of delight is blended with surprise.

I lean against the doorframe, staring at him. "I felt challenged to make something out of that painting. You could say a stranger motivated me."

Adam turns to face me, amusement etched on his face. "You should thank that stranger."

I narrow my eyes at him playfully. "Reminiscing on the events of the last few days, I believe I already have."

His chuckle fills the room.

"You know, I thought you looked lovely that day. You were wearing jeans and a T-shirt, your hair was wild from the events of the day, and yet there was something about you I couldn't ignore." Adams eyes linger over my form. "And now..." He pauses.

I straighten against his scrutiny. "And now...what?" I need him to say the right words. He rarely says something tender unless we are in the throes of lovemaking, but at the moment I need Adam Black to be my *hero* again. I feel vulnerable in my own home, standing naked before him, and one dismissive glance, one careless phrase, will break me.

"Now you look gorgeous." He strides forward and strokes my cheek with his knuckles.

The action hurts because I recognize it's fleeting. "You have to go." I say the words myself because I know they're coming anyway.

He nods. "I have to go to New York to settle a problem."

I smile at him brightly. I refuse to let him see even a small measure of sadness in my eyes. I've come to the conclusion that Adam Black is not a man who appreciates weakness, mainly because I have yet to see him exhibit any.

"At least take your sandwich," I say with a smile.

"I wouldn't dream of leaving without it." He leans down and kisses my cheek before stepping past me.

I hear him grab his keys from the coffee table and I'm fighting back tears as I turn to face the door. He has the sandwich in his hand. He looks at me as he opens the front door and enthusiastically bites into the sandwich. I laugh, because I know it's his way of saying thank you. The door closes behind him and I'm left alone.

My body is sore. It has been used and discarded. My thoughts are unforgiving. *You wanted this. You're the one that tried to seduce him. Live with your mistakes.*

"I doubt there's a girl in this world who wants to be left alone immediately after she's been thoroughly fucked," I whisper, and the words sound loud against the vacant room.

I slide down the wall and bring my knees to my chest. As I sit there thinking, something dawns on me. *He was tender. He admitted he cares— that he can't stay away. Perhaps tonight was not a defeat, but a small victory.*

The thought is enough to get me through the night.

# CHAPTER FIFTEEN

"**H**OW ARE THINGS going with Adam?"

Tina flips through an old magazine as she speaks. I know her interest is a nothing but pretext because she's the one who gave me the magazine—she already read it cover-to-cover.

We just finished baking a batch of cookies. Actually, Tina baked and I gave her moral support, because I'd burn the house down if I attempted to use the oven.

I plunge the tip of my finger into a melty chocolate chip as I stall. I don't know how to answer her question.

"Things are still going, and that makes me happy."

Tina tosses the magazine on the table. "That's not much of an answer."

I grip the cookie tightly and it crumbles. I feel like I'm on a rollercoaster that has no end. It's Wednesday afternoon and I haven't seen Adam since our impassioned meeting on Monday. I miss his voice. I miss the confidence he stirs within me. More than anything, I miss his strong arms and the way they anchor me against my insecurities.

"We texted a few times yesterday. He's busy with some real-estate problem in New York. Adam's not exactly forthcoming when it comes to his work."

I chuckle, because it's a vast understatement. Adam gives tiny droplets of information. Being with him means relinquishing control, though the thought no longer petrifies me. Feeling consumed by a relationship is dangerous, but I've arrived at the conclusion that that type of danger excites me.

"From the little you tell me, he's not forthcoming, period."

Tina's snippiness startles me. "Hey. What's wrong?"

"He's like chocolate ice cream, Evie. The taste is divine, but too much of it and your hips get wide, your stomach puffs up, and you feel like shit when you look in the mirror."

"You have the wrong impression." I put down the crumbled cookie and lick my fingers. "I would say he's more like cookies and cream. Sweet, but riddled with mystery. You never know which spoonful might offer that big piece of cookie."

Tina scoffs. "Whatever the flavor, too much ice cream is still bad for you."

"Yes, but can you imagine a world without ice cream?" I stare at her with mock horror.

Tina bursts out laughing. "You're head over heels for this guy."

*She has no idea.* It's been three days since I was in Adam's arms, and I'm going through withdrawal.

"I don't know. I try not to focus too much on me and Adam or the intricacies of our relationship."

"I know he makes you cry. That can't be good."

"I make *myself* cry, because I overthink everything. I just want to be happy."

"Are you happy when you're with him?"

"Tina, why do you ask me these questions? You're almost as bad as Dr. Davis."

With a heavy sigh, I answer her question. "A lot of the time, I am."

"What about the other times?"

"I know you want to protect me, Tina. You always have. When we were little you punched Timmy Phelps in the nose because he pulled my hair. But you can't protect me from this."

"Old habits are hard to let go."

"I'm okay, I promise. You know what I want now?"

Tina grins. "Ice cream."

We both laugh in unison and head straight to the kitchen. As I open the freezer door a sharp knock startles me. *Who could that be?* I move to the living room and open the door to discover a delivery man standing on the porch.

"Miss Evelyn Snowe?"

"That's me."

"I have a delivery from a Mr. Black."

The poor man is struggling to read off of a clipboard while gripping a large parcel. I move forward to help him. He produces an envelope from his pocket once his hands are free. Absently, I take the note and thank him.

"Good day, Miss Snowe." He turns and heads toward his car.

I open the envelope and begin to read.


*Dear Evelyn,*

*I considered sending you flowers but the thought of them dying after only a few days contradicts the spirit you effortlessly exude. Therefore, I thought giving you something simple, yet multi-dimensional, might be best.*

*Adam Black*


Tina looks at me, amazed.

I whisper the key phrase of the note and shake my head. "*Multi-dimensional. No, he wouldn't do that…*"

Like a child on Christmas morning, I eagerly open the package. Inside are eight carefully bundled photographs. My mouth opens in shock at the gift. Adam has bought me the photographs I admired at Art Basel.

"What are they?" Tina asks impatiently.

"Nick Vasquez's *Warhol's Flowers*."

Tina frowns. "What does that mean?"

I shake my head in exasperation. My heart is racing and my attempt at explaining is pathetic. I move my fingertips across the glossy photos.

"At Art Basel, when Adam and I bumped into each other I was looking at these photographs."

Tina's eyes widen as she finally understands the significance of the gift.

I'm overrun with emotions. Wonder. Elation. Hope.

*He remembered. Our meeting must be something he holds in his heart if he remembers our conversation.* This is the most meaningful gift anyone has ever given me, because it pulls at the threads of my tattered soul, disarming me. When I view something so beautiful, all the bad in my life fades and the world is filled with possibilities. For years, I've been trapped in my own suffocating self-loathing, but Adam Black manages to break through the barriers surrounding me. Like the nude painting we discussed at Art Basel, he leaves me exposed. *How does this man know me so well when I'm still discovering myself?*

Adam has been in my life for just two weeks and he's already buying me expensive clothing, and now expensive artwork. But does he truly care for me? Is this to placate me, to get what he wants from me? *What more does he want? I've given him everything!*

Tina watches the changing emotions on my face with a worried frown.

"Evie, what's wrong?"

"I need to talk to him," I say, reaching for my phone.

"I thought you were avoiding him. You said he was busy with business, he may be in the middle of something important."

Tina sounds logical. I should heed her warning, but the anxiety tugging at me makes it impossible for me to listen. I dial his number and as the phone rings I realize I have no idea what I'm going say. *Smooth, Evie, real smooth.*

"Evelyn?"

Adam's surprised voice echoes through the phone.

"Excuse me, I need to take this call."

Vaguely, I hear the chattering of other people in the background. He was probably in the middle of some important business meeting. *See what you did? You should have listened to Tina.*

"What's wrong? Are you okay?"

"I got the photographs you sent me."

"Good." He pauses for a moment. "Did you like them?"

"Why would you give me something like that?"

I try for the detached tone he effortlessly manages, but I fail. I sound agitated.

"Is the phrase *thank you* not in your vocabulary, Miss Snowe?"

His initial gentleness has been replaced with irritation. *Great, I'm Miss Snowe again.*

"I'm trying to understand why you would send me something so expensive after I told you that when you flaunt your money it makes me feel uncomfortable."

"*Flaunt?*" He growls. "I'm beginning to hate that word. We've already had this discussion. My desire to give you gifts is solely a reflection of my own selfish needs. I enjoy giving you something that might make you smile. That happens so rarely."

Regret washes over me. "I'm sorry. The photographs are beautiful, I do love them. I just…" I take a deep breath. "I miss you."

He goes silent for what feels like an eternity and a cold sweat mists my forehead.

Finally, he sighs into the phone. "I miss you, too. Friday is almost here."

The way he enunciates the words is seductive, and it makes me smile.

"Thank you for the photographs." I absentmindedly play with a strand of my hair. This man makes me feel like a hormonal teenager.

"Oh, so you *are* familiar with those words." He laughs. "I need to go. Goodbye, Evelyn."

"Bye, Adam."

I sit there for a few minutes with the phone in my hands, dazed. I finally understand that if this liaison ends, it might be because of my own reservations, my own inability to accept happiness when it comes. I make a solemn vow.

*I'm going to stop overthinking everything.*


I step out of the school and am surprised to see Adam leaning against his black Mercedes. I notice a group of teachers gawking at him. *Yep, he's gorgeous, ladies. Now back off.*

"What are you doing here? I thought Parker was picking me up."

"I got in a bit early and thought I'd surprise you," he says, his shoulders a bit tense.

I nod mutely as I enter the car. He hasn't attempted to kiss me, and the lack of intimacy between us makes me anxious. In a few minutes, we arrive at his apartment.

"Is something wrong?" I say hesitantly. Maybe his business deal went poorly. I don't want to be the cause of any further aggravation, but I'm worried about him.

"We need to get ready for Sarah's party."

He steps out of the car and moves toward the elevator. His response is not an answer, but rather a creative way of avoiding the question. My heart starts to race as I follow him. When we enter the apartment he greets Ms. Wright briskly and then retreats to his office. I stare at the older woman, unable to mask my confusion. She smiles at me, but I can tell she's also confused by Adam's mood.

"Evelyn, would you like anything?"

"No, thank you."

Ms. Wright nods and busies herself with work. *I wish I had something to do. Standing here is so uncomfortable.*

I consider going to the guest bedroom and getting ready, but Adam's behavior is too odd to ignore. As I stand alone in the hall, my fists balled, my forearms shaking, I realize I'm not only confused—I'm angry.

*What the hell is wrong with this man?* He picks me up with a massive chip on his shoulder and then refuses to explain his problem. Trying to calm down I pace near the entrance of the apartment, though the action has the opposite effect because minutes later I'm fuming. Letting my anger dictate my actions, I storm into Adam's office.

"What's your problem?" I place a hand to my hip for emphasis.

He's sitting at his desk, his face stoic. It's as if he was expecting my entrance. With narrowed eyes, he stands. "I have something for you." He retrieves a blue box from his desk.

"Are you going to answer me?"

Disregarding the question, Adam turns the box toward me so I can see the name *Harry Winston* written across the case in elegant script. *Adam bought me jewelry?*

"I thought you would appreciate a gift of this nature."

He opens the box, and inside are two beautiful thick bangles with delicate flower patterns circling their edges. Adam's voice is still low and detached.

"Let me put them on you."

*You had a good run, Evie, but the cat's out of the bag. Did you honestly think you could hide this forever?* A shudder rips through my body and my mouth is dry as panic replaces my anger. I shake my head and offer Adam a mechanical smile.

"Thank you, but I can't possibly accept anything so extravagant." Attempting to put some distance between us I take a step back, but he moves forward, invading my space.

"I insist. I'm tired of those bangles you wear. They make the most annoying jingling noise as you walk."

The stiffness of his facial features scares me. I turn to leave the room, but he grabs one of my wrists, preventing my escape. *He knows. I don't know how, but he does.* Adam pulls me against him and then speaks. "What has you so nervous?"

His eyes are a piercing cobalt. He's trying to conceal his emotions, to control them, and as always, he simultaneously intimidates and mesmerizes me.

"I think you already know," I whisper.

"I'm going to let you go, but I need you to sit." He points to the chair behind his desk, his grip on my wrist firm, and his imposing frame shadowing mine. The domineering undertones of his actions sends chills down my spine.

"Do you understand me?"

I nod, and Adam releases his hold. Butterflies have infiltrated my stomach and the room is spinning, so slowly, I move to the chair and sit. *Oh God, please don't let me have a panic attack now.*

"How did you find out?" I say, staring at the floor and avoiding his gaze.

"Unfortunately, not from you."

He tosses the box on the desk, the sharp sound echoing as it slams against the wood. I appreciate the jolt as it snaps me out of my shock, because again my privacy has been violated.

"Well then, how exactly did you find out?"

"If you're going to question me, stop being such a coward. I'm not offering you any explanations while you refuse to look at me."

"*I'm* a coward?" My head snaps up. "You're the one who went behind my back investigating my life. Tell me, how did you find out?"

"What's going on between us has moved like wildfire. In the span of weeks, we've become more than I anticipated. I make it a priority to know those I spend time with—I won't allow another woman to make a fool of *me!*"

He flinches, his head tilting sideways and his lips pressing hard against each other. His stilted movements make it obvious he regrets the admission. He swallows once before speaking.

"I told you before, I don't associate with people who lie."

"An *omission* is not a lie."

"It is to me."

"How. Did. You. Find. Out?" I punctuate the words slowly.

"I had a private investigator run a background check on you."

"You're an intrusive bastard."

Ignoring the insult, he stares at me hard-faced. "It all makes sense now. The way you acted the night we first slept together, when you woke up from that bad dream. I knew something significant in your past was tormenting you, but I wasn't prepared to learn what I did." Closing his eyes, he shakes his head and the image of him filled with pity and regret, is unbearable, because Adam has never been one to demonstrate such emotions.

"Wipe that expression from your face. Don't you dare look at me like that."

I'm on the verge of falling apart. If I don't calm down soon I'll pass out. Adam doesn't respond to my commands, in fact he keeps staring at me with muted eyes.

"So you investigate me, you find out I once tried to commit suicide by slashing my wrists and you decide to buy me jewelry? That seems logical to you?"

Air escapes his lips in a cynical chuckle. "I was in the process of buying you the bangles before I found out. I wasn't lying when I said I found the jingling noise of the jewelry you normally wear, annoying."

"You keep secrets from me." I say between clenched teeth. "I've respected that because the truth is we barely know each other. It's not reasonable to assume someone will tell you everything about them in the span of two weeks."

"We're talking about two separate situations." Adam rubs the back of his head, an action I know he does when he's stressed. "Knowing that the person you're with has potential issues—that they might hurt themselves because they're upset or unhappy—is the type of information you tell someone when you start a relationship with them."

"That's just it! We *aren't* forming a relationship here. We're sort of dating, and idly fucking each other for the time being."

My words snap him out of his somberness. "I'm so fucking tired of you saying that. Of you using that excuse to push me away, even after I've explained that what's going on between us, that this—" he flicks his wrist point at himself and then me, "—is new to me."

"Don't worry. I won't do something stupid if things between us fall apart." I swipe at my cheek, flicking away my tears. "Put your conscience at ease and feel free to do what you do best, walk away."

I need to leave. The idea of being in the same room with Adam is intolerable. I stand, but immediately his strong arms are around me.

Frantically, I struggle to escape his hold. *Why does he care? Why is he doing this to me? Why doesn't he understand?*

My chest burns, spots cloud my vision and before I realize what's happening, my body stiffens against Adam and my knees go weak. The room is spinning, and I'm reminded of the first day we met, when he held me like this at the bank, when he was my *hero*.

Adam effortlessly scoops me into his arms, carries me to the couch on the adjacent wall, and lays me down. We sit there for a few minutes—me watching him breathe while I desperately try to mimic the action. As the panic attack fades and my surroundings come into focus, I notice Adam's thumb rubbing against my forearm in small circles. I hate how gentle he's being because it makes me feel pathetic and weak.

"It's not something I discuss even with people who've known me my entire life."

Tenderly, he grabs my chin so I stare at him. "Maybe, it's something you should discuss."

"Are you offering your ear?" I say sullenly.

"If you want it, then yes. It's yours."

He stares at me, with those damn beautiful eyes—eyes that can see through everything and a paralyzing pain erupts in my chest. *He's never going to look at me the same as he did before.*

When I stay silent, he sighs, a deep expelling of air and I think he's going to tell me it's over, that he can't deal with my past, my baggage. I'm so scared, I can't move.

"Evelyn, I've been wondering, since I met you why a woman with so much to offer, lives her life like a shadow. Now I know why." He pauses, his fingers combing the strands of my wandering hair before he carefully pushes them behind my ear.

"You have every right to be angry at me—I am an *intrusive bastard*. And while I'm sorry my actions have upset you, I'm not, nor will I ever be, the type of man who can ignore a problem, especially when it gets in the way of what I want."

The statement is so far from what I expected, my downcast gaze shoots up to meet his. As our eyes connect, his hand curves around the back of my head, holding me in place.

"I care about you. And because I do, I need to tell you that if you're not honest with yourself about your past, it's bound to repeat itself."

"It won't." I deny with a strong shake of my head, but still he doesn't let go of me.

His lips tense, and his jaw stiffens almost as if he's holding back from saying something and the reality of the situation again makes me angry. Angry that he hired someone to look into my past, angry at the hypocrisy of his statements.

"*You're* not honest with *me. You're* not honest with *yourself.*"

Adam's hand pulls away, dropping to his side and his posture transforms before my eyes. The caring man who a minute ago was tenderly touching me is now hidden from view.

"You're right. I don't talk about my past, because it has no bearing towards my future. It doesn't weight me down like yours does. It doesn't inhibit me and prevent me from being successful."

He's wrong of course, his past does inhibit him, because though he's obviously successful, his reticence about his past, prevents him from falling in love. But I'm so desperate to keep us together I don't contradict him. Am I willing, in order to keep him in my life, to cede all the power in this *liaison*? Frustrated by the thought I lash out.

"Why does it matter? Why can't we be happy with what we have now?"

"Because for the first time in years, I'm not finding satisfaction with something superficial." Adam grabs one of my wrists and pulls off the bangles I normally wear. He looks at the visible marks of my past and his darken expression, the vulnerability of being so exposed in front of him makes me tremble. Noticing, he fits his fingers between mine until my muscles relent and quit shaking.

Adam glances at his watch. "We're late, and we still need to get ready. That is, if you still want to go to Sarah's party."

I nod and he gingerly pulls me up. We're inches apart, and I want him to kiss me and show me we can make this work. But his voice is distant as he takes a step back. "Are you okay?"

"Yeah…" I rub the sides of my arms, and the friction helps me focus. "That happens to me sometimes…panic attacks." Confessing that, even though he already knows from past experience, makes me feel exposed, so I quickly add, "I'm fine."

His eyes twitch and I know he doesn't believe me, but fortunately, he doesn't press the issue.

"How long will you need to get ready?"

I shrug and tell him a half hour. He nods again and then walks to the door, leaving without looking at me. His detachment makes it impossible for me to hold back my anger.

"You're wrong," I call out, and he stops, turning his head enough to look at me. "The secrets you keep do inhibit you. You're not as free as you think."

A pensive expression crosses his face and he inhales deeply.

"Maybe you're right… But I'm not sure I can fix that." Without another word, he strides out of the room.

*What are you doing here, Evelyn? The man is riddled with trust issues, and you're pretty messed up already.*

Unwilling to throw in the towel, I mimic Adam's purposeful gait as I make my way to the guest bedroom. But my aching heart makes it hard for me to get excited about the evening ahead.

With disinterest, I shower and dress. I've decided to wear the fluted dress Marian from Neiman Marcus absolutely loved. I style my auburn curls so they cascade down my back. As I'm putting on lip gloss I see Adam in the bathroom mirror. We stare at each other. I'm still frustrated, yet I can't deny the effect his appearance has on me. He's impeccably dressed and, to my shame, my mouth parts at the sight. I turn to face him and he's holding the jewelry box.

"You look beautiful. I want you to wear these." There's sincerity in his voice, though I still get the impression he's building barriers between us.

Without waiting for me to agree, Adam grabs my wrists and puts the thick bangles on me. His actions always reflect his desire to dominate me, to own me, though for some reason I don't find the notion frightening anymore. *Wake the hell up, Evelyn. You've fallen down the rabbit hole.*

He turns to leave and I grab his arm. The thought of him pulling away is like a knife piercing my already fragile heart. He looks at me, emotions I don't comprehend waging war in his eyes. Unbelievably, Adam is unsure of what to do. I help him by wrapping my arms around his body and kissing him.

He lifts me so I sit on the bathroom counter. One of his arms moves up my back, gliding along the nape of my neck and firmly settling in my tangled curls. Our kiss is filled with desperation as our tongues clash with each other. Adam bites at my lips, making me moan with want. I can tell he's as frustrated as I am, because I can practically taste his exasperation.

I forget everything and I want him to take me right here. I want him to rip the clothing off my shaking body and show me how much he needs me, wants me. He pulls back, his lips compressing with what seems like regret. His eyes shutter and then he's lost to me again.

"We need to go." Adam stares into the mirror and straightens his attire. He gazes at me with what I think is longing, though I'm not sure, and then he turns, stepping out of the room with the same purposeful walk.

I shake my head and whisper to myself, "I'm not falling down the rabbit hole. I'm already in Wonderland."

## CHAPTER SIXTEEN

A S PARKER DRIVES us in a black limo toward Coral Gables, Adam and I sit in silence. I wish I knew what he was thinking. He wanted me in the bathroom and yet he pulled away. *Why would he do that?*

"What do your parents do, Adam?" I say, in the hopes that an unassuming conversation can break the tense atmosphere.

"My father owns a medical practice and my mother owns an architecture firm," Adam says with disinterest. He gives me a quick side-glance and then turns away, his attention focused out the window.

*I hate it when he's so indifferent.*

"Oh, that's interesting." I fidget in my seat and let the quiet envelope us. A few more minutes pass and I realize that this is a make it or break it moment. If I let the distance between us widen, if I ignore the situation, I'm signing the death warrant on our brief affair.

I take a deep breath and stare at him, in possession of a bravery foreign to me. "I want you to answer a question for me, Adam."

He cocks his head to the side, his body stiff. "Whether or not you get an answer depends on the question."

*Is nothing easy with this man?*

"You've often said that honesty is important to you. I hope that if you expect honesty from me, you are willing to offer it."

"What diplomatic reasoning," he utters dryly while pressing a button on the doorframe. A dark divider rises, separating the front of the car from the back. Parker can no longer hear us; we're alone. "What's piqued your curiosity now?"

Staring into his intense gaze almost undoes my resolve. "What was the name of the woman, the one you cared for?"

"Why would you want to know that?" He scoffs. "I would think the details of my dealings with past women would be an unpleasant subject for you."

A nervous laugh shakes out of me. "Normally I would agree, but the more I get to know you, the more I realize your past is an important factor in our future." I try to sound rational, though I can't prevent the tremor in my voice. "I want to get to know you better, and to do that I need to know about her."

He sighs heavily and his intimidating gaze takes on a calculating gleam. "I'll answer your question if you answer one of mine."

*Oh no, not this game again.* I purse my lips, noting the challenge in his tone. "What type of question?"

He grabs my hand and I gasp at the unexpected action. With ease, he pulls and I am in his lap. Adam's lips rub against my neck and his breath is warm on my skin. It's hard to think when he's so close.

He pulls on my hair, forcing me to tilt my neck up, and then places his lips on my pulse in a soft kiss. "What would possess you to harm yourself?"

The beating of my heart has increased, and though I want to avoid his gaze, his firm hold makes the action impossible.

"Evelyn…" he says tenderly. "Help me understand. Because if I'm perfectly honest, I have to admit your history confuses the hell out of me. How could a talented, beautiful, clever girl who quite literally had the world at her fingertips try to kill herself?"

Adam grabs my chin and his nose rubs against mine as he stares into my eyes. "A private investigator can tell me *what* happened, but what I want to know is *why* it happened."

"Why do you need an explanation?" I say as the sting of my watering eyes burn.

"I want one because even though you have yet to realize it, I care about you. The thought of you harming yourself fucking burns." He shakes his head. "I need to understand why you would do something so incredibly…"

"*Stupid… Selfish.*" I finish his statement in a broken sob. My fingers graze his cheek and the grainy rasp of his stubble helps me focus. "Sometimes truths are too hard to talk about."

One of Adam's hands moves along my back, massaging the muscles of my spine. "Sometimes confronting those truths is the only way to overcome them."

"Have you done that? Confronted all your demons? Because from the little that I know, it seems like you're holding on to something heavy. A secret you keep locked away and hidden under this tight—" I clamp my fists together, "—suffocating control."

"I own everything that's happened in my life because I know every struggle has made me the man that I am—a man who is successful and determined. A man who knows that living under the shadow of mistakes and regret is stifling. My past relationships have molded me, but they sure as hell don't dictate my future. Don't fault me because I refused to make the same mistake, twice."

"What mistake? Would trusting me, be a mistake?"

"That's not what I meant, and it's not pertinent to what we are discussing."

"I hate when you do that," I say petulantly. "You speak as if you know everything, as if no one in the world could possibly disagree with you, all the while ignoring my questions." I close my eyes because I'm frustrated by his eloquence and my persistent inability to articulate what I'm feeling.

"And you avoid topics by pointing an angry finger at me." He sounds offended but still holds me close, the beating of his heart ticking steadily against my chest.

I need to tell him. He needs to know I can be honest, and I need to tell him because I need to know he can be kind, loving, and considerate. Maybe that's what love is, one person taking a leap and praying the other follows.

"Little girls adore their fathers. They mean the world to us." I can hear the bitterness in my voice, the sound overflowing with a sorrow I know too well. "But as time passes we grow up and we want our freedom." My legs flex in a fidgeting motion as I speak. "So one day, I told my father that I was leaving, that I loved him but I was moving out." I pause for a long moment. "My dad was a troubled soul. He suffered from a long list of issues and had been taking pills to regulate his moods since he was twenty... He didn't know how to be alone and having his little girl abandon him broke his heart."

The tears I have been holding onto fall. Adam gently brushes them away as he listens.

"He couldn't live without me. I think deep down I knew that. People do stupid things when life puts up road blocks, when you can't see the solution to a problem, and my dad did a really stupid thing." My breath is ragged. "And after I...I felt so *guilty* for leaving him alone and I..."

"And *you* did something stupid." He finishes my statement as the back of his hand caresses my cheek.

The action is too tender, and I twist away.

Adam sternly pulls me close, his body overpowering mine. My head is alongside his, and the smell of his skin is comforting. Being in his arms is all I want and my struggles lose momentum. *Enjoy it, Evie, because as soon as he can, this man will run. He's rich, gorgeous, and can easily find a woman who is not fucked up.* His words break me from my dark thoughts.

"Do you still want to go to this party?"

"Do you still want me to come?" I ask.

"Of course I do." He pulls back and retrieves a handkerchief from his pocket. With care he wipes away my tears.

I laugh with embarrassment. "I must look horrible." I pat my puffy eyes and give him a bashful smile.

"Even tear-streaked, you're beautiful."

He smiles at me and all I see is the face of the man who's clawed away at my defenses. What we have may be fleeting, but at the moment we're both here in this car and the world is a blur. Staring at Adam, warmth pervades my core and I want him, I *need* him.

I brush my lips against his, and for an instant I let them linger, my eyes meeting his deep-blue gaze. Our kiss is wet and hungry. I moan as his tongue runs along the outline of my lips, and when we both pull away the only noise echoing through the back seat is our panting.

"You're upset, I don't want to…"

I place my fingers against his lips. "What's upsetting me right now is that you're not inside me." I shift my legs over his hips, lift my dress so it's high on my waist and straddle him. As my pelvis presses against his, I can feel the bulge of his growing erection.

His hands slide up my thighs, underneath my dress and slip inside the confines of my delicate panties. He grips my ass and pulls me forward, the action making me inhale sharply.

"Mr. Black, we're here."

*Oh shit!* I'm startled as Parker's voice blares from a speaker. I forgot he was driving us somewhere.

Adam closes his eyes in frustration. He presses a button located on the door. "Avoid the valet and park toward the back." He kisses me, his soft lips rubbing against mine. "Do you really want to go to this party?"

I trail my fingers down his cheek until my hands rest on his chest. "I would never dream of making you miss your sister's birthday party. Besides, after everything that's happened today, I like the idea of mingling and having fun... Trust me, I'm okay."

He gives me one of those knee-shaking, heart-thumping smiles. "In that case, are you ready for a party, Miss Snowe?"

I give him an impish grin. "I thought we were already in the middle of a party, Mr. Black."

His chest rises as gives a throaty laugh. He whispers against my lips, "Don't worry, I promise that we'll get back to *this* party soon."

I grin as I crawl off him, and to my surprise he playful slaps my ass. It startles me because Adam is rarely so frisky.

"You cheeky bastard!"

"Bastard, yes, though you're obviously the cheeky one between us." He winks as he finishes the statement.

I shake my head with a grin and grab my purse. I comb the *I've just been fondled* look out of my hair, apply some lip balm, and straighten my dress. Adam smirks as he fixes his attire and as I watch him, I remember my original question.

"So, what was the name of the woman?"

His face hardens at the reminder and he rotates his shoulders, as if the action can eliminate his stress. "Serena Welsh." He speaks the name plainly as he opens the car door and extends his hand to me.

I take it with a smile and whisper, "Thank you."

He tries to conceal a smile as he pulls me from the car. I hook my arm around his and get my first real look at the house, my jaw dropping in the process.

His parents' home is extravagant; it reminds me of an Italian villa. Stunning trellises adorned by blooming bougainvillea outline the entrance, and vines crawling against the outward façade form a wall of immaculately manicured vegetation.

Dating this man is such a culture shock. He lives an extravagant life. It's no wonder he is evasive and demands obedience. Evidently, getting what you want from the world is a family trait.

We walk on cobblestone paths leading to the backyard, and I'm stunned by the sight. It's a mixture of *Cirque du Soleil* and *Cinderella*. Performers on the far left flutter across the air on a trapeze while impeccably dressed guests observe. To the right, other guests talk while sipping on beverages provided by the bar station near the large polished dance floor.

Sarah makes her way through the crowd upon seeing us. Her dress is short, and I catch Adam noticing, his forehead wrinkling in a disapproving frown.

"Evie, you came!"

I step back at the sheer force of Sarah's hug. She smiles at Adam and steps on her tippy-toes to kiss his cheek.

"I think your dress is a bit too short," he says with brotherly angst.

Sarah rolls her eyes and ignores him. "You guys are going to have a wonderful time. The band has been playing the *best* songs." She leans against me and whispers, "Also, the guy at the bar knows what he's doing; have him mix you an apple martini and you'll be on cloud nine in ten minutes."

Adam narrows his eyes at Sarah. Her giggle makes me respond in turn.

Suddenly, a handsome older gentleman is beside us. He has salt-and-pepper hair but his chiseled jaw is reminiscent of Adam.

"Well, son, what are you drinking?" He slaps Adam on the back firmly and has a wide grin on his face.

Abruptly, he sees me. "Well, hello there. I'm John Black." He extends his hand and I offer him my own. I think we're going to shake, but instead he lifts my hand to his mouth and plants a soft kiss above my knuckles. *Well, that's where Adam gets it from.*

"I leave you alone for one minute and you're already kissing other women?"

I turn toward the woman's voice. Her hair is a soft honey color and her eyes are a deep emerald green. I can tell by the smirk on her lips she's merely teasing John Black.

Adam rolls his eyes, annoyed by the playful banter. He pulls me against him protectively. "Evelyn, these are my parents."

"Oh, so *this* is Evelyn." The older woman looks at me with a grin. "I've heard so much about you. I'm Lillian." She leans forward and gives me a quick hug.

My eyes widen at the comment. *Has Adam talked about me with his parents?* My silent question is soon answered.

"I may have mentioned a few things." Sarah smirks mischievously at Adam, who is glowering at her.

Sarah grabs my hand. "Evie, let's get a drink."

Before I can reply, I'm being dragged across the dance floor. I catch a glimpse of Adam shaking his head in annoyance.

"I can't believe he brought you," Sarah says with a smile.

I frown at the random comment. "Why is that?"

Sarah motions for the bartender. "Two apple martinis, please." She turns to me. "Adam acts unusual around you. He's oddly protective; I'm sure you've noticed."

I nod slowly, surprised by the candid nature of this conversation.

"He's totally smitten. I've seen my brother act like this only once before."

The opportunity to get information on Adam doesn't come often. So a bit too eagerly I interject, "With Serena Welsh?"

"No way!" Sarah grabs my forearm as if to settle her shock. "He told you about her?"

"He only told me her name."

"It was a long time ago. She's the daughter of a family friend. Mathew, Adam, and I grew up with her."

"Mathew?" My eyes narrow curiously at the name.

"Yes, our brother."

"Adam has a brother?" I utter in surprise. *And he had the audacity to blow up because I didn't tell him about my past?*

Sarah laughs at my outburst. "Yes, he's two years older than Adam. He lives in New York." She shrugs. "I want to give you a warning. I'm sure you've realized Adam gets around. There may be a few women here who *know him* pretty well." She takes a large gulp of the apple martini.

*Are you fucking kidding me?* Wearily I scan the patio, letting her statement register.

"I've left you speechless." She takes another large sip of her apple martini, emptying the glass. "Being with my brother means accepting his past." Her voice adopts that calm tone Adam has mastered.

"Thank you for the information, Sarah." I say sincerely, though I'm still reeling with shock.

"I like you, which surprises me. I *always* despise his girlfriends." She utters the word *girlfriend* with a sarcastic inflection.

I open my mouth to respond when Markus suddenly slips his arms around Sarah. She leans against him with a small smile, and I instantly feel out of place.

After a moment, Markus realizes I'm standing in front of them, and he coughs lightly. "Evelyn, you look lovely tonight."

Revulsion flows through my body as he eyes my body. *Why do I find this guy so creepy?*

"Markus, how nice it is to see you." Before I can continue, I feel Adam's hands around my waist.

"I was wondering where you'd run off to," Adam says strangely. When I tilt my head to regard him I realize why. His glare is fixed on Markus, who's brazenly holding Sarah against him.

Sarah straightens her shoulders, in the process moving Markus away as the menacing expression of Adam dawns on her.

"Baby, let's dance," Sarah suggests quickly.

Markus leads her away and I turn to face Adam. His body is rigid with fury. I place my hand on his cheek. I want to ask him why he never told me he has an older brother, but our location makes it impractical.

"Hey, don't let him ruin our evening." I take a cue from his book and wink at him.

Adam smiles and grabs my hand, leading me through the crowd, pausing every so often to introduce me to some of the guests. Most of the people in attendance are mutual friends of his family, yet another thing I find daunting.

"Adam." A voluptuous redhead captures my attention. Her heels are three inches too high and her skirt is three inches too short. Though she has the body to pull off the look, she seems like walking trouble.

"Diane, I didn't expect to see you here." He gives her a tight smile and leans forward to kiss her cheek.

"Do you honestly think I would miss Sarah's birthday party? I mean, she did do her internship with me. Besides, she only has one more semester until she graduates, and I intend to recruit her."

"I'm certain she'll go on to do her master's immediately after. She'll be unable to take on any full-time positions," Adam says definitively.

Diane places a hand on her overexposed breasts and the other on Adam's forearm while she artfully laughs. "You never change; you're still so overprotective."

*Hey, who said you could touch him?* The hair on my arms prickle and a cold chill sweeps over me as I watch them. *Is this jealousy?*

Adam smiles at me as he listens to Diane, though I can tell he's not pleased. "Evelyn, this is Diane Glen. She manages the art gallery *Stir Crazy* in the Design District."

I nod at the woman and she barely pays attention.

"Oh, it's a pleasure." She sets her gaze on Adam again. "I'm so sorry I didn't return your call earlier. I was busy with a client, but I'm searching for the right piece. I considered showing you something from Mary Forester; she's a local artist, but after thinking about it I doubt you'll appreciate her work. Maybe we can do lunch sometime next week and discuss some other potential art investments?"

*He* called *her? They're going to* lunch *together?* Okay, I am without a doubt jealous, not to mention insulted on Mary Forester's behalf. She's a fabulous artist.

"I'm afraid I have to disagree with you. I think a piece from Forester is something Adam would love."

Diane looks at me with a frown, while Adam attempts to hide the grin curling at the edges of his mouth.

"She's known for her abstract landscapes and her capacity to texturize her work. Her paintings literally jump out of the canvas." I lean against Adam, like a cat marking her territory, and continue. "One piece in particular might suit your tastes. I believe it's called *You're Beautiful*. The painting is a contrast of both dark and light colors, reminiscent of what you admire in my work." I shrug casually and once again smile at Diane. "That is, of course, only my humble opinion."

Diane looks flabbergasted. She wasn't expecting me to have an opinion on the subject.

Adam places a hand at the small of my back, his expression radiating pride. "Evelyn is an extremely talented artist. She recently painted a mural in my house."

"I see." Diane's body tenses and she stands straight so she's noticeably taller than me. "What medium do you utilize?"

"I try not to limit my options, though I do prefer oil paints."

"Well, I'll have to see your work one of these days." She turns to Adam. "I'll send you photographs of Forester's paintings. It was lovely to see you again, excuse me." She turns and strolls off, her walk strikingly less self-assured.

"What was that?" Adam asks with amusement.

I shrug and give him a sheepish smile. "I have no idea what you're talking about, Mr. Black."

He does the most adorable eye roll and I'm sorry we're in the middle of a party because all I want to do is tackle him to the ground and have my way with him.

We mingle with a few more guests, and when Adam is discussing the recent developments in the South Florida real-estate market I take the opportunity to visit the restroom. Adam's parents' house is a maze, an elegant jumble of intricate rooms. It takes me five minutes to find a restroom. I put on some lip gloss and fix my hair; the humidity is wreaking havoc on my appearance. After a few minutes I shrug and exit the room.

"Well, if it isn't the flavor of the month." A stylishly dressed woman stands in front of the door.

"Excuse me?" Surely this woman is talking to someone else.

"I'm pretty sure you heard me." Her eyes flit across my form in a measuring fashion. "Where exactly did he meet *you*?"

"Lady, I have no clue what you're talking about." I begin to walk past her.

"Adam is quite a handsome man."

Her words stop me mid-step. I turn and face her. "He *is* quite handsome, though I doubt you stopped me to talk about his attractive qualities."

"We just wanted to say hello." The voice of Victoria Chase echoes across the hallway.

I laugh, because I find the entire situation ridiculous. These two women have confronted me because I came with Adam? Is my presence really such a threat? I suppose I should feel flattered.

"Victoria, I wish I could say it's wonderful to see you again." I give her a condescending smile.

"I see that he's not bored with you yet." She walks to me with a model strut.

"No, actually I think he's enjoying the *flavor* I can offer," I say pointedly.

"For now. Though he does seem *very* interested in the conversation he's currently having."

The smug statement makes me frown. I walk out the sliding glass doors to the patio and search for Adam. He's surrounded by a group of women who are laughing and leaning toward him. Adam looks as if he is enjoying himself. As I stand there, flustered, Victoria and her friend position themselves beside me.

"You'll only keep his interest for a while. Even as we speak your appeal is waning." A cynical chuckle escapes Victoria's her parted lips.

The sight of Adam surrounded by beautiful women makes me dizzy, though I refuse to let these vile women demoralize me—I do a good enough job of that on my own. I turn to them, take a deep breath, and speak my mind.

"What I have with Adam may be fleeting, but I do know one thing for certain. I will never be as *pathetic* as you two, who have nothing better to do than walk around a party and insult someone you don't know."

"You may think we're insulting you, but honestly we're trying to warn you." Victoria sighs. "Men in our circles, may slum it and find a girl like you appealing, but they'll marry someone like us—Adam will marry someone like us."

Unwilling to listen to another word, I turn and walk away. I have no desire to interrupt Adam, so I make my way to the trapeze performers. For a few minutes I stare at them, though I'm not even remotely interested in the show.

Adam's a wealthy, handsome man who can bed any woman he wants. How do I keep someone like that interested?

Listlessly, I make my way to the dance floor. I'm not paying attention to my surroundings, because I'm dragging my broken heart across the floor, so I don't see the man in my path. I crash into him and his hands instantly are around my waist, holding me up as I regain my footing.

When my eyes fix on his I'm startled by his deep emerald gaze. I place my fingertips against his broad shoulders and straighten. The thought of being caught in the arms of an incredibly sexy man by Adam does come to mind, but I'm too pissed to care.

"Are you okay?" His voice is deep and he has a five o'clock shadow on his face.

The lights finally turn on in my befuddled mind and I manage to speak. "Yes, I'm sorry for bumping into you."

"How can I be offended by being run over by a beautiful woman?" he says with a cocky smirk.

A nervous laugh escapes my lips. I take a step back to distance myself and I notice the hint of regret in his eyes as I move.

"I'm not normally this clumsy. I was just…" I sigh. "Lost in thought," I say shyly.

The mystery man takes his time assessing me, admiring my curves. "There should be a rule against thinking too much at a party." He gives me a perfectly straight smile. "Dance with me," he says authoritatively.

"Is that a question or a command?" I'm sick of being on the receiving end of demanding men and my frustration is showing.

"A sincere question. In fact, a longing hope."

"I came with someone." I give him the patented *Adam Black* tone.

"Yet, you're walking around alone." His voice is laced with arrogance.

He's right. I am alone. Adam is no doubt still surrounded by beautiful woman, not even remotely concerned as to my whereabouts. The thought makes my stomach churn. Recklessness takes control of my body, my actions.

"You know what? I think a dance is a wonderful idea. Lead the way."

His strong hand grasps mine, and in less than a minute we're swaying to Ed Sheeran's "Thinking Out Loud".

"So, is the beautiful woman in my arms apposed to telling me her name? Let me guess—you're the type that will make me work for every syllable." A carefree chuckle escapes his lips.

"Why ruin the moment with introductions?" *Shit, I'm actually flirting with this man.*

He twirls me and then pulls me close. "Playing coy?"

I open my mouth to respond when I am interrupted by Adam's curt voice. "May I cut in?"

The mystery man tightens his hold on me. "Adam, I was on my way to find you when I was stopped by this beautiful woman."

I stifle a groan. *I didn't stop him, I tripped.*

Adam looks at me with mildly controlled fury. I feel like he might combust before my eyes.

"Mathew, get your fucking hands off my girlfriend." Adams voice no longer holds even the tiniest measure of control.

I'm struck by two important facts. The mystery man is Mathew Black, Adam's brother, and the man of my dreams has claimed me as his girlfriend.

Adam's glare does not allow me the time to revel in the delight of my newly acquired title. *Oh shit...I'm in so much trouble.*

# CHAPTER SEVENTEEN

MATHEW BLACK LOOKS genuinely confused. "You have a girlfriend?"

"I don't exactly tell you everything about my life." Adam takes a step forward and grabs my hand.

Mathew smirks as he takes a step back. "Does your girlfriend have a name?" He looks at Adam when he asks the question, placing a sarcastic emphasis on the word *your*.

"I can speak for myself." I narrow my eyes at them both.

Adam's grip tightens around my hand. "Evelyn, this is Mathew, my brother." He scoffs. "Though I'm not sure why I'm bothering with introductions, since you two have obviously met."

"Actually, we never did get around to making introductions," I murmur with irritation, because I find it ridiculous he's upset.

"Yes, we were eager to get on the dance floor." Mathew has a condescending smirk on his lips as he stares at me.

"That's not how I remember it happening." I rally to my defense.

Adam pulls me closer. "Well, since you enjoy dancing, so much, please do me the honor." He looks at Mathew. "Now, if you will excuse us?"

"It's been a pleasure, Evelyn." The way Mathew utters my name holds the same seductive edge Adam often uses.

I have little time to think on the uncanny similarity as Adam's free hand moves to the small of my back and we're dancing. Being light on my feet is a skill that eludes me, though in Adam's arms I doubt anyone would notice. He leads me in a variety of spins, and more than once I find myself catching my breath at the fluidity of the movements. It's as if we're having a silent argument on the dance floor, our eyes often meeting in a fierce clash of wills.

After a deftly executed twirl, Adam pulls me against him so that I can smell the intoxicating aroma of his skin.

"Smile, Evelyn; you looked quite happy before. I would hate to be the cause of your distress," Adam says impassively.

My eyes dart up to meet his and I smile with sincerity, because even if he's controlling his emotions and leaving me guessing as to his thoughts, I'm where I want to be—in his arms.

As the band finishes the song Adam leads me toward a secluded area around the house. Throughout our brief trek he remains silent, the soft tapping of our feet as we step on stone pavers being the only noise between us. My eyes focus on our destination. The building we're approaching has a wall with a high peak toward the front, and vines are climbing over the delicate brickwork, the erosion forcing some of the stones to fade and chip. As we enter the structure I'm awestruck by the sight; it's a greenhouse. The exterior stonework extends to the far wall, but all the others are made of delicate glass. Flower pots are scattered around the room and the smell of soil and blooming roses make me smile. If Adam wasn't flushed with anger, I would assume he brought me here for an intimate encounter.

As if he were discarding his coat after a long day, he whirls me around and releases me from his clenched grip. I shuffle back with wide eyes as the top of my thighs hit a weathered table and the clank of ceramic pots echoes behind me as my fingers splay out in search of stability.

"Did you forget that you came to this party with me?" he says, adopting a cold, detached tone.

The question surprises me, though my shock quickly shifts to anger. "I should ask you the same question."

"What the hell is that supposed to mean?"

"I'm not the one who was surrounded by a cluster of scantily clad groupies earlier. If it was your intention to ignore me, why bring me at all?"

"Ignore you! I've spent the night standing by your side, introducing you to my family, to people I've known for years, and you have the nerve to say I was ignoring you?" He takes a step forward and glares down at me.

I meet his gaze, because even though he intimidates me, I refuse to be humbled by this man.

"The second I walked away you surrounded yourself with the Adam Black Fan Club. I doubt you even noticed I was gone until you saw me on the dance floor."

"You're being ridiculous. I was socializing with family friends while you went out of your way to make me jealous."

"You act as if you found me making out with some guy in a closet! It was a *dance*."

"It's the fact that you were dancing with *him*," he says with exasperation.

"Why does it matter?"

When he doesn't respond to the question, I look at him, really stare him down, focusing on the flush of his cheeks, the sweat misting his hairline, the stiff rigidness of his locked muscles. Though he's attempting to mask his expression, insecurity is written in the subtle nuances of his tense jaw and the small creases under his eyes. The realization is so shocking it dulls my anger.

"Why did you neglect to tell me you had a brother?"

He leans down and whispers, "You seriously want to discuss why I neglected to tell you something?"

My face blanches. "It's not the same."

"You're right, it's not!" His raised voice reverberates against the windows.

"There you go with your self-righteous, high-and-mighty attitude. You get angry at me for being dishonest when you conceal everything from me."

"I wasn't the one with my body pressed up against someone else." His sapphire eyes gleam against the glittering lights of the greenhouse.

I sneer at the comment. "Well, honestly, how could you press up against just one person? Your groupies virtually surrounded you. I doubt you knew which direction to lean."

"That's enough," he growls. "I was talking with people I've known for years, while you were flirting with my brother."

"People you've known for years?" A laugh escapes my lips. "You mean people you've fucked, don't you?" I stand tall, steeling myself. "Just how many people have you screwed at this party?"

"Do you want an exact number or an approximation?"

"You are *such* an asshole," I say through clenched teeth.

"My brother is a handsome man. Maybe if he compliments your paintings, you'll fuck him, too."

I don't give myself the opportunity to think. My palm cracks against his cheek. The shock on Adam's face gives me a small sense of satisfaction and I raise my hand again, to hurt him like his words have hurt me. Adam grabs my wrists and twists my arms so they are pinned behind my back. Though I'm still angry, a raw sexual energy charges the air around us.

"I didn't mean that… I'm sorry." The words rasp out of him, as if torn from the deepest part of his soul and it's hard for me to keep it together when I hear vulnerability in his voice.

"Sometimes you're so cruel, a complete—"

"Bastard. Unfeeling, ruthless prick."

I hate his acquiescing response, more because I'm not willing to end his self-deprecation than my reciprocating sentiments. And yet, faults and all, I still believe he's an incredible man—the best I've ever met.

Before I can get a grip on my emotions, his lips clash with mine. Our bodies move back and once again I hit the table full of ceramic pots, one of them falling at the sudden jolt. My head is telling me to fight back, to stop him, but my body is a slave to his touch. In a moment of clarity, I tilt my chin up to pull away and Adam bites my lower lip. It's the best type of pain, one that makes your heart race and reminds you you're alive.

I'm panting. He's only inches away and I can tell he's struggling with his own desires. How can I be so angry at him and yet so starved for his attention, for his touch?

"What's your plan, Adam? You want to get in a quick fuck before you toss me aside so I can be like one of the fawning women out there? Pining over you, hoping you'll deign to give me your attention." I pull my hands from his grip and push them against his chest.

Adam isn't fazed by my shove, though he does take a few steps back. "Evelyn, upsetting you wasn't…" he starts to say.

I interrupt him. "I refuse to be something you use and discard. Remember what I told Victoria, that maybe I was going to be the one using *you*? I meant that."

I take a deep breath, strengthening myself against the pain numbing my senses, because I know my words are a lie. I already belong to the Adam Black Fan Club. In the span of two weeks I've fallen in love with this man, and to him I'm probably nothing more than a diversion. The words of my Catholic mother echo in my head. *Don't sleep with a man before you're married…he'll never respect you.*

"You're letting emotions get in the way…" Adam's says bitterly.

Once again I interrupt him. "Well, at least I make the effort to openly express my emotions. You repress and bury them, until they fester."

He mutters a curse under his breath before his mouth covers my lips, effectively silencing me. I shift my hands up with the intention of pushing him away, but I'm lost to passion. Adam pulls back so his lips hover above mine, his strong arms holding me in place.

"Why do you keep doing that?" I say softly.

"Because it's the only way I can get you to shut up." Adam pulls back and runs his hand over his hair, frustration searing through his expression. He eyes his watch. "It's getting late, we need to go."

"I despise how you tell me what to do. I hate how you keep things from me and then criticize me for doing the same. You rage at me for keeping secrets from you, when you keep *everything* from me. You're a hypocrite."

Adam leans forward; his movements like a prowling panther, slow and frightening. "Say what you really mean. You despise *me*." The self-loathing in his gaze is sobering.

My eyes widen and I take a deep breath. I can't stand the idea of Adam thinking I hate him. I place my hands on his cheeks. "I don't know how to be the person you want me to be. I keep making mistakes without even trying."

"The person you *are*, is exactly who I want in my life."

His body freezes and his eyes dilate, almost as if he's surprised by the admission he's made. Sensing I need to make the next move or run the risk of coming to a deadlock in the conversation, in our relationship, I bite back my fear and hold on to my resolve.

"Adam, before you, I was numb, purposefully disconnected from the world around me. I could be around a thousand people and still feel choking fear, but in your arms, I feel safe. Even when I think you are being unfair, I could never, ever, hate you."

We stare at each other for a long time—then like magnets, we collide. Grabbing the back of my thighs, Adam carries me as his lips bruise mine in a kiss that tastes of the longing, the frustration, and the craving we've both been afflicted with.

My back hits the delicate ironwork of a weathered trellis and I don't bother to muffle the moan that escapes my lips. Adam's hands move up my dress and the realization of what we're doing hits me like a freight train.

"Adam, we're in your parents' house, in a building open to the public," I protest, and though I mean it, my body rubs against his, contradicting my statement.

"I don't care. I've wanted to fuck you since I saw you in this dress. It took all my willpower to resist you in the car, and right now all I want to bury myself in your sweet pussy and hear you cry out. I want to know I'm the only man who will lay claim to every inch of your body."

His husky tenor and brutal honesty makes my body warm.

For a brief moment, I note the words he chose to describe his desires. He wants to fuck me, not make love to me. Do I mind? I don't even know the difference between the two, and the truth is, I want him inside of me.

He slips his fingers inside the delicate fabric of my panties and tears them free, leaving me open-mouthed in astonishment. He takes the opportunity to claim me in a chaotic, wet kiss. The world stills.

Adam moves his lips over my chest and my muscles constrict. His hands and body continue their downward journey until he's on his knees, and to my shock, he lifts my already short dress so it bunches at my waist, exposing me. My ripped panties have long since been discarded and I'm too filled with desire to feel even an ounce of shame. With wide eyes I watch as he peers up at me, lust burning through his gaze. His lips trail kisses along my thighs, and when he reaches the apex, he buries his head between my legs as his tongue parts the folds of my sex.

I cry out at the feel of his tongue swirling along the delicate flesh between my legs. Adam's pace is slow at first, and when his fingers move against my clit the sensation makes my muscles clench. I'm close, and the skill of his probing tongue pushes me over the edge. One of my hands grips the iron trellis for support as I come, my panting cries sounding incredibly sharp in the serene greenhouse.

Adam moves up, all the while rubbing his head along my body. He holds me upright as my knees shake, and when his face meets mine he kisses me, his lips still slick with my arousal. I rub my body against him like a cat in heat, because he has the power to make me lose all sense. He pulls back and the sexy smile on his lips is dripping with masculine pride.

"Do you like the way you taste?" he says in a deep whisper.

I don't even have to think about my response. "Everything tastes good on your lips, even me."

"I want you to say it, Evelyn." Adam pushes his growing erection against my pelvis.

A small frown forms on my face.

Responding to my unspoken question, he once against thrusts his bulging erection against my body. "Tell me what you want."

"You, I want *you*." I writhe with need against him.

"Why do you want me?"

His arrogance turns me on. Between breathy pants, I respond. "I want you to fuck me…because I'm yours. You're the only man I want to be with."

His lips bruise mine as he claims my mouth and I vaguely hear the clink of his belt buckle before he pushes into me. My body is pinned between him and the iron trellis and each thrust feels like a magnificent punishment. I know he's still upset, he's exasperated with me, and he's fucking his frustrations out. One of his hands is holding the intricate iron while the other holds my hip in place, anchoring him, so he can maintain control.

A quivering moan escapes my lips as his precise lunges build me up fast. This isn't a slow seduction, but a quick fuck, the threat of being caught making the thrill sharp. I bite my bottom lip, trying to repress my screams, because the echo in the greenhouse amplifies every sound, but Adam won't allow me to hold back.

"I want to hear you, Evelyn. I want to hear every uninhibited sound you make as I fuck you."

He hitches my leg, shifting his position so his shaft slides against that special spot inside me he's so incredibly familiar with and I cry out, not even remotely concern about being heard by another party guest. In seconds, I'm letting go and coming with a heart-pounding shudder.

Adam reaches his own climax, and the sensation of his release pulsing between my legs is exhilarating. We both slide down the trellis to the floor, our bodies exhausted. Running my fingertips along the strands of his hair, I notice it's damp with perspiration, and I love that I can do this to him, leave him weak and spent. I look over to the door and realize Victoria has left.

"How you can so easily make me lose control is both fascinating and frightening," Adam gasps.

I kiss his lips affectionately. "The feeling is mutual."

He gives me one of those go-weak-at-the-knees smiles and as I gaze at him, I feel a new confidence. "Why did you ask me out to dinner that day?" It's a question I have long asked myself. Why would this man who has everything want to be with me?

His expression is tender and open, and I realize these moments are rare. "You want a truthful answer?"

I nod.

"At the bank, I thought you were attractive, but it was the way your heart pounded against mine that captured my attention. Maybe it was the situation, the adrenaline coursing through my veins, but as crude as it is to admit, I wanted to fuck you right there and then."

I open my mouth to protest, to deny his brazen admission when he presses a finger to my lips.

"I'm not done," he says firmly. "I took you home and when I realized the attraction between us was too strong to dismiss, I made the decision to pursue you. I thought I would contact you, we would see each other a few times, that I would sleep with you and sate my curiosity."

My eyes narrow. *He was only interested in sleeping with me?*

"I am, as you so aptly put it, an asshole. I've never denied this." He shrugs. "Something unexpected happened, though—I saw your paintings. Then at Art Basel, it was as if fate was throwing us together. We crossed paths and had our conversation." He grins at the memory. "The way you spoke about the Vasquez photographs surprised me. You challenged me at every turn and I knew I wanted your sharp-witted lips against mine, that if I didn't possess you it would drive me crazy."

"And now that you've conquered me? Is your curiosity sated?"

He grabs me and with little effort pulls me onto his lap. His hand grips my chin and he shifts me so I'm facing him, only inches away from his tempting lips.

"I'm not so certain you're conquered." He brushes his lips against mine in a soft kiss that rapidly gives way to passion. "Fuck... I want to be inside you again," he says between kisses, his lips caressing mine as they move.

I'm pressing my body against his when the clicking of heels makes me stiffen in shock. Adam looks amused as he stands with ease, as if the notion of being caught partially naked on the floor is not even remotely horrifying. He tucks himself in his pants, then extends his hand and lifts me onto my feet. With haste we dust ourselves off, and in the process I realize I don't have my panties. I peer over to the entrance as Lillian Black walks into the greenhouse, her gown blowing against the wind.

"Adam..." I whisper. "My panties!"

He grins and takes a few steps forward toward the tattered garment. Adam places his foot over the black lace, concealing the evidence of our intimate encounter. He turns to face his approaching mother.

"Adam, I've been looking everywhere for you."

Adam's chuckle is smooth and unperturbed. "I've been busy showing Evelyn around."

His mother nods and looks over at me. "How do you like the greenhouse?"

I have to fight the blush threatening my cheeks. "I doubt anything I say could do the place justice. It's gorgeous."

"I've considered remodeling the space, fixing the aged bricks, but part of me likes the wild atmosphere created by the encroaching vines."

"I wouldn't change a thing," I say firmly.

"Evelyn is fond of flowers, of anything dealing with nature, I think."

Mrs. Black nods with a smile. "Oh, Adam, the Children's Care benefit, you *are* going tomorrow, correct? I know your father expects you to attend."

"Yes, I'll be there, Evelyn will be coming with me."

*I will?* Adam and I seriously need to work on our communication.

Lillian Black's eyes widen. An odd expression crosses her face for a brief moment and then she nods. "Oh, that's wonderful."

My hands fidget as I watch Mrs. Black. I get the impression she doesn't want me to go, and the entire situation—my lack of panties, the *I've just been fucked* flush on my face—has my heart working overtime.

"I need to head back to the party." She turns her attention to Adam. "Mathew has decided to visit. Have you spoken to him?"

The calm expression on his face evaporates. "I had the pleasure."

Mrs. Black purses her lips as if she's going to speak, but after a few seconds she shakes her head. "Oh, and Mr. Rivera has been asking about you. Something related to a business proposition?"

"We were just heading back to the party. I'll be sure to find him."

The way Adam speaks gives me chills. This man is so disconnected from the people in his life. His outward façade usually exudes charm, and though he's always polite, moments of happiness seem fleeting. *What torments him so?*

"Don't keep him waiting long. You know he's an impatient man." She smiles at us. "Well, I better go see what your father is doing." Mrs. Black turns and walks out of the greenhouse.

My eyes drift to Adam. I move toward him, wrapping my arms around his body. I don't want him to be upset. I don't want the intimacy we shared a few minutes ago to disperse like smoke in the air.

"We should get back to the party." His hand slides to the small of my back, the hold rigid and tense.

"You seriously want to take me out there? What if a gust of wind were to hit us? Imagine the scene I'd make." I don't bother to hide the naughty grin on my face, since I learned it from him.

He laughs, his body relaxing in seconds. Adam bends and retrieves the tattered remains of my panties. "I need five minutes to placate my mother and talk to this man. Then we can revisit our pre-party activities in the limo," he whispers in my ear. "And if a gust of wind strikes, you better make sure to hold your dress down. You may not have noticed, but I can be a very jealous man."

It's my turn to laugh. "Really? You're the type that gets jealous?" I gaze at him with mock surprise.

Adam grabs my ass in a tight grip, making me squeal. "I'll make you pay for that later." He grins and gives me a quick kiss.

We walk out of the greenhouse holding hands. His strong palm against mine is reassuring, especially considering my ruined panties are crumpled in his pants pocket and the eyes of jealous women are on me as we start to mingle with the crowd. Once we reach Mr. Rivera, Adam politely introduces me. A few minutes later I excuse myself as they continue their conversation so I can visit the powder room. My recent activities have made me self-conscious. Adam's semen is sliding between my legs, and the confidence I had when I walked out of the greenhouse is slowly fading as a small measure of Catholic shame creeps up on me. *At least you're whoring it up with a handsome, rich, charming man.* I push away the mean thought.

I enter the house and make my way to the restroom when I'm once again halted by the sound of voices. I hear the loud groan of a woman and a knowing blush forms on my cheeks. A few minutes ago I was in the same position, so it's oddly comforting knowing I'm not the only harlot at the party. I push the restroom door open, deciding I'll ignore the passionate noises emanating from my left, when I hear three dreaded words.

"No. Don't. Stop!"

The voice is familiar, but the pitch is odd. I walk to the left, slowly making my way down the hall, and the sound of the protesting voice gets louder.

"Not here. We can't! It's my party, we should get back."

My eyes widen at the realization that it's Sarah's voice I hear.

"That's the fun, baby. While everyone's out there waiting for you, you're in here getting fucked by me."

"Markus, stop it. Get off me!" Sarah yells.

At this point, I'm in a panic. Should I go and get Adam? Should I barge into the room? I hear the sound of furniture grating against the floor and Sarah's loud shriek. I go with my gut and storm into the room with my eyes narrowed and my fists balled at my sides. The door bangs as it hits something and I get the opportunity to survey the room. It's a library.

Sarah is bent over a table, her dress pulled up, and though she's still wearing underwear, Markus's hands are between her legs. My eyes meet hers and the horror on her pale face is startling. Markus shifts his attention to me. We all stare at one another for a few long seconds until Sarah manages to squirm away from Markus's control. She pulls her dress down with embarrassment.

I take a few brave steps into the room, getting closer to Sarah, and when I reach her I extend my hand. "Let's go."

She grabs my hand and as we reach the door Markus closes it and stands in front of us. I pull her behind me because she's crying, her entire body trembling.

"You know, *this* could work," Markus says in a slur as he moves toward me. "We can have our own little party here, just the three of us."

I turn my face to the side as I smell the liquor on his breath. My heart is pounding like a jackhammer against my ears. *Be rational, Evelyn. Talk your way out of this.* I steel myself and stare into Markus's menacing face.

"Adam knows where I am; he'll come looking for me soon," I say with vehemence.

He laughs. "That guy is a fucking pussy. I think you could do better."

Markus moves his hand along my hip, lifting my dress slightly, and I quickly slap his hand away, though the action seems to excite him since he continues to move forward. *Shit! I'm in a room without panties, with a drunken asshole.* I have to fight the panic overwhelming me.

Markus persists in a low, garbled voice. "I bet you do all types of nasty shit when you're getting fucked. Adam is easily bored, everyone knows that. You'd have to be a little freak in the bedroom to keep him interested."

"Markus, you're drunk! Quit being such a fucking moron." Sarah's says a bit steadier, though she's still crying.

Markus blinks a few times as he looks between Sarah and me, his eyes finally gaining some measure of sense. He takes a step back and straightens his jacket. "Girls, come on, I was only messing around." He chuckles and though he appears to be calm, a hint of apprehension lingers in his voice. "It was a poor joke. I'm sorry."

I take a step back and stand next to Sarah.

"I think you should leave, Markus," Sarah says coldly.

"Baby, it's your birthday. I don't want to leave you alone." His voice is still showing signs of inebriation, though he is attempting to control his slurring speech.

Sarah opens her mouth to speak, and I grab her wrist and squeeze, stopping her. I smile at Markus. "Why don't you go back to the party and we'll follow you in a minute." I've dealt with drunk people before; it's better to placate them and make them think you agree with whatever nonsense they're sputtering.

Markus narrows his eyes on us. He looks over at Sarah and once again I squeeze her wrist, hoping the subtle gesture convinces her to cooperate. She smiles mechanically at Markus.

"Baby, go back to the party. I need to freshen up," she says in a practiced sweet tenor.

Markus grins and combs his fingers through his disheveled hair. "Don't keep me waiting. You know how I miss you when you're gone." Stumbling a bit as he walks, he exits the room.

I turn to face Sarah, who's sitting on the leather couch in the center of the room. She's shaking her head and her hands are pressed against her crimson cheeks.

"Are you okay?" I whisper.

"He's not like that very often. Honestly, most of the time he's charming, but when he drinks too much he becomes *such* an ass." Her feet are tapping nervously as she speaks.

"I'm not exactly in the position to be offering unsolicited advice, but you deserve better. You sounded…" I shrug, unsure of what else to say.

"Scared." A bitter laugh emanates from her parted lips. "I don't know what to do." Her voice is soft and her shoulders are slumped in defeat.

I move closer to her and sit on the couch. "We could tell Adam. I'm sure he would know what to do."

Sarah's eyes widen in horror. "No!" She looks at me imploringly. "Please don't say anything to Adam; he'll flip out. Trust me, you don't know him, not really. I mean, Adam was in the Marines, he would kill him."

My body stiffens. "I can't keep this from him. Adam can read me like a book."

Tears once again streak down her rosy cheeks. "Evie, please, for my birthday, don't tell Adam."

I don't have the opportunity to respond before Adam's crisp voice echoes across the room. "Don't tell me what?" He's standing in the doorway, a frown on his attractive face as Sarah and I huddle together.

## Chapter Eighteen

"WHAT'S WRONG?" ADAM looks at us both with concern. I focus my gaze on Sarah, who's wiping away the remaining tears on her face and has adopted a cool, unconcerned expression. How she can manage to appear so collected under the circumstances is astounding.

"Nothing's wrong. We were chit-chatting. You know how girls can get when they're in the same room together." Her laugh, though spirited, holds a hint of nervous tension, and her complexion looks wan as she stands up from the couch.

"Sit down, Sarah." Adam's tone is clipped.

Adam walks to the center of the room and his imposing height makes me sink farther into my seat. Sarah does what she is told. He turns his attention to me, and I avoid his gaze by staring at the hardwood floor.

"What was it Sarah didn't want you to tell me?"

"You're being a bully; if she doesn't want to tell you something she shouldn't have to," Sarah snipes.

I appreciate Sarah rallying to my defense, but the entire situation is beyond stressful. One of my hands rubs against my cheek, the flush of my previous anger and fear still consuming my exhausted body.

"I asked you a question." Adam's voice holds a firm command.

"Ask your sister what happened." I realize a little late I've shouted the words.

"Please don't fight over this, over me." Sarah's voice is strained.

Adam ignores her, grabs my hand, and pulls me from the couch so I'm standing. I keep my face cast down, and when he notices he reaches for my chin, forcing me to gaze into his eyes.

"I didn't ask my sister because I want you to tell me." His tone is chiding, yet soft.

I gulp once, because I know why he's doing this. Throughout our brief relationship honesty has been a struggle. He hates the idea of me keeping secrets, and I can sympathize. Gazing into Adam's cobalt eyes, I realize my hesitation is dissolving the little faith he has in me, in our relationship.

My eyes close under the pressure. "I'm sorry, Sarah. I have to tell him."

She sucks in a deep breath. When I open my eyes, I see the impatience in his, and I know Sarah is right—he is going to flip out. I hate being the catalyst for his anger, but more than anything, I hate having made him pluck the truth out of me in such an excruciating way.

I speak with haste, because I ramble when I'm nervous. "Markus was here. He was drunk and he was forcing your sister to do something she didn't want."

Adam lets go of me, visible rage boiling over his tense body. His fists are clenched as he turns to Sarah. "What happened?"

"Adam…" she pleads. "It's not what you think. He was being an asshole, but he's drunk. He's normally not like that…" She runs her hands over her hair. "Evelyn was trying to protect me, but I was fine. Then he started acting like an ass. I didn't think he would be stupid enough to touch her..."

Sarah is unable to finish. Adam strides out of the room, and both his sister and I are left there in shock. After a few seconds I walk out of the room, quickly moving to the open patio terrace. Sarah is right next to me, and for a second everything looks fine. People are dancing, laughing, drinking, and then I see Adam. He's walked over to the bar; Markus is there with a drink in hand. They exchange a few words and then Adam's fist swings toward Markus's chin. People scatter and the shocked gasps of all those in attendance fill the night air.

I make my way toward the swarm of people huddled around the bar, horrified expressions on their faces as they watch the fight. Though I'm not sure it can be considered much of a fight, since Markus never connects a single punch. If someone doesn't intervene I think Adam will kill him, and a cold fear sweeps through my body at the thought.

Mathew, having made his way through the crowd, pulls his brother off of Markus. The rage in Adam's eyes exhibits a wild frenzy that fills me with uncertainty. I want to run into his arms and hug him, to push my body onto his so the contact can center him, but I'm scared. He's scaring me.

Adam shrugs off his brother's grip as he eyes the groaning Markus. Sarah is crying next to me, and a slew of young women stand around her, cooing calming words.

*How did everything fall apart in the span of fifteen minutes? Can this mess be salvaged?* My thoughts, like my heart, are racing.

A cold wind hits my body and my dress ripples in the breeze. Adam's words echo in my head. *If a gust of wind were to strike, you better make sure you hold your dress down.* My hands clamp on the fabric. Though truthfully, at this point flashing everyone at the party is the least of my worries.

WE have spent the last thirty minutes sequestered in an elegant looking office. Mrs. Black has remained on the patio tending to guests as they leave, attempting to assuage wagging tongues, no doubt. Adam has been on his phone with his lawyer, and though his body is stiff with anger, he doesn't seem perturbed by the fact he might get sued for assaulting Markus.

"What the hell were you thinking?" Mr. Black looks at Adam as he paces around the room.

Adam, having finished his conversation, slips his phone in his pocket as he looks at his father. "He tried to take advantage of Sarah and Evelyn. I was making sure he never tries something like that again."

"There are smarter ways to deal with these situations," Mathew chimes in, his arms crossed over his chest.

I'm sitting next to Sarah, who's pale except for her bloodshot eyes. I squeeze her hand, attempting to give her support, though she's unresponsive.

"I don't need your shit, Mathew. I'm not even sure why you both care. If Markus is stupid enough to sue me, I'll ruin his already limping career."

"We have the Children's Care benefit tomorrow. We don't need the bad publicity." John Black runs his hands over his head and rests them on the nape of his neck. Like father, like son.

"If it's such a concern, I don't have to attend," Adam says with a hint of arrogance.

"You're the biggest contributor. You have to attend." Adam's father shakes his head as he reaches for his glass. He's drinking some type of liquor, judging by the coloring, probably whiskey.

"I wasn't going to ignore the fact that Markus tried to rape my sister."

I wince at Adam's choice of words and notice that Sarah's eyes are vacant and sad. She's listening to these men bicker over her and with each passing minute she falls deeper into dejection. I suddenly remember the birthday gift I purchased for her.

"Sarah?" My voice is cheerful under the circumstances.

She tilts her head to the side as she regards me.

"I have a gift for you." I reach into my purse and retrieve a small envelope. "It's nothing huge, but I thought you might appreciate the experience."

Sarah grabs the envelope mutely and opens it. Inside is a voucher for a month-long workshop with Camden Ross, a local artist.

She smiles at me. "An art class so I can be something more than an art enthusiast?"

"Well, you did mention it was something you were interested in doing. I signed up for the workshop as well. It's on Wednesdays and will give us the opportunity to get to know each other better."

Sarah leans over to give me a hug. As I wrap my arms around her, she trembles. When she pulls back a small shy smile covers her face.

"Sorry. I'm still a bit jumpy. I love the gift."

Mrs. Black enters the room, her face agitated. "I wouldn't be surprised if a picture of you beating Markus to a bloody pulp shows up in tomorrow's paper."

"That's it, I'm leaving. This conversation is pointless. We can't change what happened, I've already called my lawyer and made him aware of the situation." For the first time in the last thirty minutes Adam looks at Sarah and me, and though he attempts to hide his concern, worry is etched on the features of his handsome face. "Sarah is unwilling to file a police report, so there's nothing else we can do at the moment."

In that instance, I realize that while Adam is often reserved, among his family he is considerate and protective. I mean, his parents and brother are placing emphasis on the scandal created by tonight's events, the bad publicity, while Adam acted in order to protect his sister.

We quickly say our goodbyes and head out. Adam has avoided speaking to me. He holds me by the hand, his grip firm. I'm not sure if his disposition is reflecting his agitation with his family or if somehow he's upset with me.

"Are you okay?" I step into the limo as he opens the door for me.

"I'm the one who should be asking that question."

While the response is sweet and considerate, his tone doesn't match the statement. He stares at me, his gaze worried and yet something else lingers in his expression—something I don't like.

"You're upset at me," I say, voicing my sudden realization.

He shakes his head. "I don't want to have this conversation here. Making sure you're okay, is my priority at the moment."

I should heed the warning blatantly demonstrated by his stiff posture, but I don't. "I'm fine," I say stubbornly, "Tell me what's wrong with you."

He raises the divider, ensuring our privacy and then turns to face me.

"You hesitated... When Sarah asked you to keep something from me, you considered her stupid request. I can't even trust you to be honest about something this serious."

Though I forced the admission, it still hurts to hear him question my ability to be honest.

"I... I had every intention of telling you. Sarah cornered me, and then you showed up and I didn't know what to say."

"It's easy; you tell the truth."

"And I *did*."

"Only because I stepped into the room and forced you to."

"I would have done it anyway."

He nods, though I get the impression he's not actually agreeing with me.

"Damn it, give me a break!" I cover my face. "When you picked me up today you accosted me with my past, then we came to this party and I got blindsided with your jealousy. I finally think we'll have a moment of peace and your sister's boyfriend decides to screw up the night by being a complete prick. Not only does he try to force himself on Sarah, but he makes a move on me, too! And I'm still currently not wearing any panties!" I shift in my seat and tug on the dress, tucking it underneath my thighs.

Both of Adam's hands run through his hair and settle on the nape on his neck. "You're an impossible woman."

I laugh outright. "*I'm* impossible? You're the one who has me on a rollercoaster. One moment you're angry at me and the next you're not."

"I want to drive you crazy because that's precisely what you do to me. You completely ignore everything I tell you and then you do something adorable like tuck your dress under your thighs. A futile action, since I've already seen what's underneath and all I want to do is turn you over and fuck you again."

The curt, primitive declaration makes me gasp. "You are unbelievably rude. Most people have a filter, but if you have one you disregard it at every opportunity. I mean, how you can talk to people like this and still get your way is baffling."

"I rarely talk to anyone like this because I'm rarely defied."

I stare at him with narrowed eyes, and though I hate it, I can't deny the desire stirring inside of me—I want him. The top button of his shirt is open allowing me a glimpse of the tense muscles of his neck. Though I fight the impulse, my breaths become shallow.

"Thank you, for interfering and helping Sarah," he says gruffly.

"Those are the right words, but not the right intonation." I cross my arms over my chest.

"What do you expect, for me to sound happy?" he growls. "I hate that he touched you. Sarah was stupid enough to get involved with him even after I told her to stay away, but you…"

"I slapped him. I know how to defend myself."

He laughs. "I'm familiar with your slaps. They don't exactly deter me. I doubt they're effective on anyone."

"Are you upset because I didn't do a good job fighting him off or because he had the opportunity to touch me?"

"I'm upset I wasn't there to kick his ass from the start," he grounds out, in a near roar. Closing his eyes, he takes a few drawn-out seconds to collect himself. When again he speaks, his voice is husky but calm.

"I'm upset you feel the need to lie to me even though I've told you I can't be with a person who lies…I understand the omissions you've made about your past. Hell, considering how I feel about my own past, I can accept you being unwilling to talk about it—even though I think that's a mistake. But I will not accept being with someone who isn't honest with me."

"I wasn't trying to be dishonest. Sarah said you would freak out. I didn't want to ruin the party. I thought that if I waited and told you after, things would be better for everyone."

"I'm tired of saying it, but since you are obviously having trouble understanding, I'll reiterate. Don't keep things from me."

"Right back at you!" I lean back on the seat and eye him, my arms still crossed. "You want complete honesty, then lead by example and explain why you neglected to tell me you have a brother."

"What?" he utters with exasperation.

"I think it's odd you've never mentioned your brother."

"Mathew is an opportunist," he says, leaning forward the muscles of his neck taut. "He's only interested in his own agenda and that agenda often involves trampling the people around him—and if you haven't figured it out yet, that's not something I condone. Biologically I have a brother, but I assure you no love is lost between the two of us."

"Why is he like that?" I say, my pose softening because I'm concerned over the change in his appearance. I want to reach out and comfort him, though before I can, he again says something to exacerbate the situation.

"I don't want to talk about it. This topic is closed."

"That's so unfair. You have *all* the power between us."

His eyes focus on my body, shifting to the cleavage exhibited by my scooped neckline. With a simple glance he can make me long for his touch.

"That's not true. If I did have *all* the power, I wouldn't be as frustrated as I am now."

"I don't want you to be frustrated," I murmur softly. "The last thing I want to do, is fight with you."

Adam nods slowly. Again his eyes dance across my form, focusing on my curves. His lips press together, the action making the hard edge of his jawline more pronounced and the image of tracing that well-defined line with my tongue, flashes in my head. My mouth parts, my heart begins to race and the air circulating in the back of the limo, heats. It's quiet for a few tense seconds, until the deep grate of Adam's voice shatters the silence.

"Take your dress off."

I blink a few times, surprised by the demand. "Excuse me?"

"You heard me."

"And if I *defy* you again and don't?" I say, taunting him more because I can, than my desire to rebel.

His chuckle is filled with confidence. "You won't, not this time. You're rubbing your legs together, breathing heavily, and your cheeks are flushed. Your mind may be urging you to resist, but your body will win the argument." He shifts in his seat and undoes the buttons of his vest, a cocky grin on his lips.

"What makes you so damn sure?" I say.

He tilts his head as he gives me a sideways glance. "I'm very familiar with the feeling." He shrugs and the vest falls onto the seat. "Now take off the dress before I tear it off."

"You wouldn't dare." Again I utter the statement with the sole intent of provoking him, because if I'm honest, I find the idea of Adam tearing my dress from my trembling body, exciting.

His fingers begin working on the buttons of his white dress shirt and I get a glimpse of the hair scattered across his chest.

"Your faith in my self-control is astounding, considering around you I don't exhibit any." He looks amused, and the sight of his exposed chest crumbles my defenses. I pull the dress over my head and quickly unsnap my bra, then kick off my suede Jimmy Choo pumps.

"Now that you have me like this, what are you going to do?"

"You're the one who's going to do something."

His hand reaches for mine and in seconds I'm straddling him.

"You're tired of being on a rollercoaster, right? Here's your chance to take control."

There's an irresistible dare. *He's giving me free reign? I can do anything I want?* I'm like a kid in a candy store. My hands plunge into his pants and the feel of him, hard and ready, makes me lick my lips. I wait for him to take the invitation, for his lips to brush against mine, but to my surprise he sits motionless, a small grin on his face as my fingers wrap around his hard length.

I kiss him because I can't resist the urge, and though he responds, the raw intensity I've grown accustomed to is absent. I open the top button of his pants and pull on the zipper. All the while those deep blue eyes are pinned on me, and the force of his gaze makes me self-conscious.

"Why are you doing this?" My voice is small.

"I'm not doing anything." A small smile dances across his lips.

My eyes narrow at him as resolve rolls over me. "Move up so I can pull your briefs down."

Adam tilts his pelvis up, his eyes impassive. I pull on the boxer briefs and gasp when he springs free.

"What's next?" I hate how he manages to sound so reserved when I'm naked on top of him. Determined to elicit a response, I rub myself against the tip of his erection and finally his body betrays him, his muscles tensing at the contact. I dig my knees into the leather seat and bite my bottom lip as I move down on him. My body is wet and I want him, but the lack of foreplay makes the action hurt and I cry out.

Adam moves forward so the tips of my breasts graze his skin. "You're being impatient, letting your frustration dominate. You're going to hurt yourself."

"Only because you're purposely staying indifferent to my touch." I don't want to show him the hurt in my eyes, though I suspect my attempt at concealing the pain is pointless. He can usually see through the bullshit.

His hands circle my waist, holding me in place as his lips brush against my neck. He whispers against my skin, "I could never be indifferent to your touch. Though you're right, I am holding back, but only because you asked me to. You wanted control and I've given it to you."

I frown. This is not what I wanted.

Adam moves his face against mine. "The truth is, you don't want control; you want to *feel* as if you have it, but more than anything you want to give in."

His grip tightens on my waist and he pushes me against his stiff shaft. I cry out at the contact and my body trembles.

He's right. The notion of dominating instead of being dominated is alluring, but it's a hollow fantasy, because more than anything I want Adam to force my body into submission, to lay claim to every inch, every curve. The flesh between my legs is swollen for him, aching for his touch, for his measured thrusts. My mind is urging me to exhibit a modicum of self-control, but my body knows Adam can stir sensations in me that are too tantalizing to resist.

"You did this on purpose," I say sullenly.

"I did it to prove a point." He moves his thumb along my lips and then thrusts it inside my mouth.

I suck on it, my lips running over the ridges. Adam licks his lips as he watches, and after a few seconds he pulls his finger out of my mouth and shifts my body so he dislodges from my eager sex. He presses his wet thumb inside the folds of my swollen flesh, circling against my clitoris, and forcing me to respond to his skilled touch.

"Adam, please…I need you," I sputter between breathy moans, and though I hate begging him to take me, to fuck me, part of me revels in the debasement.

"Let's get you nice and wet first." His voice is tender yet authoritative.

This man knows my body better than I do. After the initial frustration of being denied, the feel of his hand cupping me, stroking me, makes my muscles tight with anticipation. I close my eyes, about to let go, when his free hand grabs my chin with a stern force.

"Look at me when you come," he orders as he thrusts another finger inside me.

I'm lost to him. I come around his hand, my eyes fixed on his pleasure-filled gaze. He gave me this, and he knows my body is his, that he's the only man who's possessed me.

Adam cups my buttocks and positions me so I slide down his length. Slick with my release, the sensation is pure pleasure. Our bodies form a rhythm and soon the wet noise of our union, mixed with the gasps and groans emanating from our lips, echo through the backseat of the limo. My nails dig against his chest as he brings me to the peak of another orgasm, and the feel of him letting go and filling me with his release, dominating me like no other man ever has, is perfection.

I sway against him, exhausted by the experience. My eyes yearn to close, but I fight the urge because I need to say something. "I'm yours and my body submits to your touch, but *only* because I willingly give myself to you."

The smile on his face is affectionate. "I wouldn't have it any other way."

I lay my head against his chest and let the exhaustion consume me.


I'M awoken by Adam's hand brushing through my hair. My eyes flutter open and I look out the window. We've pulled up to Eden Beach. I'm still naked, and Adam is still inside me. He shifts my body, slipping out, and I wince.

He frowns. "Did I hurt you?"

"I hurt myself."

Adam shakes his head and kisses my cheek. "You're too stubborn for your own good." He reaches for my dress. "Put your arms up."

I groggily follow the command and with care he slips the fabric over my head. Adam buttons his shirt and fixes his collar, though he doesn't bother to put on the vest.

I put on my suede pumps and as we exit the car I lean against Adam for support. It doesn't matter that I'm not wearing my bra because with Adam inhibitions are unnecessary burdens.

When we reach the apartment we both begin to clean up. As we brush our teeth he turns the shower on and starts to strip. I stare because he's fucking gorgeous.

"Enjoying the show?" Adam has a smug grin on his face.

I nod. "I'm thinking about all the wicked things I'm going to do to you."

His chuckle makes the hair on my arms stand on end. Ready to make good on my promise I'm slipping off my dress when the loud ringing of his phone startles me.

Adam shakes his head with mild annoyance and grabs the phone. "Hold that thought." He turns to leave the bathroom, but not before he playfully slaps my ass. Startled, I turn to face him and he has the most devious smirk on his face. He winks at me once before he retreats to the bedroom.

I jump into the shower with a goofy grin, and the warm water feels amazing against my skin. Two weeks ago I was a walking ghost, a girl living in a black-and-white world, and now every moment with Adam comes on the waves of emotions I never thought I could experience again. Life is filled with colors, and although I'm happy, my heart unexpectedly begins to thunder.

Maybe it's because my day has been wrought with emotionally draining events, but something in me suddenly snaps. As I stand underneath the shower, the floodgate within me bursts and I'm unable to handle the pressure of this strenuous day. The panic attack cripples me, and before I can brace myself, I'm on the floor, the water striking me like rocks as I lay against the wet marble struggling for air.

Adam's appears in front of me and the tears I've been holding onto all night flow down my cheeks like a waterfall. I'm embarrassed, but more than anything I'm relieved to see him there.

"Evelyn, what's wrong?"

His concern makes my heart break. I know then I've been a coward from the beginning. Starting a relationship with him was so selfish.

I open my mouth, trying to speak but I'm struggling to breath. Adam cradles me in his arms and the feel of his warmth, soothes my itchy skin. My hands clutch his forearm, and my fingertips begin to move as if on their own, rubbing against his fine hairs. The friction helps, but only a little.

"Breath with me, baby." He says in a low, steady voice.

Pushing past my trembles, I try to comply with his command. I inhale a deep stream of air and I hold it for a few drawn out seconds.

"That's it." He encourages. "Breath just like me."

The scent of his skin, his close proximity and the calming authority of his presence is enough to bring me out of the haze.

"You should stay away from me," I say between shallow gasps of breath. "I'm fucked up. I don't know how to be happy. I'm like *him*. Tormented like him, unable to just be happy. God knows I want to, but I don't have it in me."

Adam holds me against his chest, his strong hands supporting my limp body, caressing me with gentle care. "You're not making sense. What are you talking about?"

It's hard to speak. Though I want to tell him everything, I can't. I want the water to wash away my sins, to lift the guilt holding me down like an anchor so all the bad can fade away.

"Talk to me." He stares at me intensely. "Don't shut me out."

"Some people are broken. The things they've lived through pollute everything they do." Staring at my scarred wrists, I loathe the shame consuming me. "I'm sorry I did it, I really am."

"Evelyn, look at me." Adam lifts my head so our eyes meet. "That's in the past. Don't let one action define you, because it doesn't in my eyes. You are more than one bad decision. You're smart, gorgeous, caring, and strong-willed, I could sit here for hours and list hundreds of extraordinary things about you."

*I love you!* My mouth opens but nothing comes out.

Staring into the calming blue of Adam's eyes, feeling safe, I'm desperate to give him all the details about the relationship I had with my father. I want to tell him how my dad would wake me in the early morning hours, his tall frame shrouded in shadow. "I can't take it anymore. Tonight's the night," he would say. Then I'd see the gun between his fingers and I'd be terrified. For hours I would beg and plead, trying to convince my daddy not to kill himself. "I need you," I'd say, and eventually he'd relent and put the gun away.

I could always talk him down, and I did, until that cold November day—the day before I told him I was moving out. I abandoned him, because his depression and persistent drinking was drowning me, and I suffered the consequences.

For the first time in years I want to confess everything to someone, not because there's a therapist who expects me to, but because I want Adam to know my every secret. I want him to own not only my body, but my mind, my soul. I want him to forgive me, to love me, because maybe then I can forgive myself. But a crippling thought hits me. *What if his opinion of me changes? What if he never again looks at me with the tenderness he has now?* My fears get the best of me.

Unable to muster the courage to tell him how I feel, I press my lips against his in a tender kiss. Our lips brush against each other as the warm water trickles down our bodies.

After a moment Adam pulls back. "Why is it so hard for you to talk to me?"

I smile. "I guess I should ask you the same question."

Adam opens his mouth to respond and I silence him with another kiss. When I pull away, I offer him a simple olive branch and hope he's willing to take it.

"I'm working my way up to telling you everything. I promise I am, but please don't push this tonight. Let's finish our shower and screw the night away."

The briefest smile appears on his face as he grazes my cheek with the back of his hand. He gives me a small nod and it's the only answer I need. Then I'm kissing him again, drowning in the seduction of the moment, because I don't care about tomorrow, I'm too busy living for today.

# CHAPTER NINETEEN

*M*ICHAEL'S FINGERS SNAG *in my tangled curls as he guides my head down, forcing his erection between my lips and down my throat. I cough and my eyes water. My hands are pressed against his thighs and I fight the urge to push back from him.*

*He's not forcing me to do anything; I'm the one who offered to get him off. And yet the idea of his touch is repulsive.*

*Once again, he shoves my head down, driving his cock farther into my mouth so the tip hits the back of my throat. My muscles stiffen and I cave— I push off of him. I move my thumb across my lips, wiping away the spit. When I manage to fix my gaze on him he's furious.*

*"I can't keep fucking doing this shit." He shakes his head and stands up.*

*"I'm sorry." I say the words reflexively, hoping they'll defuse the situation.*

*Michael bends down and grabs his boxers.*

*"No. Please don't go." My voice shakes.*

*He ignores my plea and starts to get dressed. My arms begin to tingle as my heart struggles to pump blood throughout my body.*

*My muscles shift into gear and I stand up and move to him. I wrap my arms around his waist and lay my head against his back. He tenses and stills.*

*For a few drawn-out seconds everything is calm.*

*Michael turns abruptly and presses his lips against mine in a frantic kiss. He shoves me down on the bed and runs his hand up my shirt so he can squeeze my breasts. I freeze.*

*"No. I can't."*

*"Yes, you can. You'll feel better afterward. You want this, I know you do. Trust me."*

*His voice is low, like the vibration of an idling engine. My skin prickles at the sound.*

*He hooks his finger on the fabric of my panties and yanks them down, exposing me. My hands move to counter his, but they're soon halted by his unyielding grip on my wrists. His erection pressed against my thigh makes me panic, and I jerk my knees up between his legs.*

*"Fuck!" His hands cradle his balls and he lurches to the edge of the bed. "Fucking crazy bitch!"*

*"I'm so sorry. Please...I'm sorry."*

*The words sound foreign on my lips, because a part of me wants to claw his eyes out for trying to force me, for trying to take something from me I don't want him to have. However, between the bursts of anger a choking fear looms. He'll abandon me like my father did.*

*"You're a fucking tease, and I'm tired of waiting for you to put out." He shifts off the bed and collects his clothing.*

*"Don't go. We can talk about this. We can fix this." I lean forward and place a trembling hand on his shoulder. He shrugs off my touch and my hand drops down.*

*"There's nothing to talk about. And the only thing that needs fixing is you. You're fucked up, just like your dad."*

*I dig my nails into the palms of my hands, hoping the pain will provoke a response from me. I want to cry at his words, but the tears won't fall. Ever since the death of my father I feel frozen in place, a ghost walking among the living.*

*"Please don't leave me. I'll try to do what you want. Please just give me time." I say in the hopes of appeasing him, however I'm not sure I can give him what he wants. Since my father's suicide, the thought of sleeping with Michael, of losing my virginity to him, is disgusting.*

*"I'm fucking done with you." His eyes are cold and vacant, as if the act of leaving doesn't hurt him.*

*For weeks, I've done everything I can to please him, short of sleeping with him. I've held on to my virginity like a child does a security blanket, as if that small action will absolve me in the eyes of God for abandoning my father when he needed me the most.*

*The rattle of Michael picking up his keys from the nightstand makes me lurch up. I kneel on the bed and stare at him.*

*"Please...don't go. Please, please, please..."*

*I say over and over as my panic attack robs me of the ability to breathe. I feel pathetic and weak for needing him to stay. He nearly raped me, and I'm begging him to stay.*

*He ignores me and walks out of the room.*

*For what seems like an eternity, I lie there, caving under the pressure of all the emotions I can't confront.*

*When I recover enough, I walk to the bathroom, open the vanity drawer, and retrieve a razor.*

*I sit on the floor and do what Michael wanted me to—I spread my legs. I trail the razor across my thighs, and since I don't even feel the blade I press down until I see the crimson blood dribble down my pale skin. A shot of pain ripples across my thigh to my groin. The sensation offers me the release I need, and the tears finally fall.*

*The cuts I give myself help me cope. They make it so I can survive the day. After six cuts—I survive this day.*

I wake in a panic, Adam's arms around me. My chest heaves as I struggle to regain control of my breathing, and in the serenity of the moonlit room I feel out of place.

*What the fuck is wrong with me? Why do these memories haunt me?*

I stare at Adam. He's dead to the world as he sleeps, and it's easy to pull away from his embrace, too easy. He could slip away from me in a nanosecond, and yet in the span of two weeks he's become my North Star. He has awoken feelings I had abandoned.

I get out of bed and tiptoe out of the room. I'm naked, because I always sleep naked with Adam. Like my secrets, he enjoys stripping me of my clothing, leaving me exposed so he can explore everything I have to offer.

I've concluded I can't fault Adam for wanting to possess me, because while I have allowed him to claim my body, the tragedies of my past have remained mine.

I've tried to tell him. Like the painting at Art Basel, of the naked girl with her soul exposed for the world to see, I tried to reveal everything to Adam. I failed. I'm too chicken-shit to show the man I love my vulnerabilities, or maybe I'm too selfish. In a few weeks he'll tire of my company and toss me aside, like Michael did, and the fear torments me.

A soft, bitter laugh bursts from my lips as I walk to the piano room. I was unable to sleep before I met him, and now in this calm before the storm, sleep continues to be elusive.

My eyes scan the room; the skylight gives the space a moon-touched glow and the oddity of the antique piano displayed in this sterile, modern apartment once again draws my attention. *Why would he keep something so contrary to his tastes?*

It's been years since I sat on a piano bench, and even when I practiced frequently I wasn't good. Though I had the technical skill to play, I lacked the passion to make the music beautiful. My emotions were conveyed through my painting. That's always been my gift, not music.

I move my fingers against the keys and the first few notes of Beethoven's "Moonlight Sonata" echo in the hushed room. After a few minutes I pause, unable to remember the rest of the notes.

"My god, you look gorgeous."

Adam's voice surprises me. I tilt my head to gaze at him and the sentiment is mutual. He's naked and gorgeous, leaning against the framed entrance. His face is relaxed and I can clearly see the ridges of his abs, the definition of his broad shoulders and sculpted chest.

He gives me one of those panty-dropping grins and if I was wearing any underwear, it would have slipped off at the mere sight.

"It's the fact that you don't know how truly beautiful you are that turns me on, Evelyn." He speaks my name slowly, enunciating the syllables. "You sit there detached from the world, a specter in the room, and I'm drawn to the sight."

The hairs on my arms stand up. "Why not sate your curiosity?" I lick my lips as I watch him stride toward me.

He hovers behind me, leaning over me before he whispers in my ear, "I had no idea you could play the piano."

I smile at the statement. "I play at the piano, Adam. I have no real skill."

His lips brush along the curve of my shoulder. "Maybe all you need is practice." Adam's fingers trail up my spine and the action makes me straighten my posture. "The first thing you have to do before you play is sit correctly."

I push my chest forward, my breasts moving up as my shoulders pull back. "Like this?"

"Yes, perfect." I can hear the smile in his voice. His hands caress the curve of my waist, softly grazing the sides of my breasts before they move over my shoulders and down my arms. They hover over my wrists, and with ease he lifts them up. "Remember, when you play it's with the tips of your fingers touching the keys. Your wrists have to be elevated."

I exhale, my head moving forward in a small nod.

"Play the song again. Only this time don't stop."

"Adam, I don't…"

His authoritative order interrupts me. "Just play."

I gulp, though I do what I'm told. My fingers move against the keys and I play the first few notes of the sonata. As I play, one of Adam's hands moves around my waist and the feel of his warm touch makes me hit the wrong key. I recover, though my timing is off and I'm playing the melody at a too-quick pace. His hand continues down my body, sliding between my legs.

"I think playing the piano makes you wet," he whispers in my ear as he rubs his fingers against the opening of my sex. "Don't stop playing."

*Don't stop? How the hell am I supposed to play when you're doing that?* My fingers once again betray me and I miss a note. Somehow I manage to find my place, and even though Adam is laying claim to my body, by some miracle I play.

His free hand moves to my thigh, and with little effort he spreads my legs open while two of his fingers push inside me, making my muscles tighten.

"I can't…"

His husky voice cuts me off. "Playing the piano is all about muscle memory. Don't think about what you're doing."

As his fingers thrust into me I lean toward him, and the feel of Adam hard and ready at my back makes me moan. My fingers continue to play, but I don't even hear the music. Both of his hands are between my legs, one of them stroking that special spot as the other pushes into me at a quickened pace. My hands move off the keys, and I grab Adam's shoulders as my stomach clenches. I thrust my pelvis forward into his hand as I come and I can feel my pleasure escape me, spreading onto his fingers. I tremble against him for a few long seconds and his lips trail kisses along my neck as I recover.

"I didn't think it was possible, but you're even more stunning when you come."

He pulls his fingers out of me, and even in the dimly lit room I can see they're wet with my release. I lean against him because I'm spent, because he can do that to me, make me lose control of my muscles and leave me vulnerable.

Adam, still standing at my back, moves his arms forward so I'm nestled between them as he positions his hands above the ivory keys. He plays Beethoven's "Moonlight Sonata" and the melody is perfect. His rhythm follows the specified tempo, he places emphasis on all the right notes, and I can literally feel the passion he's exuding. I lie against him, and even though moments ago I reached an orgasm, my nipples harden and my body quickens at the sound reverberating around the room, at the sight of the slippery piano keys and the intoxicating smell of his body.

I turn, place my knees on the piano seat, and kiss him. I can tell by his eager tongue he doesn't mind the interruption. The music has been silenced, yet there's a harmonious overtone in the soft noises of our frantic embrace.

He pulls back from the kiss and looks at me, his gaze taking in the sight of my nude body. "You left a wet mark on the bench." He licks his lips and gives me a salacious smile.

I mimic his grin. "Sorry."

"Never apologize for that. I love how wet you get for me."

I lunge at him, because the need to have his skin pressed alongside mine overtakes me. We stumble onto the floor and the lone black-and-white rug in the room breaks our fall. I position my body between his legs, and by his expression it's apparent my enthusiasm has startled him. My lips run down his length, and my hands move in unison with my willing mouth. I suck on the head of his shaft and a few eager drops flood my taste buds.

"Fuck! If you don't stop I'm going to come in your mouth."

His words stir my excitement. I twirl my tongue around him and I'm relentless.

Adam sits up and tangles his hand in the wild curls of my hair. He pulls me away from him and I'm sure there's a pout on my lips, because all I want is to suck him dry. There's a primal need coursing through my heated veins that only his touch will satisfy. That only his touch has *ever* satisfied.

Before I know it, his arms are around me and I'm on my knees, facing the mural I painted for him.

"Spread your legs."

The domineering edge to his voice makes me grin as I follow the order. His erection is pressed against the cheeks of my ass. One of Adam's hands moves across my skin, cupping one of my breasts, and as he massages my nipple he presses the tip of his erection inside me. My natural reaction is to move forward, to go on my hands and knees, but the pull of his hands stops my descent. My body is pressed along his, and we're both slippery with sweat.

"Stay up on your knees."

I don't exactly have a choice. One of his hands pulls me back onto his length. From this angle he feels deeper, overwhelming, and he's carefully building my excitement. Sex has always been rough and passionate with Adam, but this time it's measured and tender.

I open my eyes and stare at the mural. The crimson petals of the flower are blossoming, and under Adam's skilled touch, so am I.

He thrusts into my body while his hand massages the folds of my sex. The feel of his hand between my legs as he fucks me is enough to push me over the edge. I call out his name as I reach my climax, and he milks his own release, pushing into me with a savage intensity as the warm rush of his orgasm spreads between my legs, down my thighs.

I fall back on him and his strong arms brace me. We lie on the rug, panting as we regain the ability to speak, his body still pressed against mine, his cock still inside of me. As I lie there on the floor, I realize what we just did can't be considered just fucking. It was gentle and giving. No one has to say the words for the sentiment to be true—we made love. The thought frightens me, and I don't understand why.

A few minutes pass. I can't face the elephant in the room, and so I rely on one of my many talents—I change the subject. "Where did you learn to play the piano?"

With care, he pulls out of me and turns my body so I'm facing him. "I've played since I was four. For a long time I thought I would do it professionally. I even dual majored in Music and Business at Columbia." He rubs his fingertips against my cheek as he holds me close. "How did you learn to play?"

My body stiffens at the question. "My dad taught me. He was a musician." I move my face into the curve of his neck as a chill runs across my body.

"You don't like to talk about your father." His hands run down my back and he pulls one of my legs over his body.

"No, I don't." I nuzzle against him.

"Did you wake up because you had a bad dream?" Adam's voice is detached because he's trying to coax information out of me. My body stiffens.

I pull myself from the security of his embrace and focus on the deep blue of his eyes. "This is the first time I've ever heard you play."

He frowns and refuses to allow me to distance myself, his strong arms pulling me close. "I don't play often." One of his hands cups my cheek. "You're changing the subject."

My eyes widen in contrived innocence. "I'm just trying to understand you better. Why would you study music and never play? You obviously used your degree in business; what happened to your passion for music?"

His hand trails down the curve of my spine. "Are you doing what you wanted to do when you went to college? You studied art and now you teach at a school."

Though his tone is still gentle, I hear a hint of reproach. "No, I never expected to be teaching. I envisioned something different." There is an obvious bitterness to my voice. "All I ever wanted to do was paint. The kids around my neighborhood would be running outside, riding their bikes and rollerblading while I worked for hours on pictures that consumed my head. My dad would say it was the same for him, only he didn't see pictures, but heard notes instead. Was it like that for you?"

He shifts back and props his head up with a hand. The smile on his face is carefree. "My parents never were into showing their emotions. I'm sure by now you've noticed it's a family trait. Music let me express myself in a way that was appropriate," he says dryly.

"Will you play for me again? Not now, but in the future." I place my lips against his cheek in a soft kiss. "Listening to you play relaxes me."

A masculine chuckle escapes his lips. "I thought having me inside of you was relaxing. In fact, right after you orgasm you get the most adorable look in your eyes. They cloud over with this languid serenity." The expression in his eyes is smoldering.

I giggle, because only Adam can simultaneously make me feel safe, calm, and turned on. "Well, we could alternate between the two."

He nods. "I always have appreciated resourceful women with good problem-solving skills."

I scrunch my nose in a playful frown. "Exactly how many resourceful woman have you appreciated?"

Adam shakes his head with a laugh. "I don't keep a running record."

I frown and straighten my arms, forcing some distance between us. "You don't take my questions seriously."

Adam pulls me close, so my breasts press against his chest. The action is sudden, and I gasp at the movement.

"Everything you say, the questions you ask, the actions you take—all of it is important to me. If I'm guilty of anything it's that I take you *too* seriously."

The look in his eyes makes me uncomfortable because it's raw. It's an intense heart-melting look that for a second makes me believe fairy tales exist.

"You have talent." He shifts so we're both sitting, his eyes focused on the mural I painted. "You should paint every day. Let the pictures in your head run free."

"Adam…" My mouth opens and I have to lick my dry lips. "Take me to the bedroom and fuck me senseless."

His shoulders lift in a burst of laughter. "I never expected you to be so blunt."

I'm reminded of the first night he made me his. I uttered similar words. I tilt my chin up and offer him the response he gave me. "You'll find I only am on special occasions."

"This is a special occasion?" Adam arches his brow with amusement.

I give a slow nod because words are useless. We don't need them. The night fades and Adam does what I want, he claims every inch of my body with tender attention.

MY phone vibrates against the nightstand. I reach for it and whimper as my sore muscles constrict. I spent the night being deliciously tortured by Adam's skilled hands, his nimble fingers, and his eager tongue.

"Hello?" I say scratchily.

My mother's chiding tone reverberates through the phone. "Evie, where are you?"

I open my mouth to offer her a lie when Adam presses his erection against my back. His hands move over my thighs and nestle between my legs. I don't think before I speak in a breathy pant. "Adam…"

"You're with him?" My mother attempts to hide the reprimand in her voice. She fails.

Adam trails kisses down my back as his fingers part the folds of my sex and gingerly rub against that special spot he's all too familiar with.

"Yes, I'm at his apartment," I say quickly because if I don't end this conversation soon, my mother will be privy to sounds no mother should hear her daughter utter.

"I see. Well, I was calling to invite you to brunch. It's fortunate he's with you. Your stepfather and I would like to meet him."

I close my eyes as my body shifts back, brushing against Adam. "Mom, I don't think we'll be able to make it to brunch today…"

Adam interrupts me. "Tell her we would love to go."

My mouth opens to protest, but my mother's voice sounds in my ear. "Perfect, how does *Brio* sound? We can keep it simple."

I shift upright and frown at Adam, who has an adorably lazy grin on his lips.

I'm panicking. Adam and my mother together, talking? The idea is disturbing on so many levels. "Mom, don't you have to go to church today?"

"Evelyn." Her tone is clipped. "It's *Saturday*."

My shoulders slump. *Duh!* Adam's chuckle makes me scowl. He's enjoying this too much.

"I'm getting the impression you don't want me to meet him."

"No, of c-course th-that's not it…" I stammer.

Adam once again speaks. "We'll meet her wherever she wants. Name the time."

My mouth is parted in shock as I hear my mother's exuberant response.

"Noon will be wonderful. See you both then."

I blink a few times as I place the phone on the nightstand. "What just happened?"

"We agreed to meet your mother for brunch." Amusement governs his expression.

I grab one of the pillows and swing it at him. Adam grabs me by the waist and flips me so my body is trapped under his. I squeal with mock indignation at his forceful restriction of my body. My eyes widen as a disturbing thought interrupts the moment. "Did I hang up the phone?"

Adam gives me one of his movie star grins. "I sure hope so, because I plan for us to make plenty of noise before we go."


I decide on wearing a simple spaghetti-strap dress for brunch while Adam opts for dark denim jeans and a button-down, the long sleeves rolled so his toned forearms can be seen. He is my little piece of heaven and the idea of sharing him with my mother, who judges every action I make, is as appealing as a root canal.

The restaurant is empty when we arrive, and yet my mother insists on sitting in the outside patio.

"We live in Florida, the weather is beautiful, and a little sun is good for you." The designer sunglasses she wears frame her oval face.

Adam, to his credit, doesn't seem to mind. With debonair flare he approaches my mother and kisses her cheek in greeting. He shakes my stepfather Nicolas's hand and exhibits the impeccable manners I've grown accustomed to.

My mother wastes little time with pleasantries. "I must admit, I didn't think we would meet anytime soon. Evelyn has been secretive lately." She shoots me an accusatory glace before picking up her glass of water.

I move the menu forward, not bothering to look at it—from her tone, I know my nerves will make it difficult to eat.

Adam doesn't appear to be flustered. I envy how self-assured he is, because I'm usually foundering in a sea of insecurity. The feeling is only amplified by the presence of my overbearing mother.

"I haven't been secretive, just busy. There's a huge difference between the two." I try to sound calm, but an edge of anger pervades my tone.

Adam has a small smile on his lips as he speaks. "I've been a tyrant with her time, Mrs. Aaron. I won't apologize for that—I doubt anyone could blame me for wanting to be around her."

My stepfather's loud chuckle and my mother's shocked expression makes me grin. I give Adam a look as he eyes the menu.

"Are you always this demanding with the women you date?" My mother's sunglasses shield the dark glare I know she is giving Adam.

*Mom!* I stifle a groan.

"Ava, she's twenty-four years old. I doubt she wants you to interfere with her love life." My stepfather rolls his eyes.

"I have a right to be concerned; she *is* my daughter." Her expression of indignation is perfectly executed.

"I am demanding in general, and from the direction this conversation has taken, I think it's safe to assume you are as well." Adam looks at my mother with frank honesty. "Though, rest assured, Mrs. Aaron, I only show such interest when I truly care about someone."

I look at my mother with a small smile, because I love hearing the gentleness in his voice. When he openly admits his affection for me I'm lost, drawn to that feeling only he can stir within me.

My mother takes off her glasses as she regards Adam. The corners of her eyes soften, the wrinkles easing. I have to stifle the laugh threatening my composure. His charm is winning her over.

"Mr. Black, what are your plans for Christmas Eve? We're hosting a small gathering at our home. Nicholas and I would love it if you joined us," my mother says pleasantly.

Adam reaches for my hand and holds it under the table. "Unfortunately, I have a business trip I can't miss. I'll be spending the holiday in New York. In fact, Evelyn will be traveling with me, and we won't be back until after Christmas."

My eyes widen at his words. *Wait...we're going where?* Adam squeezes my hand and his thumb rubs across my knuckles. I get the impression I'm supposed to nod and smile; I can't muster the energy to nod, though I manage the smile.

"Really? You'll have to forgive my surprise, but Evelyn neglected to mention this." The tension that had recently eased once again makes her stiffen in her seat.

My stepfather's cheerful voice cuts the tension. "That's the smartest decision you two could make. I'm only sorry I couldn't convince Ava to go away for the holidays. Now we have the *pleasure* of hosting a party." He sighs and shrugs.

"Nicolas!" My mother glares at my stepfather.

"What? It's true. We're going to spend hours getting the house ready, preparing the food, and then afterward we have to clean up. I doubt that's anyone's idea of a perfect Christmas."

"I think planning a trip together when you've only been seeing each other for a few weeks is unwise. I mean honestly, Christmas is less than two weeks away." My mother looks at me.

I want to tell her to mind her own damn business, but the words elude me. I fist my fingers, pressing them against my palms. Adam's grip around my hand tightens. He's getting upset, though I'm not sure if his anger is for my mother's intrusive statements or me. *Why would he be angry at me?*

"Patience unfortunately is not a trait I possess. Besides, the idea of spending the holidays without Evelyn won't work for me. I won't do it."

My mother and Adam stare at each as the phrase *"oh shit"* is stuck on repeat in my head. After a few heart-pounding seconds my mother relents. She pulls her gaze away from Adam and gives him a hard smile.

"Well, I'm sure Evelyn and I will speak about this trip at length later."

*Oh great, that's the type of conversation I'm dying to have.* I need to get away from them both. I'm being pulled to pieces by these two domineering figures.

"Excuse me." I don't bother to wait for a response. I get up and walk to the restroom. For a few minutes I stand in front of the mirror, then I wash my face with cold water and don a brave expression as I make my way back to our table.

Our food soon arrives and I pick at my salad with disinterest. My mother, of course, chides me, and as I listen to her I catch the small frown that forms on Adam's brow. *When will this disaster end?*

In less than thirty minutes we've finished our meal, and the check is placed on the table. My mother reaches for it, but Adam is quick to counter her. He slips some money in the black folder and hands it to the waiter.

The soft lines in my mother's face become more pronounced. She hates not being in control. I understand the feeling, since it's something I've been struggling with for the past two weeks. When Adam is around you have to enjoy the ride, because the moment you come in contact with him he's like a wildfire, and he'll burn until he's ready to stop.

We say goodbye, and as we pick up the car from the valet I notice Adam isn't talking to me. I don't bother to speak, because after the stressful brunch I'm enjoying the silence.

When we arrive at Adam's apartment I'm fed up with his brooding mood. "Is there a reason you're not talking to me?"

"Oh, so the Evelyn I have come to know *is* still in there. I was beginning to wonder." Adam tosses his keys on the kitchen counter.

"What the hell is that supposed to mean?"

"I can't believe you let her walk all over you."

"Wait…" I blink a few times processing my confusion. "You're angry at my mother and you're taking it out on me?"

Adam shakes his head. "I'm angry that the woman I normally see in front of me, one that is not afraid to voice her mind to me, is so damn stifled around her mother."

My fisted hands are shaking. He's right, I do suppress many of my feelings in the company of my mother, but that's only because I know the dangers of giving into them. There was a time when I thought of no one else, when I succumbed to my impulses. All that got me was several months in an institution, and for most people that would be the worst experience of their lives. For me it was one in a long string of them.

When I saw Tina's ashen face, the tearful eyes of my mother looking at me with a horrible mixture of fear, pity, sorrow and anger, the shattered bits of my broken heart were grinded into dust. I swore then I would think about my every action. I would be patient and never give in to the selfish desires I had inherited from my father.

I purse my dry lips and focus on Adam. "Sometimes it's important to stay quiet."

"Throughout the entire experience you sat idly while she voiced all of her thoughts. Never once did you offer your own opinion. When is it time to speak up?"

"I didn't have to; you were more than willing to offer opinions for both of us. In fact, you often make decisions without even consulting me. I had no idea we were going to New York."

"Let me get this straight—you're upset I didn't inform you of my intention to surprise you with a romantic getaway?" He arches his brow at me and I get the full force of Adam Black's arrogant stare.

"That's not the point," I say meekly.

"What *is* the point?" he scoffs.

"I loathe how you do that, Adam. How you can so easily confuse me. Just because you're better at arguing a point doesn't mean you're right. You do exactly what my mother does."

"I suppose the only difference is that when she does it you stay quiet."

"Is that what has you upset? That I'm docile around her and not you?"

He gives a low chuckle and I shiver at the sound. The way he regards me makes me fidget, though I refuse to give him the satisfaction of turning away. I glower at Adam with a blend of passion and anger reserved solely for him.

"If I wanted a docile woman do you honestly think it would be hard for me to find one?"

Now I want to walk away. I turn around with the intention of going to the bedroom, though I never make it past the first step. Adam grabs hold of my hand and pulls me so my body hits his.

"Answer the question."

"You are an arrogant, demanding, *impossible* man."

"Answer the fucking question."

"No! If you wanted some docile woman, I'm sure you could find hundreds who would bend over backward for you." I shove at him and take a step back. "*Happy*? That's what you wanted to hear, right? Has your ego been satisfied?"

Adam looks amused and I hate seeing his smug expression, because even though I'm furious I can't deny this man is damn handsome. He looks as if he's hiding a smile. *Bastard!*

For a brief second those hypnotic blue eyes stare at me, and then his arms are around my waist, pulling me against his body. His lips press on mine and his tongue is relentless as it probes my mouth. My hands find their way up his back, settling in his dark locks. I pull on his hair, because although I love the taste of his kisses, I'm desperate for even the smallest edge of control.

Adam bites on my lips as he's pulled away and the most adorable expression is on his face. "The truth is, I want only you." Adam shakes his head and for once I see an unsure look in those startling eyes of his. "I don't like seeing you so uncertain of yourself."

I blink a few times at his admission. *Adam wants me. Why the hell is this idea so hard for me to digest?*

I narrow my eyes at him. "So you want to take me to New York…" I press my chest against his. "How do you know I can go? Maybe I have to work."

Adam's laugh fills the room. "School's out for winter recess. I know you can go."

I narrow my eyes at him. "Don't be so sure. I may have other plans."

He pushes me against the kitchen counter as two lines form between his brows. "With whom?"

I run my tongue across my lips. "With this tall, dark-haired, blue-eyed guy."

Adam tilts his head to the side as his facial features relax. "He sounds like a catch."

I laugh. "Yes, but he does have an Achilles heel; he's conceited and bossy." Adam's lips claim mine, and though the kiss is brief, when I pull back I'm panting.

"I would think by now my true weakness would be obvious..." His words are soft, the faint warmth of his breath brushing against my cheek as he trails kisses down the curve of my neck. "Come to New York with me. I don't want to spend the holidays without you."

My mother is right. We've only been dating for two weeks and going on a romantic getaway with someone under these conditions is insane, but with his body pressed against mine I'm unable to say no.

I close my eyes and whisper the word, "Yes." When I flutter them open, Adam is staring at me with a triumphant expression. I can't help but smile at him.

Once again he kisses me, only this time the action is not sweet, but frantic with erupting desire. His hands move up my thighs, underneath my dress, prompting me to groan against his mouth.

We do what comes natural to us, what we do best—we forget about everything but each other. A perfect way to spend a Saturday afternoon.

# CHAPTER TWENTY

I'M WEARING AN Aidan Mattox strapless gown. It's a beautiful rose color and the bustier is snug. It accentuates my breasts and constricts my waist. The little fabric flower accents decorating it are beautiful, but the smoldering gaze Adam has in his eyes when he focuses on me is what makes the fairy tale complete.

"You are staring, Mr. Black." I lean back against the plush leather of the limo and cross my legs to give him a more tantalizing view.

"You can't honestly be mad at me for being mesmerized by such a stunning sight."

"I can be mad at you for being so indiscreet."

Adam laughs. "Believe me, I'm being discreet. At the moment, images of you wearing nothing but those heels are consuming my thoughts. You're lucky I'm only staring."

"I disagree." I give him a playful pout. "I'd much rather you go with your impulse."

"You want me that badly?"

I give him a slow, serious nod. Our eyes lock for a long beat and then our lips are pressed against each other. Adam moves his hand to my ankle, trailing it up my leg, and when he reaches the apex of my thighs he groans. His fingers press against the silky fabric of my panties, cupping me.

"You're already wet."

"I can't help it. Around you it's hard not to be."

Adam gives a deep chuckle. He moves the delicate fabric of my panties to the side and rubs me. Like a cat in heat, I move my pelvis forward and Adam accepts the silent invitation. He slides a finger inside me, prompting a loud moan to escape my lips.

"As much as I'd like to peel that dress off your body and fuck you, we're almost there." He moves his finger back so only the tip is invading me, and when he pushes into me again his thumb rotates along my clit.

The muscles of my core constrict and I shift my pelvis forward to meet his thrusting finger. "Then fuck me only a little." I mewl as my body gyrates against his skillful touch.

"How exactly does one fuck someone a little?" He teases as he pushes another finger inside me.

I groan at the welcome invasion. "You're known to be a resourceful man; I'm sure you can figure it out." A damp sweat creeps over my brow as my breath becomes shallow.

"I don't think you realize how convincing you can be." He trails wet kisses across my cheek. "Do you want to come?" Adam whispers as his tongue licks the edge of my ear.

I know why he's asking the question. He wants me to beg, and lost to his touch, I'm more than willing. "Yes...*please*."

His free hand moves to my breasts and with ease he releases them from the tight bodice of the strapless gown. Then his tongue is rolling around my nipples and the muscles between my legs are clenching around his probing fingers.

"I'm going to let you, because I want you to walk around this party wet," His voice is silky smooth as he speaks in an authoritative tone. "Throughout the night I want you to think about how when we return to the limo I'm going to spread those pretty legs of yours and fuck you until you're slick with my cum, until it's dripping down your thighs."

His words are like a lit match rippling across my skin. I'm burning with need for each deep thrust, for the feel of his talented fingers as they caress the parted folds of my sex and claim me with eager persistence.

"Would you like that?"

"Yes," I moan between breathy gasps. My eyes focus on his as he teases me with each stroke. He has a charming half-smile on his lips and I know why. Only he can do this to me. I'm his.

I reach the peak of my orgasm. My body stiffens and the muscles between my legs convulse as I come, pleasure searing through my trembling limbs, rocking me to my core. This is the type of pleasure you feel only when you relinquish control—when you let go of inhibitions. A frightening thought invades my bliss. *You've given him power over your body but not your person. He doesn't really know who you are. What would happen if he did?*

Adam's fingers are still inside me and the feathery kisses he trails across my neck brings me back to reality. They tear me away from my sudden melancholy. My mouth is parted, because it's the only way I can breathe at the moment.

"I love that abandoned look your eyes get when you come," he says in a slow drawl.

"We have arrived, Mr. Black." Parker's voice echoes from the intercom.

My body tenses at the sound and Adam grins. He presses a button before he speaks. "Give us a minute."

He pulls his fingers out of me and I exhale slowly. A small pout forms on my lips as I shift my dress into place so my breasts are tucked away.

"You should be smiling." He says, tugging the lapels of his suit and straightening his appearance.

"I would be, if we could skip this party and enjoy the one we have going on in here." I lean forward and grab the hand he used to finger-fuck me. "You have lipstick on your lips. Right here."

I move his damp fingers along the edge of his lips. Adam pulls me against him to steal a quick kiss. I squeal at the action and revel in the taste of my own release. I don't know why, but tasting the saltiness of my arousal on his lips is so damn erotic—I love it.

He pulls back from the kiss. "What a difference two weeks makes." He gives me a pensive stare as his hands cradle my face. "Are you happy being here with me, spending as much time as we have together?"

The question surprises me, and I want to pull away from his grasp. It's hard to focus on his gaze because his eyes have a serious expression, one that simultaneously scares and intrigues me.

I place my hands on his cheeks, mirroring his actions. "*Yes*. Being with you is the only happiness I've known for a long time."

Adam shakes his head with a smile and pulls away from my hold. His mask slips in place and the intimacy we've just shared is lost. "Shall we?"

I comb my fingers through my hair while a lingering dread builds inside me. For some reason I want to stay in the limo, but that's not an option so I give him a quick nod.

We exit the car and the flash of cameras blind me. I didn't expect to be accosted by reporters, though I suppose when you're dating one of the most sought-after bachelors in the state and you go to a high-profile event, that's precisely what's going to happen.

Adam holds me close as the reporters get their photos. After a brief pause we move past them and enter the Biltmore hotel, a stunning building surrounded by lush greenery.

As we head toward the ballroom I have to rein in my astonishment. The room has vaulted ceilings adorned with chandeliers and spectacular arched columns outlining different alcoves, housing elegant tables. Multiple second-floor terraces are rimmed with elegant iron rails, and in general the entire room boasts impressive architectural features.

The moment we enter the room people are greeting us, and I'm startled. I've spent the last few years in a bubble, and before that my experiences were limited to the normal activities of an everyday college girl. I spent my days going to movies and the mall, not being escorted to fancy charity events. I cling onto Adam's arm because I'm filled with uncertainty. *How am I supposed to act around these people?*

Adam leans to me and whispers, "You okay?" I give him a shy nod and he flashes me that perfect smile of his. "I think you need a drink."

"I think for once I agree with you. In fact, make it a double."

He chuckles and leads me to our table. It's segregated from the rest, toward the end of the room. Adam disappears into the crowd, making his way to the bar while I'm left on my own. The table is empty, and I assume all who are supposed to sit here are currently mingling. The out-of-place feeling multiplies in the seconds I'm left alone in this new, strange setting.

Sarah strolls over to the table and gives me a hug. Her skinny frame feels flimsy and the strong smell of liquor and perfume emanates from her pores. "You got roped into this event as well? Well, aren't you *lucky*."

I try to hide the frown that forms on my brow. "I take it you didn't want to come?"

"It's not that I don't support the cause, but I could do without all the snobby people rubbing elbows and insincerely smiling at one another."

I arch a brow at her comment. "It can't be *that* bad."

"You would be surprised." Sarah smoothes out the wrinkles in her dress. "Do you plan on sitting here all night?" She gives me a glance, and I note the dare in her voice.

"Lead the way."

We walk toward one of the alcoves, featuring easels holding pictures of various men and women surrounded by children. From the actions and setting, I assume that these people have contributed to the Children's Care Fund.

Sarah affectionately grabs me by the arm as we walk. I steady her as we move, making sure she doesn't fall.

"You okay?" I can't hide my concern.

Her laugh is bitter. "I'm peachy." She points to a photograph in which her father is tending to a sick child. "Did you know my family makes up the top three contributors?" She leans against me and whispers, "It's all a pissing match. Father donates because he works at the hospital and it's expected. Mathew only donated because Mother nagged him, and, well, he wanted to one-up Adam, but of course Adam wouldn't let him win. He contributed the most."

"Sarah, I doubt they would do something like that for such ugly reasons. In fact, I know Adam would never do that."

Sarah twirls so she's standing in front of me. Her eyes are holding pooled tears. "Don't be naïve; men only like that in short spurts. After a while they grow bored of explaining everything to the inexperienced."

Now I'm getting annoyed. "How much have you had to drink?"

"Not enough." Her hand moves to her pale face. "You should run far away from Adam. Everyone in this goddamn family is a lost cause. They're only interested in keeping up appearances." She wipes away a trailing tear.

"Why are you saying this?" My words are a hushed whisper. "I know yesterday was upsetting but…"

"I meant it when I told you that I liked you." She shakes her head and lurches to the side. Her hand reaches for one of the easels and it shifts, unable to hold her weight.

I lunge forward and grab her. Even inebriated she's a beautiful girl—her blond hair is straight, and her cerulean dress matches the blue of her eyes. "If I could, I would run," she says, her petite frame trembling. "Listen to my warning. Get out while you still can."

"What happened yesterday after we left?"

Pulling back from my hold, her features soften as she straightens. "I think I need to visit the ladies room."

"I'll go with you."

"No. I'm fine. Adam's probably looking for you." She stares at me an odd expression dominating her face. *Is it pity I see, or resignation?*

Before I can decide, Sarah turns and dashes off. I want to follow her, to make certain she's all right, to ask her all the questions racing through my head, but I'm in shock. Never did I expect Sarah of all people to warn me away from Adam.

I turn and make my way to the dining area when I'm stopped by a familiar image. The photograph in front of me is of Adam. He's sitting in a room surrounded by small children and he's holding a book, reading to them. I would never have pictured Adam volunteering in a hospital, and yet as I stare at the image it makes perfect sense to me. Sarah is angry at Adam; maybe she's angry at me for telling him about Markus. I'm not certain what is wrong with her, but I am sure about one thing—Adam would never donate to a charity he didn't believe in, and if I needed proof it's right in front of me.

When I reach the table it's full of people. Adam is frowning as he sees me approach.

"Where have you been?" he murmurs low, but with annoyance.

"With Sarah. We were looking at the photographs in the other room."

The furrows in his forehead soften. "Next time tell me where you're going."

"Why?" I say with genuine confusion.

"You're too sweet for the type of crowd these parties cater to. I worry someone might upset you."

"I'm not made of glass and though you like to believe you can control every situation, you can't." My tone is playful but I'm dead-serious. "Besides, what can anyone at this party do to upset me?"

Adam opens his mouth to respond but is cutoff by someone calling his name. He turns his head quickly, addressing a man sitting across from us and my question is soon forgotten.

The next half hour passes without a hitch. I'm concerned about Sarah. She's been absent for the duration of the dinner and no one at the table seems to care. Adam has spent the time talking to his father, and more than once I've caught Mrs. Black staring at me. My skin crawls every time her emerald eyes focus on me because they seem so appraising. *What the hell is she thinking?*

After dessert is served, Adam is called up to the podium to speak.

"Hearing you have developed a debilitating disease of any kind is hard to understand and to accept. However, when you're confronted with such a difficult situation at a young age, the illness does so much more than incapacitate your body; it steals your innocence.

"All of you who have contributed to this fund should feel a measure of satisfaction, because your support has allowed children who previously had no recourse to get the care they need. However, our journey certainly does not end here…"

Adam speaks about statistics concerning child cancer rates and how the donations for the Children's Care Fund are monumental for the advancement of research. After he's done with his speech, everyone applauds and brings out their checkbooks, including me.

I expect Adam to return to the table after his speech, but that doesn't happen. He spends much of the evening talking to other guests while I'm left alone. Obviously, he took my impassioned, *I'm not made of glass* comment to heart, because I've been left to my own devices. Even after getting what I wanted, I'm not happy. *You practically told him you could handle being on your own—now you have to live-up to the boast. Don't be clingy!*

My internal pep talk appeases me for five minutes and then I'm again restless. It's uncomfortable to be sitting while everyone is mingling, so I head to the bar and order a drink. "Cranberry Sparkler, please."

As I'm waiting, a familiar bitter voice makes me groan.

"So he decided to bring you along even after yesterday's disaster."

I turn to face Victoria. "Do you seriously have nothing better to do at these parties than come and bother me?"

"Don't flatter yourself." She motions for the bartender. After her drink is poured she turns to face me. "Did you have the opportunity to read the article?"

I should walk away, but her question intrigues me. "What article?"

She pulls out her phone and shows me an alarming headline, *Millionaire Playboy Starts Jealous Brawl at Sister's Party.*

"Shit." I say the curse a bit more loudly than I intended, and a few guests give me frowning glances. "That's not what happened."

Victoria shrugs. "I don't think reporters are known for their interest in the truth, at least not these ones." She smirks at me. "You've been dating him for a few weeks and already his name is being tainted by the association."

I down the drink I receive from the bartender and make my way to the restroom. I may actually throw it up. The loud tapping of Victoria's heels as she pursues me, fuels my anger.

"Leave me the hell alone."

"Did you know my mother is good friends with Lillian Black? They've often discussed how wonderful it would be if Adam and I happened to fall in love."

"I don't care who your mother is friends with. You can all waste your time together daydreaming. It's not a concern of mine. Stop following me," I keep walking, striding out of the hall.

"Does Adam know about the time you spent locked away?"

My muscles lock—I'm frozen solid. And the edges of the room are blurring as if I'm a watercolor painting, discarded in the rain. *How did this woman learn so much about me in such a short time?*

Victoria laughs with genuine mirth. "Is it like in the movies? Did they lock you in a white room and make you wear a straightjacket?"

*Don't you dare pass out! March up to this bitch and slap her. Snap out of it!* I focus on my thoughts because if I don't, I'm a goner. I'm getting a headache from holding back my tears.

I turn and slowly move toward Victoria. Even though I'm in heels, she towers above me. "Maybe they did, Victoria. Maybe I was so out of my mind that for my own safety and that of the staff they had to make sure I couldn't move. Now, do you really want to fuck with someone not all there?" I stand in front of her, my expression calm, though I'm anything but in control. I'm a hairsbreadth away from lunging forward and claw out her crystal-blue eyes.

She takes a hesitant step back. "You don't deserve him."

"Mind your own damn business."

"He *is* my business."

Lillian Black's voice breaks through the air like the snapping of a whip. "Victoria, go back to the party."

Victoria's face crumples. "I was just…"

"I know what you were doing." Mrs. Black moves toward me. "Evelyn, walk with me."

The way she speaks makes it clear she's not asking me a question, but voicing a command At the moment, I could care less. I need to get far away from Victoria, because if not I'll attack her—I'll make a scene.

Giving Victoria a final glance, I turn to follow Mrs. Black, who's already moved ahead. She leads me back to the ballroom though instead of intermingling with party guests, we climb some steps, making our way to a secluded terrace.

"I've found out some interesting facts about you, Miss Snowe."

I lick my dry lips and nod. "I imagine Miss Chase was more than happy to supply you with these facts."

She shakes her head. "It was *I* who informed *her*. Though I never expected she would be foolish enough to confront you yourself."

"How…" I swallow, pushing past the tightening of my throat. "How could you know anything about me? I only met you yesterday."

"As you grow older you'll find that life is all about who you know."

Her eyes narrow as she watches me and under the weight of her scrutinizing stare I find it hard to stay still. "You are quite beautiful, I can see why my son is taken with you." She pauses and shrugs. "But you'll soon realize, if you've naught already, men are very fickle."

She combs her fingers through her blonde locks while peering down at the dance floor. "Don't they look good together?"

I place a hand on the rail, and focus my gaze in her direction. Adam is standing at the edge of the dance floor talking with a group of men as Victoria approaches him.

She's only a few inches shorter than him. Her complexion is pale and perfect. Victoria places a hand on his forearm, bracing herself as she stands on her toes and whispers something in his ear. Adam shakes his head, and though his body doesn't lean into the sway of hers, he doesn't pull away from her touch. She says something and then everyone in the group laughs, including Adam.

They *do* look right together, like connecting pieces in a puzzle. I don't belong here; throughout the course of the night I've felt out of place, and as I watch them I know why.

The words of Tevye from *Fiddler on the Roof* echo in my head. Adam is a bird and I'm a fish. It doesn't matter that I love him, because our worlds are too different to reconcile. I will never be accepted by the people in his life.

"I normally wouldn't interfere in his affairs," Mrs. Black says. "I mean, Adam usually beds women and then tosses them aside. However, he's clearly enamored with you, and though he'll bore soon enough, by then the damage will be done. He did this once before."

"Serena Welsh," I murmur.

"He spoke of her?" A derisive chuckle seeps out of her lips. "They were childhood friends and fell in love in college. She was studying music as he was. I tried to discourage him from pursuing that degree, from being with her, but he wouldn't listen. That woman nearly tore my family apart. She broke his heart."

"I won't do that," I whisper.

Mrs. Black stiffens and an emotion I'm not familiar with crosses her face. "As an architect, I've spent my life imagining buildings, constructing countless structures and making something beautiful out of ideas. I'm sure as an artist you can relate to that sentiment."

Though the shift in conversation surprises me, I nod. "Yes, of course. Being an architect is the same as being an artist. You just work in another medium."

Mrs. Black smiles at me, and though the action seems genuine, the way her eyes narrow makes a chill run down my body.

"I have built many stunning things throughout the years. However, the greatest example of my artistry is my son. Raising him, helping him become the man he is today is my best accomplishment. One day, when you become a mother you'll understand what I'm feeling."

She takes a step forward, invading my space. The pleasant smell of her perfume contrasts with the acidity of her words.

"Would you want your son to get involved with a woman who tried to kill herself? Who spent months in a hospital for treatment for God only knows what type of issues? I'm sure you're a lovely girl, but you're not the right girl for my son."

Her words are like a jagged knife plunging into my heart—they knock the wind out of me. Everything she says confirms the fears I've been harboring for weeks.

I want to speak in my defense, but nothing comes out. I felt rage when Victoria was insulting me, but in the company of Lillian Black, I'm numb. Her relation to Adam intimidates me; she's his mother, and I'm only the woman he's currently bedding. Even though I'm already defeated, she continues to speak.

"I have to look out for him when he's too blind to realize the mistakes he's making."

I shake my head and focus on her, because I want her to see the sincerity in mine. "I love your son. The last thing I want to do is hurt him."

Her features are like ice; my words don't provoke even the smallest of cracks.

"Then walk away. Being with you will damage his reputation, potentially hurting his business associations. People will talk."

"He doesn't seem like the kind of man who cares about what people will say." A tear escapes my eyes. I lean against the arch, shielding myself from the view of others.

She sighs in apparent annoyance. It's obvious Mrs. Black, like Adam, is used to getting what she wants with no questions asked.

"He may not care what people will say, but *you* will. I'm trying to save you embarrassment. How do you think I found out about your situation?"

I blink a few times at the change of topic. "I don't care," I mutter, because the truth is, I'm terrified. *Did she find someone from my past? How much does she know?*

"As we speak, a story is being written on you and Adam. The only reason it hasn't been published yet is because I know the editor. If you honestly care for him, spare him the humiliation." She grabs my hand and shifts me so I'm once again looking at the ballroom. "The people in this room are his business associates. Believe me when I tell you they care about appearances. Dating you will only close doors for him."

I press my cold hands against my flushed cheeks as I think. A thousand ideas hit me at once. If the people at school find out about my past I could lose my job. I take care of kids, and parents aren't forgiving when it comes to those who are entrusted with the wellbeing of their children. I can hear them now. *How can she take care of our kids if she can't take care of herself?*

What could this article do to Tina? She vouched for me so I could get the job. Could she lose her job because of it? Would the people at work lose respect for her and no longer value her opinions?

*Oh shit! My mother!* She's already ashamed enough that her daughter tried to kill herself. If her business associates found out, she would be mortified.

What about Adam? Would he grow to regret being with me? Would the weeks we spent together be tainted by my past mistakes?

The revelations of what this article could mean to me and all the people I love is too much to take. I'm filled with resignation as I speak. "If the article is already going to be published, what's the point? The damage is already done."

"Your relationship is new and therefore unimportant. Fade away like the diversion you were meant to be and there won't be a story to tell. End it tonight and no one else needs to know the details about your past, not even Adam."

Mrs. Black turns, her hips swaying with grace as she saunters off, showing not even the smallest hint of remorse. This entire conversation has been insignificant to her—a means to an end.

Finally alone, the tears stream down my cheeks. Adam knows I have a past, and in the solitude of his apartment I'm sure it's not a concern, but if being with me hurts his business dealings he'll turn his back on me. I wouldn't blame him.

The idea of having my life exposed in print petrifies me. I wipe the tears from underneath my eyes and rush down the steps. Aimlessly, I move through the lobby and head outside, and at some point I become aware of my surroundings. The courtyard is barren. Arches surround me, and a simple garden is outlined in the center. The wind brushes against me, and my nose, wet with my tears, feels cold.

"Evelyn!" Adam looks winded as he clambers down the steps leading to the square.

I'm pulsing with anger and relief. I hold onto the anger, because it's the emotion that will get me through the night.

Adam moves closer to me. When I take a step back he tilts his head to the side as a look of confusion crosses his features.

"I've been searching for you everywhere." By his tone, I surmise that anger is the emotion he's favoring as well.

"Was this before or after your conversation with Victoria?" I circle the small garden at the center of the courtyard, lengthening the distance between us.

"I don't see how that matters."

"You wouldn't," I scoff.

Adam walks on the opposite edge of the garden, his eyes following me. "Is this your solution to a problem? You get upset and disappear? You disregarded the fact that I told you not to wander off without informing me."

"And you were concerned?" I don't bother to hide my sarcasm.

"I was concerned. In fact, I spend far too much of my time worrying about you."

"Oh, well, excuse me. I'm sorry I'm such a bother."

"Is there a reason you're acting like petulant child?" His stare is icy and his body is rigid.

I sigh with resignation. "You said something didn't work between you both, that she was smart and beautiful but not what you wanted. I think you're chasing a challenge, and that's a dangerous reason to be with someone."

He closes the distance between us. I want to run away, because if he touches me saying goodbye will be impossible, and I've already decided…I'm saying goodbye.

"I've known Victoria since we were kids; our mothers are good friends."

I roll my eyes, and by the stiffening of his jaw I can tell his ire is rising.

"I haven't explained myself to anyone since I was a teenager. I'm not about to start now." He takes a step forward, standing only a few inches away from me. "You should know by now that if I wanted to be with Victoria, I *would* be. As for the notion that I'm interested in a challenge, you're right—I am. I want to be with someone who provokes me into interesting conversations, not someone who is contrary for the sake of stirring up nonexistent problems. I don't have time for that."

I want to tell him how his mother accosted me, how she blatantly told me I wasn't good enough for her son, but deep down I know walking away is the only kindness I can offer Adam. He deserves to be with someone who is his equal, and I'm not. I'm royally fucked up, and being with me can only cause him pain.

"You two look perfect for each other. Cut from the same cloth even," I murmur.

"I'm assuming you're getting to a point," he says curtly.

"We're not right for each other." I focus on the flowers in the garden, because I can't face his scrutiny. I've never broken up with someone, and the idea of walking away, of returning to the black hole of my previous life, makes me feel lost.

"Why are you doing this?" One of his hands grabs my chin and roughly tilts my head back so I'm facing him. "You're starting a petty fight with me for no reason. What aren't you telling me?"

I hate how he can see through me, and yet it's why I've fallen in love with him. He's pulled more truths from me than anyone, but not today, not now.

"Adam, you don't really care about me. You've spent the evening talking to everyone *but* me. Sure, behind closed doors I'm interesting but here..." I spread my hands open. "I'm a novelty you're getting tired of." I think back to Sarah and her warning earlier. She's right, men don't like naïve girls.

"If I'm getting tired of anything, it's of your damn insecurities." He lets go of his hold on me and turns, his hand resting on the nape of his neck as he gives me his back.

"There are days I still think about it, about hurting myself, and I don't think it's a feeling I'll ever get over. The truth is, it's a constant struggle," I say, hoping I can show him I'm not worth being upset over. I want Adam to think of me as a mistake, because I do love him and I don't want to hurt him.

Adam eyes clash with mine, his face ashen. "Evelyn..."

"I'm going home. This isn't going to work; it's over," I blurt out quickly, because my resolve is wavering. This conversation needs to end.

I take a few steps to the left when Adam's hands grab hold of my arms. He pushes me against a stone pillar and his gaze cold and impassive.

"This can't be because I had a conversation with a woman who means *nothing* to me," he says incredulously. "I know when someone is running away from a problem; I've done it often enough. What are you keeping from me?"

The smell of his body is intoxicating my senses, the scent and situation provoking my eyes to burn with the sting of impending tears.

"We both knew this was a short-term liaison," I say pointedly. "You're only upset because I'm the one leaving first."

"Stop changing the subject. What the fuck are you keeping from me?"

"*Everything!*"

Adam moves back as if I have struck him. "You're right then, it's over. I can't be with someone I don't trust, and you sure as hell don't trust me. I guess all we had between us was a couple of good fucks."

I want to curl into a ball right there and bawl until my eyes are swollen, until the well dries and I have nothing left. Trust is the main thing he wants from me and I have denied him that again and again. In that moment I want to tell him everything that happened throughout the night. He deserves to know the truth. "Adam…"

"It's my own damn fault for letting it get this far. When I found out about your past I should have ended things."

His expression is vacant. His voice unfamiliar; it's cold and foreign and the distance between us makes me clam up and stay silent.

"I almost did. When I took you to the apartment yesterday I was going to tell you it was over, but the way you reacted—you had a panic attack, your body was shaking and the expression in your eyes was so haunting… It made me want to take care of you." He stares at the ground for a long moment. "I couldn't turn my back on you."

"So what your saying is that you've always *pitied* me?" I spit out. "I don't need your charity. It's never been something I wanted."

"What the hell does it matter now?" Adam looks at me, emotionless. His hands are tucked into his pants pockets and everything about his posture screams of a person who's indifferent.

I'm about to respond when Victoria rushes toward us, her face more pallid than usual. She's focused on Adam, her gaze never meeting mine.

"You have to come now!" she sputters. "Your sister's unconscious. We think she took something and we can't wake her up."

My heart skips a few beats, as the seconds trickle by in slow motion. It's as if the air around me is compressing. I'm going to shatter.

*How did I not see this?* Sarah was crying out for help and I was too caught up in my own bullshit to notice. And then a horrible thought crosses my mind—maybe I *did* notice. Maybe I didn't think twice about it, because going to that extreme, hurting myself, self-sabotaging, is natural to me. It's my go-to instinct. I kept silent about my father's suicide-talks, his late-night drinking binges, his emotional and psychological abuse, because I grew up thinking those conversations and experiences were normal. But they're not.

After years of therapy and months of being institutionalized, I'm aware society says it's wrong to hurt yourself, yet I can't reconcile that truth with my twisted view of free will. And now, because of my inability to understand what so many people intrinsically know—Adam's sister might be dead.

# Chapter Twenty-One

"WHAT THE FUCK are you talking about?" Adam roars.

Victoria is crying as she speaks. "They found her in the girl's bathroom, foaming at the mouth as if she had a seizure. They think she took some pills. We can't wake her up."

The three of us race to the main hall where a large cluster of people have congregated at the far end, by the bathroom entrance. Adam shoves his way through the crowd, while Victoria and I follow.

Sarah is lying on the floor, gray vomit covering her delicate face, and her mother, a woman who is obviously known for her impeccable appearance, is a mess. Her mascara has run, her hair is tousled, and her gown is full of wrinkles.

I focus on Adam, and he's the epitome of composure, ready to do everything and anything to make sure this incident is a hiccup in his baby sister's life. In seconds he's on the phone, and in less than five minutes the throng of ogling bystanders is dissipated by personnel he's no doubt commanded to do his bidding. However, a flicker of worry is in those cobalt eyes. It's an expression only those who know him would understand.

Is this how my mother acted when I tried to kill myself? Was Tina composed or was she crying? Seeing Sarah on the floor, floods me with emotions—emotions I've repressed for years.

Guilt makes the bile in my stomach churn. People say suicide is selfish and in some ways it's true, but what most don't understand is that a person who is depressed, thinks it's selfish to remain a burden to those they love. They think their family is better off without them. They don't see the immediate aftermath of their actions.

The paramedics arrive and Sarah is whisked away, her father riding with them.

As Lillian Black rushes to follow, her tear-blotched face turns to me. "Victoria saw you talking to her! What did *you* say?"

She lunges forward, grabbing my arms and pinning me with her grief-stricken stare. Mesmerized by the sight, because the image of my own mother in the same situation comes to mind, I begin mapping out the creases of her frowning face as her tears fall. The vacancy of her expression, chills my bones and makes it hard for me to move. *Did my mother look like this?*

"A-All I did was listen to her." I stammer, unwilling to turn away.

"Listen to what?" Adam asks, his decisive demeanor faltering under the strain of confusion.

Mrs. Black's fingers dig into my skin, the sting distracting me from Adam's question.

"Why didn't you come get me if she was upset, why didn't you…" Her words fade and her hold on me stiffens to the point that I know I'm being bruised.

Adam, pries his mother's finger from my arms and she clings to him as he engulfs her in a strong hug. "It doesn't matter who she spoke to before. Sarah needs us now."

"She was crying when she was with *her*," Victoria says as if she'd just presented a jury with a smoking gun.

I don't bother to look at her, but I sigh, because of course she would still be here.

"She stumbled when she was with you, almost falling to the floor." Victoria shrieks the accusation while turning to face Adam and his mother. "I was so worried I thought to follow her, but I was detained…"

*Detained, accosting me!* I want to scream the statement, but the terrible reality of what's happening—Sarah might die—holds me back. Ignoring Victoria, I focus on Adam because I want to be here for him, but the shadow I see in his eyes as he holds his grieving mother, is so reminiscent of doubt, I'm paralyzed.

"If you knew my sister was in trouble, why didn't you tell me?" He asks in a hushed tone, and it may be my imagination but I think I hear disappointment in his voice.

*Is it my fate, my destiny in life to have everyone I care for, find me lacking?*

"There wasn't any time and I didn't know she was—"

"You should've found the time." Victoria hisses.

"Why would *you*, of all people, be the one to talk to her?" Mrs. Black, pulls away from her son, her erect posture determined.

"None of this is important now," Adam says as he grips the back of his neck, and my heart hurts for the obvious stress I see in his taut body.

"This is a mistake, a miscalculation," his mother rambles. "Sarah would never have done this willingly. She must have not read the label on the pill bottle. She's such a smart and accomplished young girl."

I've remained quiet thus far, because I want to respect Lillian Black's pain. But the hollow justifications and clear misconception as to why her daughter has harmed herself, hits a nerve. My future was as bright as Sarah's when I tried to kill myself.

"She knew exactly what she was doing," I don't mean to sound so hard and certain, but I do.

"Evelyn, don't. Not now." Adam looks at me, his gaze unyielding.

I refuse to listen because I've lived this moment, I've heard the excuses people made for me and I can't hear them again, even if they're directed at someone else.

"Maybe she did it because she was nearly *raped* yesterday. Maybe it was something brewing for years. Honestly, I don't know. But she knew what she was doing and you shouldn't make excuses... Not if you want her to get better."

"Sarah wouldn't do this because of yesterday's..." Mrs. Black lowers her tone, and her eyes dart from left to right, surveying her surroundings. "Because of yesterday's unfortunate incident. She's not that dramatic."

Lillian Black's slanted priorities and condemning scrutiny disgusts me, and she notices. Shaking her head, her expression adopts an air of superiority, her pert nose raising loftily. "You know nothing about my daughter or my family."

"I know you were more worried about bad publicity yesterday than supporting her. Don't make that same mistake today. Now more than ever, she's going to need unconditional support."

"How dare you judge me."

"The same way you've *dared* to judge me."

"What are you talking about?" Adam steps forward. "Evelyn, don't make this about you, because it's not. My mother is upset over what's happened with Sarah; she's not judging you."

The naïve comment makes me laugh, because I've always been the naïve one among us. He doesn't know about the conversation me and his mother had. And while that memory is very present in my mind, it's not the reason I've said what I've said—someone has to be Sarah's advocate. If they ignore this and try to hide it, if they pretend it didn't happen, that it's not significant, her existence may end up being as hollow as mine has been for years. I don't wish that on anyone.

"Smart and accomplished young girls aren't immune to harming themselves," I whisper. "In fact, depression doesn't discriminate."

"And you would know, wouldn't you?" Mrs. Black's lips curl in a smirk full of vitriol.

"Yes, I would," I say vehemently, for the first time not feeling remorse about my past but rather a somber acceptance.

A dark gleam shines from Adam's hard sapphire eyes as he stares at his mother. "This conversation is over." He growls between clenched teeth. "I don't know what the fuck has gone on tonight, but I'm going to find out."

"Yes, and while you're investigating, be sure to learn what exactly *she* said to my baby."

Without acknowledging his mother, Adam grabs my hand and begins walking, but my nagging fears won't let the issue lie. I tug my hand free and look at him, my chin lifted in defiance. "Do you blame me for your sister?"

"No," he states flatly. "However, I know your judgment concerning a situation like this can be skewed and I don't fault you for not—"

"Now, you're making excuses for me!"

"You're twisting everything I say because you're agitated and not thinking straight."

He's back in control and his calm stance, the cool effectiveness of his steely composure makes me want to shake him and throw him off balance.

"It's not my fault," I cry out, and in the recesses of my mind I know I'm not talking about Sarah and her actions, but my own. "I'll be dammed if I let you criticize me in order to feel better about your own collective apathy."

"*Apathy?*" Adam moves close, so we're inches apart.

"That's rich, coming from you. You've lived your life avoiding difficult decisions and embracing apathy. When something overwhelms you, you run and hide. It's what probably happened when you spoke to Sarah, and it sure as hell is what's happening now."

I shove my index finger against him. "Keep pointing an accusatory finger at me. Maybe if you point long enough you'll feel better about your own choices. Maybe you'll forget that your passion doesn't lie in a real-estate contract, but in piano keys. That you've lived your life as repressed, as sheltered. That you've made mistakes as misguided and as big as my own."

"Stop talking." Adam closes his eyes for a long second, and when he opens them the most bittersweet expression radiates from his heated gaze. "Stop talking, before you say something you'll regret."

At this point I'm seeing red. I can't stop. All the emotions I've controlled and bottled up throughout the night are demanding release.

"Yes, I think of hurting myself—often. Every day of my life, to be exact. But you know what I don't do? I don't look down on people. I don't throw stones like you and yours while you sit perched upon your high and mighty pedestals."

"I've never thought less of you." He says huskily.

"Of course you have!" I ball my fists, desperately trying to reign-in the urge to lash out, because for a man who can easily wade through bullshit, in this respect he's blind. "You hired someone to look into my past, you've demanded the truth about the darkest, most vile moment in my life while being unwilling to reveal your own sorrows."

A small sob escapes my lips, and when he reaches for me I step back because I know his touch will burn. It's painful to realize that after all we've been through together, I've never had his confidence—I doubt anyone does.

"I could forgive it all, Adam, if it weren't for what I know you're thinking now about your sister, what you probably have thought about me since you've learned the truth."

The steady hammer of my heartbeat echoes like thunder against my ear, egging me on. "What bothers you most, all of you, is not that Sarah hurt herself, it's that the image you have of her is now *tarnished*. That type of vanity is more a sin than her actions."

"You little bitch—"

Adam cuts his mother short. "Mother, go to the hospital with Victoria."

Mrs. Black tries to protest, but is once again silenced. "I'll be there soon."

Victoria and Lillian walk past on my periphery, but I refuse to turn away from Adam. When they're no longer in earshot, he speaks.

"What bothers me, Evelyn, is that after all this time, after everything I've uncovered, I still don't know you. I've only ever seen shades of the person you are. And you know what, Evelyn? What I did see was beautiful. But looking at you is like staring at the *Mona Lisa* through a hole in a wall. It's *infuriating*."

"The sentiment, Adam," I say slowly, the catch in my voice making it hard to complete the sentence, "is mutual."

I think it's pain I see in his expression, but the moment is so fleeting I'm not sure. He shakes his head. "I've given you more than I've given any woman in years."

Without a doubt, I know the statement is true. This strong, intelligent, totally alpha man in front of me has broken his rules—but it's not enough. His reticence about his past, the hypocrisy of the truths he demands from me while keeping his secrets, has erected a wall between us I'm not sure I can break. And even if I could, even if I pushed past his barriers completely and got the full story, it wouldn't be enough to secure the fairytale. Even with his faults, I believe he deserves so much more, than what I can offer. He deserves the full painting.

"It's over." My mouth is dry as I press my lips together. "Let it be over. Save your sister. Get her the help she needs. Don't waste your time on me, because I'm a lost cause."

Again, I see that flicker in his gaze—that flash of pain and concern. But in a blink, it's gone.

I shake my head and move to his left, only to be halted by his hand on my wrist. His touch feels like fire on my skin. Not because the grip is reconstructing, but because there's no affection behind the action.

"Parker will take you home," he says with finality as he pulls out his phone.

"I can get home on my own."

Adam ignores me. He speaks to Parker and tells him to bring the limo to the entrance. After he finishes the conversation he stares at me from head to toe and the expression on his face makes me squirm. I don't feel beautiful anymore; I feel uncomfortable and ordinary.

He grabs my hand and leads me out of the hotel, never once speaking a word. My eyes are glued to the floor.

By the time we reach the entrance Parker is there. Adam opens the limo door for me and my heart is racing. This is it; this is the end.

He leans down and kisses my cheek. The action is void of the emotion I've felt since we first met, and this is the worst punishment, being denied his passion. He's pretending my presence doesn't affect him, and then a scary thought strikes me—maybe he's not pretending. I don't have time to dwell on the thought.

"Goodbye, Evelyn." His voice is formal, and the way he says my name lacks the seductive quality I've grown to adore.

I hear nothing in his voice, not a touch of regret or longing, only emptiness.

"I hope your sister is all right." I genuinely care about Sarah's wellbeing.

"Me, too."

He ushers me into the car. I open my mouth to speak, but I don't know what to say and before I can figure it out, he closes the door. I look out the tinted windows and watch him turn and enter the hotel. Then the car pulls away and nothing matters anymore.

A few hours ago I was in this limo with Adam, his hands were under my dress and the promise of more lingered in the air. Now, I'm alone, and it's nobody's fault but mine. Yes, I had coercion and threats from his mother and his ex, the stress and anxiety of coming face-to-face with my past mistakes, my growing resentment over the secrets he's keeping, but deep down I know I've ended things because I'm scared of what the future might bring. I *have* been apathetic; because that's the only way I can control the urge to cut. Adam's presence in my life has thrown me off balance, like a planet without an orbit. I'm lost.

The tears come then. Between the sobs, my mind chimes in with words of wisdom.

*How can anyone love you when you're too scared to love wholeheartedly?*

# CHAPTER TWENTY-TWO

THE SCANDAL AT the Biltmore has made the local news. As noted by the press, "The beautiful heiress Sarah Black is in stable condition and should make a full recovery." They report that the incident was an unfortunate accident and that further investigation will follow. It's apparent, at least to me, that her family is orchestrating what is being reported in the media.

I don't have the courage to call and tell Adam I'm happy his sister will recover. Mainly because I know a "full" recovery is not possible. Events like that remain with you forever, especially when those who love you are more interested in denying the severity of your actions, than confronting them.

Miserable, again feeling hollow, I just lay in my bedroom with the lights turned off and the curtains closed.

A week later, on Christmas morning, Tina barges into my room, her face full of determination. She yanks open the curtains, letting sunlight permeate through the room.

I groan at the intrusion and place a pillow across my head.

"You've wallowed in self-pity long enough. Get up, Evie!"

I close my eyes and remain motionless. I'm not ready to face the world. A few minutes pass and I assume she's relented. I'm wrong.

Tina grabs me by the arms and yanks me to my feet. Her dark eyes narrow as she watches me.

Standing at five-foot-three, Tina's shorter than me, and yet when she is determined to do something nothing will stop her. Somehow she manages to drag me to the bathroom. I stumble over the shower step and shake my head. Before I can react, she turns the water on.

"Shit! It's fucking cold!" The water clings to my clothing, and for the first time in days I flush.

Tina ignores me and squirts body wash on my drenched body.

"We're not letting this happen again. Do you understand me? People break up all the damn time and they don't starve themselves and become hermits. Now, get cleaned up."

"Leave me alone." I run my hands through my wet hair. All I want to do is crawl back into bed and sleep.

"Like hell I am. Six days to New Year's, and if you start the year like this, you're screwed. You know the saying, right? Start the year how you plan to go on—and you are not spending it dirty and in shambles. Pick up that razor, shave your legs, and wash your hair."

Tina doesn't bother to wait for my response. She turns and slams the bathroom door shut behind her.

I'm not sure why I listen. I suspect that I just don't want to hear her bitch.

Fifteen minutes later, I'm clean and presentable. I walk out of the bathroom with a towel wrapped around my body and my toothbrush clamped between my teeth. An outfit has already been laid out for me.

*How fucking convenient. I've time-traveled to grade school.* I put on the outfit because I'm too tired to argue.

Tina has been busy cleaning my house, opening windows, and airing out the musky abyss I've been residing in for the last week, since the breakup. She knows the story. The next day, between shots of Grey Goose, I'd confessed every sordid detail of Saturday's calamity. She'd been silent since then and I'd assumed it was to let me get over the shock. Now she's in my house cleaning, and I'm getting dirty looks.

"What's your problem?" I pull out one of the chairs from the dining set and sit.

"*You!*"

"What the hell did I do to you?"

"It's what you are *not* doing. You let Adam's bitch of a mother railroad you. You let his sister's actions scare the hell out of you, and you just *quit*."

I'm surprised by the vehemence in her tone. "It was never going to work. You even told me he was like chocolate ice cream. You gave me some bullshit explanation about how too much of anything is bad for you and that I was losing myself."

"I meant you should be careful, not be a pushover. You fucking walked away without putting up a fight." Her stare is frigid as she wipes the dining room table with a damp cloth.

If it were anyone else, I would have pounced like a lion. However, this is Tina, the one person in the world who has never let me down. The type of loyalty she's always given me deserves better than my anger.

"His sister just attempted to commit suicide. He doesn't need to be around someone else who's a total basket case. I would be an embarrassment to him and would damage his reputation."

She tosses the cloth on the table and points a finger at me. *"Bullshit!* You're scared."

"Well, thank you for the Christmas visit." I stand and start to walk to my room.

Tina follows me and her voice is louder than ever. "I want you to say it, because I doubt you've ever spoken the words aloud."

"Have you been drinking?" I cock a brow at her. "What are you talking about?" I start to organize the items on my dresser. Doing something simple helps me stay in control.

"You're in love with him. Say it."

I turn to face her. "What does it matter? You want to hurt me; is that it? You want me to break down and curl up on the floor because I can't have what I want?"

"I want you to be honest. You never tell me the truth…" Tina has tears in her eyes. "Three years ago, during the holidays you—"

"I took a razor to my wrists. Is that the honesty you're looking for?" My eyes swell with suppressed tears.

"No," she says softly. "I asked you before I left that day if you were okay. I was petrified for weeks, thinking you might do something stupid, but you said you were fine and I fucking *believed* you." She wipes at the tears cascading down her cheek. "You weren't honest with me then, and you're not being honest now."

"I didn't hurt myself because of you, Tina." I say the words because I feel she needs to hear them. "I was unhappy. I didn't want to keep living with the guilt of abandoning my father, of being the catalyst for his fucking suicide. I wanted to stop thinking of all the things that had gone wrong since his death. Like when Michael would try to leave me and I would suck him off to placate him, even though I fucking couldn't stand his touch. Or how after he tried to rape me, I begged him to stay! Who the fuck *does* that?"

I swing my hand against the glasses on the dresser and they fly off shattering against the wall.

"I wanted the pain to stop. It had nothing to do with you or my mom."

Tina takes a step forward. I know she's about to hug me and the thought makes me cringe. I take a step back. I can't stand the idea of being touched right now. We both stare at each other, our bodies frozen. Tina is the first to break the silence.

"That's not the point. You had people who cared about you—you had me. I could have talked to you about what you were feeling. Your mother and I, we could have gotten you help. You pushed us away and you're doing it again. You're pushing *him* away."

"Adam has kept me at arm's length from the very start," I yell. "He kept his past a secret, while not only demanding truths from me I wasn't ready to reveal, but going out of his way to search for them."

"So instead of standing your ground and calling him on his bullshit you ended it before he did?"

"Since when are you his advocate?"

"Since he shelved his arrogance and called me," she blurts out.

"W-What?" My heart does a weird skip and suddenly feeling lightheaded, I place a hand on the dresser to support myself.

"You wouldn't answer his calls. He wanted to make sure you were all right." Her voice softens. "I imagine, for a man like Adam Black, who is used to getting his way, it must have been hard to call the best friend of the girl he was seeing, just to know how she's doing. You've said it yourself, the man isn't known for demonstrating his emotions and yet, he called someone he barely knows, because he was worried about you."

"It doesn't matter," I say breathily, my chest hurting, because of course it does. "What I feel isn't important, because it doesn't change anything." I raise my hands, splaying my hands in a futile attempt at restraining the anxiety taking hold of my body.

"It's important to me, because I love you, and I know it's important to him. A man doesn't introduce a woman to his friends and family if he doesn't care about her. He wouldn't have agreed to meet your mother… He wouldn't have called me." She takes a deep breath and gives me a hard stare. "If you walk away now, you'll never know if it could've worked. You'll live with that regret for the rest of your life."

"So what's the alternative? You seem to have all the answers. Tell me what to do." The sarcasm in my voice leaves a bad taste. "What the hell do you want from me?"

"I want my fucking *friend* back! It's what I've wanted for the last three years. I don't know if all the *happily ever after* shit really exists, but I know if you walk away now you'll quit living again."

I shake my head. "I can't call him. I can't see him. I wouldn't make it a minute before I fell apart and begged him to take me back. I would lose what little pride I have left because I'm in love with him. And I can't lose the little I have left, because I won't be able to go on, and I know I have to, for you and my mom."

"No, Evie, *not* for me and your mom. For *you*! Life is not worth living for others."

Tina really missed her calling. She should have studied psychology, because I swear she's more adept at getting me to face facts than anyone else in the whole world.

I take a deep breath and will my body to relax. "I'm sorry that it's your shitty lot in life to pick up my pieces. I'm not even sure why you do it. We both know when the pressure builds I crumble. It doesn't matter how strong I want to be, because I don't have it in me."

The sobs I've been guarding against burst free. Voicing the words aloud is cathartic and yet bittersweet.

Tina moves forward and I let her wrap her arms around me.

"Do you remember when we were in high school and Kevin and I broke up?"

I frown at the question. "Yes."

"You convinced a bunch of us to go to Orlando for an impromptu road trip to get my mind off of things. And my shitty day got better. The girl who was always ready for an adventure is still inside you waiting to be let loose. You're stronger than you think, Evie."

My arms tighten around Tina's petite frame and I owe her more than an apology. I owe her an explanation. "I'm sorry. I've been selfish and preoccupied with my own problems. Sometimes I wish you would leave me alone so I wouldn't feel so guilty for being such a horrible friend."

"You're not!" Tina pulls away and scowls. It's the type of reaction I would expect from her and the familiarity of my best friend, the girl who's been like a sister to me since we were kids, is comforting.

"Own the day. Don't let another minute pass you by."

I'm not sure I can accept her advice. We sit there in silence as time trickles by, and we do what best friend and almost-sisters do best—we enjoy each other's company.


MY iPod has shuffled to Leona Lewis's "Bleeding Love". As I listen, I wonder if I'm crippling myself, if the self-doubt I harbor is like a festering wound that never heals.

Adam's family and friends think I'm shit. They want me to stay away. Though, if I'm honest, they're not the problem. I'm scared of being found wanting, of getting so enamored I won't survive if he abandons me.

Tina has gone home to get ready. We're spending the evening with my mother, and the idea of facing her makes me queasy, so I lie on my bed and listen to the song.

I'm wearing a blood-red dress. The color suits my complexion, and though it's the first time in the past few days I've taken interest in my appearance, I feel anything but pretty.

I remove the platinum bracelets Adam gave me and focus on the scars I will forever wear. The truth is, with each passing day, new scars are being made, they just aren't the type people can see.

I think of him as I inspect the bracelets, of his sculpted lips and his gorgeous eyes. With my fingertips I trace the flowers etched on the edges of the platinum bangles. Light bounces off the bracelets, and I see they have an inscription on the inside rim. Adam never mentioned he had them inscribed.

I pale at the words.

*Hide from the world...but never from me. —AB*

A few hours ago, Tina told me to stop running and confront him. Someone can show you the right path, but you'll never follow it unless you see it for yourself. Staring at the inscription, all I want for Christmas is to tell Adam I love him—that I'm full of imperfections but around him my flaws aren't so stifling. I need to tell him he makes me want to be a better person. If I'm willing to take the risk of baring it all, then maybe, he'll reciprocate.

He's in New York and what I have to say can't be explained over the phone. I rub my head in frustration. After a few minutes of contemplation I decide to write my thoughts down, something I haven't done since I was little. The words pour out of me in minutes, and somehow I manage to capture in words the emotions I've repressed.

*Dear Adam,*
*You're the last person in the world I want to hide from. I see you and my heart skips, because I know you can see through me.*

*I'm scared I may never lay eyes on you again, that the warm sound of your laughter across my skin will soon be nothing more than a distant memory. More than anything, I'm scared your opinion of me has changed.*

*Being in a bank hold-up was the best thing that ever happened to me, because I met you.*

*I still wonder how you can blame me for bottling up my feelings, when you yourself are guilty of the same? How many secrets can a person truly confess in the span of a few weeks? How can two extremely different people make something destined to fail work?*

*Maybe I did let my fears control my actions. Maybe I shouldn't have walked away. However, the reality of being with you for only a month loomed always in the background. When you expect something to fail, you take steps to make sure it does.*

*I refuse to apologize for my inability to tell you everything about my past, because your demand was always unreasonable. The only thing I am sorry about is that I never told you how much I cared. I never said the words, because every time I utter them to a man, they disappeared, but since you're already gone, it doesn't matter anymore.*

*I love you.*

*Evelyn*

I leave the house with only my keys and cellphone. The walk to Eden Beach only takes me a few minutes. The gentleman at the reception desk smiles; he's seen me a few times with Adam. I offer him a quick lie about needing to go to the penthouse to get something.

"They're expecting me." I smile and straighten my posture. *Look like you belong.*

He nods and in less than a minute I'm riding up the elevator to Adam's apartment. He mentioned he would be in New York until after Christmas, so I figure it will be easy enough to slip the letter under his door.

When the elevator opens into the foyer I feel a twinge of apprehension. I move forward and crouch down by the door. It opens. With rounded eyes, I stare at Ms. Wright.

*It's Christmas. Why is she working?*

"Evelyn?" she says with astonishment.

"I'm sorry. I didn't expect anyone to be here." My cheeks burn. "I wanted to drop something off."

Ms. Wright looks at me with an expression I'm unable to gauge. She probably thinks I'm a lovesick girl pining over her boss. *Is she wrong?*

"You must think I'm out of my mind." I fiddle with the envelope. "I need to leave Adam a letter and I want to make sure he gets it." I push through the embarrassment, and meet her gaze.

For a long moment she looks at me—her expression pensive. She opens the door wide.

"Come inside. He's not home at the moment, but you can leave it in his study."

"Thank you." I say hesitantly. The expression in her eyes makes me nervous, as if she knows something I don't.

Ms. Wright turns to leave, but before she can take a step she blurts out, "He's been playing the piano. For years I've seen it sit there, untouched. I've dusted it off and seen it get older and older, its potential wasted."

The affection she holds for her employer is obvious as she speaks.

"How long have you worked for him, Ms. Wright?"

"Long enough to know when someone is good for him." She purses her lips and looks uncomfortable as she continues. "It's not my place to say anything. I don't know what happened between you two, but I do know when you're in his life he's happier. You wouldn't be here if you didn't care. Don't give up on him."

"Maybe he's the one who'll give up on me."

She gives me a small smile. "Well, that's the risk we run when we care about someone, isn't it?" Ms. Wright doesn't wait for an answer, disappearing toward the kitchen.

I make my way down the hall to the study, and the moment I enter, images of Adam flood my head. At least Ms. Wright didn't suggest I leave the envelope in his room. The memories that would plague me there would make it hard for me to go. I place the letter on his desk and turn to leave.

My mouth drops open when I see him standing in the doorway, dressed to impress, his dark locks pushed back and his eyes registering the same shock I'm no doubt exhibiting.

I speak his name because it's the only word I can manage. "Adam..."

He frowns. It seems like the man who always knows what to say is speechless. His eyes never leave mine as he closes the door, and the action is intimidating.

"What are you doing here?" I say with reproach as I take a step back.

"I *live* here." He tilts his head to the side as he regards me.

I swear my IQ drops ten points when I'm around him. I feel awkward standing in front of this gorgeous man who leaves me unable to form sentences. Lucky for me, he breaks the silence.

"Why are you here?" Adam asks softly.

His striking blue eyes move down my form, and for a split second I wonder if he likes my dress.

"Is there a problem? Are you all right?" A hint of concern is in his eyes.

"I'm okay." I pause for a moment to think. "I thought you were in New York. I wouldn't have disturbed you if I knew you were home." I hate that my voice shakes. "I have to go." I take a step to the side and head to the door, but Adam moves to counter me. He stands before me like the most charming wall in the entire world.

"Like hell you're leaving now."

I pause and then burst into laughter. For the last few days I've been starved for his touch, for the sound of his voice, so even if he's scolding me I can't deny the comfort stirred by his emphatic statement.

Adam arches a brow in surprise. "Is something amusing?"

I give him a shy shrug. "Nothing, I should go."

"You came for a reason, Evelyn."

"How's your sister doing?" I blurt out, because I want to avoid his question.

"Recovering." He sighs with exasperation. "Stop avoiding my question. Why are you *here*?"

"I came to drop something off. I never expected you to be here."

"What did you want to drop off?"

I bite my bottom lip and close my eyes in frustration, because drawing attention to my letter is embarrassing. When I finally focus on him, his expression is expectant. "Nothing important."

Adam grabs my hand and yanks me farther into the room as he strides to his desk. In seconds, his gaze falls on the envelope.

"Sit." He barks the command at me and pulls me to the chair at the head of the desk, his chair.

"Hey, you don't get to…"

With one glance he silences me. I sink into the chair, my eyes never wavering from his.

Adam grabs the envelope and looks at it for a long moment. He turns his attention to me. "What does it say?"

"Read it," I whisper. My heart is about to leap out of my chest. The idea of having my letter read in front of me is terrifying.

Adam sits on the edge of his desk, and I see a hint of anger in his eyes. He tosses the letter on the desk and faces me.

"It's easy to leave a letter, because you can avoid a person's reaction. It's easy to be honest in print, and the last thing I want is for you to take the easy route. Why are you here? What do you want to say?"

"My God, you're such a hypocrite. You want to talk about easy? It's easy to demand honestly and expect someone you barely know to pour her heart out at the snap of your fingers, especially when you have no intention of doing the same. How can anyone live up to that?"

"So you wrote me a fucking letter to tell me that? To tell me how hypocritical I've been?"

I'm slightly shocked by his fury. "No. I just wanted to be honest with you."

"Then tell me why you broke up with me that night. Tell me what the hell happened, because I was there, inches away from you as you fell apart before my eyes, and I still don't have a fucking clue as to what triggered the breakdown. Does it have to do with the conversation you had with my sister? Did seeing her in that situation remind you too much about your own past? Help me understand." He stares at me with uncompromising determination.

"Yes...No...I don't know." I sigh. "You scare the hell out of me, and I don't mean because you're intimidating, though you are. You yelled at me for going off with Sarah and then almost immediately went off to give a speech. I was overwhelmed by everything. I didn't feel like I belonged, like I was right for you. Then Sarah did what she did, and I was angry. I felt like everyone was judging her, like..." I shrug, unwilling to finish the sentence.

"Like you feel you were judged after your suicide attempt?" Adam says softly.

I nod, my gaze glued to the floor. He moves from the desk and then his strong fingers are gripping my chin, so he can tilt my head and force me to stare into the blue of his eyes.

"I made the decision to keep seeing you after I found out your past because the idea of losing you over something that happened years ago was not an option. I don't make decisions about the people in my life based on the opinions of others. You just gave up."

"You blamed me for your sister." My voice raises an octave.

"I did not blame you and I said as much." He let's go of my chin, to rub the side of his head.

"Your eyes told a different story. You looked at me with doubt and disappointment."

Again he's close. His hands are wrapped around the arms of the chair as he looms over me, the imposing nature of his proximity taking me by surprise and wiping-out all my thoughts.

"Since you're such an expert at gaging what a person is thinking based on their expression, look at me now and see if I'm lying."

The sharp grate of his words, and the perfection of the lips uttering those words, lips that have roamed my body possessively and indiscriminately, have me captivated.

"My baby sister had just overdosed on pills and I was upset. I was trying to understand what had happened. If I seemed confused or as you put it I looked at you with doubt, it was because I *was* full of doubt. I was questioning *my* actions the previous night, wondering what I could've done to prevent Sarah from harming herself."

He moves back and mutters a curse under his breath as he shoves the suit jacket he's wearing off of his shoulders and tosses it on the desk. "And yes, I wanted to know what you said to her, and what she said to you. I wanted to better understand the problem so I could fix it."

*Damn, that makes sense.*

Adam is the type of man who tries to fix a problem, no matter how insurmountable the odds are, and the thought makes me sad, because though I see him as my *hero*, even hero's meet challenges they can't overcome.

"There are some things even you can't fix," I say quietly.

He crosses his arms over his chest and a small smile fits his lips. "You're right, and you and me being together is one of those things, isn't it? I can't make you stay by my side. Being in a relationship with someone is a decision you have to make, it can't be made for you."

"We were never meant to be in a relationship."

"Fuck!" Adam raises his hands in the air. "We're still on that?"

"It's a big issue, Adam."

"So you ran away because of the threat of our liaison ending?" he says incredulously.

"I don't know. Everything is better when we're alone. When we go out and interact with people, it all falls apart. I was fine until everyone at that party told me I wasn't right for you."

"Who is everyone?"

I blink a few times, finally registering what I've said. My mouth parts, and Adam doesn't give me the opportunity to think. His deep voice radiates throughout the room.

"Who the hell is *everyone*?"

I stand and square my shoulders. "Sarah, Victoria, *your mother*. I was accosted from every direction. First, Sarah warns me that everyone in her family is fucked up, and that I should run away. Then Victoria insults me about my past, which she found out about through *your mother* since they're fucking best friends. Then your mother tells me I should leave you alone, because I'm not good enough for you."

Adam runs his hands through his hair. "How the hell could you keep that from me?"

*No fucking way!* I raise my hands in shock. "Are you *kidding* me? You're upset with *me*, not your mother and Victoria?"

"I'm fucking furious with them, and believe me, I'll deal with them, but you were the one I was with. It was your responsibility to talk to me."

"What was I supposed to say? 'Oh, by the way, Adam, you mother just told me I'm the wrong girl for you and is threatening me with the release of an exposé on my sordid past if I choose to continue dating you?'" I roll my eyes. "When was I supposed to say this? Right after your sister was found unresponsive?"

He takes a deep breath, and I know what he's dealing with; he's trying to reign in his rage. I take a deep breath, mimicking him, and for once I'm the one in control, or at least not the one about to blow.

"Don't be mad at me," I breathe, as my body stiffens with stress.

"I'm *furious*. I don't know how to process you being in front of me. What we're doing here, what we've been doing since we met, all of the fights. It's not something I've ever experienced. My life is organized. If I want something, I take it. But in the span of a month you've thrown my life off balance."

"Adam…"

His voice, sharp like a whip, cuts me off. "Now I find out my mother tried to blackmail you into not seeing me, and my sister and Victoria were somehow involved? How the hell am I not supposed to be upset, when you obviously have such little faith in me? You broke up with me and didn't even bother to tell me the truth."

His words frustrate me, because they're so unforgiving. I was the one who was demeaned and insulted, so when I speak I don't bother to hide my sarcasm.

"Oh, please educate me on the appropriate course of action. How was I supposed to react?"

"Like a goddamn adult," he snarls.

"I can't believe I came here. I'm leaving."

I turn to walk away, but Adam's question stop me dead in my tracks.

"Were you scared of people finding out about your past? Was that the real reason you left?"

"Yes, I was scared. I still am, though that's not the reason I left."

"Then why?"

"Adam, I have to go."

"Not until you tell me why."

He has the ability to make my world stand still, and the incredible part is, I welcome the frozen feeling. I love this man. I love the alpha in him— the way he makes the world bend to his will. His imposing nature and probing stare have since the beginning, been my kryptonite.

Sensing he needs a particular answer to his question, I dig deep, trying to build up my courage. And as I drown in his ocean-blue eyes, all the fear I've been harboring melts away.

I'm tired of fighting these emotions, of being a coward. The difference between a person who is happy and a person who is sad is the way that person reacts to the challenges they're confronted with. I'm not sure why I'm willing to take the risk. Maybe it's because I've already lost him, but I can't leave without confessing my feelings.

Moving toward him, I commit his image to memory. The outline of his handsome face, the contours of his chin as his lips press against each other in a firm line—he's a work of art. Anger and passion filter through his startling eyes, as he watches me. Weeks ago I would have been petrified by the intensity of his stare. Now the muscles in my body tingle with anticipation, because I know my presence affects him in a primal way. I submitted to his passion long before I had committed to the love I felt for him, and I don't regret one moment.

"Adam, the idea of having my past published frightens me, but more than anything what scares me is the idea of you suffering for your relationship with me because of my past—that's what made me leave. I wish I had the resolve to stay away, because even the remote possibility of hurting you tears at my heart. It makes it hard to breathe, to think, to do anything. I've done more living since I met you than in the past few years combined, and I won't be able to sleep at night if I don't own up to the fact that I've fallen in love with you." I pause for a second to catch my breath. "I don't expect you to reciprocate…"

Adam denies me the opportunity to finish my declaration. I'm pulled against him in a flash as his tongue brushes my lips in a ravenous caress and I sway in his arms.

I speak against his lips because it's the only latitude he offers me. "Adam…"

His husky, commanding voice interrupts me. "Shut up and kiss me."

Once again his lips take mine. He nips at them and the sweet sensation makes me moan. His tongue invades my mouth, claiming me with lustful strokes.

Suddenly, angry voices intrude. I push away from Adam's embrace, though the strong hand on my waist makes it so the curves of my body are still pressed against him.

"Miss Thomas, you can't go in there." Ms. Wright's voice is high-pitched.

"Adam has kept me waiting long enough."

The door to the study is pushed open by a well-dressed blonde. She peers across the room and her thin lips press together as she glowers at me. Ms. Wright is behind her, glowering with equal hostility at the woman.

"I'm sorry, Mr. Black."

"Don't worry about it, Cadence."

Adam releases me. He runs his hands through his hair, and the muscles in his forearm tighten with tension. He's frustrated by the situation, though I don't know why. For a few drawn-out seconds the three of us stare at each other. Adam is the first to speak.

"Evelyn Snowe, this is Ashley Thomas."

I try to muster the energy to smile, but I'm confused by the presence of this beautiful woman. *Why is she here? Why didn't he tell me she was here? What's going on?*

Adam's frown mirrors my own. "Ashley is an old friend. She studied at Columbia with me."

"Those were good times." Ashley shoots Adam a knowing grin.

Her lips curve and small smile lines form at the corners of her eyes. This woman is older than me, though she carries her age well.

"I'm sorry to interrupt." Her gaze once again falls on me, and though she still bears a smile, her rigid stance exudes insincerity. "I was under the impression we were only stopping at your apartment to pick something up before we went to the party."

That's when it dawns on me. Ashley is upset because I have intruded. She had a prior arrangement with Adam and my brash actions have not only ruined their evening but made me look like a complete fool.

*He was going on a date!* I hate that my body trembles with unhindered mortification. I want to crawl into a hole. I want to make myself invisible. A thousand impossible desires filter through my thoughts in the span of seconds. I need to get the hell out here.

"It's been a pleasure to meet you, Miss Thomas, but I have to get going."

My voice is mechanical. My actions are instinctual and precise. I'm not even thinking as I make my way to the foyer. As I press the elevator button I become aware of Adam's presence behind me. I turn to face him.

"Please don't waste your time on my account. You're obviously busy with a prior engagement." I press the elevator button again. It's taking too long to get here.

"You're overreacting."

The back of his hand tenderly grazes my cheek. Tears swell in my eyes.

"You let me pour my heart out like that when you knew there was a woman not twenty feet away? Why would you do that?"

"You surprised me. We started talking and I was focused on getting answers from you. It slipped my mind."

Adam's hand trails down to my waist and he pulls me into him in a gentle embrace. My hands rest on his broad shoulders, and in those seconds I enjoy the scent of his body wash, of his skin.

"She doesn't mean anything. I've known Ashley for years. She happened to be in town for the holidays and we decided to get together. It's nothing more than two old friends catching up."

I cry into his shoulder. Finding him here in his apartment with another woman forces me to face one of my biggest fears. How can a simple girl like me maintain the interest of a man like Adam? Even if we were to stay together it would only be fleeting.

"Your mother was right. You and I don't fit. I can't compete with women like Ashley Thomas or Victoria Chase."

His arms tighten around me, his embrace ridges as he holds back his anger.

"You're right, because you're out of their fucking league." Adam grabs me by the chin so that I'm forced to face his gaze. "You're the flower in the mural. I've known it since the day I met you. You have the potential to be so much more and you constantly cave under the pressure. You run away from your problems. You shut down and find ways to avoid them instead of facing them."

I tilt my head to the side, shifting away from his grasp. "You're so familiar with my faults. What about yours?"

"I settle for less," he whispers.

The loud ping from the elevator makes me jump. The doors open and I shift my body to enter but Adam refuses to let me go.

"I need to go home."

"I'll drive you."

"I'd rather walk."

"We need to talk. So I'm either driving you or we're walking together." He speaks with that authoritative voice that implies I don't have a choice.

As the elevator doors close Adam pulls me by the hand to one of the chairs in the sitting area adjacent to the foyer, his expression filled with concern. I'm a mess. I've been crying for days so my eyes must be huge and red. My skin is blotchy from the stress and I feel frumpy.

"I'll be right back. Do you need anything? Are you thirsty?"

I shake my head.

Adam leans forward and presses a soft kiss on my forehead. It's such an odd action coming from him.

"Evelyn, I want to take care of you. I don't want anything to ever happen to you." He takes a deep breath and I can tell it's hard for him to make the next statement.

"When I saw my sister on the floor, almost dead, the image of you lying beside her, popped into my head. And I can't get it out."

I place my hand on his cheek. Even though I haven't hurt myself, I haven't cut myself in a long time, my previous actions have still managed to hurt him.

"I can't let that happen to you. I won't. I need to protect you," Adam says with finality. "I've tried to give you space. It's why I only ever called this past week, even though the urge to go to your house and breakdown your door, was driving me crazy."

I rub my fingers along the edge of his chin and as the grate of his stubble scratches my skin, I'm reminded of the day we met at the bank. I touched him like this, with a sense of enchantment.

"Tina said you called her."

"She convinced me to stay away, by promising she'd make sure you were okay and if not, she'd call me."

Maybe I should feel blessed to have two amazing people like Tina and Adam, strategizing about how to stir me out of my depression, but I'm not.

"Evelyn, after what's been said in the last twenty minutes, I don't want to stay away from you. I want to be the person you lean on. There are so many things I want to show you, so many things I want to do with you. It's been a long time since I've found someone worth caring about. We've both fucked up, but it's not too late to make this right. We can figure it out."

Sincerity is exuding from every inch of him. And as I stare into his eyes I know this man, who is unable to say the words, loves me. In his own way, Adam loves me.

For a moment, the notion of him taking care of me is sweet and perfect, but only for the briefest of moments. Being a burden on those who love me is not my aspiration in life. Tina and my mother have shouldered that responsibility for far too long, and the last thing I want is for Adam to remain by my side due to a sense of obligation or fear. He's the type of man who needs to protect the people in his life—it's one of the many honorable traits that make him so incredibly special. But he can't be my crutch. What would start as a pure need to help someone he cares for, would soon become a choking burden. This isn't how two people should start a relationship.

As I stare into the warmth of his eyes, I have the realization every young girl needs to have before she can consider herself a true woman. The people in your life can help you, love you, and yes, at times protect you, but they shouldn't dictate what you do with your life. Eventually, you need to take up the reins, and take care of yourself.

"What if I told you I needed more space, more time. What if I'm not ready to be in a relationship right now."

He squeezes my hand, almost as if he's scared I'll pull away. "I'm not a patient man and I certainly won't make compromises I know can potentially be disastrous. Us being apart, is the last thing you need. You *need* someone to take care of you."

His words have never hurt me more than right this minute. It's weird, to have a man tell you all he wants is to take care of you, and be saddened by the sentiment. I imagine many women would jump at the opportunity to be kept by the man they love, sheltered and nurtured, but it's not what I want. I didn't escape the prison of my hollow existence, to now find myself trapped in a gilded cage—I won't allow my *hero* to become my warden— no matter how much I love him.

I've done this to myself. I've allowed Adam to railroad me throughout this *liaison*. He's always been in control as is testament by the fact that he has yet to truly confide in me about his past relationship with a woman named Serena Welsh, a woman who royally screwed him over. Adam thinks of me as this weak woman, albeit, one who according to him has potential, and the realization is disheartening.

"Your friend, she's waiting for you," I say absently, feeling suffocated in his presence.

Adam's eyes narrow and again he squeezes my hand. "I haven't trusted a woman enough, to be in a relationship in over ten years. What we have is special to me. I don't want to lose you."

"I know." I don't have the heart to tell him his statement a minute before, contradicts his admission. Adam doesn't trust me, not really. Sure, he trusts I'll allow him to run our *relationship* as he sees fit. But he doesn't trust I can take care of myself and honestly, how can he? When in the last three years have I taken care of myself? If I stay now, there would be no equity between us, he would be in charge... That's not the life I want.

Adam's not the type of man that makes concessions. If I'm going to be happy, I need time to become a strong, independent woman. A woman who can manage the impulse she has to hurt herself, because though I hide it well, the impulse is still there.

Realizing this will likely be the last kiss I ever share with the love of my life, I make it count. Our eyes lock and my hands cup his face, which by his small flinch surprises Adam. When our lips meet in a tender kiss, the world stops. It's a bittersweet experience.

"I'll only be a minute."

As he walks down the hall, I know he's going to talk to her. He's probably going to give her some type of explanation as to why he can't go to the party. It's irrational to be upset. I broke up and abandoned him. But I'm heartbroken by the situation. I'm disappointed that in the span of a week he already made a date. I'm disappointed that I need time to get my life together, and that Adam doesn't seem like the type of man who knows how to wait. But more than anything, I'm disappointed, both Adam and I are riddled with flaws and that the path for our happily-ever-after, is obscured.

Taking a deep breath and with a resolve month ago I would never have had, I wipe away the tears pooling in my eyes and head to the elevator. I press the button and fortunately it's still on this floor. It opens immediately.

I enter the elevator and as the doors close I see his panicked face.

"Evelyn!"

"Goodbye, Adam." My voice is so faint I doubt he can hear the words.


I take the beach exit out of Eden Beach. Adam will rush toward Collins Avenue. He'll assume I'm going home. His expression as the elevator doors closed made it apparent he wasn't going to let me walk out of his life easily. As the sun sets, I run down the coast.

When I show up at Tina's apartment, my shoes are in my hands, my hair's a tangled mess and I'm in pieces. Only this time I'm going to pick them up. I'm going to seize the day.

Throughout the next few days Adam calls me constantly, but I refuse to answer the phone. Though I want to explain why I had to leave, I know if I hear his voice, I'll submit to my desires. I'll immediately do what he wants, even if it's not the best thing for us both. He has a control over me, that both excites and scares me.

Adam deserves a woman who can handle her shit, who's successful in her own right. And I deserve a man who will be patient and will wait for me… By his own admission, he's not a patient man.

I'm not ready for love.

The day I was in a bank hold-up, I began to live. After tasting the sweet nectar of happiness, I've come to realize that to truly own that feeling a person needs to be the master of their demons. I will never be able to offer someone selfless love if I don't learn to stand on my own two feet.

Tina is right. I don't want to start the year in shambles, grasping at the tattered shreds of my life, tying them together in the hopes that I can make myself whole. I'm not that good at mending—I doubt anyone is. I need to do what any true artist would do with a million broken pieces—make a mosaic, a masterpiece.

While Tina drives us to my house, I think of everything I want to do with my life. I want to commit to my art and create an exhibit. I want to reach out to artists, establish new friendships, and work on a new beginning.

My musing is short-lived, because as we pull up to my driveway we're both awestruck by the sight of my lawn. Thousands of flowers have been planted in intricate patterns. Every color I can imagine is in a magical rainbow of petals and pollen. It's a glimpse of Eden.

*I paint flowers because they can tell all types of stories. A flower can make you smile, it can make you cry, and it can even be an unspoken promise.*

Adam has always been able to see straight into my soul, as is testament by the beauty before me.

Surrounded by this garden, which is undoubtedly a gift from the man I've left, I find myself drowning in emotions.

"Wow," Tina says as she shifts the car into park.

"He's making this so hard." I whisper while exiting the car. Tears are blurring my vision, threatening to fall and then my phone vibrates. As I look at the screen I lose the battle—I'm crying.

THEY SAY ALL GOOD THINGS COME TO THOSE WHO WAIT...

DON'T KEEP ME WAITING LONG.

Adam Black, *Mr. East Coast*, who has often claimed he doesn't possess patience, isn't a man who makes concessions, and yet he just did—for me. It's an ambiguous statement, because I'm not sure how long he's willing to wait and yet, his words leave me full of hope.

Thousands of unspoken promises are lingering in the air. My future is, for the first time in years, filled with possibilities. I don't feel pessimistic or scared as I stand there surrounded by perfection, because I know without a glimmer of doubt, one day I'll fall back into the arms of the man who awakened me from the black.

**ADAM AND EVELYN'S STORY CONTINUES
IN THE EMOTIONALLY INTENSE SEXY SEQUEL IN THE
UNINHIBITED SERIES,**

# FADING TO BLACK

**COMING SOON!**

For up-to-date information join my mailing list by visiting my
website https://vhluis.com/

---

### Author's Note

Thank you for reading WAKING to Black. I hope you have enjoyed
Adam and Evelyn's story so far. If you have a minute to spare, I
would really appreciate a short review on the Amazon and
Goodreads websites. Your help in spreading the word is invaluable
and appreciated. Reviews from readers like you make a huge
difference to helping new readers find stories similar to WAKING to
Black.

\*Link to my Amazon page:

https://www.amazon.com/dp/B07C9CBV67/

\*Link to my Goodreads page:

https://www.goodreads.com/book/show/39670435-waking-to-black

Thank you!

V.H. Luis